HARLOT QUEEN

Also by HILDA LEWIS and
published by McKay:

WIFE TO THE BASTARD

HARLOT QUEEN

Hilda Lewis

DAVID McKAY COMPANY, INC.

New York

HARLOT QUEEN

First published in Great Britain, 1970
First American edition, 1970

LIBRARY OF CONGRESS CATALOG CARD NUMBER: 76-108713
MANUFACTURED IN THE UNITED STATES OF AMERICA

To Edith M. Horsley with my warmest thanks for the understanding, the knowledge and interest she has shown throughout the writing of this book.

ACKNOWLEDGMENTS

My grateful thanks to D. Alice Clarke of Nottingham
University for her unfailing patience with all my enquiries
and especially for finding me the copy of the King's poem.
To the Marquis of Bath my thanks for allowing me to see
the original MS. at Longleat. My thanks also to L. F. Craik
for finding me the drawing of Isabella's coat-of-arms, to Captain
P. A. Burgoyne for allowing me to use his fine painting of
that coat-of-arms and to Grant Uden whose kindness made this
possible.

Foreword

I, Isabella of France,
in the sight of God and of this congregation
do hereby plight my troth . . .

The child, fully aware of the importance of the occasion, though not at all of the implication, repeating the words after my lord bishop of Narbonne, declared her willingness for this betrothal between herself and Edward of Carnarvon, heir to the great first Edward. At her left hand stood my lord earl of Lincoln, at her right, my lord count of Savoy—proxies both for the absent groom. Quiet and grave she perfectly played her part; but behind her still face the thoughts ran tumbling. Was she to wed these two lords—and they so old? And both at once—and how might that be done? And where did Edward, Prince of Wales come into this? She had thought it was him she was to wed; she had looked to be Queen of England one day. Still, the King her father must be obeyed. So now she put one hand within that of my lord of Lincoln and the other within that of my lord of Savoy. And, troth plighted, went to make her curtsey to her father, to her mother and to the lord archbishop.

A pretty, obedient child. Who could guess at the dark chapter this betrothal should now unfold? Not the King nor Queen nor archbishop; not the groom's father eager for the marriage, still less the young groom; and, least of all, the puzzled little girl herself.

The date was the twentieth of May in the year of grace thirteen hundred and three. The place was Paris; the unknown groom nineteen, the promised bride nine years old.

Part One

The King and Gaveston
Queen's gambit

Chapter One

Edward, new-come to the throne of England, Scotland and Ireland, lord of Normandy, Ponthieu, Gascony and Aquitaine stirred and flung out his arms. His hand touched the head of the sleeper at his side. He turned on his elbow, keeping the fur bedcover about him, for the January morning was cold; his hand went out to stroke the dark head and then drew back lest it disturb the sleeper; he settled himself down to the warmth of the bed and the beloved body at his side.

Piers. Piers Gaveston. He'd got Piers back. It was the first thing he'd done after his father's death; the breath hardly out of the old man's body—and there was Piers back again in England. Last winter his father had driven Piers away . . .

At the thought of the old King the young King's face darkened.

The old man, old and cold and fierce and hard. . . . I was always afraid of him. So big, so tall. When I was a child he seemed to reach up to the sky—as though he could thrust his head through the clouds and talk to God. I used to think God did surely whisper in his ear; he knew everything—everything a boy did or even thought. And of course he did know everything—though it was not God that told him. And everything a boy did or thought was wrong. And it was always discipline . . . *discipline*. I sickened at the word. I used to think blood didn't flow in those veins of his but some dark physic . . .

But it was the treatment of Piers that turned dislike into hatred. Ungrateful for gallant service in his Flanders wars, the old man sent Piers across the seas; banished. And yet, once he thought well of Piers; made him an esquire in the royal household. And then because Piers was poor and proud sent him to join the palace boys, young nobles all, being trained with me, myself, for knighthood. . . .

Edward lay back remembering the first time he had ever set eyes on Piers—the handsome face, the friendly face. Friendly. It was the thing that made Piers different from all the others.

. . . A prince has no real friends. People were respectful; or, when they dared, despised me . . . and still they do because I like to take life easy. And why not? When there's work to do—I do it. I did well in the Scottish wars though I didn't like fighting and never will. Even that hard-bitten old soldier, that father of mine, praised me. Till Piers came I hadn't a friend. Those palace boys! They bowed their backs because their future lay in my hands, but no-one was ever my friend; too scared of the old man. But Piers was different. He wasn't afraid of anyone, ever! The first moment I set eyes on him I wanted to run to him, clasp him in both arms, to call him *brother* . . .

And he remembered how, overcome by sudden love, he'd stood dumb; and how, in that moment when Piers had bent to his prince's hand, a flame had sung in his blood, and not all the winds of persecution could put it out.

And he remembered how Piers had stood out above all the palace boys. He was the oldest; he was skilled in every manly sport. He shone above them all—above his prince even, himself no mean sportsman. Everyone had liked Piers . . . at first. He had held them all by his charm and by his wit, and by tales of the fighting in Flanders.

. . . He kept us all in fits of laughter by his wicked wit. But what he didn't understand—and doesn't understand—is that people laugh only when the needle pricks others; when it pricks themselves it isn't so funny. And another thing they held against him—and still do hold—is what they call his greed. They didn't understand and never will, his poverty. Those things others have as a matter of course, were never his. Between his wit and his need, his charms wore thin. And so the mischief started. It wasn't hard to turn my father against him; Piers' pride, Piers' tongue—his own worst enemy.

But not for me. I held him dear. I hold him dearer now; of all men dearest. I stood by him, I defended him, yes even to my father; I was stung by the old man's injustice. I asked for the rewards Piers' services deserved; I asked for lands in Ponthieu with all their honours, all their moneys. Too much, perhaps? But others had got more and done less—so much less. Result—the old man's cold rage; banishment for Piers, and for myself . . .

Even now in the warmth of the bed he shivered, recalling those dark days robbed of his friend, weighed down by the King's cold anger.

. . . Days best forgotten. Days made hateful by the thought of Piers poor and shabby. I sent him all I had—moneys, jewels, my own clothes even. I went shabby myself that he might shine brighter. I tried not to hate the old man for putting the sun out of the sky, tried not to wish him dead, not to long for freedom, for summer after long winter. Well, that's finished now, God be thanked! And Piers is back again; and back with every honour his King can give. I showed then all who's King. In face of everyone, barons and bishops alike, I made him earl of Cornwall. *A Royal earldom, meant for a royal prince. Sir, your father meant it for your brother the lord Thomas* Walter Langton, sour-face bishop of Lichfield, the old man's chief adviser, one that had spared his prince no reproaches. Well his prince is prince no longer. He is King. *The lord Thomas has been well-looked to. And, if we speak of brothers, Piers Gaveston is the brother of my heart.*

So now Piers is lord of Cornwall with all its lands and castles. with all its dues, its moneys and its mines. I raised him higher still. I married him to royal blood—my own blood. I gave him my niece to wife; my sister Joanna's girl. Her brother was none-too-pleased. *It may not please you,* I told my nephew Gloucester, *but it pleases me; and it would have pleased your mother well.* And so it would. Because the girl is in love with her husband. *Take love where you find it!* she used to say.

He sighed for his sister dead these nine months.

But—and he brightened again, Piers' wedding! That was a wedding worthy of any King. There'd been feasting and merry-making and a riotous putting the bride to bed. And there'd been wedding gifts for Piers—a dozen castles, a dozen market-dues, a dozen licences for fairs.

But for all that it wasn't easy to give Piers into the arms of a woman—especially Margaret, so young, so charming, so much in love.

He sighed again, remembering the long nights he'd lain awake sick with jealousy, unable to endure the thought of Piers in any arms but his own.

. . . Yet it had to be done; Piers must raise up an heir for his great possessions. But I haven't lost by it. Piers is kind to his young wife yet he loves his friend best. Two months since that wedding and I have Piers back again. And for that he'll reap his reward! I'll show them all—the backbiters, the haters, the jealous haters! And if the old man knows as much wherever he is, as he knew when he was alive, I wish him joy of his knowledge!

Lying there in the warmth of the bed he recognised that his joyous giving to Piers was sweetened by revenge against his father. Nor had revenge stopped there. He'd brought back all those his father had put from their high place. And those his father had trusted, his son had removed; he could not work with them. He had to shake off that iron grip from beyond the grave.

First to go had been Langton of Lichfield, his father's treasurer. Finished at last with sour reproaches for extravagance. And close on his heels had followed the sanctimonious bishop of Chichester. He'd once complained that Piers had broken into his park. The old fool should have kept his fences in better order! That complaint had been the last straw; it had brought about Piers' banishment. Now Chichester could whistle for office!

But Bek of Durham and Winchelsey of Canterbury—proud prelates his father had called them—were not too proud to obey a new master; they'd come at a whistle; they'd had enough of royal displeasure. Useful men, both! Reynolds of Worcester was another bishop the old man hadn't liked; but Reynolds had been the first to welcome Piers back—and that was enough recommendation! And now Reynolds was proving himself a useful treasurer.

Everything pleasantly settled.

King at last. Twenty-four and healthy; handsome—he couldn't but know it. And free. All set to enjoy life.

But . . . within a day or two he was to be married.

A shadow fell across his joy.

Well, in this at least, he was carrying out his father's commands; and, like all those commands, it brought him little pleasure. But to marry was a King's duty—he knew that! And marriage, what was it after all? It hadn't made much difference between himself and Piers. And, since marry he must, there was surely no bride to equal his. Never had a King of England so royal a wife. Isabella of France was not only the daughter of Kings, she was daughter to a Queen in her own right—Jehanne, Queen of Navarre. She was pretty, the young Isabella, they said, pretty and well-dowered. There at least, his father had served him well—though for looks the old man had cared little. For the dower he'd cared a good deal; and for a firmer friendship with France, a smoothing out of irritations between the two countries—for that he'd cared most of all.

But . . . the business of sleeping together! Too soon to trouble one's self for that. The girl was young, fourteen at the most. A couple of years would arrange that matter; time always did.

He stretched voluptuously, throwing out his arms. The sleeper stirred, opened a drowsy eye and came awake at once. That was one of the endearing things about Piers. No yawning, no wondering where he was; a half-open eye—and then wide awake!

'Well!' Piers sat up in the bed, his admirable body lean and golden against the peacock lozenged pillows; Edward had chosen them for that very reason. 'So today you sail for France!'

'You'll catch your death!' Edward said, pettish; he didn't need reminding of that! 'The room's cold as death.' He pulled Piers down into the warmth of the bed.

'They say—' Piers spoke with his mocking grin, so delightful when it mocked at others, 'you're in such haste to be wed that you've called a halt to the fighting. They say it'll cost you Scotland.'

'They couldn't be wider the mark! If fighting holds no charm for me, marriage holds still less! But—the thing must be done!' Edward shrugged.

'A reluctant groom! Can it be that Edward of England's frightened; frightened of a little girl?'

Piers at his mocking again! Edward's mouth, sensitive and sensual—a woman's mouth—tightened.

'Frightened!' And he laughed a little. '*No!* But . . .' he hesitated'
'how if she takes it ill . . . about you and me?'

'She's too young to understand such matters. Besides, I'll win her,
never fear. I never failed to win a woman yet.'

And that was true enough. That Piers was the King's sweetheart
didn't lessen his attraction in the eyes of women. It was a charm that
didn't extend to men; Piers made many enemies. If only he'd guard
his tongue a little! But with women he was debonair; his wife was
hopelessly in love with him; she was complaining that she saw
nothing of him. Well, what could she expect!

Edward said, a little sulky, 'It's a poor lookout if I can't handle a
wife, a child of thirteen.'

'Fourteen,' Gaveston corrected him. 'Between thirteen and
fourteen there's a world of difference. In a year a child grows to be a
woman. As for handling her—a wife isn't a hound, nor yet a mare.
Believe me, of all God's creatures, a wife, even the most loving, is
the hardest animal to handle.'

'I am the King!'

'And she's the Queen—and as royal as yourself; mark it!' Then
noticing the King's frown said, with a sudden change of subject,
'I wish I were going to your wedding, Ned. Of all things, I do like
feasting and junketing!'

'I'll not risk to carry you into France; this is no time to set French
tongues wagging. And after all I leave you as Regent; there's
greater honour in that! And, if you may not come to my wedding,
you shall shine at my crowning; I leave it all to you! Well, it's time
to rise; I ride within the hour.'

He called aloud and a page came running to pick up the tumbled
clothes, no expression on his young face. Afterwards he would tell
the others how the King and his sweetheart had been so eager for
bed they'd flung their clothes to the floor, which clothes had lain
themselves embraced like lovers.

Now came the servants bearing fresh linen, bearing ewers and hot
water and fine towels, the barbers at their heels. And now travelling-
clothes for the King—fine woollen cloak, soft leather riding-boots;
and for Piers garments of velvet gold-embroidered, fit for a King's
favourite.

'Adieu,' the King said, his lips on Gaveston's. 'I leave everything with you—the crowning and the feast, and above all my heart!'

Edward was looking from the ship's forecastle and staring down into the grey restless water when Madam Queen Margaret came from within wrapped in a fur cloak against the sea-wind. He thought again how young she looked; but then she was not yet twenty-seven —a few years older than himself. He'd always thought it strange she had been content to marry his father; stranger still how truly she mourned his loss. She had never seemed like a step-mother; only like a wise, kind, elder sister. In her gentle goodness she reminded him of his sister Joanna—save that Joanna had been lovely and Margaret was no beauty but none the less lovable for that! *Margaret good withouten lack* they called her.

'Sir,' she said; and then, 'Son, you are not happy about this marriage.' And it was scarcely a question.

'No.' And he could not lie into those steady eyes. 'But, if marry I must, this is as good as any!' He turned his eyes upon the grey and tumbling sea. 'It isn't because of Piers,' he said. 'If there were no Piers it would be just the same. I don't like women.'

She had long known it; her calm unshocked look encouraged him to speak further. She was glad of it; he might, a little, ease his heart.

'All my life there's been too many women. All those sisters! Eleanor and Blanche and Joanna and Margaret and Mary and Elizabeth; and all their women and their women's women. A child *smothered* with women. I had my own household; but I wasn't allowed to be alone in it, ever. Women; always women! Afterwards when I was older and the palace boys came it was too late; the mischief was done.'

'Surely not beyond repair!' But she feared it, she feared it. 'In a little boy it's easy to understand; but you're a man now, free to come and go. Surely you can't hate us all.'

'Not hate; but I get no pleasure from women. Hate, *you?*' He lifted her hand and kissed it. 'And Joanna; Joanna I loved; she died too soon. She gave me courage. *Never be afraid,* she used to say. *But, if you must be, never show it!* And she lived by it. I never saw her afraid in my life.'

'Nor I, neither. She had a great spirit.'

'Never to be afraid, not even of my father!'

'She had no need; nor you neither—if you had known. Gentleness begets gentleness.' She sighed; others had called her husband harsh and cold, his own children even; but between him and her there had been much kindness.

'Well,' she said, 'there are few sisters to trouble you now!' and sighed again. 'All dead or far away, save Mary and Elizabeth.'

'Dear Elizabeth. She was—and is—forever my friend. She was a brave one, too. When I angered my father—and that was all too often—she always stood by me. That time, when I angered him over Piers; remember? He cut off supplies, I hadn't a shilling; and he threatened to punish any that should comfort me. She sent me her own seal, the Hereford seal; and bade me take what I would, if it were to her last shilling. There was courage if you like.'

She nodded. 'My husband's anger was no light thing—though myself I never knew it. Could you not like women a little, for the sake of those two?'

He shook his head. 'Not even for you that were, of all women, the kindest to a lonely boy—and you not more than a girl yourself. I love you, all three, forgetting you are women, remembering only your goodness. But the rest—women! When I was a child there were times I couldn't breathe for women; and I would remember the brothers that died. Three little boys; and each one of them to have had the crown . . . and not one of them to live to have it. And I'd think, *The women are alive; but the boys, the little boys are dead.* And I was sure I must die, too. I was to have the crown; should I not die like my brothers? It seemed to me there was death on the crown. Women the crown and death—they went together.'

'But,' she reminded him gentle, 'it was Joanna that died; Joanna and not you. And childhood is over; you must put away childish things.' That his life had been shadowed by women she had always known; but his childhood fear of the crown—of death in the crown, that she had not dreamed.

'Well,' she said with a brightness she was far from feeling, 'you have the crown—and you are far from dying. And, if you fear women, you cannot fear your wife, that pretty child. She's loving and obedient; you may make of her what you will. Come, sir, let us go within; there's hot wine in the forecastle.'

She saw his face brighten; he liked wine and drank more than was good for him. Still this was an occasion for rejoicing; she'd not have him show himself glum.

He was smiling as he followed her up into the forecastle.

Chapter Two

Isabella, daughter to the King of France, stood looking out of a narrow window in Boulogne Castle. Standing on tip-toe, for she was not tall, she could see little but the dull sky. She brought a stool and, so standing, could see the tents spread for the reception of Edward King of England. Today her groom was crossing the sea to make her his wife.

His wife. She knew well what that entailed; she was fourteen and marriage-ripe. She desired ardently to be wed to the handsome young man; equally she desired to hear herself called Queen of England. But for all that she was a little frightened; fourteen, after all, is not very old. All night she had not slept; once she had come from her bed to pray heaven would be kind to her husband—as she herself would be kind. She had gone back to bed thoroughly chilled and less than ever able to sleep. Even now, her whole body would suddenly start and tremble like the plucked strings of a lute.

She was well pleased with her match. The King of England was well-endowed. He was lord of Normandy, of Guienne, of Aquitaine and Gascony—though for these he must do homage to her father. He was, besides, King of Ireland, King of Wales . . . and King of Scotland. At that last she frowned. She'd heard whisperings. Too much in haste to claim his bride, they said. Had he tarried a little longer he must have thoroughly defeated his rebellious Scots; now the crown of Scotland threatened to wobble upon that handsome head.

In haste to wed his bride; she could scarce quarrel with that! But when they were wed she'd send him north again. And she would ride with him—as his mother and step-mother had done, both of them—to keep him in good heart and to share his triumphs.

She argued childishly knowing nothing of policies, still less of the machinery of war. All she could see was herself—the crowned Queen riding beside her King to battle. A tale of chivalry come alive.

But if her reasoning was that of a child, her will was that of a woman, not to be set aside save by love alone—and not always then. She was used to having her own way. Whatever she wanted was immediately put into her hand; whatever she commanded, immediately done. But she had a shrewdness that forbade her to push her luck too far. Quick to hide her anger at rare refusals she had won a name for gentle obedience. But her women could have told another story. Let one of them prove clumsy or forgetful, and displeasure would be clear, retribution certain. Even Théophania de St. Pierre, the governess that Isabella truly loved, trembled before this formidable child.

The girl, herself, was perfectly aware of her own nature. It pleased her to know the strength of her hidden will; pleased her to know she could control her anger or let it fly as she chose. But occasions for anger were few. Who would presume to argue with the Princess Isabella, *Madame of France*? Yet from her governess she would take guidance; where Isabella loved she could be won. But Madam de St. Pierre rarely offered advice; her pupil's wits were sharper than her own. And the child was charming, her manners beautiful. Madam de St. Pierre was well-satisfied with her charge.

From her place at the window Isabella turned to the clatter of small noises in the room beyond. A page came in carrying wine and white bread wrapped in a napkin. Madam de St. Pierre, at his heels, cried aloud seeing the girl kneeling all but naked at the window; she cried louder still at the dark-ringed eyes.

'No, I did not sleep. Did you expect it?' Isabella shrugged. 'But I am well enough!' She broke a roll in two and spread it thick with butter and honey; Madam de St. Pierre poured the wine. 'How could a girl sleep expecting her groom—and he the handsomest man in Christendom? At least so they say; but I'll not believe it till my own eyes tell me so. Princes are forever flattered. Myself now. They swear I'm the beauty of France; but I know for myself the truth of that! There's my cousin Marie—all blue eyes and bright gold hair;

angel-face! And there's a dozen I could name all handsomer than myself.'

She waited for Madam de St. Pierre to contradict her; Madam de St. Pierre said nothing.

'Wouldn't you say so?' Isabella asked.

'You're not full-grown. They're in the prime of their looks. A year or two—and there'll be none to touch you!'

Isabella was piqued. She longed to hear that here and now she was the fairest woman in France. She picked up a hand-mirror, her most cherished possession; not because of the cunningly wrought back and handle but because of the glass the jewelled frame enclosed. Glass was a rare possession; it reflected one's beauties—and one's blemishes, were one so unfortunate as to possess them—more clearly than any burnished metal.

She examined her face in its clear depths.

A pretty face. But more; surely more. Unusual. Framed in the pale hair, green-gold, not such another to be found in all France. She looked with love upon the skin, pearl-pale through which light seemed forever to flow—so one of the troubadours had sung only this last week. And what of the strange eyes? Changing eyes; now green flecked with gold, now gold flecked with green. She could narrow them so that the green-gold shone, arrows of light between thick fringed lashes, dark by heaven's own miracle. She could widen them so that the pupils threw up the splendour of the iris jewelled in emerald and topaz. And, young as she was, she knew how to use them—open and innocent or veiled and mysterious—to get her way with any man.

'I cannot wait two years, or even one!' She said, finger-tip smoothing the fine winged brows. She had thought once or twice of plucking them in the fashionable way. But plucked brows gave the face a stupid egg-look; her own brows gave her a fay look, as though any moment she might fly away—so the latest chanson assured her. No need to follow the fashion; fashion would always follow obedient at her heels. 'Suppose he find me not woman enough?' Her hands went to her small budding breasts.

'Then he'll be a fool!'

'You talk of the King of England!' the girl reminded her, severe.

'He's but a man like the rest!'

Like the rest! Reassuring thought. If this unknown husband were truly like the rest, life would be pleasant, indeed. She nodded and smiled to herself in the looking-glass.

'Madam is well pleased with her match!'

'Should I not be? The blessed Virgin has, I think, a care for me. For, being of some account in the marriage-market, I might have been forced to wed an old man,' and she shuddered in disgust. 'My Aunt, Madam the Queen of England—the *Dowager Queen,*' she corrected herself, 'was wed to an old, old ancient man, and she no older than I am now! He would have frightened me into the grave!'

'It was a happy marriage! When the old King died she was desolate—and still is!'

'She'll soon dry her tears.' The girl spoke with startling precocity. 'There's not a young widow will weep for an old husband for ever ... save she cannot get another! But,' she shrugged, 'that concerns me not at all. I'm to wed a young man, handsome and pleasant, they say.'

'There's other things they say. Extravagant; money runs through his fingers like water through a sieve.'

'I'll not quarrel with that as long as he spends it on the right things.' Her laugh rang out soft and full; a pretty laugh. 'If he love a good horse, hound or hawk; if he love fine furnishings, fine clothes, fine food I'll like him the better! Well now, what more of him?'

'Nothing, Madam, nothing you don't already know.'

'I think there is. I hear about a favourite; a Gascon or a Béarnais. But, ask as I may, I find out nothing. Yet something's to be found, or why this silence? Come, tell me what you know!' It was half command, half entreaty.

'I, Madam? I know nothing.' Madam de St. Pierre, sallow cheeks flushing, spread deprecating hands.

'I know that tone, I know those hands, and I know that blush! Come now, if there's anything to know, I should be warned.'

'It's the young man, the King's friend, they call him greedy. He knows what it is to be poor—and means never to be poor again.'

'Very wise. All men take what they can get—but let him be wise in his taking!'

'He's very proud ...'

'Let him bear himself as he will—as long as he bear himself seemly to his Queen. What else?'

'A sharp tongue they say.'

'It could be amusing—as long as he keep it from me. Is there more?'

'No, Madam ... except that the old King advanced him for courage in the field and thereafter took a dislike and banished him. The young King brought him back. There's nothing more except that ladies find him charming; and, oh yes, his mother was burnt for a witch.'

'And was she a witch?'

Théophania de St. Pierre shrugged. 'Who knows?'

'One hopes she was, since she was burnt for it. I hate injustice. Maybe that's why folk purse their lips and say nothing when I ask about the son. Maybe they fear the curse from the grave. Well, and one thing more. The name of this handsome, proud, spendthrift gentleman with the sharp tongue?'

'Gaveston, Madam. Piers Gaveston.'

'Piers Gaveston.' The dark winged brows flew together. 'I shall remember it!'

They looked at each other—groom and child bride. Beneath her quiet, her heart exulted. He was everything her husband should be. He was very handsome—no courtier's flattery there; golden looks and grace of person. And if she missed the weakness about the mouth she was scarce to be blamed; fourteen is over-young to judge of men. For his part he saw a pale, pretty child—no more. And if he missed the strength of mouth and chin it was not surprising; he'd never been a judge of character.

Her father spoke the words of welcome; she went down in her curtsey and the young man bending from his tall height to raise her, saluted her hand. That was all. But it was enough; enough!

She had not, as yet, spoken with him; but she had spoken with Madam Queen Margaret her father's own sister. She remembered her aunt not at all; she had been but four when Margaret left for

England. She was glad, indeed, to talk with her aunt—there was very much to learn.

She was no beauty, Madam Queen Margaret—the only plain one in the handsome Capet family. Her nose was long and her eyes small. But for all that it was a comely face, wise and kindly; she was one, Isabella thought, to trust. She was twenty-six now; and, even to Isabella, twenty-six was not very old. Twenty-six and her husband above seventy when he died! Yet still she mourned for him. When he died, all men died for me, she told her niece.

That was, of course, absurd. A young woman should weep as was seemly—but not for too long. Thereafter she should dry her tears. 'We shall find you a new lord,' Isabella said, reigning Queen to Dowager.

'My niece is kind. Let her not trouble her heart for me!' And Margaret pitied the girl that knew so little.

'We shall see to it . . .' the girl began. Something about her aunt forbade further talk on the matter; not well pleased Isabella bent to that gentle authority.

Margaret, seeing the hurt given for kindness meant, said quickly, 'All England is wild with excitement; they talk of nothing but their new Queen. At Westminster great preparations are going forward. The royal apartments have been competely rebuillt; they were damaged by fire last year. The stonework is new and everything's bright with colour—scarlet and gold and blue; very gay. And your tapestries have come. The royal arms of France look wonderful; they're hanging in the Queen's chamber to welcome you. And the furniture is new and splendid. The great bed's a marvel of carving; the tester and the curtains are all green and gold.'

Green and gold. Green brought out the colour of her eyes, gold the colour of her hair. She'd look her best in bed . . .

'The gardens at Westminster, I've never seen them so fine. The lord my husband cared little for gardens; he was a soldier first and last. But his son's different. He tells the gardeners what they must do and sees they do it. And he's always right; he has green fingers. I think at times his fingers itch for the spade.' She saw amazement in the girl's face and did not repeat what they said of him—that, give him the chance, he'd turn his hand to spade or bellows, to chisel, to hod or any other unkingly thing. A pity, they said, he didn't show the same love for his own craft—ruling and fighting; a King's craft.

'And the King has commanded a new landing-stage; it's called *the Queen's pier*. And anchored there you'll find your own boat. She's called *The Margaret of Westminster*.'

She should be the Isabella . . . The girl's face spoke clear.

'She was my ship; my husband's gift to me,' Margaret said, softly. 'And now I give her to you with all my love. She's a lovely ship, very swift; a bird of a ship. She's new-painted—red and gold and white; and so, too, her barges, all three. She's smooth and strong—even to cross the sea. You will like sailing down the Thames to Windsor, perhaps as far as Oxford. It's a gay river . . .'

Isabella's mind, quick-darting and impatient, had had enough of gardens and rivers. Now she asked about the most important thing of all.

'Great preparations for the crowning,' Margaret said. 'You may imagine! They say a King and Queen of England have never been crowned at one and the same time. It will be magnificent.'

'Who has charge of our Kingdom in our absence?' The question came sudden and unexpected.

Margaret was tempted to smile at the girl's self-importance; but the young are tender and must be tenderly cherished.

'The earl of Cornwall.' She had no more desire to smile.

'I have not heard of him!'

'He's but new-made.'

'And who may he be, this new earl of Cornwall?'

Margaret said slow and unwilling, 'It is Piers Gaveston.'

The winged brows flew upwards. *Gaveston again!*

'The King holds Gaveston dear,' Isabella said. 'But others, I hear, do not share this liking. The man I'm told is insolent; he pays little respect to any—scarce even to his King. He has a spiteful tongue, a tongue to draw blood—I've heard that, too. Well he'd best carry himself respectful to me and watch that tongue—lest he lose it altogether. But—' and she laughed a little. 'I have no fear of him—nor of any man. There's no man in Christendom but I can win him.'

'Gaveston is not like other men,' Margaret said troubled. 'He doesn't like women; you cannot hope to win him. As for threat of punishment—niece, niece, have a care. My son of England is easy enough in his nature, save in this. If you would live pleasantly with him, you must accept Gaveston.'

She saw the fine jawline harden; the eyes glowed green as a cat's. 'Have patience, niece,' Margaret said. 'It is a madness; the King will grow from it.' But she did not sound hopeful.

Chapter Three

January twenty-fifth, in the year of grace thirteen hundred and eight, Isabella and Edward were married. Never in Christendom so splendid an assembly—four Kings, five Queens, princes and arch-dukes three to the sou! The great church lit by a thousand lamps and tapers, the gilt crosses, the robes, the jewels, the swords of state—a fitting background for those two that knelt at the high altar.

So handsome a couple—the groom not as yet twenty-four carrying his magnificence with grace; the bride, the pretty child almost extinguished beneath her own glories. From her narrow shoulders a cloak of cherry velvet lined with gold tissue fell back from a gown of cloth-of-gold; beneath the light coronet the straight, pale hair flowed like water either side of the small face. So white she was, so still, so earnest she might have been a little stone saint.

Madam Queen Margaret watching, chided herself for a troubled spirit. Surely these two were made for happiness. If the bride were so little a girl, she would grow; and if the groom were not overwise, he would by God's grace come to wisdom. Two such blest young creatures were bound to aid and comfort each the other . . . unless . . . unless . . .

Piers Gaveston.

Did Edward, too, think of him in this moment? She crossed herself against the thought.

They had put the bride to bed with all the ceremony of custom—the games, the jest, the drinking by bride and groom from one cup. And now the nuptial blessing given and all custom duly observed, the guests, reluctant, departed. In the stillness they had left behind, the groom came from the bed and reached for his bedgown. She looked at him with unbelieving eyes. Could be he leaving her. But he must stay! The lewd jest, his splendid nakedness had excited her. She wanted to sleep in his arms—no more than that; she had to feel her way into womanhood. He bent to take his Goodnight; she put her thin child's arms about his neck. 'Will you not stay ... a little?' Gently he unclasped them. He had no desire for women and she, mercifully, was a child.

'Not tonight,' he told her. 'So long a day; I'll not weary you. God keep you in his care.' He kissed her courteously upon both cheeks and was gone.

A full fortnight of ceremony—public prayers, processions, feasting and tournaments. But for all their gracious smiling, neither bride nor groom was happy. She was pricked with desire for her husband. The sight of his maleness, the mere naming of her as *wife* had forced her, already precocious, into too-early blooming: and making more painful her desire, pride burned that he had no desire for her. As on their bridal night he commended her to God and left her. Free of demand upon his manhood he was already wearying for Piers. Nor had it pleased him to kneel to his father-in-law in homage for his French lands. It seemed to him unworthy of a King of England to kneel before a King of France. As her pride burned with neglect so his with the homage given. He could not quickly enough leave for home.

February the fifth; and all ready for the journey. 'Home!' Edward said with joy; 'We are going home!'

Isabella said nothing; already there was question in her eyes. She carried with her a vast retinue, but of the gentlemen she found comfort in her uncles alone—Charles of Valois and Louis of Evreux; of the ladies in Madam Queen Margaret and Théophania de St. Pierre.

'I am glad of my uncles,' she told Théophania. 'They will be fathers to me in a strange land.'

'What need of fathers?' Théophania said, troubled. 'You have a husband now!'

'Yes, I have a husband.' She said no more. Resentment was hard within her; a hardness ready to melt at the first sign of warmth.

Kindness and courtesy in him were never-failing; but of warmth, of loving—never a sign.

A smooth journey but cold, cold as the cheer in her own heart; she remained within the forecastle with Madam Queen Margaret.

On the deck the King paced with ever-rising excitement. There they were, his cliffs, faint on the skyline! Soon he would hold Piers in his arms again. Piers, Piers!

He turned from joyous contemplation to see his Queen wrapped in a fur hood that framed her small wind-bright face. He took himself from the thought of Piers to consider the child he had married.

'Home!' he cried out and pointed towards the land.

'Yes,' she said. There was about her an air of desolation. For the first time it came to him that she might need reassurance.

'I hope you will be happy!' He took her by the hand. 'Mary and Elizabeth long to meet their new sister. Mary's a nun but she's often at court. She travels a good deal; she has an especial dispensation. She'll give us all the news—she's a gay person, you'll like her. And Elizabeth's the kindest, the best of sisters. You'll find the chief ladies of our court waiting besides; they were summoned at our command. They ask nothing but to serve you; you will like them all.'

You will like them! not, *They will like you!* Neither for the first time nor the last was he to wound her with his careless kindness.

She stood by her husband, a lonely little creature, smitten into shyness at the company drawn up on the shore. Edward brought up the ladies one by one; and down they went in their curtseys upon the wet stones. The Princess Mary she knew at once by her nun's habit. Elizabeth she knew, too, by her likeness to the King; she looked to be about the same age, and like him as two peas—save that her charming face held more warmth.

'This is Margaret, wife to Gilbert of Clare, my nephew of Gloucester.' He gave his hand to a very young girl scarce older than the Queen herself. Isabella caught the moment's shadow on his face and remembered that Gilbert's mother had died less than a year ago; of all his sisters the King had loved Joanna best.

And now the King led forth my lady of Lancaster, my lady of

Pembroke, my lady of Norfolk, my lady of Lincoln—their husbands she had already met in Boulogne. Lady after lady . . .

She stood there smitten into an appalling shyness, overcome with the need to weep for her most shocking loneliness. But, child of her breeding, she forced her mouth to smile; and they, seeing the pretty, gentle-seeming child, smiled back from joyful faces. And no-one could have foreseen the future; least of all the forlorn child that stood smiling from a stiff, cold face.

It was only later, in face of the King's expressed disappointment, that she realised Gaveston had not come to greet his King; neither he nor his lady.

'It's his way,' Elizabeth, my lady Hereford, whispered in her ear. 'He keeps the King waiting to send up his value—if that could be!'

'And his wife; is she so proud she cannot come to greet her Queen?'

'No. She's gentle. I know her well; she's my niece—my sister Joanna's girl. But she does what her husband bids her. And, besides, they're new-wed; she cannot bear him from her sight.'

'Respect to her Queen comes first!' Isabella said. It was her first prick on account of Gaveston.

Yet still she was prepared to like him; at the very least to accept him. He did not care for women? She would teach him better. They would all three be friends: her husband's friends must be her own.

When she saw the man himself she was not inclined to take him seriously. His handsome looks, his airs and graces did him no good in her sight. He came swaggering in a mantle and suit finer by far than the King's And the cut of his clothes scandalised her.

Her first thought was that he had forgotten his cote. He wore a tight-fitting jacket that reached no further than his waist, where, beneath the hose his virile charms were clearly displayed; and, as though to attract further attention to those charms, one leg was striped blue upon green, the other green upon blue. Never had she seen such odd hose nor so short a jacket. Even in Paris where they wore the cote shorter than here, the most fashionable of young men carried it midway between thigh and knee. Yet surely this must be his outer cote, for there were the long tight sleeves of his undercote showing beneath the long, wide sleeves extravagantly dagged and sweeping to the ground. And if the scandalous cut of his cote didn't call enough attention to itself, the material of rich silk ran in crossways stripes of blue and green. Such a fantasy of dagging and striping she had never seen before; it made the head spin. She was to hear later from an admiring King that this most daring of garments had come direct from Italy, leader of fashion in the courts of Christendom.

He came walking gracefully with a slight kick forward to avoid tripping over the absurd points of his shoes, the longest she had ever seen. He wore his fantastic clothes, she must admit, with elegance. He did not bow to the King but flinging his arm about Edward's neck, *Brother! Brother!* he cried—and even the King's own brothers had not dared as much. And there they stood, hugging and kissing like a pair of sweethearts and a fine pair of fools they looked! They offended her fastidious taste; nor was the offence less that they behaved as though she were not there at all, she, Queen of England, *Madame* of France.

Margaret of Clare, Gaveston's wife, made her reverence. Isabella could have liked her—the shy, elegant creature, the King's niece and now her own. But she must allow herself no kindness for this charming girl scarce older than herself.

'She was born honest but she's mad for love of her husband. He neglects her and she'd sell her soul for a kind word from him!' Elizabeth had said. 'I love her dearly but I must warn you—watch your words; be sure they'll go straight back to him!'

Nor did Isabella find her annoyance with Gaveston less as they took the road to Eltham there to stay until preparations for the crowning were complete. After that first meeting he had tried to win the offended Queen. He had been over-gallant, over-familiar. A certain look in his eye she found both offensive and disturbing. It was a look half-ardent, half-amused, and wholly disrespectful. His eye would linger upon her thin body, and especially upon the budding breasts beneath the tight gown. She was conscious of her immaturity; did he admire or did he mock? She would feel her breasts tingle and rise—and for that disliked him the more. Nor did his biting tongue amuse her; she doubted not at all that, alone with the King, he spared herself nothing of his wicked wit; nor that, so far from reproving, the King would smile his lazy smile. Even in this short time she had wearied of the man—the swagger, the flaunting of his power over the King; and she was ashamed, young as she was, of the familiarity between them—the sickening fondling.

And now they were for London, Gaveston fantastically riding in dagged and lozenged velvet. A foolish fashion for the miry roads, Isabella thought; it showed poor taste and poorer sense.

The great procession took its slow way upon the rutted roads and, lumbering in its wake, came the baggage-trains carrying the new Queen's furnishings—the carved beds, the chairs, the chests and presses heavy with clothes, with household linen; the carpets, the cushions, the tapestries, the feather-beds; and the two baths without which she never travelled.

Already homesick, Isabella looked out upon the winter-bound countryside and wondered if, at this rate, they should ever reach London; and whether she should find it gay as Paris. She sat within the red-and-gold charette with Madam de St. Pierre while Gaveston rode with the King, those two bending towards each other laughing and chatting. Her anger against them both grew steadily. She longed to be riding with the King instead of being shut within the cold and stuffy charette. More than once she had invited Madam Queen Margaret, but at the suggestion that she should get to know her husband's sisters, she had invited Mary and Elizabeth. Mary, a gay and gossipy thirty, could tell a good tale—not always suitable in a nun; she liked rich clothes and rich food. The wonder was that she had ever become a nun. 'I had no choice,' she said. 'At five years old I was offered to God. No, the rigours of the cloister trouble me not at all. I am free to come and go as I please. And, indeed, there are so many family occasions—betrothals, marriages, births and deaths—I am scarcely in my convent at all! And Mother Abbess approves; the convent is always the richer for my journeys. I come back with my hands full of gifts.'

Isabella found Mary amusing and sent for her often. But even more she liked Elizabeth; warm and gay she made a charming companion. She knew everybody; her advice was wise, tactful and to the point. Once Isabella thought of inviting Gloucester's sister; the girl was, after all, her own niece by marriage. But the girl was

Gaveston's wife; the Queen had no mind for a constant watch upon her tongue.

Day after day shut within the charette save when they came to a town; then she came forth to ride beside the King, and Gaveston must fall behind. The people would press forward to cheer and kiss their hands to the pretty child. Her tender years, her ready smile, her slight and childish grace moved all hearts; and the King, popular and charming, was showered with yet more approval for his most happy choice.

London at last. And the Mayor and sheriffs and all the guilds riding out to meet them, to bring them into the city where the gay colours of holiday dress, the tapestries floating from the windows, the ribands and evergreens turned winter into summer. And, warm as summer, those two felt the joy, the blessings called down upon their young heads. Never so well-loved, so well-graced a couple. Everything set fair.

And so to Westminster. Used though she was to the luxury of the French court, Isabella could find no fault with the Queen's lodgings. The fresh stone, the walls new-painted with fanciful devices pleased her well; her own tapestries worked with golden leopards and lilies upon scarlet gave her a happy sense of home.

Time, a little time; and she would woo the King to her bed and send Gaveston packing. Here her new life began; it should be a happy one. She was singing under her breath as she watched the women about their unpacking, the clerk to the Queen's Wardrobe standing by.

First the gowns and mantles, with Madam de St. Pierre watchful to see them shaken and laid within presses. Such gowns, such mantles! Scarlet-cloths of every dye; deep-piled samites and lighter taffetas, gold and silver tissues and most beautiful of all six gowns of marbrinus; she liked the white one best, its stiff silk marbled with gold.

Out came the furs—minniver and mink, ermine and vair; and now piles of shifts fine enough to pass through a wedding ring, and with them gorgets and headveils transparent as water. Half-a-dozen men staggered beneath the weight of heavy linen; one hundred and forty yards of it to hang about her bath for privacy.

And now for the jewels, casket after casket. Coronets to hold the headveil in place—seventy-two of them, some simple, some heavily jewelled. And two crowns; one for state occasions set with great gems, emeralds and rubies, sapphires and diamonds; and the other for lesser occasions set with pearls to sit light upon a young, small head. Out came brooches and clasps, bracelets and rings. The winter sun struck forth arrows of rainbow light.

Quite suddenly she was tired of it all; the rest must wait until tomorrow.

'I have the list of Madam the Queen's household plate,' Théophania told John of Falaise, Master Clerk to the Queen's Wardrobe. 'Twelve great dishes and three small ones, together with forty-eight porringers, all of fine silver for Madam the Queen's daily use. For great occasions, six great dishes of pure gold and six smaller ones, likewise of gold. Of porringers . . .'

'If Madam the Queen will make choice of things for her immediate use, the rest shall go to the Tower; the Queen's Wardrobe is stored in the northern turret. We shall need, I fancy, ten wagons.'

She smiled her gracious thanks, glad that so honest a man and one so faithful to her service should have in charge these precious gifts.

Master John dismissed at last, Madam de St. Pierre watched the women change the Queen into a gown of fine green scarlet-cloth, for the air struck chill in this palace by the river. The clear colour of the gown brought out the green in her changing eyes; should she, she wondered, wear her hair free-flowing? She was a married woman and should enclose it beneath a guimpe; but some married women wore their hair flowing free. And besides, she was a virgin; she might do well to remind her husband of the fact! She preferred her hair hanging loose; beneath the guimpe her face appeared too thin, too young. Madam de St. Pierre loosed the long, pale locks and set the lighter crown upon them. She handed her mistress the looking-glass, stopped to arrange the folds of green and bowed herself from the room.

Patient, Isabella awaited the King. Surely he would come to welcome her this first night in her new home, to lead her down to supper.

He did not come. Into the great hall she went alone, Théophania at her right hand and the page carrying her train. She took her place by the King; but all she got of him was his turned cheek and back as he bent to Gaveston.

She sat there cheeks and pride aflame, picking at the food offered upon bended knee. When the cloth had been cleared and the jugglers come, she rose and curtseyed to the King. He did not rise to lead her from the room, he did not even see her. Absorbed in his friend he had forgotten her.

In her chamber she bade the women undress her and go. Minutes passed to hours; hours stole the night away. But still he did not come. He had forgotten even the cold courtesy of the Goodnight salutation.

She was beginning to understand why the King did not come to her bed.

That passionate affairs existed between men, young as she was, she had long known; one couldn't live at her father's court without knowing. But that a King should so demean himself filled her with shame; that such a one should be given her for husband filled her with fear. Turn him from Gaveston, win him for herself she must. Fear and shame whipped her on.

'Patience,' Madam Queen Margaret said. 'Time is young and the King is young; and you, niece, youngest of all.'

'Twenty-four; I cannot think him over-young!' Isabella said hurt and stubborn. 'As for me, I doubt Gloucester's wife has much advantage in age; nor Gaveston's neither. Fourteen is the right age to bed with a man. And time? It is not so young, neither. Six weeks married; it is time enough!'

'Yet still be patient; time is on your side!' Margaret said and prayed that her words prove true.

Time is young . . . time is on your side. But time went by and things grew no better. The King was kind—when he remembered her existence; behind his kindness she sensed his indifference. She was ready to love him—if he would let her. But she saw him at board only—and then his face was turned from her to Gaveston; in bed she saw him not at all. It was that she found hardest to forgive. He shamed her not only as a Queen but as a woman.

Madam Queen Margaret spoke to him on the matter.

'Sir,' she said; and then, 'Son; things are not good between you and my niece. Oh you are kind enough—when you remember! But my niece should receive from you more than kindness. She's your wife.'

'A child!' He shrugged.

'She's no child. At fourteen many a girl's a full woman. She's a Capet—and in us passions run high. And she is, besides, of Navarre; there girls ripen early and blood runs hot. Your wife is a full woman; you may believe it!'

He threw out his hands in rejection. The idea of bedding with a woman was at no time pleasing; but to bed with so young a girl, to teach her the business of marriage! The thing repelled him. He could not do it.

'You have hurt her pride. She has been well-taught her duty and is ready; the more so that she sees others as young as herself not only wedded but bedded. You shame her in her own eyes and in the eyes of her father; he'll not take it kindly. Well, by God's grace it is not too late. All this time she has asked nothing but to give herself; and, believe me, she has very much to give. But, mark it, son; hers is not a nature to stand still. If you do not take her now she is hot, she'll grow cold. Go to her; show yourself man to woman! Let her grow cold and she'll turn against you. And then, I know her nature and her stock—you had best beware!'

'You make too much of the matter. I tell you the girl's too young!'

'It is not my niece you consider in this. You do not want her or any woman. Your heart's elsewhere . . .'

He swallowed in his throat. 'If you mean Piers, then say so!'

'I do mean . . . Piers.' Her mouth was distasteful about the name.

'You cannot divide us!' He was suddenly passionate with hot Plantagenet anger, 'We are one.'

'Then,' she said, 'I cannot think which of you three I pity most. I think it is you, my son.'

Chapter Four

Preparations for the crowning were going on apace; Gaveston had complete charge. In the short time she had been in Westminster she had not only seen enough of Gaveston, she had heard more; more than enough. They were saying everywhere that the King was mad to entrust any sort of ceremony to him, let alone a crowning. They were saying that Gaveston looked to make a pretty penny out of the affair. They were saying another thing too—that the best part of the wedding-gifts, not the King's alone but her own, too, had already come into his hands. That her father's gifts to the King should be lightly handed over to another she found hard to believe; that her own personal possessions should be given away—and no word to herself—that she found incredible.

She began to use her eyes. The great S. chain her father had given the groom she saw adorning Gaveston; he wore—her father's gift also—the gold clasp of fleur-de-lys. That she had coveted for herself but had not dared to ask; now here it was fastening Gaveston's cloak.

'You wear our lilies, my lord?' she asked cold as snow.

'I love whatever comes out of France, Madam!' he said, very quick, and raked her head to foot with that long impertinent stare.

She turned a furious back upon him. She went straight to her rooms to demand her jewel-casket. When she unlocked it with shaking fingers she found it half empty.

'My lord King had the keys of me,' Madam de St. Pierre said, distressed. 'It is but two days or three. It was wise, he said; women are careless with keys.'

She went storming into the King's closet; Piers was there, elegantly lounging.

'Sir!' she cried out and in her anger did not wait for his nod nor go down upon her curtsey.

'Madam the Queen forgets her devoir to the King,' Piers said, insolent.

Of him she took no notice. 'Sir,' she cried out again, 'some thief has been at my jewels.'

'Then you had best question your household.'

'Sir, I have. I am told, that you, sir, took the keys.'

'Why so I did; and returned them again. But that is not in question. I am no thief, Madam, since what is yours is mine; and what is mine I do with as I choose.'

She saw the small smile lift Gaveston's lips; he put up a hand as if to hide it; and there upon the little finger shone the great ruby ring—her mother's parting gift. He saw her whiten. He said, bowing, 'I told you, Madam, I love all things that come out of France.'

His smiling, his false courtesy was the last straw. In that moment, hatred for him was born.

She turned her back upon them, defying etiquette, she went stumbling upon the long points of her shoes; the long train, also, threatened to trip her, but she gave it no thought. She could not quickly enough reach the shelter of her own chamber. In the solitude of her private closet she put her face into her hands and wept. Her tears surprised her; she did not easily weep. Anger got the better of her tears. She would stay to be insulted no longer. She would write to her father, tell him of the insults they had put upon her—those two; tell also, of the insult put upon himself—that even now his gifts were adorning the favourite. She asked advice of none. Madam de St. Pierre, she knew, would stop her, saying it was unwise for so young a bride to complain thus quickly; and certainly Madam Queen Margaret would say the same. In hot blood the letter was written and despatched before either lady knew of it.

The first Madam Queen Margaret heard was when the King came storming into her apartments the day the messenger arrived from France.

'A toad, a snake, a wife that knows no loyalty!'

'She is scarce your wife,' she reminded him.

'Nor shall be until she learns to behave herself!'

Isabella had done herself little good. She had angered her husband to no purpose. Her father's remonstrances were politely answered—and there it ended save that a strain had been put upon the friendship between the two Kings; the new precarious friendship. She must learn, she saw now, to go more secretly, more subtly about her business.

Her anger was no longer a child's; jealousy and humiliation were turning her, all too soon, into a woman. And it was the more hurtful because she could not look upon her husband's high and handsome looks, his elegance, his grace, without a quickening in all her blood. Had he meant to torment her with jealousy he could have found no better way.

One consolation she had. In hatred of Gaveston she was not alone. Save for the King there was not one that did not hate him; and greater even than hatred was scorn. He was a foreigner and his birth humble. Let him declare his birth gentle; what was he but a country squire and poor with it? Compared with the peers of England he was, for all his new earldom, no more than the dirt beneath their feet.

She was beginning to learn them—these earls, these barons; beginning to know how to flatter them.

'Henry de Lacy, he's earl of Lincoln—our premier peer, and of course older than the rest. He's honest to the core but slow to move!' Madam Queen Margaret said, not dreaming that her niece was weighing each word for her own use. 'A kindly man that considers well before he acts.'

The girl nodded. *Show myself patient and gentle and helpless . . . win his heart for the ill-used little Queen.*

'He has no son of his own. His son-in-law Thomas of Lancaster is his heir.'

And he hates Gaveston. The King's cousin he may be; but he's my own uncle, my mother's brother.

'A man of contradictions,' Queen Margaret said. 'He'd like to lead the earls, he'd like to rule the Council; he'd like to rule the King. He can't wait for his father-in-law to die that he may step into his shoes. He opposes the King in everything good or bad; and the King hates him. He's an angry man, Thomas of Lancaster, and bitter. The whole world's his enemy; and the one he hates most, more even than Gaveston, is de Warenne.'

'I dislike him myself; a stupid brute of a man.'

If I want Lancaster and Lincoln I must keep clear of de Warenne. But never offend him; the pricked bull is dangerous.

'I like Pembroke best,' Isabella said.

'And may well do so! He's the pick of the bunch. He has a quickness to think and to understand that most of the others lack. He's no angel though! Self-seekers all; but he's the best.'

'Gloucester I find charming.'

'Charming he is; but more than that he's honest and generous and kind. He takes after his mother—the King hasn't got over her death yet. Gloucester's going to be important one day; he's too young at present, not above sixteen.'

She was thoughtful leaving her aunt's chamber. Lincoln, Lancaster, de Warenne, Pembroke and Gloucester—she'd got them clear in her mind. The others—Arundel, Richmond and Hereford—she knew little about them, except that they were the King's friends; indeed she scarce knew them apart. There remained Warwick; no forgetting him! Sour mouth, shifty eyes and chin like a rock. A man to watch. A clever woman would know how to use him. She was not clever enough yet; she was clever enough to know it.

To all of them she would show herself sad, brave and ill-used . . . the gentle little Queen.

She felt anger growing steadily against the King; and hid her own. The top and bottom of his offending was Gaveston. Gaveston had been recalled against the old, good King's expressed wish. Gaveston had royal honours heaped upon him. And Gaveston's tongue had a cutting edge that spared no-one. Their own personal affronts the barons scarcely mentioned; they took a nobler line. The Queen's dignity had been insulted. She must take second place to the foreign upstart—if any place at all. He wore her jewels, he treated her with an abominable rudeness, he kept the King from her bed. Their resolve went forth. As long as Gaveston remained at court they would not attend the crowning. The King should have a week to consider of the matter.

Not attend her crowning! She had not meant them to go this far! In after years mightn't it be forgotten that anger against Gaveston had kept them away? Might it not be put down to some offence within herself?

Fear sent her flying to her aunt's chamber; and there she found them both—Gaveston restless with annoyance so that he could neither sit nor stand but must wander fingering this and that; and the King, blue eyes ablaze and the rest of him white and cold . . . cold as death.

'Let them stay away!' Gaveston was crying out, his voice thin and shrill. 'What odds as long as we find a bishop to crown you. What can they add to the business, the loud-mouthed bullies?'

'It is unthinkable they should be absent!' Madam Queen Margaret said.

'I care not how long we postpone it, I'd liefer have Canterbury do the job; but he's in Rome. Give him a week and he'll be back. As for absenting themselves—let them do it till Kingdom come. I'll give up Piers—never!'

Isabella stood pale and silent; some inner voice warned her to silence.

Margaret said, 'I cannot think it good to put off the crowning, sir. To my mind it's a bad beginning. Get yourself crowned as soon as may be. This is a trial of strength between you and your lords; to put it off from day to day—that's no policy at all. No! Meet them friendly, listen to their demands; some demands are best met.'

'They make no demand save that I give up Piers; and that I'll never do! Send my brother from me? Never!' And his arm went about Piers' shoulder.

'There are other complaints,' Margaret said, 'and some are just.

The debts for instance; and nothing to meet them! That's scarce your fault—left as you are with debts from your father and his father before him. But you have added to them—considerably. You might,' and now she spoke slowly, 'perhaps spend a little less.' And her eye rested on Piers.

She saw the King's jaw go rigid and knew it for anger. She said, 'If you cannot meet their complaints, tell them it is because time is short, that you can do nothing before the crowning. When you are crowned—and if they come seemly to your crowning—you will listen to their requests.'

But not grant them! Isabella caught the sly smiling between those two, Piers and the King.

'Sirs,' the King told his peers assembled, 'You would slight your King, willing though he is to listen to your demands when this present press of time is over. But, are you willing to slight Madam the Queen that has offended no-one?'

'Sir, we are not!' Henry of Lincoln spoke for them all, his son-in-law Lancaster adding in a whisper that could not but reach the King, 'Before God she has slights enough!'

'Sir,' Lincoln said, 'we will come to the crowning, we will renew the oath of allegiance. But afterwards let the lord King keep his promise.'

It was by no means the end of the trouble.

Edward came striding into his step-mother's bower: he was bone-white, leper-white.

'They *dare!*' And the voice choked in his throat. 'They seek to alter the oath; the oath the King makes at his crowning!'

Something of this she had heard. She sat quiet above her stitching and let him speak.

'Always the King makes his own promises; in his own words he makes them. It is our custom. But they would bind me with *their* promises; make me speak *their* words! Am I less than my father?' and he screamed in his rage.

She could have told him; she bit back the words.

'Here, in England, the oath has never been exact—so much is true,' she said. 'Now the barons would have it set down, the self-same words handed down from King to King. It is nothing against *you* . . .'

'Is it not?' he cried out, passionate. 'I'll take no oath but of my own devising!'

But they knew both of them he would repeat the oath his lords devised—exactly worded, exactly promised.

Chapter Five

February the twenty-fifth, in the year of grace thirteen hundred and eight, the King and Queen went to their crowning. A grey and sullen day to match the King's mood; he was coldly, viciously angry. It was for the King to promise, freely to promise; not to repeat, obedient as a child, the words put into his mouth. With this oath they struck at the heart of majesty.

But for all his sullen anger he looked handsome beyond all men Isabella thought; and she herself, in cloth-of-gold, the mantle lined with ermine matched him well. Gaveston appeared and her good humour broke. He was dressed finer than any prince of them all, finer than the King—the King that was to be crowned. He drew every eye with his fantastic splendour. She shut her eyes against him and his magnificence.

They had spent the night in the Tower; now they were to ride through London to Westminster to show themselves to the people. Already the King had broken his fast; Isabella caught the wine on his breath. To eat before the sacrament of crowning! So wanton a challenging of God struck at her careless young heart.

And now the procession was about to start. First came the priests and monks, crosses held high and chanting, leading the princes of the church in gold embroidered copes, jewelled croziers lifted before them. Upon their heels rode the peers of the realm led by Thomas of Lancaster and his brother Henry by right of close kinship to both King and Queen; and between them Henry of Lincoln premier baron of them all. Behind them the Queen's uncles from France led the foreign princes. Now came the royal family—the princess Elizabeth of Hereford and Mary the nun, followed the King's half-brothers Thomas of Brotherton and Edmund of Woodstock riding to right and left of their mother. Gallant boys and good to look upon; at the sight of all three a cheer went up, for Margaret the good Queen was well-loved.

And now, by themselves, the King and Queen. At the sight of those two, so handsome and so young, his weaknesses forgotten, the cheering swelled to a roar. It reaches to the sky, Isabella thought; the whole world is full of joyful sound. Her heart beat high.

Her joy was all too soon cut short. For there was Gaveston, riding from his place and pressing close to the King—Gaveston handsomer than any man has the right to be, more insolent than any man has the right to be. In that split second she felt the mood of the people change ... *He will turn all hearts from the King.* Angry, a little frightened, she bent her young head, smiled her gracious thanks.

Through garlanded and beribboned streets the slow procession passed; and all the way the sweet of the people's welcome was spoiled for the Queen by Gaveston; and through the whole of this great day the thought of him came pricking.

Ar Westminster the King and Queen alighted and into the palace they went while the procession rearranged itself to enter the abbey. All were in their places when hand-in-hand the King and Queen came forth to walk—according to custom—beneath the blue silk canopy ajingle with bells.

Within the abbey it was not the peers alone that waited, but their ladies with them. The King had commanded their presence also. It was the first time the wives of peers had been summoned to a crowning; the King had thought of it in one of his gracious moments —a charming gesture to do greater honour to the Queen. And, for this she was ready to forget all slights, to love him again.

The King walked alone in his ruined world. *With this oath they insult me in the eyes of Christendom.*

Within the glowing jewel of the abbey those two walked to their places; the congregation rose and the voice of the choir swelled in angelic praise; but the King was like a dead man walking. Obedient to the bishop's hand he allowed himself to be shown to the people. Scarce heeding he heard their joyful acceptance. The words of the bishop, the exhortations fell upon deaf ears. He waited for the dreaded moment.

And now it was come: the oath must be sworn. In one thing, at least, he had had his way. It was to be sworn in French instead of Latin. Some Latin he had; and besides he knew the accursed oath by heart, but he dared not risk anything being slyly slipped in at the last moment. Even now he found himself wondering what, if they played that trick, he should do.

My lord bishop was standing now before the King and, in the utter silence, his voice rose.

'Sir, will you guard and keep and by your oath confirm to the people of England, the laws and customs granted them by their ancient Kings, your righteous predecessors, under God? And, in particular will you confirm the laws, the customs and the freedoms granted to the clergy and the people by the glorious King, Saint Edward?'

And the King's voice colourless, each word dropping cold as stone, 'I grant it; and will keep my promise.'

'Will you keep peace according to God and His holy church, towards the clergy and the people, perfectly and entirely and with all your might?'

'I will keep it.'

'Will you, with all your might, cause true justice to be done—and to be seen to be done—in wisdom, in truth and in mercy?'

'I will do it.'

'Do you promise to hold by the laws and rightful customs which the people of your realm shall determine; and will you defend them and enforce them to the honour of God and with all your strength?'

At this he hesitated . . . *the laws which the people shall determine.* Then what became of the divine right of Kings? But the silence waited and he must reply.

'I promise; and will abide by my promise.'

The first King of England to take that oath. Yet so simple the oath, so right, so proper, how could any man—even the King himself—fault it? Yet its very simplicity hid the full meaning. Few there understood its power to control the King—not even the King himself, resenting, only, the affront to his pride. But those that had framed it, barons and bishops weaving each word into a rope, knew well the strength of each strand. Let the King break one strand, one strand only—and what was he then but a King that had broken faith? And to such a King it could be right and proper to break one's own faith?

And now came the sacred moment of the anointing. But not even sacred oil upon his head, his hands, his breast, was balm to soothe his wounded pride. And all the while he lay prostrate before the high altar, offering himself to God, he nursed his bitter pride. And when they raised him and robed him in the long white robe and put upon him the tunicle of red bordered with gold and the dalmatic of shot gold and silver, he stood longing to strike the hands that touched him.

And now came Thomas of Lancaster bearing the Sword of Mercy and the bishop buckled it about the King's waist. And Henry of Lancaster came bearing the Rod of Peace and the bishop put it into the King's left hand; and Thomas of Lincoln brought the golden sandals and knelt to fasten the spurs.

The great ceremony was drawing to its end. They fastened upon the King the square mantle of majesty; they placed upon his finger the ring that wedded him to his people. And now came Gloucester bearing the sceptre and the bishop put it into the King's right hand.

So far, so good.

But what was this? Who was it that came carrying the St. Edward crown? Who but Gaveston making ridiculous this highest moment, belittling the King in his great robes of majesty. Inscrutable in the silence the bishop took it; inscrutable placed it upon the King's head.

Sitting there grave and still a, small image of majesty, Isabella knew the anger rising in the abbey; knew it by the anger in her own heart. Hateful the oath forced upon the unwilling tongue but needful; needful to curb this foolish King. Yet it put the power into the wrong hands—the barons' hands. Power belonged to the King. Then whose were the right hands? Not her own. She was but fourteen and . . . a foreigner. But she could learn; learn these people and their ways. Yes, she must watch, she must listen, she must learn; forever learn. One day—not too far distant—she might help this foolish King. It was her coronation oath to herself. One thing she had already learned during these uneasy weeks. Patience hid beneath a child's helplessness is woman's most potent weapon.

One by one the peers came to kneel. She did not find the long procession tedious. She sat intent watching each man, weighing him, considering his possibilities.

And now it was her own turn to be crowned. The ceremony was short, the anointing upon the hands only. But it was done. She was an anointed, a crowned Queen.

There remained now only the King's formal offerings in gold; and out they came, blinking a little, into the grey of the February daylight.

Isabella was tired; the great mantle dragged at her shoulders, the crown weighed heavy upon her head. And she was faint with hunger; she had not yet broken her fast—she had due regard to what one owed to God.

They returned to the palace to find all in disorder. The tables were spread but of food there was no sign save the stench of burnt meat. She sought her own chamber to rest until all should be ready; but, when the King came to lead her to the feast, the tables stood empty as before. The great golden salt-sellar glittered upon the gold-fringed cloth; but of food—nothing; not even the piled bread.

The guests were already seated. There had been some disturbances, places had not been assigned; now seated with no order of precedence, they looked upon the empty tables. In their black looks and angry buzzing, anger was plain.

Gaveston has charge of all. Well, let him take full credit! Faint with hunger, Isabella yet found satisfaction in the thought. Even the King, besotted as he was, could not pretend that Gaveston had done well; he had not even troubled to apportion the honours of serving the King on his crowning-day. Where was the baron with basin for washing the King's hands, where the baron with the towel? Where the earl with the ceremonial cup of wine to open the feast, where the earl with the ceremonial gloves?

Of them no sight; nor would be. For now, at last, they were carrying in the first course. The young page kneeling—since no baron had been appointed for her service—offered the cup. Beneath its silver cover the soup was cold. Now came a boar's head glazed, white tusks shining; it was tough and over-spiced and she put it by. Venison followed but the sauce was lumpy, the cream sour.

Dish after dish. Heron and swan and a great pike cooked in wine; the birds were not over-fresh and the great fish raw at the bone. The first course ended with a huge pancake; it lacked sugar but she was glad of anything to assuage her hunger.

They were bringing in the second course. So there was to be no subtlety! She had looked forward to the pretty figures of sparkling sugar which should end each course.

Now came geese and bittern; the birds were greasy and under-cooked. They were followed by a great venison pasty, its raised crust embossed with the arms of England and France. By some miracle it was good to eat. Beef and mutton were carried in next. She was glad she had eaten the pasty for the beef was black as cinder and the mutton running with blood. Now came the centrepiece of the feast—a peacock carried high on a silver platter, and dressed in all his glory; but the tail feathers drooped into the sauce; it had lost its attraction. The second course was over; again there was no subtlety.

The feast was but two-thirds over and already food was running out. *Gaveston has skimped both food and service to fill his own pocket.* She caught the rumour as it spread from table to table. And she could see it was true. Not only were some plates empty but what food there was, all but thrown at the guests.

She sat there, cheeks burning; she was not the only one out of humour. She caught sight of her French uncles glowering; the barons bent black brows. Only the King sat smiling; he was not sorry, she thought, to affront his magnates. He and Gaveston would, no doubt, sup cosily in the King's closet. She was sick with fatigue, with hunger and with shame. If only she might rise and go weep away her distress.

But still it went on, the noise and confusion.

And now the King's champion came riding to announce the King's titles and to challenge any that should question them. There was such a jostling and a pushing and a screaming to get out of the way of the horse's hooves, it was a mercy no-one was killed. Impossible to hear the words the champion spoke. There he sat high on the great horse his mouth opening and shutting—and no sound. So shameful a thing had never befallen in all the time since Norman William had brought this handsome custom to England.

In came the third course; she caught the stale whiff of crabs and lampreys as she waved them away. Cranes and curlews stuffed; antelopes and conies cooked in wine. The air was heavy with the smells of meat and fish. And now to end the feast, mercifully to end it, a subtlety. It was carried high upon a dish of gold. Two sugar figures represented herself and the King; she guessed it by their crowns, for already the sugar that should have been as hard as ice and glittering was soft and sweating; a sugar child kneeling, offered a scroll.

The King turned about, and, for the first time, spoke to her reading the rhyme aloud.

> 'In your glance
> Queen from France
> England rejoices
> With all her voices.'

She could not force a smile at the wretched lines.

It was over; over at last. My lord bishop had pronounced the blessing. Had she thought the long misery over? The King was adding the crowning-piece. He was leaving the table affectionately entwined with Gaveston—and both of them staggering.

He had left her to make her exit alone; again, again he had forgotten her. She rose in her place; her ladies picked up the train. Charles of Valois came from his seat to take her by the hand. She passed between the standing guests; save for her whiteness she gave no sign.

Unsmiling, unspeaking, she let the women undress her; they removed the crown, loosed the long, pale hair, put her bedgown upon her. Théophania brought her wine, white bread, cold chicken and the little almond cakes she loved. She did not even see them. And now, all of them dismissed, she sat alone. So she had sat too many nights; but this night of her crowning she had thought must be different. She gave herself to bitter thought.

The crown of state she had worn earlier lay upon its cushion; it drew her eye. *The hateful, vulgar muddle is nothing, is less than nothing. The crown, the crown is all . . .*

She rose and step by slow step walked across the room to take it in her hands. Again it surprised her by its weight; yet already she had felt it heavy upon her head ... the crown, the crown.

She turned it about, eyes fascinated, lips drawn to a thin line, jaw set so that the bones strong and beautiful showed clear.

She raised the crown and set it upon her head. Now she expected the weight; now she was ready. And so standing, crowned and indomitably proud she was beautiful; she was formidable. Had her husband come upon her now he must have seen the truth of Queen Margaret's words. No child this, for all her tender years, but a woman purposeful, not to be set aside. But he did not come. He was in his closet toying with Gaveston.

For some moments she stood; the crown grew heavier still upon her head, the young neck began to tremble. With reverent hands she lifted the crown from her head and set it again upon the cushion. She sat down and could not take her eyes from its glory.

Of a sudden hunger took her. She fell upon the food, swallowing bread, chicken and wine; since there was none to see, she picked up the crumbs that, in her haste, she had let fall upon gown and floor and ate them too. And now she could sleep. She fell asleep at once, and in her dreaming smiled—for a hand, bright as a sword, reached down from the sky to set the crown upon her head.

Chapter Six

Early in the morning her French uncles came to bid her farewell. Feasts and tournaments had been prepared for their entertainment. But of English hospitality they had had enough; she could not blame them. *Gaveston has insulted the majesty of France. The King of England cares more for his mignon than he does for his wife.* Unspoken the message passed between them. Her father had considered her too easily offended; he had made little of her letter. Now her uncles would show him that, without cause, a princess of France had been insulted. Surely, now, he would bring this foolish husband of hers to his senses.

The rest of the guests had departed, the court seemed empty. The King, for the most part courteous, remained cold; both courtesy and coldness enhanced by letters from France. In this court of strangers Isabella knew not who was to be trusted, who avoided. That she must be careful in word and deed she needed no telling. All courts were hotbeds of scandal; and in this court, where Gaveston had the King's heart, more than most. The King had appointed four ladies to her bedchamber. 'Two of them you must watch,' Madam Queen Margaret said. 'Gaveston's wife and Despenser's wife. They're Gloucester's sisters and good girls both. But they are not married to good men . . . and a woman's first duty is to her husband. Gaveston's wife would put her own neck under the axe for him, never mind another's.'

'I could have liked her,' Isabella said, regretful.

'You may still like her; and pity her, too . . . an open nature driven against itself by such a man! Like her, pity her—but never trust her. Trust her sister still less. She was well enough until she married.

Despenser—ambitious as Gaveston and as greedy; but not so warm-hearted and cleverer by far. And Eleanor's under his thumb. Five years under that thumb! It plays havoc with goodwill and honesty.'

'Five years married? She looks too young!'

'She's full eighteen.'

'Thirteen when she was wed. Did her husband sleep with her?'

Margaret shrugged. 'He's one to take what he wants; a brutal young man.'

'Is a man a brute to sleep with his wife?'

'Each man must do according to his nature. Now for the other two. You may trust them both. There's Elizabeth, the youngest Gloucester girl, she's her mother Joanna all over again; a most lovely person. The other's Gloucester's wife; she's steadfast and true. Pure gold those two; but they're very young. Discretion may not equal honesty.'

'I like them both. Gloucester's wife certainly sleeps with her husband and she's no older than I am.'

'Full fifteen; a whole year older.'

'My age when she began to sleep with him. She's to have a child; no need to tell me, I use my eyes. All four of them living with their husbands as a wife should live. How much longer must I endure the slight the King puts upon me? Every man to his nature—as you say! And the King's nature I begin, alas, to understand. But what of woman's nature; what of *my* nature—answer me that!'

'It is woman's part to be patient—especially in such a matter.'

But the girl was right: Edward was a fool.

Between the King and Queen things were no better. To win her husband, a man cold to women, to turn him from love of Gaveston to love of herself—it was a task an experienced woman might well fear; for Isabella it was hopeless.

The advice concerning discretion she did her best to follow. With her ladies she was pleasant, endeavouring to show no preference and guarding her tongue even with those she might trust. But she was too young to be forever on her guard. All about her she felt the watching distrust of Gaveston's wife, of Despenser's wife.

To Gaveston, himself, she meant to show herself gracious; yet there were times when she must bite upon her tongue not to retort upon his flippancy, his rudeness. Her courtesy to Gaveston went unnoticed by the King; unnoticed by him, also—though not by others—the mignon's scanted courtesy to the Queen.

To the King she showed herself debonair, readily obedient, resentment hidden. And he was pleasant enough, affectionate, even, with the affection he might show a small hound. But beyond that—nothing. And Gaveston kept his eyes upon them both. Let him suspect she was with the King and he made it his business to join them; even into her private closet he would come unasked and unannounced. And, so far from reproving, the King welcomed him with outstretched hands. Yet still she showed herself friendly, thrusting down anger but, for all that, her eyes betrayed her. She could not know how fierce her eyes, glowing amber-green. *Like a cat, a little wild cat,* Gaveston would say laughing. And of all this she kept her close account.

The Princess Elizabeth came up from Hereford; she found the little Queen peaked and unhappy.

'Madam,' she said, 'sister—if I may call you so—you have the wit and the will to save us all. Gaveston—he's no more than the sugarplum my brother never had, and in his childhood should have had! So bleak a childhood, he and I. We never had a home, forever on the move; never the safe place that's home.

'When Edward was two, our parents left England. They were away three whole years. He was five when he saw them again. We went to Dover to meet them. We were both excited; Edward was sick with excitement. *Father, Mother.* He kept saying that over and over again; what it meant to him God knows!

'And what did he find? Our mother—just another woman. She hardly knew us and she was shy; we thought it a coldness in her. I was disappointed; but Edward! And when it came to our father—there was tragedy! The child had expected to find something younger, warmer, kinder ... *human.* And what did he find? An old man. Fifty, my father was—and older than his years; a life of fighting leaves its mark. Think of it! So little a child . . . and the old man, the old stern man. He shrank back. I saw him. And I saw my father's face. *My son shrinks from me.*

'It was the beginning of the trouble between them. My father didn't understand children; his girls he loved—he didn't expect too much of them. From his boy he expected too much; the courage, the endurance of a grown man. He tried to strengthen the child with the whip; and that didn't make things better. Edward was just beginning to know our mother, to go to her for comfort—and then she died. He was just six.

'So there he was—a motherless, frightened child, the object of his father's deepest love. . . and deepest fears. A handsome boy, very strong. He rode well, he made good showing with his little sword; in every sport quick and skilled. But he lacked something; princely dignity, my father thought. Well, that was no wonder! While my father lived Edward was never his own master. When he was too old for a whipping, he'd be punished another way. Humiliated by harsh words, his allowance stopped, forced to trail at my father's heels like a dog expecting the whip. He lost faith in himself. He began to seek the company of low fellows; and he found some comfort using his hands . . . making things. He'd plait a basket, or hammer a piece of iron, or make a pattern for my needle. He could stitch better than I could. Once he took my work from me to unpick a fault and my father caught him at it. He snatched the work from my brother and his face went black. In Christ's name, he roared out, what do you call yourself—a lad or wench? And the contempt in his voice was terrible.'

'Can you wonder?' And there was contempt, also, in Isabella's voice.

'Yes, you can wonder! To see some beautiful thing his own hands had made—it was a need in him. Oh he's man enough with sword or spear; but it's the skill he likes, not the blood. He'll fight if he must; and give a good account of himself. Even my father admitted it.

'For eight years after my mother died, my father grieved; a lonely man. And then he married again. Not for love; he loved no woman ever save my mother. He married for peace; peace with

France. A good marriage. It meant more to my brother than he'll ever know. My father's wife was so good to him. And she was young—seventeen to his fourteen; and that helped. But she had to feel her way; he didn't trust her. She'd married the enemy—and she was a woman! But she won him. He loves her and he trusts her. And she? She loves him and she fears for him.'

'She may well do that!' Isabella said, a little spiteful. 'Gaveston turns all hearts from the King.'

'Then you must turn them again; you can do it! Madam, try to understand. Gaveston is come to be the joy in my brother's life, all the sweetness. Gaveston dazzles him. And, above all, to cherish Gaveston is a symbol of revolt; revolt against my father, still more against those barons that like my father would curb him. It is for you, Madam, to teach my brother a new joy.'

'Teach him to play the man in his own bed?'

'Women are wiser in such affairs than men. And you are all of a woman. He's twenty-four and you, fourteen. Yet still you are older. Bear with him, Madam, and teach him. So you save yourself and him and all England. I beseech you, think upon it.'

'I have thought and can find no answer. That a man should love another man above all women, it is hard to understand; harder still to bear. Yet I will try; I will try, I swear it.'

Elizabeth took the Queen's hand and kissed it.

Chapter Seven

The wisdom of Elizabeth's advice Isabella accepted. With a patience foreign to her quick and wilful nature she set herself to woo the King. These days she was learning her craft; the craft of a clever woman exploiting her every charm. She was gentle with a gentleness learned from Madam Queen Margaret, she was gay with a gaiety learned from Madam Princess Elizabeth; and she was discreet beyond her years. Above all she made the most of her budding beauty; she was enough to delight any eye that could tear itself from contemplation of Gaveston.

But still the King looked upon her as a child, albeit a precocious one. When he came, as was now his custom, to bid her Goodnight, she would put forth every art to coax him to stay that he might not go to Piers. Sometimes he would allow himself to be coaxed into bed . . . but no further. Then she would turn to him with passion, locking him in her childish arms. Gentle, he would free himself, kiss her upon both cheeks and take himself off to a more congenial bed. Every failure still further lacerated her pride. But still, though often in despair, she went on trying.

'Were he set upon a woman,' she told Queen Margaret, 'I could, I think, win him. It would be a challenge! But to win him from a man—and such a man! It is a challenge I cannot meet.'

'Handsome enough; but stupid. One day he'll make his blunder.'

'The King's blind with love; he'll never see it.'

'But others will see it; and others will punish. They bide their times, our lords. They'll not endure for ever the way he stands between them and the King so that it's hard for them to come at the King's private ear. Nor will they long endure the way he speaks to them as though they were his servants—this petty Gascon squireling . . .'

'... whose mother was burned as a witch. *A pity they didn't burn her litter with her!,* that is what my uncle of Lancaster says and doesn't care who hears him!'

'Yet he should have care. It is not wise, even for Lancaster, to offend Gaveston.'

But, indeed, Lancaster and his brother Henry of Derby had their own added grievance against the man. Uncles by blood to the Queen —sons of her grandmother of Navarre—they were not likely to countenance rudeness to their niece.

Gaveston and his rudeness was not the Queen's only cause of distress. Great Edward, piling up his glory, had piled up, also, his debts. About those the King was not disposed to trouble—he had enough of his own making. There was no money in Treasury or Wardrobe, but still he went on crazily bestowing gifts upon his friend—lands and titles, jewels, horses, hounds, and hawks, whatever he deemed worthy of acceptance. And now it was May; four months since her marriage and the Queen had received nothing of her revenues. When she complained to the King that she had not the wherewithal to pay her servants, he retorted, Gaveston prompting, that her French household must go—ladies, women, priests, knights, esquires and pages.

'Sir ... my *friends!*' Hands flown to her breasts she turned her frightened eyes upon the King.

'It is not unusual,' he said. 'When Madam Queen Margaret came from France my father, within a little, sent her ladies home. Nor did she complain.'

She had no need. She was her husband's dear companion. She bit back the words. She turned on him the look of a little frightened animal, a cornered animal, so that his heart a little relented.

'Madam de St. Pierre you may keep; and your confessor, also!'

She thanked him for that, grateful smile and bitter heart.

This, this, too, she would add to the long account with Gaveston! Alone in her closet—narrowed eyes, teeth caught upon her underlip—she swore it.

She gave no sign of her anger. She went about white-faced and quiet; her quiet must have warned a wiser man. Madam Queen Margaret was not deceived. She went to the matter roundabout.

'Madam the Queen has not received her revenues,' she reminded him. 'She has no money . . .'

'She may save it upon her servants; these French—spendthrifts all! And for what also does she need money? She has gowns of tissue, gowns of silk, and gowns of scarlet-cloth. She has cloaks for summer and cloaks for winter and furs more than I can count. What else does she need?'

Margaret could have told him of many things, including the freedom to reward those that had rendered especial service.

'And the jewels? And the gold plate she brought with her? They are not in her possession nor yet safe in the Tower. Where are they?'

No need for him to answer. She knew—and everybody knew—the answer. That the mignon might go richer the Queen must go poorer.

He shrugged. 'What am I to do? I can get no more from the Wardrobe. You cannot squeeze blood from a stone!'

She sent him a long glance. *Let Gaveston need aught and the stone will bleed.* 'Then give her the revenues of Ponthieu and Montreuil,' she said.

His face darkened. He remembered—as she had meant—that once he would have given Ponthieu itself to Gaveston; that over this very matter he had quarrelled bitterly with his father.

She said, 'Ponthieu and Montreuil—you had them from your mother. It is fitting, I think, they should be given to your wife.' And when still he hesitated she put the matter plain. 'You would have given both cities—not merely the revenues—to Gaveston that had no right. Shall you do less for your wife that has every right?'

He sent, sore against his will, for Lancaster. 'Cousin, we are pleased to assign the revenues of Ponthieu and Montreuil to Madam the Queen for her own use. See that the seneschal of those towns have their orders.'

Madam the Queen said her thanks; she said them prettily . . . but her heart burned. These were her rightful revenues. They should have been given without this delay, this show of gratitude; nor could it compensate for friends sent away. That Gaveston had urged both the despatching of her friends and the withholding of her revenues she knew well; it was common property. That he was angered by this turn of affairs was clear. He showed himself sullen to the Queen; he behaved more rudely even than before. For this, also, Gaveston should pay one day! And, to judge by her uncle of Lancaster, that day would not be long coming.

The day had come. Parliament had spoken.

It was full summer now; six months since the King had sworn the oath of his crowning. Yet nothing had been done towards keeping it; nothing would be done until the head of all offending was removed.

Gaveston must go. Peers and commons alike demanded it; demanded it with threats. Before a Parliament so united, the King must bow his head. Very well, go Piers should . . . but in a way his enemies would not relish.

'Gaveston must leave at once,' my lord archbishop of Canterbury told the king. 'And if he should return, mark it, sir, he shall be excommunicated and damned. I have sworn it!'

He had sworn it, Winchelsey that the King had brought back from obscurity! He must be pretty sure of himself. Well there was a neat little surprise in store for him!

'I cannot think he would wish to return!' the King's mocking eyes met those of his archbishop. 'He goes to govern Ireland. I trust it will please my lords.'

He saw the archbishop's jaw actually drop. He read the priest's thought plain. *The King thumbs his nose at us. He gives Gaveston the richest plum in the administration; royal honours and unlimited opportunities to make his fortune. And, most cunning of all, he sends the fellow not too far away* . . .

'You see—' and he all but laughed in the priest's shocked face, 'I keep my word.' And now, driven by one of his sudden gusts of anger, he could not stay his tongue. 'My lord of Cornwall—and beware priest how you forget his title—goes provided as a King should go. He shall have precedence and every honour that belong to his high position. He stands in the King's place.' But even in his anger he judged it wise to say nothing of revenues from Aquitaine, of blank bonds pressed upon his friend—gifts for which Gaveston himself had not dared hope, nor the King name.

But such news is not to be kept quiet. It was spread, in not unnatural triumph, by Gaveston himself. The black brows of barons and bishops alike, amused him. That it would not be so amusing if ever he fell into their hands did not trouble him—for he never should! He was the King's friend.

Piers was departing like a King, indeed; with knights and esquires and men-at-arms, with lords and ladies to form his court, with servants unnumbered, with horses and hounds, with baggage-trains scarce to be counted. The King, himself, in full procession of lords and ladies took the way to Bristol. Simple folk might stand agape but those with an eye for affairs noted that the great barons and the most part of bishops were absent. Absent, too, was the Queen; she had pleaded woman's sickness and not all the advice of Madam Queen Margaret nor the black looks of her husband could induce her to ride in this triumphal procession.

The King was back from Bristol. He was gloomy, he missed Gaveston intolerably; for him all joy had fled the court. And things were worse between himself and the Queen. He still resented the letter she had written home and her father's rebuke, mild though it had been. More bitterly he resented her dislike of Gaveston. Most bitterly of all he resented that she had not ridden with him to honour his departure. Nor was his anger the less that, because she was so young and because she made no complaint, she had won the good-will of his lords—won it at his own expense.

And still she carried herself—a gentle, helpless child. But it was no child that dwelt within that ripening body.

She was forever at her uncle of Lancaster with her subtle words—a dove that would peck to the death. 'Gaveston departed more glorious than a King. Surely that touches the honour of my lords the barons! And surely to keep him in such state costs gold and gold and yet more gold.' She forever pricked him with Gaveston's success. 'He wins golden opinions in Ireland. Everywhere they call him *King Gaveston*. How will it be when he returns again?'

And every time Lancaster answered, 'Let them call him King of Ireland—and of England, too! So he stay away I'll not complain.' But she knew very well by the restless turning of the great head upon his hunchback's shoulders that every word of hers pricked home.

The King was growing more and more difficult. To every demand for the redress of grievances he had but one answer. *When my lord of Cornwall returns I will consider it.* Gaveston was more present in absence than in the flesh.

A gloomy court; barons, bishops and King all alike morose. The Queen, as far as her husband was concerned, might not have existed. To him she was still a child; of no importance.

And yet a little kindness to his Queen might have won him comfort from her and approval from his barons. To win her now would not be easy; he had humiliated her overmuch. He had taken no account of a heart ready to love him. It was not so ready now; but still she might have been won.

But how could he find kindness for anyone at all, sick as he was with longing for Piers? 'He cannot have the plaything he wants,' she cried out to Madam de St. Pierre with all a woman's bitterness, 'so all other things must be broken—even if that thing be my heart!' And when Théophania would have comforted her, broke in quick and fierce, 'Never counsel me to patience—though, by the Mother of God I have tried. Or shall I kneel beseeching him for favour? I am no serving-wench, I, but daughter to the King of France and he should know it!' And before Théophania could take breath to answer, was gone, but not before the older woman had seen the brightness of tears.

Save for her aunt, save for Théophania, she must keep her anger to herself. She must guard her tongue; but she thought the more. She would sit pondering the word that should move this baron to anger on her account, that one to pity. Pity she resented; but it was needful—a weapon she could not afford to lay down.

The pity the whole court felt for her was driving still further a wedge between herself and the King, between the court and the King.

Every word of pity or of praise, even, was condemnation of the King. Queen Margaret watched with an ever troubled heart. Deliberate unkindness towards her was not in the King; nor in her any hatred . . . but already the seeds had been sown. Nourished alike by his indifference and her resentment what fearful fruit might they not ripen?

April in the year of grace thirteen hundred and nine. A spring sweet with violets, with primroses, with scarlet tassels of hazel and hanging golden chains. But for the King there was little sweetness; he languished still for Gaveston. Ten months since Piers had gone . . . and every day of them black for lack of him, black with his own bitterness against his barons. Could they not see how unjust their accusations against his friend? For the first time within memory Ireland was quiet. Piers had beaten her rebellious kings; he had taken their homage. As well as battles he had won hearts. All Ireland rang with his praises. His king's choice had been justified; but here in England no-one would admit it.

And still the old miserable ding-dong. Parliament was demanding redress of grievances according to the coronation promises. Grievances there were aplenty, and the most pressing the removal of officials of the King's household. They were his personal friends— and for that purpose chosen. They wasted the country's revenues— and nothing to show for it but the clothes upon their back. Of the King's own extravagance Parliament had, as yet, said nothing. Put others in the place of Keeper of the Wardrobe and the Wardrobe Clerk—and the King's extravagance must find itself curbed. All Parliament pressing upon the King in this matter—barons, bishops and commons alike; and always the same answer—*Recall my lord of Cornwall and I will consider the matter.*

'They'd be fools to believe him; his word is not to be trusted,' Isabella cried out. 'God send they stand firm and keep the King's sweetheart away! By God's Face I wish the man were dead!'

Shocked by the bitterness in the young voice Théophania said, 'Madam . . . Madam, my darling.' She cast a swift look round. 'I implore you, watch your words.'

'I say what everybody says; no more! Well, Parliament's to meet next month and the question settled once and for all. I cannot think the King will win.'

For nigh on a year the King had languished moody, resentful. Now, suddenly, and for no reason, he was cheerful. What had brought this sudden turnabout? Isabella asked herself disquieted. Nor was her disquiet the less that the younger Despenser had been much with the King of late. Two Despensers there were at court, father and son—and both of them Gaveston's friends, and both of them she distrusted; nor was she alone in her distrust. The younger man she thought might prove—give him the chance—as dangerous as Gaveston. He was sly, he was greedy, he was good-looking though he lacked Gaveston's undoubted charm. And he was clever; cleverer than Gaveston, cleverer than the King, cleverer than his own father, that shrewd man of affairs. She watched disturbed. Between the King and this sly, clever young man what game was afoot?

The year had moved into June; roses were sweet in the Queen's garden at Westminster, the river ran clear, green with mirrored trees. Within a little, Parliament would meet at Stamford to settle the matter of Gaveston once and for all.

Isabella came into the chamber of Madam Queen Margaret; she was taut as bowstring and lambent with anger.

'*He . . . he . . .*' and she could not speak the hated name. 'Back. He's here. Here . . . in this house!'

'I know it.' Margaret put by her stitching.

'He digs his own grave; and no-one may bury him—an excommunicated man!' Isabella said, vicious.

Margaret looked at her with pity. 'Excommunicate no longer. The Pope has annulled it. The King's been busy in the matter this long time!'

'Dear God!' The girl beat her hands together. 'Is the Pope, God's mouthpiece, to be bought for a handful of gold?'

'He chooses the lesser of two evils. Let the King take his stand with an excommunicated man and his own excommunication must follow—the lord Pope has no choice. And what becomes of the King then? And what becomes of you? And what becomes of England?'

Gaveston had been back a fortnight. He had conducted himself with propriety. He was courteous to barons and bishops; to Madam the Queen he carried himself with so deep a respect she could not tell whether he mocked or no. And now it was time for the journey to Stamford. Isabella had looked forward to it, to the bustle and the change; and, most of all, to the kindness in people's eyes. She was, she knew it, a well-loved Queen. Now all was spoilt by Gaveston's hateful presence. There he rode beside the King, handsome, arrogant and over-familiar. She saw how, as those two passed, folk turned aside to spit. It was for Gaveston the insult; but it came all too near the King. For herself as she rode, there was nothing but kindness; she read it in the eyes of gentle and simple alike. How easy to win the love of these good people! Her eyes rested upon those two in front. How easy to lose it!

Gaveston was a continual pricking at her peace—and it was worse when he behaved well; that charm of his inclined others to forget their grievances. He had, since his return, behaved so well that she forever asked herself, *Will Parliament stand firm against him?* When she spoke to the lord earl of Lincoln, oldest and wisest of the peers, he was, she thought, evasive. 'Gaveston has, I fancy, learned his lesson!' he told her. Yet more troubled she went to Pembroke, of all the peers most honest. She found him even less reassuring. 'Parliament is no longer of one mind in the matter! With fair words and promise of good behaviour both for himself and his friend, the King has won the half of us. We must wait and see!'

She was desperate when she went to her uncle of Lancaster. There was little love between him and Pembroke, for Pembroke and de Warenne were fast friends; and of all men Lancaster hated de Warenne most. Lincoln might be, in name, leader of the barons; but for all his wisdom he was old and tired, his mantle had fallen upon Lancaster. Whatever Lancaster said she must believe.

He had no comfort for her. He said, slow and bitter, 'It is true; we are no longer united. God knows I loathe the fellow, the rat that gnaws the foundation of the house. But, if the most part of us agree to give him this last chance, I'll not say *Nay*. I'll not split Parliament.' And when she stared, eyes disbelieving, he added roughly, 'That could mean civil war; of all wars the most hateful— for in that war no side can win. And what becomes of the King? And what becomes of us all?'

Chapter Eight

Gaveston would be pardoned; by the time they reached Stamford the Queen's mind was prepared. Her mind; but not her will, still less her heart. That first night the King came, as usual, to bid her sleep well . . . and left her to eat her heart out with bitterness.

From her window, next morning, she saw them crossing the court-yard, the handsome pair, come, as she guessed, from one chamber. The sweet day was poisoned for her. There they strolled, laughing, arms intertwined, towards the Parliament chamber; behind them a young esquire carried the crown upon a cushion, two pages carried the robes. She doubted the King would trouble to put them on; wearing the crown meant fasting—and he was not one needlessly to fast. She saw the shadowed doorway swallow them all and took in her breath. She had expected Gaveston to turn back. But no! He was actually going to outface them all. How very certain they must be, Gaveston and the King.

She turned back into the room; she paced backwards and for-wards, strange eyes glowing now green now topaz as the light caught them. And, as she paced, she prayed that they would send Gaveston into exile. If God would grant her this she would forget every slight, every unkindness. And then, Gaveston gone, Edward would surely turn to his wife. It did not trouble her overmuch that, during the months of Gaveston's exile, the King had turned not to her but to the young Despenser. Let God be kind in this; it was all she asked. During these months she had grown in beauty and in woman's wiles; there should be no fault found in her. She could not fail.

It was her uncle of Lancaster that told her how the matter stood. He had been unwilling to speak but for all that she had it out of him. The King had put forth all his charm. 'There he stood promising, promising . . . no longer commanding, no longer bargaining, but humble, throwing himself upon the goodwill of his Parliament. Impossible not to believe him!'

'Did *you* believe him, uncle?'

He shrugged. 'Not at first—nor did the best part of us. But one by one he brought us over.'

'You too, uncle?'

'I said, Madam, *all* of us!'

'*All* of you?' she repeated it a little sharp; it was a thing she dared not bring herself to believe.

He did not answer; she waited inexorable.

'I'll not split Parliament, I told you!' he cried out suddenly impatient. 'No-one spoke out against the King save Canterbury.'

'Good priest. Would God there were more like him!'

'Would God there were—he's the stuff of martyrs. But martyrs are not known for commonsense; and by them a country is not to be saved. Wise men wait their time. All those promises—lapdog and master! We know those promises! Our time will come soon enough!'

They were back at Westminster. Restored to full honours, my lord of Cornwall still carried himself seemly. But soon there he was, flaunting himself as before, dressed as extravagantly and hung about with jewels—and some of them the Queen's own. And the King, more besotted than ever, could see no fault in him. And it went from bad to worse.

'He will kill himself with his tongue!' And Queen Margaret sighed.

Isabella nodded. 'He gives them all the most insulting names— names of animals or infidels. Warwick's *the black dog;* and, indeed his lips do lift above his teeth like a *dog* and that makes it worse—the names strike home. Pembroke's the *Jew,* and every day he grows darker and his nose more hooked. My uncle of Lancaster's the *mummer;* it's because he makes fine speeches that don't come from the heart.' 'There's scarce a man of the King's council that doesn't smart under some piece of vulgarity.'

'Certainly the man's tongue will be his death!' Margaret said again.

'God grant it; and soon!'

Thomas of Lancaster lifted a bitter face to the Queen; his dark glance dismissed Madam de St. Pierre.

'It is enough, enough! I am finished with this low fellow. There shall be no more grace for him! He has broken my word for me, he has shamed me in the eyes of honest men. I gave the promise of a place to a man to whom I was beholden—it was in my gift. Now Gaveston, though he knows well my commitment, gives that same place to some fellow of his own. And the King says nothing. If I do not punish Gaveston for this I am shamed in my honour. No man can shame Lancaster and live.'

'There's no man alive can shame Lancaster; his honour shines too bright!' Isabella said. 'The man's a fool!' She set the wine before him. 'He lets his tongue run away with him!' She pricked at his wound reminding him of the hateful name Gaveston had given him. 'He has a wicked . . . wit!' She drove the last word home that it might prick more deep. 'Madam, my aunt, says he will kill himself with his tongue!'

'Why so he will. Black dog will not be slow to bite nor mummer to play his part.'

The mummer was playing his secret part. To the King he made no complaint; to Gaveston no reproach. But among his peers he went whispering; reminding them of the King's promises and of Gaveston's promises—broken, all; reminding them of the lies Gaveston put about setting friend against friend, reminding them of the hateful, spiteful names.

And still Gaveston went on flaunting and Lancaster whispering.

In September when leaves were turning and plums bursting with sweetness, the King summoned his Council to an October meeting in York. Some half-dozen, headed by Lancaster, refused . . . *because of Gaveston,* they said; that matter must be dealt with first.

The King's surprise was real. The rudeness of Gaveston he had found amusing; amusing, too, the anger of his barons. A man should learn to laugh at himself said the King who had never laughed at himself in his life. The whole matter he thought unimportant; well, let them stay away if they would; things would go easier so!

The scandal was growing. Men spoke, though not openly, of the King and his sweetheart. For the King they had scorn, as yet good-natured; for Gaveston anger at his bare-faced extortions, his wanton extravagance.

Whispering had swelled into open speech. The King could not, if he would, remain deaf; and besides, Gaveston's reproaches against those that spoke against him were fierce—traitors he called them. The King ordered the arrest of any that should speak scandal of my lord earl of Cornwall.

'He cannot make England one vast prison,' Margaret said.

'Nor would it help,' Isabella told her. 'Scandal thrust into the dark is like a plant that grows tall reaching for the light!'

Scandal was driven underground. Deep-rooted in resentment, it grew stronger, spread wider.

For Christmas the court went to Windsor; an unhappy festival for all. Piers and the King went about linked and laughing; but the listening ear could catch the uneasy note. They were aware, both of them, of trouble brewing.

Isabella was wretched and disappointed. How much longer must she wait for the King's kindness? How much longer for Lancaster's promised vengeance? Her humiliation went deeper now than in earlier days; the King could no longer pretend she was a child.

The sight of those two forever linked was constant laceration to her pride. Once, catching the King alone, she burst out, 'Two years! Nigh on two years since we were wed and I am a woman now; a full woman. The country looks to us for an heir but you . . .' She heard herself aghast, but anger drove her on, 'As long as that man is with you you cannot use a woman!'

She had dared overmuch. At the sight of the blazing eyes, the face twisted with anger she backed a few steps and fled.

It was true. He was honest enough to admit it. The country rightly looked for its heir; and as long as Piers was with him he could not use a woman. He would come to the Queen's bed determined to get her with child; but it was all useless. He had no pleasure in the business and she knew it. She lay beneath him rigid; with her he was impotent.

'He is guilt-ridden and I am angry and it is all useless! He writes his pious letters to my father trusting I'll prove fruitful. But how? *How?* I am not the mother of God; immaculate conception is not for me! Tell me, Madam Aunt, do the people blame me? If they do, by God, I'll take a lover and teach them better!'

'Madam!' Margaret cried out in fear. 'Such talk is treason!'

She watched, troubled for all three. Gaveston she must pity. A man greatly gifted yet for all his gifts, doomed with a doom he had brought upon himself. For Isabella her concern was deeper. Even the King could not deny she was a woman now. She had been patient; more patient than one could have believed of that passionate nature. And she had been clever. She had won not only the barons to her cause; wherever she showed her face the people cheered and blessed her. The King's folly they knew; the more their pity, the more their admiration for her gallant bearing. But how long could any woman endure so unnatural, so humiliating a life?

And the good Queen's fears went deeper still.

Isabella's nature was as yet unplumbed; and the record of her family on the Capet side was not edifying. No worse, perhaps, than that of many a royal line, it yet had a long record of treachery and murder. How far might she not be driven—beautiful, clever, wilful and passionate; humiliated and unsatisfied? She might have been her husband's lover, his closest friend; her strong will a support to his weakness. But with her there was no half-measure; she bade fair to be his enemy. Quicker than he, more vigorous and more ruthless— an enemy to be feared.

It was for Edward that Margaret feared most. She loved him as her own son and saw great trouble for him; trouble that would not stop at Gaveston, nor even at himself. Trouble that affected the King must trouble the whole realm. She shook her head over the folly of men.

Chapter Nine

In February the peers received their summons to Parliament. The summons was refused. Gaveston had thrust himself into the last Parliament, he was only too likely to repeat his behaviour. They'd not go through that farce again. But to attend Parliament, the King reminded them, was my lord of Cornwall's right; and their own duty. When the King commanded, come they must; distasteful as it was, that duty they would do. But so violent their anger, the King commanded them further; they must not come in arms.

Anger was added to anger. Let the King burst; to Parliament they would come as they chose!

Open defiance.

The King and Gaveston affected still a devil-may-care, walking, talking, laughing together; but Isabella could see they were more than ever disturbed. She caught it in the little nervous movements of the King—the head turned sharp upon his shoulder, the quick movement of hand upon his sword-belt. Gaveston showed it in yet greater magnificence, greater arrogance—if that could be; in a sharper edge upon that sharp tongue. And maybe they had some reason to fear! Thomas of Lancaster had whispered in her ear; a promise to cherish . . . if one could count upon it!

She was more than ever dissatisfied. As the King's wife she was nothing—except the sport of Gaveston's jests. At home they had called her *the Fair*. She had not deserved it then; but two years had ripened her green beauty—her mirror told her so; that surer mirror, the eyes of men told her so. What then did she lack that brought even a plain woman her lover? Was there some ugly flaw beneath her beauty? She could not think it.

No. The fault was not in herself but in the King. She gave herself to sweet hope. Gaveston out of the way as her uncle had promised, surely the King would turn to his wife? True she loved him no longer. But what matter? He was handsome enough to be acceptable without love. And, when things went smooth, he was good-natured enough; Gaveston gone, she could manage the King. All she wanted was his own good; to lead him with better wits than his own. Within her, power unrecognised, began to stir.

But Gaveston was not yet gone.

Parliament had met and met in arms.

'The end of Gaveston! Soon, soon I shall begin to live!' Isabella cried out joyful. Madam Queen Margaret said nothing; she looked with pity at the girl young enough and ignorant enough to believe that anything Parliament might do could take the flaw from the King's character; the fatal flaw.

Parliament made its complaints clear.

'Sir, led by evil counsel you have perverted justice. You have im-poverished yourself, the crown and your subjects. The country's wealth runs like water through a sieve.'

You have . . . you have . . . you have . . . a long, long list ending with the loss of Scotland. 'Sir, you have dismembered the crown, you have lost Scotland.'

The King tried to reply but they gave him no chance. Whenever he tried to speak they shouted him down. Nor was there one there, not even among his own friends, to stand by him. Gaveston had not, this time, dared show his face.

'Things move; they move!' Lancaster told his niece. 'The King was forced to agree to our demands.'

'*Demands?*' Her voice came out sharp. 'Other than the removal of Gaveston you have no right to demand anything. You go beyond your office; you blow upon the dignity of the King!'

'Dignity of the King!' And he laughed that sour laugh of his. 'It is for us to preserve it for him since he cannot do it of himself. We are to appoint certain lords—Ordainers we call them. They are to examine the laws. They are to have full power—amend those they find bad or sweep them away altogether; they may make such new laws as seem to them good. They shall have power, also, to put an end to abuses not only in the state but in the King's own household.'

Interfere with the King's household! There was but one abuse to be disposed of—let them dispose of Gaveston! As for the rest—impossible!

'The King will not agree.' And she was actually smiling.

'He has agreed; he has no choice!'

The smile froze on her face.

In the painted chamber at Westminster the Ordainers were chosen.

Twenty-one of them! Isabella considered the list. A good choice, balanced and fair; princes of church and state equally represented.

Isabella considered the prelates. My lord archbishop of Canterbury, Winchelsey that feared no man. He'd sworn to excommunicate Gaveston and would have done it too, save that the Pope had interfered. Langton of Chichester. He favoured the King ... up to a point; but he wouldn't allow himself to be *pushed*. Edward must be careful there ...

Her eye went down the rest of the bishops. A round half-dozen; would they defer to Canterbury? They owed him spiritual obedience. But, in matters of state? She did not know.

She turned to the list of barons.

Lincoln, of course and her uncle of Lancaster. Young Gloucester, the King's nephew and friend ... and his sister married to Gaveston; not much doubt where his interests lay. Richmond, Arundel, Hereford and de Warenne; the first three honest enough; de Warenne, though—his honesty was in question. All four the King's friends; but how far, in the face of his enemies, would friendship stand? They must reckon with Lancaster bitter against the King, with Warwick sick and sour against the King; reckon also with Pembroke that moderate man to keep the balance even, reckon still most of all with old Lincoln failing in strength but not in mind—and their spokesman still.

'Watchdogs to bite their master!' the King told Piers.

Of one thing the King was certain. Piers would be the first

object of their attack; they'd waste no time dealing with him! By God, he'd not let them touch a hair of that beloved head!

Gaveston had disappeared from court.

'The very name of *Ordainer* is enough to send him flying; the air is sweeter for his absence!' Isabella told Madam de St. Pierre. 'The King has sent him north—where they don't know him as well as we do! But they'll soon find out. Well, the further the better; as long as he stays there I am happy!' She took a dancing twirl about the room.

She had spoken too soon of happiness. The King showed nothing of his usual easy-going temper. Bereft of his sweetheart, humiliated by his lords, dreading when and where his watchdogs would bite, he grew increasingly difficult. Isabella learned what she had not known before—in his sudden rages he could be vicious. Whippings and maimings were everyday affairs—and no reason save that it pleased the King. Humiliated, he sought to humiliate others. My lord bishop of Chichester, Chancellor and a Lord Ordainer, he ordered like a dog to heel. Chichester rebelled; and the King dismissed him from office—from the rank of Ordainer he could not dismiss him. The King's a fool, Isabella thought; he has turned from him a good friend. Walter Reynolds stepped into the vacant place; a dog obedient to his master's voice.

Through the countryside rode the King, his new Chancellor with Great Seal and all his Chancery tagging at his heels, the judges with all their clerks, and whatever high official his whim saw fit to command, seeking to blind the people with an empty show of power.

He went on making a show of defiance. He was wasting what treasure he had left, giving it away with both hands; and upon the absent Gaveston he bestowed more grants, more privileges. It was as though he sought deliberately to worsen matters between himself and Parliament.

The King was for Scotland. To put down rebellion, he declared. *He cannot keep from his sweetheart,* his enemies said. The most part of the barons were left behind; they had refused to follow him.

'If I were King, by God's Face I'd not endure it!' Isabella cried out.

'And how would you remedy it?' Queen Margaret asked.

'I'd not need remedies. I'd carry myself so that the situation could never arise. But the King, it seems, cannot learn.'

'How you might have carried yourself, I do not know! How you carry yourself now, I know very well. Unseemly. Remember, Madam, you speak of the King!' Margaret said, sharp with her fears. For the girl was right. But if the King were not clever enough, mightn't the girl be . . . too clever? There were signs of change in her. In spite of that innocent air, her judgments were growing sharper, harsher. There was a suggestion of slyness, too; a watchfulness to seize her chance. But there was nothing gained by antagonising her; and she had plenty to put up with. 'Forgive me, Madam niece, but I grieve for the King.'

'Then grieve for me, also! He leaves me that he may run after his sweetheart!' Isabella lifted a white and furious face. 'Christendom laughs at him. And at me . . . at me! Nigh on three years married—*married,* God save the mark! Yet I'm neither maid nor wife and there's plenty to call me barren. And I must endure their insult and their laughter!'

Together they watched the royal train ride out—baggage and servants for the King's comfort, lions and Genoese fiddlers for his amusement, captains and forces for the business in hand. He had kissed his Queen Farewell with less warmth than he had shown his step-mother—he knew well his Queen's deep desire that the barons should make an end of Gaveston. He had bidden the older woman look well to the younger.

'Yes, look to me well!' Isabella cried out, the door scarce closed upon him. 'If he drive me far enough there'll be none to hold me. For, mark this, Madam Aunt, I cannot go on like this for ever! I'm no barren tree. If my husband give me no chance to prove it I'll make my own. I'll take a lover. I've said it before and I'll say it again. And never tell me it's treason and wickedness! It is a wife's right to have her husband for her body's comfort and to give her children. I cannot nor will I go hungry for ever!'

The second time she'd made that threat! Yet she would not carry it out lightly, of that Margaret was sure. She must be even more desperate before she took a lover—her own pride must forbid;

she would refuse, body and soul, a child not wholly royal. But if Edward drove her far enough, if she were desperate enough. . . .

Margaret sighed deeply; the matter was beyond her wits.

The King and his armies were moving ever north. Daily the messengers rode in. Wherever the lord King passed he was greeted with joy. So it would be, Isabella thought, remembering his handsome looks, his agreeable manner, his training in kingly courtesy. In that charm they would forget the promises broken.

The King was over the Border; he was at Linlithgow.

'A dreary place,' Madam Queen Margaret said. 'I remember it well. At best it's bleak enough but in this weather—!' She turned from the window and the Thames sullen beneath a heavy mist, back to the bright fire and the gay tapestries. 'The King is right. It is better for you at home.'

'Does he leave me for my good—or for his own pleasure? As for himself, he might as well be here for all the good he does! He swore to flush the Scots out of their rat-holes; but does he offer battle? No. But he amuses himself with his beasts and his fiddlers; and at night, no doubt, lies snug with his sweetheart!'

'Niece, you are unjust. Some harrying of the Scots there has been; you know it as well as I. And who led the forces? Who but Gaveston! A good soldier, very brave; my husband that was the first captain in Christendom told me so.'

Isabella said nothing to that. The man was brave and daring. She must, to her innermost self, confess to some grudging admiration. It did not make her love him better.

But for all Gaveston's daring there was nothing gained. They had moved to Berwick—and still less pretence of fighting; nothing but skating and feasting and all winter joys.

In February Henry of Lincoln, Regent and the King's loyal friend, died.

'Uncle of Lancaster, I grieve for you!' Isabella said very courteous —and no sign of grief upon either of them. For the old man's death had taken from the King a powerful and true friend. Lancaster it had lifted to the long desired seat of power. Now, as well as Lancaster, Leicester and Derby, he had the earldoms of Lincoln and

Salisbury. He was premier earl now ... and Gaveston's bitterest enemy.

'Now,' Isabella told Margaret, all joyful, 'my uncle of Lancaster will make an end of Gaveston!'

'Do not count over-much on Lancaster! He's a man of power ... on the outside. But, I know him well; there's a core of weakness within him. When all goes well, he's a lion; show him a fierce front and he may well turn tail. Or, his pride insulted, he may, sulk in his tent and let his chance go by!'

'Between husband and uncle I am like to be well-served,' Isabella said, bitter.

From Berwick the King sent to appoint Gloucester Regent—Gloucester young and very inexperienced. Lancaster took it for the insult it was. Edward's a fool, Isabella thought. He should be taking Lancaster by the hand; but no, he must needs drive him further, She was not alone in thinking so.

Winter had gone and spring and now it was early summer. And still the King diverted himself at Berwick, hunting and hawking and drinking eternal brotherhood with Gaveston.

June. The King was coming home; at long last coming home. Reluctant he had torn himself from his sweetheart. And it was not his Queen's charms nor his kingly duties that brought him all unwilling from his pleasures. It was distrust of Lancaster; it was lack of money. Money he must somehow squeeze out of Parliament. He knew well what Parliament would say. *You squandered wealth untold on Gaveston.* It was all nonsense of course. A King was bound to reward service; and the gifts were but a drop in the huge ocean of his debts, debts he'd inherited along with the crown. But still they'd be on to him insulting him with what they were pleased to call extravagance. Extravagance—and he as poor as a churchmouse! He'd been glad to pawn the crown jewels for a miserable four thousand marks—there'd be trouble over that! Even greater trouble because he'd ordered all customs to be paid not to the Exchequer but to himself direct. Yes, a devil of a row! His one hope to catch Parliament in a good mood; the cursed Ordainers might give him the chance. They'd finished their ridiculous work; now they were pressing to present their efforts to Parliament. He couldn't take them seriously; but if he showed himself agreeable, granted them a trifle here and there, he would surely squeeze something out of them.

In Westminster Palace the Queen herself went short. Her full dower had never been paid—the best part of it had gone the way of her jewels. Her uncle of Lancaster had promised to look into the matter; meanwhile she must sit and shiver, for even in summer the high stone-walled rooms struck chill.

These days she was restless. She disliked the Ordainers; she was bitter against the King that had made them necessary and now must humble himself. It seemed to her that a vast and dangerous engine had been set up to crack one small nut. Of the true issues involved— the duties of a King and the rights of a people she understands nothing, Margaret thought watching the girl restlessly pacing. She has shrewdness but no wisdom—Between this King and this Queen how shall the country fare?

'Let the King be what he may,' Isabella said suddenly, 'it's wrong that he must show himself obedient to his subjects!'

'A King must rule, or be ruled; he must be obeyed or else obey. One or other; there's no half-way.' Margaret sighed, remembering that strong man her husband. Yet, she must ask herself, had he shown himself less strong, might not his son show himself less weak? And if great Edward had spent less on his wars, mightn't his son be in better case now?

The King was home again . . . and the watchdogs ready and waiting. His courtesy to both Queens was scanted; he dreaded the coming ordeal and his missed Gaveston beyond enduring. If the barons had their way he must go without Piers for the rest of his life. But that was impossible. Without Piers he could not live.

'He keeps his sweetheart safe in Bamborough,' Isabella said sharp with disappointment at the King's greeting. 'He hopes, no doubt, if Gaveston stay quiet all will be forgotten. But it's the King that forgets. He forgets the anger of the barons, he forgets the bitterness of Lancaster . . . and he forgets me.'

'Madam,' Queen Margaret said. And then, 'Child! Beware how you speak. You can do yourself no good and much harm. To the barons the King must give way; but not to others . . . and not to you. He is still the King. If he desires to punish, punish he will, even though it be the Queen. You'll get no kindness from him if there's anger on your tongue.' She paused; she said, very slow, 'This could be the time to make a fresh start. Whether he will or no, the King must part with his friend. Gaveston will I think content himself—if his pockets be well-lined; already he has sent for his wife. But the King will not take it easy—love between those two is unequal. He'll need some comfort.'

'He'll not look for it in me! As for Gaveston, how long will he stay away? Until he find a hole in his purse; then back he'll come smiling to plague us all. As long as the King have gold to stuff into that mouth, that mouth will go on smiling.'

'He'll not dare to return. Be satisfied!'

'How can I be satisfied? I am torn two ways. I pray God for the man's departure; but I pray it may be by the King's own will . . . his humiliation is my humiliation. This unnatural love—it sickens me. And you are right—between those two, love's unequal. It's the King that loves and Gaveston that endures it—but no longer than he must. He's already sleeping with his wife . . .'

'There at least you should have no quarrel!'

'But still I have. I've no wish to see my husband cuckolded— for that's what it is! I want him free—even if he cannot turn to me; I want him free of this lying, greedy, vicious fellow!' She choked upon her anger.

Margaret's heart was torn with pity. 'Hatred my child, will get you nowhere.'

Chapter Ten

When he faced his Parliament at last, it had been sitting for several days; his discourtesy did nothing to sweeten the anger against him.

The Ordainers had set out their grievances and remedies . . . and it was worse than he had feared. He listened in a growing nightmare while they read the endless charges. All his household censured; all, all! And, first and foremost—Piers.

'Piers Gaveston—' and they did not name him by his great title, 'has led the lord King astray and deceitfully persuaded him to do evil. He has gathered to himself all the King's treasures and the most part of it he has sent out of the country. He has dominated the King and the Crown to the destruction of the King and Kingdom. Especially, he has turned away the lord King's heart from his liegemen, despising their counsel. Good ministers he has removed from their office and set up persons of his own familiars both foreign and otherwise that shall, unjustly at his command, break the law of the land. He maintains robbers and murderers and obtains pardon for them from the King, he encourages evil-doers to greater crimes . . .'

Some of it they exaggerate and most of it is false; and to all I must listen . . . the King must listen . . .

'Piers Gaveston persuades the King to make war without the consent of the barons to the danger of the King and the destruction of the realm. He has made blank charters under the Great Seal to the fraud and impoverishment of King and crown. All these things he does cunningly to the disherison of the crown and the destruction of the people.'

How much more do they find against him? Will there never be an end!

On and on . . . Telling them how the King himself—had banished the man by common desire of the whole realm; and how the man had returned, not by common consent but pardoned by the King— the King alone.

And now they were coming to an end. The King sat stiff and cold in his place.

'Therefore on account of these misdeeds and to encourage good harmony between the lord King and his subjects, we the Ordainers, by virtue of royal commission have ordained . . .'

He fought down the sickness rising in his throat, gathered his every faculty to face the judgment,

'. . . that Piers Gaveston as public enemy of the King and Kingdom shall be utterly and for ever cast out and exiled, not from England, alone but from Wales, Scotland, Ireland and from every land beyond the sea that is subject to the lordship of the King of England. Before the feast of All Saints he shall leave and utterly depart the realm of England and every lordship of the King . . .

I'll not accept it: never, never!

'And if the said Gaveston delay beyond the appointed day he shall be treated as an enemy of the King, the Kingdom and the people. And,' Lancaster turned and spoke directly to the King, 'whoever shall contradict this ordinance or delay the said exile shall suffer as seems expedient!'

The session was ending; tomorrow they'd indict himself—the King—and much he cared for that! He'd say nothing now; by tomorrow he'd have found some bargaining point for Piers. He betook himself to his closet, he would see no-one. He must think, think, think!

'So Gaveston's exile is decreed,' Isabella said thoughtful. 'For my part I give thanks to God; but will the King let him go?'

'He has no choice,' Margaret said. 'It is a hard thing to throw a friend to the hounds though the friend be bad and the hounds deserving. He'll fight . . . and he will lose.'

'God grant it!' the young Queen said.

He sat again in his place; he wore the great robes, the crown he had put from his weary head. To the indictment against himself he listened; he thought it all a great nonsense, but still he must listen. Granting some of their unjust demands he might yet save Piers.

They were censuring him, their King, together with all his officials, his household and his friends for wilful, wanton extravagance. By God's Face it was hard to take; no King had ever been so insulted! Yet take it he must if he hoped to save Piers.

'The King has impoverished the Kingdom with wrongful gifts to his friends ..

'The King has perverted justice; he has used the privy seal to pardon criminals . . .

'The King has taken into his own hands the customs due to the State . . .'

Well he'd expected that; they hadn't lost much time about it!

'All such customs shall, in future, be paid straight into the Exchequer and a sufficient allowance made the King.'

Sufficient? What was sufficient? Who was to judge? On and on the indictment; on and on the restrictions to cage a free, crowned King.

The King must not leave the realm without consent of his Parliament; without that consent he must not go to war . . .

The King must no longer choose his own officials, great or small; appointments both in the royal household and in the state to be made by the barons in Parliament. All present appointments—and, in particular, Keeper to the Wardrobe—must be reviewed. Every official high or low, sheriffs, magistrates and judges must take the oath to observe the Ordinances.

He listened; he listened. They lied in their throats. He was the King to reward, to appoint his household officers, and his officers of State; to elect his judges and sheriffs were his inalienable rights. To make war as he chose—not that he ever would choose—was his inalienable right. But for all that he'd bargain with them, give up rights and freedoms so he could save Piers.

They had made an end of speaking; they were waiting for his reply. He rose in his place.

'My lords, those things I have done are within the King's rights; and have been his rights from immemorial time. Yet time moves on and makes his changes. To these Ordinances I will consent; but upon one condition. and one only. You shall make null and void the sentence you have passed upon my lord earl of Cornwall, restoring to him every honour, land and due.'

He saw by their faces they were going to refuse: he lost his head entirely. He burst into a frenzy of speech. Pardon Gaveston and he'd sign anything; anything at all. If not—then nothing, nothing, nothing!

And still they sat, dark faces of stone.

Lancaster came carrying the parchment, carrying the quill. The King dashed it aside; in direst grief flung himself out. They hated Piers, all, all! And the wife that should give a man comfort—she was the bitterest hater of them all! That he had given her cause, and cause enough, he did not consider. Suddenly he remembered one person's kindness, one person's truth.

Into Queen Margaret's closet he burst distraught.

'Their demands—endless, endless!' He threw out shaking hands. She nodded, grave. *Of course endless; like his abuses, endless.*

'It is not the law they seek to change, but me, me the King. Nor is it the people they mean to better, but themselves, only themselves. These *Lords Ordainers!*' He was bitter with contempt.

She thought there was some truth there. The barons had much right on their side but would they use it rightly? They were, she had iong thought it, looking less to the welfare of the country than to the Increase of their own power.

'Me and my household censured! And first and foremost—Piers!' He leads me into evil ways, if you please! What am I—a child? As for evil ways! They should talk! There's more than one of these same loud-mouthed bullies has his pretty chamber-boy. But let them burst for all I care. Piers and I—we're not the public business; we're our own private business!'

'The King has no private business.' And would he never learn, this foolish, headstrong, beloved stepson of hers? She hesitated; she went steadily on. 'Indeed, sir, this business between you and Gaveston is very much public business. It concerns the Queen ... and the lack of an heir.'

This he would have taken from no-one else; yet furious as he was, bitter and harassed, still he knew her for his friend.

'You must expect some bitternesss against him on that score alone; but there are other accounts, also!' She grieved to add to his hurt; yet she must spare him nothing to make him see more justly and so save him. 'They say Gaveston lays hands upon the royal treasure— and God knows we're poor enough! They say he's sent it across the sea to Gascony!'

'It is his. I gave it to him. He has the right.'

'But was it yours to give? Was it not rather yours to hold in trust?'

'It was mine—the King's!' He was obstinate.

She let the point go. 'You gave; but a true friend would not have taken.'

'Piers is myself; between us there's no giving and taking! But there's no accusation too absurd. They say he's turned my heart from the people; that's not true!'

'No,' she agreed, 'it is not true!' His heart had never been with the people. True it pleased him to measure his skill against a humble fellow here and there, to seek their company. But for their welfare he gave no thought; for his craftsmen, his merchants, his gentry— he cared nothing, save as he might get money from them. He must mend his ways if . . . she stopped shaken by a thought; *if he hopes to keep his crown*. She looked at him with pity for the fate that made him a King. He would have done well enough in the unremarkable life of a country gentleman. He loved country ways and country crafts. But fate had pushed him—a square peg into a round hole.

'They say he led me into war without consent of Parliament. Well *what* war? None of my making! For that you must blame my father, the hero that saddled me with war and all the debts of war. Me! I hate war! But this Parliament of mine! No way of pleasing them—none!'

He didn't seem to understand that he had never tried to please them; never tried to please any but himself . . . and Gaveston.

'They say . . . they say! Does it matter *what* they say? White's black and black's white—as it shall serve their turn. For their jealousy, their spite, Piers is to be banished. Out of the country by All Saints' Day! Well, we'll see . . . we'll see!'

'What shall we see?' she asked grieved with his grief, his helplessness. 'If he should delay—he'll die . . . a traitor's death.'

His hand went to his throat to thrust down the sickness.

'I tell you there's no fault in Piers!' And now his voice came out heartbroken rather than angry. 'But he's a foreigner; there's the top and bottom of his offending. Out with the foreigner!'

'There's more to it than that! *I* am a foreigner; and the Queen is a foreigner. Yet we have met with nothing but love and respect. No, sir, it is the man himself! The pride that admits no man his equal— scarce even his King; and the strange value you set upon him. Sir . . . my son; do not, I beseech you, stand against your Parliament in this. On my knees I implore you!' And would have knelt save that his hand stayed her. 'You could split the country into a most bloody war.'

He looked at her unbelieving, yet stricken, so that she longed to give him comfort, were it but a single word. But comfort there was none—save what he might make for himself.

He would not desert Piers. Was it so ill a thing for men to love passing the love of women? So it had been with David and Jonathan —and the holy writings had found no fault.

Again and again he came into Parliament. With a patience new to his high Plantagenet spirit he listened to their complaints, their scarce-veiled abuse of himself; he said no word in his own defence. He swore upon his kingly word to grant them anything, anything at all, so they showed grace to Gaveston.

He abased himself in vain.

'He has no shame!' Isabella told Madam Queen Margaret. 'He accepts all insult, all humiliation that he may keep his whore!'

'Gaveston is more than that to the King; much more. You should respect faithfulness.'

'Faithfulness! Does he keep faith with his country or with his barons? Or with me? No, we may all go hang ourselves so he may keep his bawd. All Christendom is laughing; and by God I could laugh too . . . if the fool were not mine!'

'Pity him; pity him rather. He must lose his friend.'

He could not desert Piers . . . but in the end he was forced to desert him.

'I will never let Piers go!' he cried out in the quiet of his closet, a Despenser on either hand. 'Let the barons cut each other's throat, let the country swim in blood, they shall not touch a hair of his head. I can no more forsake him than I can forsake my own soul!'

'Sir,' the older man said, 'there's a time to give way and a time to stand firm. If you do not give way now it is not only your friend you may lose .. but your crown, also!'

He was forced to smile at that. 'Even my great-grandfather—and there was a bad King for you!—didn't lose his crown.'

'No, sir. But there was Magna Carta; he was forced to sign it!' the old Despenser reminded him. 'And, if he didn't lose his crown it was because he lost his life in the midst of an evil war—such a war as the barons will bring upon us now!'

'Sir—Ned!' It was the younger Hugh now, arm about the King's shoulder. 'If you would keep Piers, let him go . . . for the present. Even a King must shelter from the storm; when the storm is over you shall send for him again!'

The old man nodding, smiling; the young man whispering, promising . . . and both of them hoping the sun would never shine again for Gaveston, hoping for that light to fall upon themselves.

'You are my good friends!' the King said at last, and took a hand of each. 'You two I trust; to you I must listen. But to part with him even for a little—it is like parting with my own life!'

He had signed and the decree proclaimed the length and breadth of the land. At Paul's Cross and in every market-place, the people heard it with joy. There were some that did not know the nature of the love between Gaveston and the King; but all had felt the pinch in their bellies and knew whence the pinch came.

'All Saints' Day!' Isabella made a little dancing-step, skirts lifted above long-toed shoes. She counted the days upon her fingers. 'Let him linger beyond the time but one little, little day—and he suffers the fate of all traitors.'

'Would you see him hang, drawn and quartered?' Margaret asked, grave. The girl had reason enough to rejoice, yet there should be, if not pity, then at least some decorum.

'I ask no more but that he should go. If he disobey?' she shrugged. 'I'll not quarrel with the sentence. The man's a traitor to the King and to the State. For what is he but a traitor that prevents the King getting a lawful heir. Even when the King is so obliging as to lie in my bed, his mind is forever on his friend; we cannot come together to get us a child. And once—and for shame I have never said it—the fellow came bursting into my bedchamber to drag the King from my bed. And the King went with him!' She stopped, choking with shame. 'I tell you he casts a spell upon the King. In France they burned his mother. The son, I swear it, inherits her filthy spells!'

Margaret said, unwilling, 'That he has bespelled the King is true; but there's no witchcraft in it. Have you thought... that much of the trouble lies within the King himself? We're none the worse for facing the truth. And here's a truth you may have to face. How, if Gaveston gone, the King find another such; or worse?'

'There can be no worse; nor yet another such! Let me be rid of Gaveston and I'll thank God forever.'

'For ever's a long time!' the older woman said.

Gaveston must go, but there was all of two months for the King to show his love. Piers should have safe conduct from the north to come to his King. These last weeks they should have together; not a moment to be wasted day ... or night.

Gaveston was back in Westminster and no man could say him nay. The barons, detesting this thumbing of noses, made no complaint; the limit of time had been set. Gaveston, himself, gave no sign of impending doom. Easy optimism buoyed him up. There was time yet—the King was the King. But if go he must he'd not break his heart. There were pleasures enough in the courts of Christendom; to pay for them he'd sent gold out of the country ... and the King would always send him more. To tell the truth he'd not be too sorry to part with Edward; the man was cloying in his affections and the atmosphere about them far from pleasant. He'd not be sorry to part with his wife, neither; women were tiresome creatures. To live free of friend and wife—the prospect was far from uninviting. So he carried himself arrogant as ever, his tongue wagged as sharp; there was no sign of grief upon him.

The Queen kept her apartments and counted the golden autumn

days. She sat with her ladies; Gaveston's wife she had excused from attendance.

'The man is shameless,' she told Madam de St. Pierre. 'Still he flaunts himself in my jewels, still he urges the King to greater extravagance. And the King, knowing they must part, cannot enough aid and abet him. God knows what parting gifts the fellow will take with him!'

'There's a courage in both of them, Madam. It is hard for you; but never grudge them this last, short time together.'

'Who knows *how* short? Twice has Gaveston been banished and twice returned. God knows what trickery those two hatch together.'

'You may leave my lords the barons to deal with it. Sure it is the man must go and the King cannot follow him. And Madam, may I speak that guided you as a child and would die to see you happy? Be gentle with the King. Let him remember your gentleness in his sad time and cherish it!'

Useless for the Queen to keep to her room. In Gaveston would come lounging with the King; and, remembering her governess's advice, she would receive him with courtesy. He had not lost his old habit of teasing and, in spite of anger against him, she found it not wholly unpleasing; there were times when she must laugh at his wicked wit. He was at his old game of nicknames; and the King encouraged him.

'How would you name Madam the Queen?' The King asked once.

She sat over her stitching, her narrowed eyes green-amber. So far he had not dared! She was conscious of a prick of excitement.

'I would call Madam the Queen . . . a kitten.'

She stiffened with annoyance. She had expected something rare and regal; a little dangerous, perhaps. A tigress or a panther. They treated her like a child, both of them!

'A kitten grows to be a cat,' the King said. 'I do like a sleek well-fed cat.'

'It is a little wild-cat!' Piers laughed into her slitted eyes.

'A wild cat. It is of all creatures to be avoided,' the King said.

'There's one worse.' And Piers was laughing still.

'The lion? The tiger?' the King asked.

'No. Those we may catch and tame; you may go feed them in the Tower! There's a creature you cannot tame nor keep from blood—and that's the wolf.'

'A man would be a fool to try?' Isabella said, very sudden. 'It is a coward that runs with the pack. At home we hunt him with dogs. But the werewolf—that's another story.' And she spoke as from a dream. 'The creature we know . . . one of ourselves . . . yet not of ourselves. It lives with us, sleeps with us, smiles from a bloody mouth. Beware, my lord, the werewolf!' And was it to Gaveston she spoke, or to the King? She did not know; she knew, only, that she had given some warning.

When they had gone and she, herself, a little calmer, she found herself troubled. *Had* she meant a warning? And to whom? And of —*what*? And still she did not know. Loneliness, neglect and frustration were growing like a canker within her; they brought thoughts to frighten her . . . thoughts too bitter for the mind to bear.

Chapter Eleven

Gaveston was gone. Upon her knees the Queen thanked God. The King had kept his friend with him until the last moment; and then, unable to endure the parting, had ridden with him as far as the coast.

The King was back looking sick and sad; he could eat no supper but sat drinking more than was good for him. He sat listless, upon his knees the beribanded lute Gaveston had left behind. Now Isabella could feel for him some pity, for herself some hope. Surely his forlorn state must bring him to her bed.

That night he did not come; nor the next night, nor the next. He sat within his closet the lute across his knees, plucking now and then upon a string so that it wailed throughout the room.

November was wearing to its end; the land was full of rumours; they echoed in the Queen's sick heart. *Gaveston is here. He did not go. Never an end to his mischief save by death* . . .

'It is all a piece of nonsense—would God it were not!' the King said. 'He's in France, or Brabant, or Italy; who knows?'

'*You* know!' she said. 'He is here.'

He is here. She had no reason to suppose it; but she knew it in her blood. Why else had the King not turned to her—his wife. Nigh on four years married and she nearing eighteen . . . and no heir nor any chance of one!

The rumours grew.

Gaveston was in Cornwall, he was in Somerset . . .

'No!' Isabella told Queen Margaret. 'He is nearer, nearer.'

He was in his own castle at Wallingford . . .

'No!' The Queen said. 'Nearer, nearer.'

The barons commanded a search for *Piers Gaveston, supposed to be wandering from place to place.* He was not to be found.

'He is here,' the Queen said, sniffing the air like a wild thing, 'here, nearest of all; like a worm feeding upon my life.'

And so he was; he was in the King's own apartments safe-hid.

For the Christmas festival the King and Queen went to Windsor; and there, openly to meet them under safe-conduct from the King— who but Gaveston? And not Gaveston alone; his wife was with him. Isabella's heart all but died in her breast. Bitter the sight of Gaveston, bitterer still—if that could be—the sight of his wife. Margaret could not be accused of wanting to flaunt herself—she was an elegant girl, well-bred; but her condition did it for her. She was with child. The thing for which the Queen longed, longed and prayed, had been given to Gaveston's wife. The sight of the girl was a sword in Isabella's heart.

'He wasted no time at Bamborough!' she said, bitter.

'What did you expect?' Madam Queen Margaret shrugged. To make a show of pity would be further insult.

Winchelsey kept his word; he pronounced excommunication. But still Gaveston remained, laughing with the King, making music and dancing as though he hadn't a care in the world.

'The King doesn't mean to part with him ever again!' Isabella told Queen Margaret. 'Excommunication. They laugh at it. You'd think they had the Pope in their pocket. They mean to build up a party to overthrow the rebel barons. The Ordainers, the King says, shall ordain nothing but their own deaths.'

'He dare not do it. He has sworn the oath!'

'When did he ever keep the oath that irked him? And he'll find support too! The barons are always at odds. Each looks to his own. Yes, the King will find support; the right word in an angry ear, the clink of gold in a greedy ear—' Isabella shrugged. 'He means to carry his sweetheart north out of harm's way.'

'So much I've heard; and more. I hear he takes you with him!' Isabella gave no sign of pleasure.

'You'll be near him at least,' Margaret said. 'Take your chance!'

'Woo him further? I sicken at the thought.'

'Once you asked for just this chance. Use your wits, child, and take it!'

Immediately after Christmas the royal train set out. Lacking her aunt, Isabella felt forlorn. The journey was slow; they were forced to a snail's pace by the frozen roads and by the baggage-carts lumbering ahead, heavier than ever this bitter weather with mattresses with pillows and coverlets, with gowns, with cloaks and furs. And the number of the royal wagons were outnumbered by those of Gaveston and his wife. Of food they carried little; they would honour the countryside.So they rode—the King and his sweetheart, the Queen and her servants, the captains, the men-at-arms, the King's caged beasts and his fiddlers. And many a town and village, and many a household great as well as small, had reason to dread their coming.

Beneath sables from Muscovy the Queen sat silent and would speak to none; not even to Madam de St. Pierre. Her anger was continually pricked by the presence of Gaveston's wife, riding by the King's wish in the royal charette. The girl, Isabella must admit, was subdued enough, her spirit crushed beneath the Queen's displeasure. Had the girl's husband been any other, Isabella would herself have invited her into the greater comfort of the charette—the King's own niece and her baby expected by the end of the month; it was a courtesy due. But she was Gaveston's wife; the Queen would grant her nothing. Yet, for all her awareness of the Queen's displeasure, she was even more aware—this wife of Gaveston—of her own dignity, the importance of her pregnancy. She is proud, too proud, the Queen thought, envying the girl, resenting the girl. Nor was her resentment lessened by Madam de St. Pierre, who, in common kindness, looked to the girl's comfort, moving here a cushion, there a rug; still less when, at every halt, the mid-wife came to enquire of her lady's comfort—Mary Maunsel that had brought the King into the world and should have brought the King's son. And, at every halt, too, and between halts, Piers and the King would come riding back to enquire of her while she smiled out of pale lips and told them all was well.

A long and tiresome journey. The horses slipped on the glassy roads so that the charette slid and jarred; and each time Margaret's hands flew to her belly to protect the unborn child. Once or twice the Queen's mouth opened to a kind word; and closed again, the word unsaid. And the journey was slower, even, than the weather allowed, for Gaveston's wife must not be too many hours on the road. They would end the day's journey at any hour did she show signs of fatigue; or a comfortable-looking house, be it castle or monastery or simple inn, come into sight. And the first thought of everyone was for the girl; the King, her husband and the midwife anxious for her comfort; yes, Madam de St. Pierre, even, that should think first of the Queen.

No end it would seem to her humiliation. For when the people came out to greet the Queen and bring her into their city, they did not always know which *was* the Queen. She was young and fair—so much they knew; and who should it be but the fair, pregnant girl? When they understood their mistake they would come with all ceremony to welcome the Queen. In spite of all their welcome she knew they asked themselves why she had given them no heir—and she four years wed! This was the hardest of all to bear. On this long journey, thrust into second place, exposed to humiliation, she came to hate Gaveston's wife.

At York she was free of the sight of the girl at last! Here, the King come to meet his household and chancery officials, must remain several days; but Gaveston and his wife he commanded north with sufficient escort—the girl was near her time.

It was peaceful in St. Mary's Abbey where the King and Queen were lodged; away from the sight of that hateful pair she knew some peace. But not for long.

When she heard the news she could not, at first, believe it.

Gaveston was no longer a banished man; he was free to go or stay as he chose!

The King had declared by proclamation to his sheriffs throughout the land that Gaveston had been exiled against the laws and customs of the land—which laws and customs the King was bound to maintain. My lord of Cornwall, therefore, was by royal command restored to liberty; and with his freedom was restored all lands and titles, all offices, dues and honours.

Such a public breaking of his oath—how could she believe it? That he would break any oath if it pleased him she had long known; but that he would dare thus to flout his princes, to set against him the church—she had not believed even he was so witless. She caught the troubled looks of those few she knew to be his friends; saw the black looks, heard the angry words of his enemies and trembled. Now she must believe it.

But the King did not tremble, not he! His own defiance had gone to his head; there was no holding him.

'These Lords Ordainers—' and he made of the name an insult, 'think to treat me like an idiot. I'll not endure it! I'll dismiss no official, no servant, still less any friend at their command. No, but I will choose my own officers, my own servants, my own friends.' And to prove he meant it and the pleasure of angering his barons intoxicating him still further, he recalled those household officials especially offensive to the Ordainers. And even that was not enough. To feed their anger he went further still; he bestowed upon Gaveston yet more honours, more lands, more wealth.

Utter defiance; barefaced thumbing of the nose.

Pembroke, that moderate man, thrust down his rage. To Parliament assembled he spoke; but all his quiet could not hide his bitterness. Because he was a moderate man, and wiser than most, they listened as they did not listen to that rash and angry man, Lancaster, premier earl that should be their leader.

'When the King recalled Gaveston that was, of itself, a declaration of war. Yet we sat still, we said nothing. Now he heaps upon the man more wealth and yet more; the country bleeds—and to that bleeding there's no end. If we do not call a halt now we are lost; and all England is lost. For to Gaveston's greed and the King's foolishness there's no end.'

Recalling Gaveston had, indeed, been a declaration of war; the King knew it and cared little. He was glad, rather, in his mad Plantagenet pride to force the issue, to cut the bonds that irked his vanity.

'The King forces war upon us; he throws down the gauntlet!' in Parliament Lancaster cried it out. 'He makes Gaveston governor of Scarborough Castle and on terms that's plain declaration of war. He is to yield it to the King alone and to no other man. And more; more yet!' Lancaster's grin was a mask of rage. 'If the King should die, the castle is for Gaveston and his heirs for ever. His *heirs!* He'll beget no heirs—the eunuch!'

'You've been from court too long!' Gloucester could not forbear the smile. 'My sister was brought to bed of a daughter three days since.'

'We'll not congratulate you!' Lancaster told him, sour.

'There's more important things to trouble our heads. The King drums up his armies in the north . . . and not against the Scots!' Pembroke stopped; he said slow and quiet, 'He has sent to the Bruce, *the Bruce,* mark you! He offers friendship in return for help, help against us—his own lieges!'

Sell out to the Scots! And for such a reason! They looked from one to the other. Not to be believed even of this selfish and foolish King.

'He would if he could but he can't!' Warwick barking above the clamour justified, in some degree, Gaveston's mocking name. 'Have you heard the answer?' His surly face was split by a grin. 'The Bruce said, *How shall I trust a man that cannot keep faith with his own liegemen?*'

'By God, I could love him for that!' Lancaster said. 'Well, it's war —civil war, Christ save us! But it is the King that lets it loose. We march for the north!'

Wife and child safe in Bamborough, Gaveston had seen to it that Scarborough Castle was well defended; a strong retreat at need. He thought there would be need; he was a soldier and no fool. Now, awaiting the King at Newcastle, he was aware of distaste for the meeting. These days there was a new seriousness upon him.

His wife had borne him a child. He was a father; what that could mean he had not counted upon. It was as yet less tenderness than a dawning sense of responsiblity—remembrance of what his priest said. *The fathers have eaten sour grapes and the children's teeth are set on edge.* Would this little one have teeth on edge by the grapes of her father's eating? Even for himself those grapes, once deceitfully sweet, were already turning to verjuice. He was beginning to question the worth of his wealth, his titles and his treasure. Would not men say they came from a tainted source? And was it not a blot upon his honour, this friendship with the King? What would she make of it when she was old enough to understand—his daughter? There'd not be wanting tongues agog to make the situation clear. And himself; what could he say to explain to her . . . or to his son? For surely there must be a son to inherit his great position? Better his son should despise him, execrate him than grow like his father! He had dishonoured the King; he had made of himself an object of contempt, and bitterness to the barons, to the churchmen a thing utterly to be contemned. These things he had long known. But how deserved that contempt, that detestation, he had not known.

And now he knew one thing more. He had not understood it until he saw his wife, the baby at her breast. To the Queen he had offered the worst of insults, the most cruel of wrongs.

He must break with the King. But not now; this was not the moment, when the King risked all for his friend; so much loyalty he owed. But the Queen. He wanted to kneel before her, to entreat her pardon, to swear he'd offend no more.

But they were still in York; he could do nothing. He was sorry . . . but not too sorry; he guessed that, accustomed to fatherhood, he might find his grapes sweet once more.

It was growing towards March and the barons, led by Pembroke and de Warenne, moved steadily north. They were grim, they were determined, they were of one mind.

Lancaster had charge of affairs at home. He had seen to it that the whole country was securely locked against the King and that the barons held the keys. Gloucester, hitherto so loyal, held London and the south, Hereford held the eastern counties; and to Lancaster himself fell the west. In the north Henry Percy had already deployed his forces; he was watching the Border lest Gaveston attempt to escape.

It was Gaveston they wanted. And to lay hands upon him could not be difficult. When it came to it, there'd be none to help him, except the besotted King; for who would dare help an excommunicated man?

The King and Queen had left York. The late March weather was little kinder than January. The cavalcade rode through high winds that parched throats and blinded eyes; it was cold enough to freeze the rain as it fell, but nothing could damp the King's ardour—he was riding to his friend. He snapped his fingers at his barons; he threatened, by God's Face, any that dared lay finger upon Piers.

Isabella was sullen at this long journey made on Piers' account. And she was fearful at the outcome: England's princes in arms—church no less than state—what chance for the King? She was the more troubled that, at York, she had received word from Lancaster that he had not forgotten his promise. When first he had made it—how long ago?—she had been comforted; now she was troubled. It was more than Gaveston the barons attacked, more than the King himself. It was the sacred rights of royalty. If they should succeed what became of those sacred rights . . . and what might become of herself?

She sat alone in the charette with Madam de St. Pierre; she was free, at least, of Gaveston's wife! But when she remembered the new-born child, grief and anger all but overthrew her. Her rage smouldered against the King that had forced the issue with the barons for his worthless friend. And with every step northwards her grief increased that Gaveston's wife had borne a child while she, the Queen, looked to be a barren tree. And all the time she raged against the King without words. *You have broken the sworn oath for this worthless man.* Had he been successful, this would not have troubled her unduly; with her, as with him, expediency was a word more pressing than honour. But he was not successful; he never would be. She wished with all the bitterness of her passionate heart that she had never set eyes upon his handsome face—nor yet upon this wild country through which they rode.

As they journeyed March gave way to April. The wind was keen still but the rain no longer fell hard and cold as stones. It fell bright as silver spears and, when the sun shone out, trees and hedges flamed with tongues of green fire. But sweet Spring could not soften the Queen's mood. With every step that brought her nearer to the sight of Gaveston anger flamed in her the more.

Almost as if he felt her thoughts upon him, the King came riding up. 'The wind has dropped,' he said, 'Madam will you be pleased to ride with me?'

Madam would not. The rough winds had chapped her face and lips. She was petulant, refusal given before she knew it. He had turned and gone before she had time to recall her refusal. She did not need the look on Madam de St. Pierre's face to tell her she had been a fool!

'Madam, the Queen has been riding less of late,' Théophania said.

'Yes', she said. 'Yes . . . the rough moors tire me.'

But . . . so tired? Isabella stiffened suddenly. Last month her rhythm had been broken. She had thought little of it; fatigue and distress had broken it before. But now it was April . . . and the rhythm not renewed.

She began feverishly to count.

These last weeks the King had come once or twice to her bed. He had needed comfort and that comfort she had tried to give. Since then she had given the matter no thought. She had supposed him impotent; or, at best, ineffectual with her. But was he impotent? Had Gaveston's absence released the manhood in him? Had she been given the chance, at last, to clear herself of the monstrous charge of barrenness?

Now Gaveston mattered little. Turned in upon her new, her terrible joy she was confident that now he must be thrust from his place. *I carry the heir. Now the King must, in honour, cast off the man! And, if of himself he will not, then the barons will settle the matter . . .* Of one thing she was certain. She must grow in importance— mother of the heir to England; and that growth nothing could stop.

Théophania, in whose ear the laundress had whispered, sat very still lest she intrude; this moment was for the Queen alone. And it was indeed for the Queen alone. Even in this first moment of her joy she considered the child a pawn only in the Queen's advance.

The King and Queen had reached Newcastle; and there was Gaveston debonair as ever. Some of the newness of fatherhood had rubbed from him; he was more or less himself again. 'I left my wife at Bamborough,' he told them. 'I could not bring her or her babe into the hazards of war however well-fortified we may be!'

'You are right. War is no place for women and babes!' the King said. Isabella nodded and made her mouth to smile . . . But, Gaveston's wife to be cherished, to be made safe! What of herself then? She no longer wanted to accompany the King; his work was done. She

wanted to be home again, to cherish the body that bore her child—
her pawn to power.

'Gaveston's wife must be kept safe!' She went storming to
Madam de St. Pierre. 'But what of me? Me he brings into danger?'

'He does not know the Queen is with child. Madam, you should
tell him.'

'Should he not cherish me for my own sake; am I not a woman?'

'Yet still, Madam, my darling, you should tell him.'

'Not now.' And she would not, all angered as she was share with
him her secret. 'A wise woman makes certain. I'll wait till May is
out; then he must send me home again—the weather will be fitter
for travel. He must send me from this hateful north, from the sight
of Gaveston and the dangers of war!'

At first she thought Gaveston unchanged; yet soon, she was
forced to admit it, he was different. He was quieter in manner; she
found a new courtesy in him. It was the King that had not changed.
He could not be near his sweetheart without touching; Gaveston
neither invited nor encouraged it.

'My master desires, humbly, to be received by the Queen's grace.'

Her eyes narrowed at the sight of the boy wearing Gaveston's
intricate quartered arms. She was puzzled . . . *humbly desires* . . .
Gaveston had never sought her company without his master, nor
ever asked permission. Always he had come unasked, at the King's
heels; he had spared her none of his lewd jests, his stinging taunts.
And now . . . *humbly desires*. What was this turnabout?

Before she could make an answer, there he was, the man himself,
kneeling before her. He knelt not upon one knee as a courtier but
upon both knees—a suppliant.

'I have done Madam the Queen great wrong and I beseech her
pardon. Soon I shall take myself from her sight to trouble her no
more.'

She was utterly taken aback. Was this some new jest? She could
not think it; could not mistake the truth in his voice, nor the way he
knelt completely humble. Nor could she pretend not to understand
him. He was asking pardon for the wasted years of her life. How

could she forgive him that? Yet, as he knelt debonair and contrite, her heart, in spite of herself, grew gentler towards him. She could afford to be generous; she was with child and this, her enemy, swore to trouble her no more. The wheel of her life was turning towards the sun.

She stretched out a hand; she said, scarce believing this new turn of affairs, 'Why then we might learn to be friends. But as for taking yourself from our sight, we must, first of all, take ourselves from this place. The barons are on the march!'

The King burst in upon the sight of Gaveston kneeling before the smiling Queen and kissing the hand graciously extended. Already distraught, the sight added to his distraction; the world was spinning too fast!

'Up, up!' and he grasped Gaveston by the collar. 'We must fly. Within the hour Lancaster, God damn him, will be knocking upon our doors. There's but one way out. Down the river to Tyneside!' Devil-may-care was out of him; it looked less of a game than he had supposed.

'Sir,' she said, 'let Gaveston go alone. It will be safer for him. And for me, too. I cannot go!' And how could she trust herself in a small boat on the deep river in her condition?

He said nothing, only he grasped Gaveston by the arm. For the moment she did not understand. Then, 'Do not leave me behind! You must not leave me!' she cried out, desperate. For what might Lancaster not do, that angry man, finding his quarry gone— Gaveston and the King, both? He might lay hands upon herself; since he could not trust the King's word, hold her to bargain with.

'They will lay hands upon me!' *Hands upon my hallowed body!* Unreasonable with the fears of a pregnant woman—and one to whom pregnancy meant so much, she clutched at the King. 'They will hold me to ransom!'

'Then we will pay the ransom!' None-too-gentle, he pulled himself away. 'Besides—' over and above his fears for Gaveston, pricked with jealousy, he added, a little spiteful, 'you've put yourself on the right side of these rebellious lords of mine! They'll not touch a hair of your head! It's Piers they want—and more than a hair of his head! And that they'll not get! And me they want also, to bargain with; and me they'll not get neither!'

And when still she cried out, clutching him again by the sleeve, once more he pulled himself away but this time so roughly that she stumbled and all but fell. It was Gaveston that put out a saving hand, Gaveston looking from one to the other. They could hear, all three, Time's wings beating in the room.

Gaveston came and knelt before her. 'For this, too, Madam Queen, forgive me!'

She said no word. Eyes dark in her head with fear she watched them go.

She was glad, afterwards, she had made Gaveston no reproaches; their peace had been made.

Chapter Twelve

They had escaped; but by the skin of their teeth. Captains gone, the garrison made no resistance; at the first note of the trumpet the castle surrendered.

Lancaster greeted his Queen with due respect; but the eyes in the great head were pin-pointed with rage. One hour; one little hour and his hand would have closed over them both!

'Gaveston makes for Scarborough—it is his last hope!' His voice was heavy with anger. 'God send he be taken on the way!'

He had expected instant agreement; but there she sat, silent.

He cast upon her a sour look. He had expected her warm thanks; but nothing from her, nothing. He said, the voice grating in his throat, 'Let him reach Scarborough—which I doubt seeing Pembroke and de Warenne are on his heels if not already there and waiting—and he'll not leave it alive. Or let him bribe his way out—he'll find every road a death-trap!'

And still she said nothing. Since those last words with Gaveston she was not unwilling he should have another chance.

It was some time before he thought to ask of the King.

She shrugged. 'I cannot say. They escaped together.'

'Leaving you without protection?' The question was, as he meant, an insult.

'He knew I would be safe in your hands, uncle!' And, indeed, in Lancaster's hands safe she was. He was master now of this castle-fortress and everything in it—the Queen, the men-at-arms, the horses, the weapons, the treasure. All, all within his hands.

'Why yes, Madam,' he said at once. 'Safer than with the King! With you we have no quarrel. You are free to go where you will; you shall have escort and honours due to the Queen.'

The King and his sweetheart were not together; they had parted for greater safety. Now the King was safe in the strong town of York; and there, as far as the barons were concerned, he might stay. It was Gaveston they wanted.

Through the green-and-white maytime southward went the Queen's procession. She remembered how she had come this way eaten with anger against those two; now she was returning to Westminster touched with pity for them both. She had gone despairing; she returned high with hope.

Scarborough Castle had been taken. Gaveston had held out a full fortnight—longer than any man could expect. Lack of men, of food, of firing had forced him out at last; they had eaten the last of the meat raw.

In York the King waited for news of his heart's friend. In Westminster the Queen waited with a strange anxiety for tidings of the man she had once hated. News, when it came, was more favourable than even the King had dared hope. Pembroke and de Warenne, in the name of the barons, had sworn to guarantee Gaveston's safety until he should be brought to trial; meanwhile his own men were allowed to hold the castle. If by August no pronouncement had been made against him he might return to Scarborough to take undisputed possession.

'I am glad of it,' Isabella said, 'if only for the sake of his new-born babe.'

'He has, it seems, a gift to charm a bird from the tree!' Queen Margaret said drily. 'But on that charm he'd do well not to count. He deals with men driven by hatred . . . and there are three months yet to August.'

'Still he need not fear. Pembroke and de Warenne have sworn to his safety on the blessed Host.'

'But Lancaster has not sworn, nor has Warwick sworn; no, nor many another!' Margaret said.

They were taking Gaveston to his own house at Wallingford; but though they were sworn to the prisoner's safety, they were not sworn to his comfort. They set him upon a sorry donkey too low for his height and saddleless, Gaveston that had ridden fine and free.

From Scarborough to Wallingford is a weary way; yet, though they had neared Oxford, he made no complaint. But he was weary to the bone; and the pain from blisters rubbed raw where his feet scraped the ground was greater than many a battle-wound. At Deddington, so weary he looked, so wretched, that de Warenne being for the time absent, Pembroke took pity; a pity sharpened, perhaps, because the lady his wife, that he had not seen these long months, lay nearby at Brampton.

'You are worn with the journey,' he told the prisoner, 'and I have business near at hand. There's a pleasant house here where you may rest in safety; none shall harm you, I swear it! But you must swear, also! Swear you'll not attempt to escape—though escape is not possible. Try it—and it will be worse for you!'

'I thank you for your courtesy; you have my word!'

The rectory at Beddington was large enough to hold both prisoner and escort. In a pleasant chamber overlooking the road Gaveston fell upon the bed and, in spite of his fears and the pain from his blistered feet, fell asleep.

A man like Gaveston cannot be brought through the country and the news not spread; in town and village there had been many to jeer at the King's mignon brought low. Guy Beauchamp of Warwick heard the news; heard it, at first, with disbelief and then with fury. Gaveston lay in a small house with a small escort; Gaveston daring and desperate.

He wasted no moment.

June the tenth, in the year of grace thirteen hundred and twelve; and the sun slanting through the heat-mist of early morning to give promise of a perfect day. Beneath the heaviness of exhausted sleep, instinct struggled to warn the sleeper. Gaveston stirred, started, leaped from bed to door. Beneath the heavy bolt it did not move. The window then?

From the garden below the faces of armed men turned upwards; foremost stood Warwick, fierce face agrin.

'Get up traitor, you're taken!' Harsh and sharp he barked like a dog; Black dog of Arden.

For a moment Gaveston stood staring down; then, with a shrug, reached for his doublet.

'Do not stay for shoes!' Warwick cried out. 'A thief goes barefoot.'

Gaveston heard the bolt grate in the socket; he was smiling a little as he came down the stairs with that easy grace of his. The sight infuriated Warwick. He snatched the bonnet from the prisoner's head. 'A thief rides barehead!' he cried out, 'And thief you are! We found the jewels in your baggage; the jewels you stole from the King and Queen. They're worth a King's ransom; but they'll not ransom you!' With a sudden, vicious movement, he tore off the belt of knighthood; and stood booming the laugh that was like the baying of a hound. 'Neither horse nor shoes nor belt nor bonnet for a common thief. March!'

Gaveston that had lived soft in the King's company set his feet upon the cruel roads. Now one could see blisters upon feet that had known the soft leather of Spain; there was blood where he walked.

Walking, walking . . . like a man in nightmare dreaming. And here and there, a peasant wiping the sweat from his brow in the heat of the summer day would stop to wonder who this might be and what he had done, the prisoner, stumbling white-faced, eyes closed.

Half-way to Warwick it was clear he could walk no more; so once more they set him upon the wretched donkey and there he sat, bare feet dragging in the dust, ribbons slack in his hand, letting the donkey carry him onwards. And so they came to Warwick town; and there crowds stood and laughed at the sight of the fine gentleman that had played the harlot in the King's bed.

In the dungeon, dark and cold, even this bright summer day Gaveston shivered and tried to comfort himself. *Pembroke swore to my safety and Pembroke is honest . . . but Warwick did not swear.* Already he knew his end.

He was not to know, lying there in the darkness, how Pembroke, all dismayed to find his prisoner gone, ran hither and thither on useless errands to redeem his word and his honour; Pembroke imploring the barons and especially imploring Gloucester whose sister was Gaveston's wife. But Gloucester's honour lay with the barons. He said, *You acted without our counsel; you have only yourself to blame!* From the barons to Oxford, beseeching priests and justices, beseeching the university; but their honour was not in the matter, either. They had no love for the favourite; nor did they relish taking arms against grim Warwick for such a one. Let Gaveston stay where he was!

Warwick, also, wasted no time. His hand had closed over the fellow; what now? One answer, only. But . . . kill the King's friend —and not even the pretence of a trial! Bold as he was, he did not dare. At Kenilworth, a stone's throw away, Lancaster, Hereford and Arundel were gathered in company; and there Warwick rode. Let four backs bear the burden.

Nine days Gaveston had lain in the dark cell. Nine days as the world goes; but, to the prisoner, time eternal. He lay there and thought of the King's love and cursed it. He thought of the Queen he had injured and might have won for friend, and cursed himself. He thought of the young wife he had not given himself time to love and pitied her. And most of all he thought of the young child that must grow lacking a father. Ah well, without such a father a child was best!'

He was half-asleep when he heard the bolts of his dungeon drawn; hope caught him by the heart. One look at Warwick's face—and he knew his doom.

'This is your last day on earth,' Warwick said. 'You have one hour to make your peace with God!'

Gaveston's face moved like still water when a stone is cast; he said no word, but, Warwick being gone, he wept in the dark cell. *Where is my friend for whose love I now must die? The King's love has brought me to my death.*

And now in the dark cell where Time's wings beat to eternity he remembered another King long forgotten, in Whose kindness there might yet be hope—if not now then hereafter; and addressed himself to Him. Then, like the brave man he was, he accepted his fate, saying Let the will of the earls be done!

Within the hour they came for him. After the dark cell, sunlight smote upon his eyes like a sword; it struck sharp across his bare neck. Had the sword of the executioner fallen then, he had not felt it and gone easy to his death. But since it was not so, and seeing sweet summer all about him, he fell to his knees in the dust and cried to Warwick for mercy. 'Take him up!' Warwick said; that and no more.

So the sad procession came to Blacklow Hill that lies between Warwick and Kenilworth. This was Lancaster land, Lancaster having declared himself willing for the responsibility. Now he was glad to feed his grudge against de Warenne that had sworn also to Gaveston's safety; glad thus to stain his enemy's honour.

On the hill-top Lancaster was waiting together with Gloucester Hereford and Arundel; two of Lancaster's men stood by swords bared.

'We grant you an honourable death because of your kinship with my lord of Gloucester. But for him you would have been hanged, drawn and quartered like the traitor you are!' The Black dog of Arden bared his great teeth.

Gaveston bowed his head, courteous in death as never in life. Then he knelt in the grass and bent his head, that head the King had so often kissed; and one fellow ran him through the body and the other took his head. And they brought a bucket of sand to cover the blood; but the blood ran through and stained the sweet grass. Then the two fellows bore the head to Lancaster; he would not receive it but turned his back and left it lying. The executioners took up the body—the handsome body the King's love had brought to its death and carried it together with the head to Warwick Castle.

But Warwick, it seemed, had lost his nerve. He had put to death a great earl upon whom the King had set his whole love. So there it lay in the heat of the summer sun, the headless body and severed head, until news coming to Oxford, the Dominicans, of their charity, went in slow procession to carry the poor remains to their monastery until the archbishop should speak. Bury it they dare not; the man had died excommunicate.

Isabella lifted a shocked face.' They have broken the sworn oath. They have blackened their honour. Murderers all!'

Margaret's brows lifted. Once the girl had desired this very thing, desired it above all else; and those that had done the deed she would have called by a nobler name.

'They have killed a man without trial; they have stained their honour breaking the oath Pembroke swore for them all—so much is true,' Margaret said. 'But it was not murder. They had the right; Gaveston himself gave it. The man was an outlaw, a public enemy. Any man might kill him on sight. It is the law!'

'Yet it was murder,' Isabella said, strangely desolate. 'What the King shall make of this, or this of him, who knows?'

'Only God knows. But one thing any man can foresee—undying anger against the lords; and especially against Lancaster and Warwick. Those two he'll never forgive. But you; you may pluck some good from this! He's shocked and bereft; this could be your time. You should tell him about the child.'

'I had rather choose some happier hour. If he take the news without gladness I think I shall hate him forever!'

'Grief takes men divers ways, the King's grief is heavy and shocking. Comfort him even a little and you may win him—to his happiness and your own!'

'I doubt any happiness can come to me from him!'

'Then throw your doubts away and use your woman's wits.'

The King was in York when he heard the news. He took it badly. At first he did not seem to understand. He rose in his chair and stood speechless, words strangling in his throat, as though taken by apoplexy. *God! God! God!* he mouthed. *God! God! God!* Louder and louder until he was screaming. And then, out, out it came, a never-ending dribble of words, in his misery blaming his heart's darling. 'Piers, Piers, you fool, you *fool!* Had you listened to me you had never fallen into those cruel hands. *Do not trust them!* I said it again and again. *Do not trust them!* Had you listened to me you would not now be lying dead. Piers, Piers, I *told* you, I told you . . .' In his grief he seemed not to understand that Gaveston had been constrained by force. 'Oh Piers, Piers, Piers . . .'

On and on blaming them all—the dead man, also; all but himself who from first to last had played chief part in the tragedy.

Talking, talking, talking; shattered, broken, ignoble. Until he had spewed forth his sorrow in words he could do nothing, be nothing; for words transmuted his sorrow into anger, such anger as was not to be borne.

And now, his grief a little abated, the King called his Council. Pembroke was there and de Warenne with him, each burning to avenge his smeared honour; De Beaumont was there and some others that, for all they were Ordainers, disliked the manner of Gaveston's death. But Lancaster was not there, nor Arundel nor Warwick whose hands had been in the killing; nor Gloucester, nor any of those younger lords that had allowed the thing to happen.

'Sirs,' the King said, white and ravaged above his mourning, 'we must avenge the cruel murder of an innocent man. For innocent he was. The jewels they found in his baggage were his own. I gave them him, I, myself. And more. He was bringing them back to the Queen—a free gift; mark it! And for this he must die!'

Then Pembroke, all bitter with his wrongs, burst out, urging the King to his revenge upon the perjured lords, the murderers. And so, also, Hugh le Despenser the younger, who saw his own chance now Gaveston was dead. And it was seen how the King took the pretty youth by the hand—all-unknowing it would seem—and held it as though to draw comfort from the handclasp.

But the Council was divided, some standing by Pembroke; but others, knowing that the most part of the country would stand by Lancaster and Warwick in this matter, besought the King to peace. No good could come of such a struggle, but evil, only; the miseries of a country divided against itself.

And now the King knew not what to say. He burned to avenge the death of his friend; yet he was unwilling for such a war—not so much that he feared its miseries but that he feared defeat, not knowing how many would stand by him. He must, he said, consider the matter.

The King was home; no man had seen his face. He had covered it with his cloak as he entered; he could bear no man's gaze. Now he was in his private closet . . . alone.

This was her chance—so her aunt said. But suppose her aunt was wrong? Suppose this was the worst possible moment? And, if she had no comfort for him now, never in this world would they find comfort in each other. But how could she make him believe she truly regretted Gaveston's death? She had hated Gaveston, and with cause; and all Christendom knew it. Of his last words to her, of reconciliation and friendship, the King could not know—Gaveston was the last person to tell him. What should she say to him now? In her mind Isabella tried out this word and that; and always they seemed insincere, worse than useless. And, even if she could find the right words, how could she go to him unasked, unsent for; go into that private room he had shared with Gaveston, that cried aloud of Gaveston? And if she went might he not refuse to see her? And how should she bear that humiliation?

Even while she sat considering, mother-wit got the better of her. Before she knew what she was about she was hurrying, gown lifted in both hands, towards the King's apartments. The ante-room was empty and she went across to the closet; the high beat of her heart clamouring in her ears, she pushed open the door.

He was seated on a low stool, still in his travelling-cloak. His face was hidden in his hands; across them and across his breast the bright hair fell. He lifted his face. Such a face she had never seen—eyes and mouth dark holes in an empty mask. She stood for a moment, frightened; then she went running towards him.

'Oh,' she cried out, 'sir . . . sir . . .' that and no more. There was no mistaking the sorrow in her voice and he looked at her surprised; this from her he had not expected. She came and knelt by him. She said no word. She took the bright head and held it to her breast. The empty mask crumpled; tears rolled from the dark holes of his eyes; she felt them warm upon her own face, her own breast.

It was the first time he had wept since Gaveston's death; and now, it seemed, he could not stay his weeping. The cruel waiting, the shocking death, flowed from him in tears. The wound still bled; it would bleed and go on bleeding until he found some other sweet friend. But the scar would remain; forever remain. For the moment he was blessedly eased. Of her great news she said nothing; it was too much for him, in this moment, to bear.

That night he came to her bed and stayed till morning; no need to slip away to his own chamber, no-one awaited him now. They lay together like friends; quiet and gentle, she told him her news, quiet and gentle he listened. There was, she thought, a gleam of happiness upon that ravaged face; and for that she could forgive him much. She told him too, of her last speech with Gaveston and he wept again. 'They shall embalm his sweet body and we shall bring it in all honour to King's Langley, the house he loved best. My lord archbishop of Canterbury shall say the service—Piers is dead and the excommunication broken. And, if it is not, by God's Soul, he shall still be buried with every Christian rite. And the house that received him—God's House it surely is—I shall reward; the good friars that received his body I shall never forget. And those that betrayed him with false swearing I'll not forget, neither—Warwick and Lancaster that did him to death; nor all those that raised no finger and stood by to let it happen. Let them beware; all of them beware!'

So they lay whispering and weeping; and for the first time he found her woman's body sweet and took comfort from it, so that she found him neither laggard nor listless. At last, dawn lightening the room, he fell asleep, but she lay awake wondering how long this new kindness would last; or how soon he would find himself another Gaveston.

Part Two

The King and the Despensers
Check to the Queen

Chapter Thirteen

But for all that, she had not won him. He came often to her bed; but it was less love for her than loneliness for Piers that brought him—and she knew it. Yet the promise of an heir had pricked him into some awareness of his manhood; he was roused to play a husband's part. How long this happier state of affairs would last she did not know; she was not hopeful—his eyes for ever turned to the boyish charms of the young Despenser. Yet still he brooded upon his wrong; he grieved, she thought, more for the wrong done to himself than for the wrong done to Gaveston. She was beginning to know him.

The summer days went by. In the gardens of Windsor the Queen, great with child, stretched herself indolent, triumphant. After five fruitless years she carried the heir to England; she had given the lie to the reproach of barrenness. If still she had no finger in affairs of state she had increased her stature; to her the people looked with ever-increasing love, in every church they prayed for her.

She enjoyed her greater consequence, but her pregnancy she did not enjoy. Restless, irritable, she would turn upon the person nearest; she showed, at times, a disregard for others such as she had never shown before, a desire to punish however unjust the punishment. The natural peevishness of a breeding woman, those about her said; it will pass!

But how if it does not pass? Madam Queen Margaret wondered. How if it grow with the years? I see in her her father and her grand-father.

The death of Gaveston had strengthened the King's position. It had split the ranks of baron and bishop. Against him, stiff in self-righteousness, stood Lancaster, Warwick, Arundel and Hereford whose hands still smelled of blood. 'Sir,' Lancaster told the King speaking for them all, 'the man was a traitor thrice exiled. He knew well that to set foot in England meant death. It has always been the right of the King's greatest subjects to take the law into their own hands for the safety of all, should the times require it. The times did require it. Gaveston's death was just and lawful. Be content, sir; do not, I pray you, let loose the dogs of war.'

At the King's right hand stood Pembroke hot to mend his damaged honour and de Warenne whose spotted honour had been further stained. On his left hand de Beaumont—a great lord but not the greatest—speaking for all those that have cause to fear when the King's greatest subjects take the law into their own hands.

'Sir,' de Beaumont said, 'the thing was ill-done. There was no trial and no justice.'

Pembroke said nothing. No need. All had been said before.

'Sir,' Lancaster said again, 'do not, for the love of Christ, let loose the dogs of civil war!'

'It is overlate for *you* to speak,' the King said and turned his back.

London was for the King; it promised fighting-men, horses and arms—not for love of him but in fear of his greatest subjects. And still the more level-headed of his barons implored him not to plunge the country into civil war.

'Indeed, sir, how shall you fight?' Walter Reynolds bishop of Chichester, King's treasurer and toady, asked. 'The treasury is empty; wardrobe receipts have fallen heavily . . . and war costs money. Wait a little; the matter will settle itself.'

The King stayed his hand and glad to do it. He had waved the big stick, he had no great stomach for fighting, and Reynolds spoke common sense. So back to Windsor he went.

It was Autumn now. Like a ripe fruit herself, the young Queen ripened. Pregnancy became her. She had been too thin, now she had a sleek voluptuous look. She was no longer a pretty girl; she was a woman—and beautiful.

Winter came in. At Windsor November mists rose from the river; within doors logs blazed, braziers stood everywhere lest the Queen take cold. These last days of her pregnancy the King made much of her; between the Queen and the young Despenser he was, they said, forgetting Gaveston. She could have told them better. More than once, in the night, lifting herself upon an elbow, she had turned to see whether he slept. There he lay silent and still; but the tears ran from under closed lids, down into his mouth.

It is time to forget. She sent out her will a little despising him. *It is time . . .*

The Queen's labour had begun. All through the night lights burned at Windsor. She lay in bed, pale hair tangled and dark upon the pillow. A hard birth; she was small-made and the child large. When the pains took her, wrenching flesh and bone apart she bit into that full underlip of hers so that it showed bruised and swollen. So quiet she lay that, in spite of the jerking of her anguished body to reject torment, and the low moan forced through bitten lips, those that watched thought she slept.

On the thirteenth day of November, in the dark of the morning, in the year of grace thirteen hundred and twelve, the cry of the new-born babe bleated in the Queen's bedchamber. The King's son, heir to England, had opened his eyes upon the world.

The cry thin, protesting, infinitely moving, caught at the father's heart. He stretched out his hands, the strong, fine craftsman's hands, and took the child; and the young mother, lifting weary lids, marked the tenderness with which he looked upon the little one and was content. Maybe now he would forget Piers.

Prayers and processions; bonfires and fountains of wine in the streets. And all hearts turning to the King again, forgetting his weakness and his vices; and all hearts turning with yet greater love to the Queen, the fair young Queen, that had brought a little King into the world.

A fine child, handsome and lusty; a true Plantagenet. Four days later he was baptised with royal pomp in St. Edward's chapel at Windsor. To the great joy of the people he was named after his famous grandfather, his handsome father. Surely this little one, uniting all men in joy, would of himself bring peace into the troubled land.

The King's delight in his son amazed even himself; he could not enough honour the child. Upon the four-day infant he bestowed the great title of Chester with all its lands and appurtenances, together with the county of Flint and Gaveston's castle at Knaresborough. For Gaveston's young widow, for Gaveston's orphaned child, he cared little; Gaveston alone he had loved.

These days he was at his best, handsome and laughing, giving with both hands—gifts for the church, gifts for those that had honoured the ceremony of baptism, gifts for the midwife, and nurses; gifts for the messengers that had carried the news—and all, all beyond reason. The treasury was empty; what of it? Money would be found; Reynolds, for all his chatter, would find it! No end to the King's giving; he seemed to delight in the senseless pouring away of money. Once he came upon the Queen's tiring-woman dressing her lady's hair and stayed to watch the painting of lips, the shadowing of lids and lashes to make more lustrous the green-gold eyes. In his delight —a craftsman's delight—at beauty made perfect, he gave the woman twenty pounds on the spot and as much again annually to make her, and her husband that looked to the Queen's coifs, comfortable for life, but many that had rendered greater service went unpaid.

These days the Queen made herself content. She would never again love her husband as on the day she had stood with him at the altar and worshipped not God but his handsome looks. Yet, if he would continue kind, she would build what happiness she might.

But he could not forever dally at Windsor; nor, for all the Queen had given him a son, did he much like women ... and at West-minster Hugh, that pretty boy, waited. So back he came to find things much as he had left them—himself at logger-heads with his barons; and they at logger-heads among themselves. Lancaster and Warwick were, as always, fermenting trouble; the King, they pro-claimed, had no cause for quarrel, they had done their plain duty by a traitor. Between King and rebellious barons lay a bitterness that threatened to devastate the whole country.

The King sought to keep his enemies in check. Upon the barons there was constant restriction, they responded with instant anger. They were forbidden to move about the country carrying arms. Put by their arms! Such a thing had never been heard. How could a traveller defend himself at need? Without arms they'd not attend

Parliament nor any council whatsoever; they did not trust the King.

In the midst of the unease archbishop Winchelsey died. The King let out a great sigh of relief. 'There goes my most dangerous enemy; more dangerous than Lancaster or Warwick because more honest, more able; he led the church by the nose. Well, he's gone; and whether to heaven or hell it's all one to me!' Into the dead man's shoes stepped Walter Reynolds, servile priest, the King's tool.

Edward and Isabella were for France; unbelievably for France! Her father had invited them for Easter; a great celebration to knight his eldest son and crown him King of Navarre.

'France!' the Queen said; it was a word of love and longing upon her tongue.

Edward was surprised; he knew little of his wife—and cared less. Madam Queen Margaret could have told him how, in the empty years, she had longed for home; and how, though she died of her longing, nothing would have induced her to set foot there—a barren, humiliated Queen. Now her son was born and she was afire to go; pride was a splendid mantle to hide the shabbiness beneath.

Gowns and crowns, jewels and furs; knights and courtiers; horses and hounds; beds and bedding, the Queen's two baths and all the thousand things to make ready for the royal visit.

'Do not go, sir,' Pembroke besought the King, de Warenne and Percy besought him, and all that favoured his cause. 'Your barons are at odds. That—and your absence may bring Scotland about our ears! And then what confusion, what disaster! Wait until there's peace amongst us!'

'Then you may wait till doomsday! Go sir!' said Reynolds that had no desire but to please the King and to line his own pockets. 'A holiday is, God knows, needful; after a holiday a man works better!'

To the voice of pleasure the King was always ready to listen. And so to France. First to Aquitaine that England held of France, where they were received with flung bonnets, with garlands and with feasting. Thence through the green-and-white countryside to Paris, where Philip the Fair waited to welcome them. So handsome a family these Capets—Philip and his sons and his new-returned daughter!

Feasting and jousting, pageants and progresses. What Philip thought of the man beneath the handsome figure of his son of England, he kept to himself. He paid them every honour so that Edward, and even Isabella that had a little forgotten the splendour of her father's court, were alike dazzled. Happy days, free of the constant gnawing, *How shall we pay? Where do we turn for money?*

Days passing, weeks and months. Edward put aside all thought of trouble waiting at home; Isabella had no concern save for her own pleasure—she had given England its heir, she had done her duty! But of their duties came constant reminder; and when it could no longer be ignored, home they must go.

Back to autumn England, back to pinching and paring, to unresolved quarrels and an unsettled country.

'Men will be forever at each others' throats if women do not stop them!' Isabella said admiring her long, fine hands in the brasier's light.

'And what can women do?' Margaret drew the bright wool through the linen.

'We have our weapon—our tongue. We can coax and cajole; we can *talk* . . .'

'Then beware *how* you talk! A word can kill a man as surely as a sword!' She was thoughtful looking at her niece. The girl had beauty, wit and goodwill; she was discreet beyond her years. Ever since she had set her feet in England, six years ago, a child, she had not put one foot wrong. King and country together were blessed in such a Queen.

'You are over-young for such a task,' Margaret said, gentle. 'There's too much bitterness, too much deceit, too much self-seeking. Try, if you will; but do not look to succeed!'

'Cousin,' the Queen said, very loving with Lancaster, 'you are the greatest of the barons. They look to you for guidance; yes, even those upon the other side. For the sake of our kinship, come into the King's peace. You'll not lose by it; by God's Face I swear it!'

And when he said nothing, having no mind to bandy words with so young, so ignorant a creature, she said, 'You could make your own party—take the best, both sides. All men honour you and would gladly follow where you lead. You could . . .' and now she spoke softly, 'rule all England.' And when still he made no answer but went on scowling, great head sunk between high shoulders, she bent forward and kissed him upon both cheeks.

To Warwick and to Hereford she spoke also, smiling and coaxing, showing them that obedience to the King—or some show of it—was not a humble poor-spirited thing, but brave and difficult . . . and rewarding; but whether rewarding in the spirit or in this world's goods she left them to guess. To Pembroke, to de Warenne, to Arundel and Percy she spoke likewise, beseeching them to end the quarrel, cozening them that then there would be but one party—and that party strong to have its way in all things.

And all the time she whispered in the King's ear. 'Sir, forgive your rebellious lords; or, if you cannot forgive them—then make a show of it. Gaveston's dead and all your grief cannot bring him back. Think, sir, how desirable to have but one party, the great good to yourself! For, if any man propose to set himself against the King, then, the King's friends will privately inform him. It could mean the end to the Ordainers—' she named them with scorn, 'and their so-called Ordinances. Sir, you would rule—their King and master.'

So with her pretty looks and her coaxing and her flatteries and half-lies; and, most of all, with her appeal to each man's own advantage she won them—for the country's good and for the King's good and for her own good, also. For civil war—it could mean the fall of a King!

She had made peace—of a sort. The King had published his pardon for all that had taken part in Gaveston's killing; never mind how direct the hand.

. . . Pardon and remission is granted by the King through the prayers of his dearest companion, Isabella Queen of England.

How could the people not love her, beautiful and gracious; Isabella the Peace-maker.

Into Parliament came the insurgent peers to kneel, every one, before the King. He gave them the kiss of peace . . . but peace was not in his heart.

'It is the King's victory,' Isabella told Queen Margaret. *And mine, mine too!* 'Ordainers and their Ordinances—finished!'

'Not finished. Laid aside for a time because the barons choose it so. Ordainers and Ordinances still stand. Make no mistake! Not one baron—and Lancaster least of all—will accept defeat.'

'Lancaster!' Isabella shrugged. 'He has a flaw of weakness in him—you told me yourself; such things I don't forget. He'll go so far and no further. He'll crack . . .'

'. . . like a louse between my fingers!' The King had come upon them unaware. There he stood handsome and arrogant and laughing. Rising from her curtsey Isabella thought one might almost believe in his kingship. But had he learnt anything from his experiences? Would he ever learn? Well, no matter! Her part to cover his foolishness with her wits, his weakness with her strength. If he would but listen to her, men would forget the emptiness which lay beneath that commanding figure.

If he would listen . . .!

Chapter Fourteen

Peace between King and barons, Ordainers and Ordinances forgotten . . . so it seemed. King and Queen were, alike, happier. He felt himself stronger than before, freer of his barons; she knew herself to be of consequence. If there was no love between them there was, on her side, goodwill and ambition for him; on his, friendship and some trust. The present tranquillity she laid, rightly, to her growing influence with both husband and barons.

And in himself the King was calmer. He was over the worst of his grief for Gaveston; but never would he forget his friend nor forgive the manner of his dying. And still loneliness drove him to his wife's bed. And still he would start up crying out the beloved name, sometimes with joy mistaking the sleeper at his side, sometimes all broken with grief. But the occasions were less frequent, the company of Despenser, the handsome young man, comforted him more than a little.

But his greatest comfort lay in his small prince. He would send for the child, and taking him from the nurse, would fondle the little one, calling him love-names the while. Isabella thought it unkingly, unmanly. A man should love his child; but in reason, hiding his love. She, herself, loved the child; she loved him because he added to her stature, and because he was a kingly child and because he was her own. She safeguarded him as she might any treasure; but she had little fondness for children and, as long as he was healthy, cared not overmuch how little she might see him. But, from the day of his birth, his father called him by his little name—Ned. The babe—he swore it by God's Body—even in those first days turned to the sound of that name and smiled upon his father. And, certainly, within a little, he did smile and jump to come to his father; towards his mother he made no move, preferring the warm, milky smell of his nurse.

Had she loved the child with passion she still could have had no time for him. She was sworn to her husband's service—to cover his weakness, his vacillations; no mean task. And she must keep her image constant in the public eye—the good Queen, the peacemaking Queen. But, above all, she must woo the barons. The pardon they had been forced to ask, did not make them love the King more or distrust him less. Nor could she blame them! He was not one to keep a promise against his inclinations. She must forever with soft words and gentle smiles soothe their angers.

This was her work. That it was formidable she knew but not beyond her powers; none but she could carry it through.

So far so good. But now the King was to be removed from her influence. Trouble with ever-troublesome Scotland had broken out afresh. Early in February they had the news. Robert the Bruce had broken the sworn oath. He had crossed the border; with utmost savagery he had destroyed crops, burnt houses great and small, put to the sword men, women and children. Now, back in Scotland, he was raiding towns and castles that stood by their rightful lord, the King of England. Already Perth had fallen—town and castle; now Stirling, that great stronghold looked to fall also. Mowbray, the governor, had sent his urgent messengers to Westminster.

'We march for the north!' the King cried out, glad of any change, even though it involved the discomforts of war; and called upon his barons.

But it was not to be so easy. The Lords Ordainers, so long silent, lifted their voices. *The lord King must not make war without consent of Parliament.*

'Much good your advice!' he cried out white and raging, to Isabella. 'Now you can see where pardon has led! One party, you said! *One party!* My friends are still my friends and my enemies my enemies. My friends will come, and willing; my enemies will not stir until Parliament give them the nod. By God I'll not be held back! I'm no child to be constrained.'

'The man that takes you for a child's a fool!' she said, shameless. 'The child acts without thinking; the wise man acts with caution— and such a man are you! You will—I know you well—make a show of consulting the barons; thereafter you'll do as you think right!'

'Let those that will not come rot in Hell!' And he was not to be
mollified. 'I'll not wait upon their yea or nay. There's enough to
march with me—Gloucester, Pembroke and Hereford! Clifford
and Beaumont stand ready, yes and many another. By God's
Face I'll not stand to lose Scotland for any man's spite!'

To march at once was right; she'd say no more. Already he
blamed her for his pardon of the barons. He did not ask her, as she
had hoped, to go with him. A pity! Yet, staying behind she might
do much—smooth down the angered Ordainers, woo the laggard
barons, stir up the common people to the King's cause. In the cold
and frozen north she could do little; she was no captain of forces.

May, in the year of grace, thirteen hundred and fourteen, the King
rode out; those friends he had named rode with him. Pembroke had
been sent ahead with sufficient men to deal with any ambush. A very
great force had been mustered, forty thousand at the least and well-
equipped. So through the early summer countryside went the great
procession—wagons lumbering, high-stepping cavalry, infantry at
the ready, fife and drum sounding, banners and pennants flying.

From a high window the two Queens watched them go. 'The
King shows himself his father's son,' Isabella said. 'And I thank
God for it. There are over-many to twit him with playing at
soldiers.'

*He is over-hasty. It was ever his way. Over-hasty to begin, over-hasty
to make an end.* Margaret bit back the words.

The army was making its steady way north. By the end of the
second week in June it had reached Berwick. It had crossed the Tweed
no man offering to bar the way. The King was in high spirits, he
and his captains in good accord.

The King had confiscated the estates of two Scots lords and given
then to the young Despenser. First breath of discord upon general
good humour.

That last piece of news set Isabella thinking. Why? Despenser had
done nothing for the King except to weep with him in the matter of
Gaveston. But Despenser was a handsome fellow—if you admired
those fair girlish looks. Could it be possible . . .?

The sickness at her heart warned her that it could! The friendliness the King had shown the young man was warming into something quite other!

Was the Despenser boy destined for Gaveston's shoes? In that case it was out of the frying-pan into the fire for those that had slain Gaveston. Gaveston had been greedy, but it had been a poor man's greed, fear of known penury; and he could be, at times, generous. The greed of Despensers, father and son, was quite other; it was a cold and calculating greed; greed of rich men who could never have enough. They were careful, those two, they were cautious, and above all they were *able;* able as Gaveston had never been to devise policies—and always for their own good. There was no heart in them, no warmth. What their elevation could mean to herself she dared not think. Gaveston she had won—though, alas, too late. This father and son she could win—never! Now she must watch them both, seizing her every chance. If they were clever, she must be cleverer yet. Never would she lay down her hard task—but they made it so much the harder.

And now it was the third week in June. In Edinburgh the King made a short stay to replenish food, to overhaul weapons, to look to shoes of horses and men. And then no stop until Falkirk twenty-six miles away.

Daily the messengers rode in to kneel before the Queen.

'Madam, the King has left Falkirk for Stirling; he takes the Roman road. The Scots are few in number; some say six thousand, none puts it above ten. And we with our forty thousand; who can doubt the victory?'

The next news was not so reassuring.

'Madam, the Bruce guessed our men would take the Roman road. He ordered potholes to be dug to the depth of a man's knee and well-hid by branches. Down the road our vanguard came marching, Sir Humphrey Bohun at the head . . . and there the Bruce met them. Madam, he wore a crown upon a helmet all of leather; a *crown* as though he were King of Scotland. He! The sight enraged my lord Bohun—and can any man wonder? He went spurring forward to his death. For the Bruce, old as he is and a leper, with one blow felled him.'

'And then?' She gave no thought for Bohun save as it might affect the cause.

'His men fought on. Madam, they were brave! Yet they were but a small part of the army and their captain dead! In the end they must give way. So, Madam, they turned at last; and, as they fled, they stumbled into the accursed pot-holes. And some escaped and some were taken . . . and those that were taken were at once put to the sword.'

'How many?' She was less concerned for those that were dead than for the number of those that were left to fight.

'Almost the whole contingent. But let not Madam the Queen lose heart! It is but the beginning. We left the Roman road to cross the river further down—the Bannock, Madam. The upper course runs wild and swift through rocks; the lower course is quiet; it runs through pool and marsh and none the less deadly for that! And still we outnumber the enemy three to one; Madam, be of good cheer.'

But of cheer she could find little. The Bruce, for all he was old and sick, was a warrior; her husband, for all his youth and strength, was not. The Bruce had a firm purpose—to free Scotland and to rule it, her independent King. But Edward? Who knew how long his purpose would stand? But even were he firm of purpose, he did not know the terrain; he was, besides, too little patient, too careless, too confident to trouble about such a thing! On the other hand he out-numbered the Scots three to one at the least; that must surely count for victory.

'Madam, we crossed the river a mile below the Bannock village; when we left each man was busying himself for the morrow.'

'The morrow?'

'Yes, Madam; to meet the Scots in battle.'

The morrow! Then already the battle was fought; already lost and won. It had taken these messengers above a week riding in relays, day and night to reach her today!

'Tomorrow, or the next day, Madam the Queen shall have the news!'

Tomorrow? How does one live till tomorrow? Her anguished eyes turned to Queen Margaret.

'We can pray.' The older woman said.

We can pray. And pray she did—if one can call it praying, the bargain she sought to drive with God. She knelt, offering masses, offering jewels, offering plate to God's service, offering a chapel, offering a church; offering, offering. The half of the kingdom could scarce pay for it; yet still she went on offering. Such offers surely God could not refuse!

God had refused.

The English had been routed; the great army drowned or dead or fled.

'Madam,' and the messenger could not lift his eyes, 'God be thanked the lord King is safe!'

Yes, he would be safe! But how far did he shame himself and me . . . and me?

She could not ask but she must know; she must know!

He felt the pressure of her will upon him; he said, unwilling 'Madam, the King left the field . . .'

He left the field, oh God he fled!

'Madam, there was no other way. He returns by way of Berwick and thence by sea!'

'Tell me of the battle.' *And if he showed some spark of valour, in God's name let me hear it . . .*

'They fought, Madam, where the river turns north. It is all black marsh; evil ground. The Bruce drew up his men in four close squares; their pikes stuck out like bristles of a hedgehog—full eighteen feet in all directions. Such a thing was never seen. Impossible to get near them.

'The most part of our captains, Madam, urged the lord King to wait one day at least—the men were weary with the long, forced march. But he would not listen. Then my lord of Gloucester urged further, but still the lord King would not listen. He called the earl a coward. . . .'

She drew in her breath. Gloucester had spoken good sense. He was no coward nor ever had been. It was the King that was the coward; he had feared to wait until his courage should cool, the King that had fled the field!

'At that, Madam, the lord Gloucester rushed into the battle; he threw himself against those murdering pikes . . . and so he died.'

Gloucester killed. Driven to his death by the foolishness of the King; dead in his springtime, the brave young man. She felt tears prick in her eyes.

On and on the dreadful tale, the appalling slaughter.

'Again and again our men flung themselves against the murdering pikes. The lord Robert de Clifford died upon them, so also the lord Beaumont and many another. Gone all of them to join dead Gloucester. Hereford they took; he struggled like a lion in the net. They took also the lord bishop of Lichfield together with his clerks and all the records . . .'

'And the seal; the privy seal? Lichfield had it!'

'That, too, Madam, in Scottish hands.'

She closed her eyes. Shame upon shame!

'Madam, the men—the common soldiers—they fought; they went on fighting. Heroes all! The King was gone, the leaders dead or fled; but still they went on fighting. But it was all useless; it was worse than useless. Our cavalry could not move; it was caught between their deadly pikes and our own archers. Nor could our archers shoot; for then they must wound our own cavalry in the back. Madam, it was horrible!

'And there was no stopping the Scots. They pressed on in solid blocks screaming their warcry—a wild sound to curdle the blood. They forced our men back—riders and footsoldiers; back, back, . . . into the marsh. And the marsh, the evil marsh took them. And that, Madam, was the most horrible sight of all. In battle a man expects to die—by sword or spear or arrow; a clean death. But this! Madam, Madam . . . the fine men sinking down into the mud, choking and suffocating in the mud . . . dying their fearful death . . .'

He stopped, sickened on the thought; and she sickened, no less than he. She wished to hear no more; the rest she knew. And wished to God she did not know.

He guessed her thoughts—as how could he not? Unwilling to leave her to shame as great as misery, he said—but he kept his head low, 'Madam, the lord King could do no other. Those whose place it was to advise him, besought him to leave the field.'

How much beseeching did he need? She sat stiff in her place; she she could not take this easy comfort.

'Madam—' and it was as though he asked pardon for his own fault, 'at first he would not go. But they entreated him saying, *When the King is lost, all is lost.* So then he did quit the field. Then such lords as were left, when they saw the King leaving, the standard carried before him, followed him. But—as I have told Madam the Queen—the men, the common men of England, still stood to the enemy. And some died in the marshes, and some in the river, and some upon the pike; and some few, by the especial grace of God, escaped. Madam there were no cowards.'

Was there not one coward?

The thought beat upon her sick heart.

Chapter Fifteen

Madam Queen Margaret said, and she white as a bone, 'At Berwick, at Dunbar, at Falkirk, my husband carried the day. Had he not done so they had brought him home on his shield. If the dead know aught he is shamed this day!'

It was the first time she had faulted the King—and he not there to hear. She had, at need, spoken outright to his face; but she had allowed no criticism behind his back—not from herself, nor from any other, not even from her niece the Queen.

Isabella said, shocked, 'If you, Madam Aunt, allow yourself such words, what words shall they use that do not love the King? What shall Lancaster say? What Warwick?'

Margaret said, 'You are right, my child. There's no word of mine can alter by one hairsbreadth what has been; or shall be!'

Long before the last of the news came through they were to learn both of them, what the barons thought, what the country thought and what Christendom thought. Edward of England, son to great Edward, was branded coward; a fainéant that, through easy living, had lost Scotland, chiefest jewel of the crown.

And now the last of the news came through. It was not Scotland alone that was lost; it was the flower of England's manhood. To the great names of the dead were added other names—knights and high officers of state together with names of simple folk beyond counting. Now it was not only the loss of Scotland that England mourned, nor yet the death of her chivalry; in countless homes men wept for their dead . . . uselessly dead.

Isabella felt herself spotted with the King's disgrace. Her last, lingering regard had turned to contempt—contempt the world must never see, not for his sake but for her own. She would scant no sign of respect, nor fail in any duty as a wife. But if, his eye wandering to the young Despenser, he did not call for wifely duties, so much the better! She had borne a son; no further need to prove her womanhood. Now she would never willingly give herself to her husband nor shed one tear if he deserted her for a mignon's bed. She had rather sleep with the Bruce himself—old and leprous as he was than with her fainéant husband.

'Now the Bruce is the hero of Christendom!' she told her aunt. 'And well deserves it, the sick, indomitable old man!' No need to add that, by so much as Bruce of Scotland's honour grew, Edward of England's honour lessened. 'All England shall rue Bannockburn . . . and I think the King will rue it most!'

The King was home again. And now he was at the mercy of his barons as never before; defeat had delivered him up bound hand and foot. Pembroke, captain of his forces, sharing the blame for Bannockburn, lost much of his influence; a pity, he was a moderate man. Now Lancaster openly led the ever-growing ranks of those that neither liked nor any way honoured the King. Friends and servants in state and household were put from their places; Archbishop Reynolds himself, the chancellor, sent packing.

'My friends dismissed, my household broken up! By God I'll not endure it!' the King cried out.

But endure it he must, and a good deal more.

It was not only the high officials centred at Westminster that were driven out. All over the country, lesser officials—mayors, sheriffs, magistrates and judges, even, were put from office and men obedient to Lancaster put in their place.

First of the King's friends to go were the Despensers, father and son. Able men, both, that might have been good servants to the state but for that greed to which honour and reason were alike sacrificed. It was the most popular thing Lancaster had ever done: he was the best-loved man in England. When he rode through London bonnets waved, cheers rose in the air. All England hated those two that with their extortions had made the country poorer; and especially they hated the younger that looked to take Gaveston's place in the King's love.

And to all Lancaster's decrees the King was forced to submit; for Gloucester was dead, and Hereford and many others prisoner in Scotland and Pembroke's power diminished. The most part of the barons—and especially bitter Warwick whose hand was hot yet with Gaveston's blood; the most part of the princes of the church together with the common folk of England looked to Lancaster, Guardian of their rights. It was Lancaster that gave instructions to the new officials himself had chosen—to Chancellor, Treasurer, Keeper of the Wardrobe; and to him they held themselves responsible. It was Lancaster that issued commands for the conduct of the realm, that gave or withheld pardons, that decided upon life and death. It was Lancaster that spoke for the barons with the King— and spoke like an equal prince.

Lancaster supreme.

These days Isabella hated her uncle because, diminishing the power of the King, he had diminished the power of the Queen. Had she thought to influence him, to rise on the wings of his power? The more fool she! She'd not be so fooled again. One day he should pay for this. Meanwhile he was all-powerful and she must show herself gracious and friendly.

Torrential rains ruined the harvests. There was neither meat enough nor corn enough, nor any to be bought in Europe; for all Christendom suffered likewise. Prices rose; they went on rising. Wheat was eight times the usual price; oats, peas and every common food followed the wheat. How soon, men wondered, would even the coarsest food be weighed in the balance against fine gold? And the corn—however much one paid—was of wretched quality; it must be baked in the oven before it could be ground. With hunger, with bad food, pestilence fell upon the land so that many died.

Misery upon misery.

'They are eating horseflesh which the church forbids; they are eating cats and dogs and mice and whatever vermin they can lay hand upon,' Isabella said. 'I hear that men murder each other for a little bread. And when they get it—no virtue in it!'

'There are some that eat human flesh!' Margaret shuddered. 'Dear

Christ, that in a Christian country man should eat man!' She crossed herself; these days she wore a thin and stricken look.

The sad year moved on. To hunger and sickness was added anger, bitterness and unrest. The King, frustrated and furious, distrusted his Council; the Council, grimly determined upon its rights, distrusted the King. And all the time food less and less, and all the time prices rising. In the fields where they had gone searching for rotten turnips, men lay down to die praying for death before the wild beast found them.

The King and Queen fared none too ill. They travelled the country; the larders—such as they were—in one house emptied, they betook themselves to the next. A fretful Edward complained of quality, of flavour, of cooking; Isabella made no complaint. She had learned to complain only where she might mend matters; this matter was beyond her mending.

The bitter year was nearing its end; the King was morose and sullen; he would give way to sudden, unpredictable rages. Those that had offended—and many that had not—he punished with cruelty. Afterwards he would regret what he had done, though that he never would admit.

He would take no advice; he could scarce bring himself to listen when others talked. Frustrated in his power to command great issues, he set his whole will upon having his way in small ones.

A fews days before Christmas he declared his intention of removing the body of Gaveston from Oxford where all this time it had lain.

'Foolish, foolish! It will anger Lancaster and Warwick still further; reminder without words of their treachery!' Isabella cried out to Queen Margaret. 'Madam Aunt, could you not speak with him on this matter of Gaveston? To you he might listen!'

But even to her, though he choked down his anger, he would not listen. 'Leave the body where it is! Let the barons forget the thing they have done! And I, am I to forget it, also? No! Nor yet the oath I made to avenge his murder and thereafter to give him a King's burial. Two years have gone by—and still the murderers go unpunished. Punished they certainly shall be; but for that I can wait no longer. No! There shall be a solemn procession to carry his body home to the house he loved above all others!'

At Oxford the great procession assembled—the King, the Queen, Reynolds that, though Chancellor no more, was still Archbishop of Canterbury; and following him four bishops and priests aplenty, together with the Despensers and others of the King's friends—few alas! And so they came to King's Langley and there the body was interred with high ceremony . . . but barons and princes of the church were, for the most part, absent.

The King shrugged their absence away; but he would remember it. The funeral over, he went to Cambridge, seeking the company of those he liked best—peasants, simple folk that had no part in politics. There he matched himself against them in all country sports; in skill and strength and grace he outdid them all, so that they worshipped him as he might be a god. Such warmth, such adulation touched him to the heart; he felt himself magnified so that he carried himself as though he were, indeed, a god. But he made no attempt to win the burghers, solid folk whose goodwill might have served him well.

And now it was a new year; the year of grace thirteen hundred and sixteen. *God grant us a better year than the last!* Isabella made her prayer; Margaret and the people of England, gentle and common, prayed likewise . . . all save the barons. Apart from the famine and the sickness it had been a good year for them. With their Ordinances they had brought the King beneath their thumbs.

'We must see that we keep him there! He's as slippery as quicksilver!' Lancaster warned them, Lancaster bent on humiliating the King, bent on showing all Christendom who ruled England.

Later in the month the King must meet his Parliament in Lincoln; no help for it. The barons were, for the time being, his masters. Reluctant he tore himself from the delights of Cambridge. He commanded the Queen's company and she went unwilling. She had neither love nor respect nor any hope to influence him. Nor did she relish the cold, troublesome journey; she fancied she might be with child. Yet go she must; and with a good grace. She was well-liked by barons and simple folk alike. It was good for the King to be seen in her company.

In the bishop's house at Lincoln he cooled his heels waiting for Parliament to assemble. Some barons had arrived—those that were the King's friends and they were few enough; Lancaster was not there nor any that were of his mind.

'I'll say no longer; it's a studied insolence to gall me!' the King cried out.

'Yet wait a little,' she said. 'Men are delayed for this thing and for that, against their will. Give them yet a little time.'

Day by day she sought to keep him in Lincoln. 'Sir, the weather is bitter; wait until the wind changes.' Or, 'The roads are bad; floods as high as a man's knees.' And when she could delay him no longer with her excuses, said, desperate, 'Sir, I think I am with child!'

For that he would stay; but he would not stay long.

Day after day; and still no Lancaster. And still she kept him with her prime excuse. *Sir, I am sick. I dare not venture.* Keep him she must lest he anger Lancaster further; such anger must bring him yet more humiliation. And waiting, there might be some gain. A show of courtesy might wring some advantage out of Parliament. Her pride was as great as his, but she was quicker to learn. She was learning to weigh every hairsbreadth of advantage in the scale against pride.

The King had waited above a fortnight, he would wait no longer. She could not blame him; she made no more attempt to keep him. They were on the point of departure, bag and baggage already on the move, when Lancaster saw fit to arrive.

The King's temper—she had suffered from it these last days—was flayed raw. She sought, before those two could meet, to gentle them into some show of friendship.

'Sir,' she besought the King, 'show some goodwill to Lancaster. For the moment he rides high; it will not be for long. He's top-heavy with pride; soon he must overbalance and fall.'

And to Lancaster, 'Dear Uncle, if you love me, show due respect to the King. I ask it for your own sake. There are some—and not a few—that dislike a show of disrespect to him; the King is still the King. Take his hand in friendship; so you keep the goodwill of all to do whatever you may choose.'

He looked at her in some surprise. Always he had seen her as a wilful, coaxing girl, of little importance. Now, for the first time he saw her—a woman; possibly a clever woman. That she was beautiful he did not notice; to women's looks he was indifferent. But she had spoken good sense; he might do worse than make some sort of alliance with her. But, could he trust her? Might not the sharpness of her wits turn about to wound the man that trusted her? It was a matter to require thought. But for all that he smiled and kissed her hand and vowed himself to her service.

And she? Could she trust him? His wits were not sharp nor was he honest; but what he lacked in both he made up in pride. Flatter his pride—the sure way to manage him!

'Dearest Uncle!' she said and bent forward to kiss him upon both cheeks.

Now the King and Lancaster must woo each other with false and flowery words. In open Parliament the King declared, 'Dear Cousin of Lancaster, doubt me no longer. In all things I am your good friend as I hold you to be mine. I pray you be chief in Council to direct all my affairs.' And he wondered that the words did not blister his tongue.

And Lancaster, no whit behind in false compliments, 'I thank my lord the King. For love of him I consent to lead the Council.' Yet he must add, 'But if the lord King shall not heed my advice, I must hold myself free to leave the Council.'

So, smiling above his hatred, the King must swear again to observe every Ordinance. And more bitter than ever it was, for they had added fresh demands. Now he must agree that any member of his Parliament who gave him what Lancaster called *bad advice* must at once be dismissed. *Yes* and *Yes*... humiliating himself, humiliating his friends.

In Parliament it had been *Yes* and *Yes*; but when he burst into his wife's closet it was *No* and *No*!

'Lancaster seeks to chain me beneath his obedience—presumptuous fool! Let the fool beware!'

She laid a finger to her lip lest with an unguarded tongue he might yet, in spite of all humiliations, undo himself. She lifted the arras and looked into the empty ante-room beyond. She said, very low, 'Sir, this is Lincoln and Lancaster is its lord. Say nothing now; wait till we are back in Westminster. Pembroke has better wits than my uncle, and Pembroke is our friend; Pembroke will know how to deal with him! Between those two there's no love lost.'

Pembroke was wise and Pembroke was loyal, but Lancaster was supreme; she knew it, and within that knowledge she must work.

Chapter Sixteen

The worst of the famine was passing. Trees were breaking into healthy leaf, corn was growing straight, uncankered. Yet there was misery enough. Sickness still took toll and there was not enough food—nor would be for some time. The misery of the people showed itself in unrest; unrest everywhere. And with unrest—violence; violence spread like a plague throughout the country. Good honest folk, solid burghers who, in happier time had set their faces against crime, now supported gangs of robbers that supplied them with food. In the north the misery was even more intense. The Scots, drunk with success at Bannockburn were over the border, with every raid they struck further south; slaughter, rape, arson—the north knew it all. And, following the Scots' example, the Welsh poured over the border and the west suffered with the north.

Lancaster did nothing to put the violence down; he was facing trouble in his own household. For this reason he had not, as yet, come out in open enmity to the King.

Division in Lancaster's household! Isabella considered the matter. That must certainly hamper his plans for a while. Wise, perhaps to show him less kindness; wiser still to find out the truth.

'Why this trouble among your husband's people?' she asked my lady of Lancaster.

Pretty Alice, born de Lacy, lifted a pale face.

'It is the steward, Madam; a violent man and greedy. He extorts as he will and punishes as he will; he does not stop at murder.'

'And Lancaster allows it?'

'Madam, he is much occupied with affairs. As long as the fellow fills his master's pockets as well as his own, there's no question asked.'

'A hard man, Lancaster; a man not easy to love!' She fixed Alice with a meaningful eye. Pale Alice went a shade paler.

'I know well what you suffer at Lancaster's hands,' the Queen said, 'but is it wise to leave Lancaster for de Warenne?'

The red came up in Alice's pale cheeks. 'It is not de Warenne, Madam. It is his esquire . . . it is L'Estrange.'

Isabella stared, unbelieving. The lame man, the landless man! Did the fool think to throw away her place, her fortune and her honour for this?

Alice said, 'A little kindness, Madam—it is all I ask; all I have ever asked . . . and L'Estrange is kind. Madam—' and now she spoke with passion shocking is so pale a creature. 'I am more than an animal to breed upon. But Lancaster! Even using me he has no tenderness. Nor would I welcome tenderness from him now. My flesh creeps at the sight of him!'

'Can you hope to escape Lancaster—his anger and his revenge— you and your lover, both?' Queen Margaret looked up from her stitching.

'De Warenne will help us, Madam; he has promised.'

'I knew your mother,' Margaret said, 'and I speak for your good. De Warenne helps you not from kindness but from hatred—hatred of Lancaster. To take you from your husband for himself—that had been bad enough; to take you for another man—and that man poor and humble . . .'

'A gentleman, Madam; he loves me!' Alice said gentle yet proud with the pride of the great house of de Lacy.

Envying the woman, despising the woman that cast away everything for love, Isabella said, honey-sweet, 'If you are sure of your heart then follow it.'

'What have you done?' Margaret asked when Alice had made her curtsey and was gone. 'You send that woman to disgrace.'

Isabella shrugged. 'If she wants her cake let her eat it and not complain of bellyache later!'

'You did it not out of kindness but to stir up angers between Lancaster and de Warenne.'

'It needs no stirring.'

'Then in God's Name, why?'

'Lancaster's too proud. All the world laughs at the man that wears the horns; such laughter will help to bring him low.'

Margaret stared as though she had never truly seen the girl before. So devious a mind, so ruthless a will, such quickness to seize upon her chance . . . and still so young. How would she grow with the years? What strange fruit might her tree not ripen?

Lancaster's wife had left him—and for so low a man!

He was, he said, well content. Her rich lands, the titles her father had left were secured to him and to his house for ever. He was well rid of a strumpet; he said that, too. But men said otherwise. *He shall he hope to rule any man—let alone the King—Lancaster that cannot rule the one creature all men should rule; his wife?* Men asked the question laughing the while; but the laughter was behind his back; to his face they did not dare. But Lancaster knew well what they said of him and burned against the whole world.

Now, as though at a challenge, he thrust himself ever forward; he loomed over the whole country like a black sky. Blind to the law, deaf to the law, he played the king, punishing whom he would and how he would. He set himself against the King in every way; and it was not ambition alone that drove him. Personal bitterness against both King and Queen went deep. He suspected she had encouraged his wife in her flight; and the King made no attempt to hide his amusement. 'If no wedding, at least a bedding for Cousin Thomas's wife!' he said once where Lancaster must hear. They should pay for it—King and Queen, both! Lancaster swore it. Now he stirred up trouble wherever he could.

Trouble from the Scots gave Lancaster his excuse to march; march through Yorkshire where de Warenne sat thumbing his nose. Private quarrel between those two threatened to break into civil war.

Lancaster command the armies; disaffected Lancaster! The King would have none of that. Himself would take command to punish the Scots. But already Lancaster had departed. Now with his forces he sat in his own city of Lancaster to stop the King's advance. He blocked roads, he broke bridges, he dared to imprison the King's messengers. Unlawful disturber of the peace, he declared it his duty to guard the peace of the realm.

The King's party was weak, Lancaster's strong. The King must go to the wall unless ... unless ...

'Pembroke could save us all—if the King would let him!' Isabella told Queen Margaret. 'He could put Lancaster down and set himself again in the leader's place.'

'I have long thought it. He took overmuch of the blame for Bannockburn. Lancaster's all noise and bluster. But Pembroke has a wisdom beyond most men. He's clear in thought and moderate in demand. He's reasonably honest and he's steady; he doesn't chop and change. He keeps the middle way ... a good middle man.'

'He could lead a middle party ... *a middle party!*' Isabella said, thoughtful, and coined a new name.

A new name; a new party.

In the ever-growing enmity between the King and Lancaster, Pembroke was steadily coming into his own. A man to be trusted. It was not only the two Queens that had come to recognise his virtues. He had stood unwavering by the Ordinances, he had never, since Gaveston's death, shown friendship for Lancaster; yet he had not shown hatred, neither. A moderate man he had friends in both parties. Now these friends were turning towards him—their one hope; they were forming a party to put an end to the incessant quarrels and to all the miseries quarrels brought.

'The church rallies to Pembroke,' Queen Margaret said. 'He's got both archbishops in his pocket, yes even Reynolds that knows which side his bread's buttered; and with them, naturally the most part of the bishops. He's got de Warenne, of course; they're brothers in this!'

'Many of Lancaster's friends have left him—if you can call them friends! They don't trust him. Folk say everywhere that he had his own secret understanding with the Bruce; and because of it we lost Bannockburn. Hereford vouches for it; he heard it in Scotland while he was waiting for ransom. He says he'll have nothing to do with my uncle. And he's not the only one.'

'You may count on the Despensers! Give them the chance and they'll be back; Lancaster will have to reckon with them too!'

Margaret told her. 'Never look so black. And don't underestimate them, neither! Greedy they are and insolent; but able, able both. Useful men—if the King would but show himself reasonable in his love of them!'

'*Reasonable*—can you expect it?' Isabella was silent, biting upon her lip. 'Better for us all if he keep them at a distance; and for the King best. The people hate them; and hatred has spilt over upon the King. Now goodwill turns to him again; God send he doesn't thrust it back!' she cried out passionate. 'The tide is turning, friends and servants are creeping back to the Treasury to the Wardrobe and to the Household . . . have you marked it?'

'I have marked it; and I begin to hope,' Margaret said.

In the summer of the year of grace thirteen hundred and sixteen the two Queens went to Eltham; there in mid August, Isabella was brought to bed with her second son.

Food might still be scarce and misery rife; there might be little in Wardrobe and Treasury. But the King's son had been born and the King's friends were back in office and there was enough money to fling about. The messenger had a hundred pounds for bringing the news, the midwife enough to keep her in comfort for the rest of her life. The Queen ordered a gown of white velvet, very rich and fine, five pieces went to the making of it; and all trimmed with minniver and pearls. Very lovely she looked when she went to her churching. There were some to mutter against her extravagance; but it was an extravagance most could forgive. She had given them a second prince; she was but twenty-two and well-liked. The mutterings were lost in the louder cry of love.

Chapter Seventeen

A new name had been added to Pembroke's supporters; an unexpected name. Uncle and nephew had sent from the Welsh marches with assurances of friendship, of help at need.

Mortimer! It was a name Isabella knew. A great name on the Welsh border. The uncle was Mortimer of Chirk, the nephew Mortimer of Wigmore; and baptised Roger both. One never saw them at court; their hands were full. Most powerful of marcher lords they kept peace on the Welsh Border. Isabella thanked God they had come in to Pembroke.

The year moved on; the new year came in.

Lancaster more bitter, more intransigent than ever still rode high in the saddle. But Pembroke's Middle Party gathered strength, bishops and barons forever swelling its ranks. Mortimer; it was a name often heard now and Isabella listened with care, stored the information. Mortimer of Chirk was in late middle-age; a strong man of great authority. Mortimer of Wigmore in his early thirties was his uncle's heir and both were very rich. Bonny fighters both of them; and the younger, one that knew how to use his wits. He was, they said, ambitious above all men. From Madam de St. Pierre the Queen had the personal, intriguing gossip about the man.

'Women hate him or run mad for him!' Théophania said.

'And he?'

'No woman-hater, certainly!'

'Married?'

'But certainly, Madam. His wife's a good and pleasant lady—our country-woman. De Joinville she was; Jeanne de Joinville.'

'A name I know. I hope to meet its pleasant owner soon.'

'She'll not come unless you command her. She's not fond of courts—she has a growing family. They say he's as faithful a husband as you can expect from a soldier—but he's a man to like variety in women; and he's able to take his pick!'

'I hope to see this challenging man one day!' the Queen said, indifferent.

'Since, Madam, he's of the lord Pembroke's party he must soon come to court!'

'Then let it be soon! Before God, I'm sick to the soul of the faces I know—the greedy, suspicious faces. Should this Mortimer prove no better than the rest, at least he's something new!'

The year of thirteen hundred and seventeen had worn its dreary way to December. Christmas was not enlivened for the Queen by the knowledge that she was once more with child. Nothing for it but to resign herself as best she might to the situation. Of her sons she saw little. Edward, turned five, and John, half-way through his second year, lived each in his own household. They had their governors and their tutors, their household officials and servants. Their father saw more of them than she; he liked children and little Ned he loved with an all-devouring pride. He visited them both whenever he could, he sent them playthings—a tiny boat, or a hound himself had carved with loving care, his strong, fine hands holding the knife with precision. But she? As long as the childen were well she cared not how little she might see them.

Of a third child she saw no need; two were enough to secure the succession. She resented the coming child; as with the others there had been no joy in its conception; this time, indeed, she had resented her husband yet more. Had he come to her in love or even in plain lust she might have welcomed him—it proved, at least, some need of her; she might have welcomed, also, the fruit of this need. But it was no such thing and everybody knew it; everybody knew of his passion for the young Despenser. It was the old story. Having sported with his love the King might remember his duty; at such times he would come to her bed to take her with indifference. Then he would be off and nothing more seen of him for weeks.

Now she must count the weeks to June, watching the thickening of her body, enduring the discomforts of pregnancy. She was wearier than ever of Westminster, wearier of the faces about her. She thought she must scream at the sight of Lancaster back from his fastness, with his great hump and the great head sunk between his shoulders, and the fantastic clothing hard even for a handsome man to carry. She was sick of the sight of Pembroke, saviour though he might be, Pembroke with his yellow face and his beak of a nose. How aptly Gaveston had named him! She sickened still more at the sight of the Despensers—the father with his clever weasel-face and the pretty son with his girlish ways. And most of all she sickened at the sight of her husband with his grace, and the handsome, smiling face that hid the cold heart. Warwick, thank God, had gone to his grave. *Blackdog;* men need fear his bite no more. She found herself, to her surprise, regretting Gaveston; with him laughter had fled the court.

The Middle Party was growing ever more strong. Lancaster must hold on tight lest he fall from the saddle. Isabella longed for the day. But a question troubled her—this new party once in power, would it, too, crack the whip over the King? She wanted him to be ruled— but by herself; her foresight, her wisdom covering his weakness, his instability and the light breaking of his promises; and the way he gave his heart to unworthy men—and the country's treasure with it. The spectacle of the King of England bending to the barons' whip was unendurable. Partner such a man she could not!

She took her trouble to Queen Margaret. 'Shall a new party treat the King with more honour than the old? To crack the whip, beat down an anointed King—it sickens me!'

'You may trust Pembroke. Lancaster would have the King dance to his command; Pembroke will restore the King's dignity.'

Restore what was never there; it's beyond the power of a man! Isabella bit her tongue against the thought.

'Lancaster had best look to himself!' Margaret said. 'If he's wise he'll come in with Pembroke now—while there's time. But he isn't wise. He's losing ground and he doesn't know it. He thinks he can go on for ever flouting the law as he thinks fit, allowing none other to speak for the barons but himself, himself alone, treating the King with insolence. I tell you, madam niece, Pembroke will not tolerate it much longer.'

'By God's Face I weary of Lancaster and Pembroke alike! I weary of all those that set themselves to govern the King; and, most of all,

I weary of the King that needs such governing!' Isabella spoke with the irritability of a breeding woman; but for all that Margaret caught the ring of truth.

Isabella was wearier of the court than ever. Madam Queen Margaret had gone into the country. She had not been well of late; unable to sleep, unable to eat, she could no long support the struggles and the quarrels and the fear of saying too much. She longed, instead, to set her thoughts on holy things; the pain within her breast of which she never spoke told her it was time. She was now at Marlborough Castle, her own house, where, free of court restriction, a sick woman could rest and make her peace with God.

'You will come to Woodstock to be with me in June?' Isabella had asked and it was less a question than a certainty. Margaret had been with her at the birth of both her sons; it was Margaret's kind hands that each time had taken the child from the midwife, Margaret's voice that had spoken the joyful tidings—*a son*. To go through her ordeal alone, alone to bear this undesired child—it was not possible.

'I will come . . . if I am let,' Margaret had said.

Then all was well; for when the Queen commanded, who could say *No*?

Now Isabella had no-one to comfort her with good advice. Madam de St. Pierre she could trust for a loving heart and for discretion; but scarce for understanding affairs of state; Théophania had not the keen wit to pierce through policies and come at the truth. Isabella longed for Margaret and her wisdom.

In the third week of February, in the year of grace, thirteen hundred and eighteen, *Margaret good withouten lack* died. She was thirty-six.

Isabella took the news with disbelief. She had not thought, she had not *dreamed* . . . Her aunt had tired easily of late but the peace of Marlborough would mend all! But Marlborough had not mended; it had ended. Forced, at last to the bitter knowledge that her aunt would come no more, Isabella gave herself to her grief. But grief was for herself; there was none to spare for the King, nor for Margaret's two sons—Thomas of Brotherton eighteen years old and Edmund a year younger. Men all three! They had no need of woman's comfort in woman's ordeal But she... *she*! She felt herself cheated that Margaret could not be with her for the birth. One greater than the Queen of England had said *No!*

The King had taken the news with grief, grief greater, he was sure, than that of Margaret's own sons. As always, with him, grief flowed in easy words. 'She was my mother, dearer to me than my own. When I offended my father—and dear God how easy he was to offend!—she would speak for me; without my asking she would turn away his wrath with gentle words. And now she is dead, my dear mother. There was never another so kind, so good ... *Margaret good withouten lack*, and, Yes, Isabella said, Yes, letting him talk himself out until the flow of grief died with his words.

'I will make a memorial for her, the most splendid in Christendom. There shall be continual offerings made in her name. I shall give an altar-cloth of crimson samite worked all of gold.'

I shall ... I shall.... He had talked himself cheerful again. But for all that he missed her intolerably; only toying with the young Despenser could he forget the one creature that had loved him with a pure heart; and a wise one.

May deepened into June and the Queen ripened with the year. Early in June she betook herself to Woodstock to await the birth of her third child.

Mid-June she was brought to bed of a daughter; boy or girl, she cared little. She was done at last with the inconvenience of pregnancy and her body come again to its sweet shape. But the King's joy was deep; the birth of a daughter released in him a tenderness he had never known nor expected. Women he did not like; but this baby daughter filled him with an almost feminine love. And with it came gratitude to his wife; a gratitude he had not known since the birth of his heir. He could not do enough to pleasure her. He sent her three hundred pounds to spend on new clothes; he sent her a silver-gilt box of sugared violets for which, in pregnancy, she had developed a craving. He ordered new cushions for her charette—flame-coloured silk and gold tissue to become her beauty well. He could not stop sending her gifts. There were three pieces of satin worked with gold, and with them he sent shoes dyed to the same colours with tassels of pure silk and tags of silver-gilt. He sent her a message, also; the first message to come from his heart. He longed to see her and his daughter; he would have come at once, had, indeed, been upon the point of starting. Instead, he must, alas, meet his barons at Leake; he scented trouble.

He did not ask her to join him, he had all a weak man's vanity—but he prayed she would come of herself. With the grace of recent motherhood, added to the affection in which already they held her, she could surely influence the barons in his favour.

The same thought had taken possession of Isabella.

His kindness had come too late; she wanted none of it. But power she did want; and this was a step towards it. But dare she take it? Dare she join the King, unasked? And what of the barons; might they not resent her? Opinion had hardened against the King; her task would be more difficult than before. Was she ready?

Margaret was no longer there to advise; it was a matter to think out for herself.

... She was cleverer than the King, so much was certain; cleverer than any man of them all, more subtle, than Pembroke, even. Crooked was a word she would never admit of herself. She was clever, she was subtle, others were crooked. She and Pembroke together—she guiding! She could do it.

For the first time she was not sorry that Margaret was dead. With Margaret she had pretended to goodness; pretended that her heart was set to help the King—that and that alone. She need pretend no more!

She felt within herself like the stirring of a child, the stirring of freedom—freedom to act without pretence, to do exactly as she thought fit. Like a birthpang she felt within her the strong, unfolding will. Will to power.

Mind and will; these were woman's hidden weapons; with beauty she made immediate assault. Isabella searched her face in the looking-glass, knowing with love, her own beauty. But what of her shape after this third birth? Hands upon high, white breasts, hands sliding to slender waist and rounded hips, she was, she knew as fine as ever.

And now she was for Leake. Had she been weary of the court? Now she could not get there fast enough! Would there be newcomers to charm? Had the Mortimers come yet from Wales? And if they had would she find them useful? Her mind took her again and again over the barons; some she could assault with her beauty, others undermine with her subtlety. Power. Power for herself! She would be satisfied with nothing less. To wield it in the shadow of the King would no longer serve. Power she must have within her hands to hold it fast. She and she alone.

Chapter Eighteen

Things were unpleasant at Leake. The King was irritable and troubled, he and his barons distrusted each other. And among themselves they were divided. Pembroke made it clear that he meant to be master; Lancaster was bitter, intransigent. But beneath his unbearable pride Isabella sensed fear. Had his slow mind grasped at last the possibility that, if he did not come in to Pembroke, Pembroke would act without him? Bend or break.

She did not wish Lancaster to break. Pembroke must not have it all his own way. When a man, be he never so moderate, rises to power, how long will he content himself with moderation?

Lancaster must join the Middle Party. Outside it he would find himself over-ridden; within it he must be listened to; he was still a great prince. Lancaster she must have—a brake upon Pembroke. Only within the party could they balance each other, weaken each other. And the King would lose nothing. Whether those two were reconciled or not, he would have to accept the Ordinances, be made to dismiss those friends so lately creeping back—above all send the Despensers packing. On the other hand, with Lancaster and Pembroke working against each other within the same party he might gain much—if he had the wit to be guided. And what better guide than she with her new-found gift to reconcile enemies. To hold the balance even between Pembroke and Lancaster, to settle the King and barons in peace; to work, a hidden influence, for the country's good— the thought filled her with a sense of power.

But ... reconcile those two! They bristled like angry dogs. Well, angry dogs can be coaxed; or else—the whip. One way or the other dogs be brought to obedience.

She had time to consider that problem. There was little diversion at Leake—no feasting, no gay riding-parties, no hawking ... and no new faces. The Mortimers had not come from their marcher lands; and that was something of a disappointment. They had made their legend those two and she longed to see them for herself. That the younger Mortimer had a way with him to turn the heads of women interested her not at all; she had no wish to have her head turned. She saw her way clear—and meant to keep it so. She had, besides, nothing but scorn for women that would lie down for the asking. It was the possible usefulness of the Mortimers that she meant to assess—usefulness to herself.

The dull days stretched on. Pembroke and Lancaster were still immovable, the barons still distrustful and the King irritable. But to her he was pleasanter than ever before. She listened to him with seeming kindness, her cool, unfriendly mind at work. How best might she turn this to further her end—to reconcile those two fierce dogs?

She came upon Lancaster, surly as a dog, walking the August garden, great head sunk between his shoulders, the whole man stiff with iron pride. Yet her subtle wits guessed at the indecision beneath the pride, the teetering of fear . . . *Bend or break!*

'Uncle!' She went across the grass, both long, jewelled hands holding the rose-and-gold gown above the dewy grass, her feet in the rose-coloured shoes themselves like roses upon the grass. 'Why waste your strength fighting Pembroke? He's not worth it; not he nor any man! We need you, Uncle, your strength and your courage. We need your wisdom to put a spoke in Pembroke's wheel—and that's not to be done by quarrelling. Take his hand; why not? The things you two want are the same things—that the King observe the Ordinance as he has promised; and shall promise again for you, for *you*, Uncle! And to rid himself of evil friends—that you can deal with, also, as you dealt before. You rid us of Gaveston; and I and all Christendom say it was well done!'

She heard, with satisfaction, her smooth tongue utter those last words. She had meant to say them but had feared to choke upon them. Now, out they came clear and simple as truth. Devious she had been; need had taught her. Now, for the first time she truly perjured herself, denying the truth of her inmost being. She felt no shame; nothing but pride that she so well spoke the lie.

'The Despensers are back, Uncle!' she pricked at him sharply.

'But your hand can thrust them where they belong. Without you, this poor country is torn between them—the ravening hounds.'

His lips lifted above his teeth; she thought he had the look of a ravening hound himself. She guessed at the thought that poisoned his whole being—the thought he would die rather than utter. *If I take Pembroke's hand, I must take de Warenne's also.*

She said, 'Take the hand of your enemy—if it may advance you. Within the party you may more easily punish de Warenne. And by God's Face punishment is due. All Christendom knows that he laid hands upon your wife to shame you both; and that to shame you further he gave her to a fellow of no account, a servant of his!' So she pressed upon his pain adding for good measure, 'But she—she knows no shame!' And that last was true enough. Alice, she had heard, was honoured and happy as never before. 'No, she delights in her low pleasures and has no care that she bespatters Lancaster's proud name!'

She saw him swallow in that thick throat of his as though at some physic indescribably foul. She sent him a long look from her strange eyes. 'Uncle, you know the saying that we have in France, *Take one step backwards to leap two steps forward.* Show friendship with Pembroke that you may thrust him from your path—he and de Warenne with him!'

He looked at her and his heavy face did not lighten. Women. You couldn't trust them. This one, for all her loving words, had encouraged his bitch of a wife. Yet for all that what she'd said made good sense. He needed Pembroke . . . for the moment. But she should pay for her humiliating advice, pay for encouraging his bitch! And the King should pay for his coolness and Pembroke should pay. But first and foremost de Warenne should pay, and most of all that bitch should pay! But first he must take Pembroke's hand. And this chit of a girl had shown him how to do it without loss of face.

He bent his great head over her hand. 'Madam and niece, when the Queen asks, how shall a man refuse? Already the country calls you *Peacemaker.* An honourable name if—' and he was bitter, 'the peace be honourable!'

'I would advise nothing to your dishonour, Uncle, and that you know! Take Pembroke's hand and cut through the tangle in which the jealous lords would bind you!'

She stood there smiling and friendly; yes and respectful, too. He nodded.

The Queen had saved Lancaster's face. Give way he must—and she had made it easy. He had, he proclaimed it aloud, given way to Madam the Queen's entreaties. What more right and chivalrous than to obey his Queen?

Peace between Lancaster and Pembroke was followed by peace between Lancaster and the King. Kneeling and humble, Lancaster forced himself to the Kiss of Peace, though his juices turned to acid. But the Kiss meant pardon not for himself alone, but for six hundred of his followers. And the King, longing to strike this man that would have dared outking his King, bent his mouth to his cousin's cheek.

Isabella, that peace-maker, sat beside the King; behind her still face thought rode triumphant. *I have done this, I! And not for your sake Uncle of Lancaster, but for my own!*

Now the Ordinances must, indeed, be honoured; like Magna Carta binding upon the King. Now those friends that had come creeping back into high places must away back to the wilderness. Now was the time, Lancaster thought, to strengthen his own hand, to build up within the King's very household his own party. And he had the right! High Steward of England, it was for him, did he wish it, to choose the King's household; and, in particular, to choose the chief steward—the High Steward's deputy. He did so choose. He knew the very man to stand by him, to report to him, to identify himself with his chief.

'Cousin of Lancaster,' the King said very courteous—and the Queen all but laughed hearing him repeat the words she had put into his mouth, 'we shall enquire into the matter. If it be your right to appoint our household, none shall take it from you. Give us a little time.'

A little time . . . and a little time; and the matter—as she thought—quietly shelved.

These days, Isabella told herself, she was content. Life had taken a turn; she, herself had given it a twist. Life was not all love and passion—nor did she wish it so! Any woman—even the plain and the foolish—could get a man in her bed; power was for the few, the very few. But Théophania noting the restlessness, the brittle brightness, wondered how long this young woman, ardent and ready for love, would endure her empty life. She needed love, needed cherishing; the lack of these things was already twisting her nature out of true. Where would it all end? The fire that slept within the Queen must one day burst forth. And then? Everyone would be hurt—not least the Queen herself.

The Kiss of Peace had cost the King more than he or she had dreamed. The barons had elected a new Council; without its consent the King could not carry out his most ordinary duties. To this Council, led by Pembroke, all of the great barons had been elected. Save one. They had had enough of Lancaster; he, alone, had found no place.

He made the best of a bad situation. 'I have no wish to row in such a boat!' he told the Queen. 'So many captains will bring it to grief. I can afford to wait; I am the hidden rock. I have my friends in this Council, friends that sicken of Pembroke—Bannockburn is not forgiven him yet! He will find himself every way obstructed. Events move in my direction; you will see!'

She did not believe in his power to sway events; but still she murmured her approval and her praise; one must not underestimate his mischief-making—nor his treachery.

The Council had strengthened itself with new names; it had gone further afield to find them. The Mortimers had been summoned, those marcher lords of power; to Westminster they came to kiss hands.

They were in the palace—two new faces and each man a legend! Isabella had herself dressed with especial care. The gown of gold embroidered upon green set the green and gold of her eyes aflicker; the pale gold hair gleamed through the transparent lawn of her headveil—a beautiful but quite shocking fashion she had borrowed from Italy. And the same lawn, transparent as water, revealed the high white breasts—a fashion from Italy even more shocking . . . and more beautiful.

A small gilded statue she sat beside the King; the elder Mortimer came to salute the King's hand and then her own. She summed him up. In no way remarkable; his legend did him too much grace. In early middle-age and clearly a gentleman of good birth. Shrewd, she would judge, rather than clever; brave, honest up to a point and not over-delicate in his dealings. A typical man of his class; she could pick half-a-dozen such and not stir a step.

The young Mortimer she could not so lightly dismiss. Her first impression was one of disappointment. He was not tall, scarce above middle height and looking shorter by reason of his broad shoulders; a thick-set man. A bullet-head well-cropped, defying fashion, red and bristling. A cold blue eye, nose of a hawk.

The mouth she could not judge; he held it close-pressed above a chin like a rock, for wearing no beard, he again defied the fashion; she liked him for that! And the sun falling upon reddish-gold stubble of head and chin gilded him with a fiery light; it lent him a fierce, an urgent look. When he knelt to the King he did it with more grace than she could have expected from so thick-set a man. When he spoke she saw that the lips were full, and, contradicting the eyes, sensual; his voice lifted in the musical lilt of the Border.

He was not handsome as the King was handsome, as Despenser was handsome, as Gaveston had been handsome; and for that she liked him the better. There were no airs and graces about him; a soldier determined and commanding. What was there, she found herself wondering, to stir the longing of women?

When he knelt to the Queen, when she felt that full mouth hard, vicious almost, upon her hand, she understood. She felt the moment like a rape . . . but it would not be rape; the whole of her body consented to him. So shocking a desire for any man she had never imagined. He was the most virile, the most male man she had ever seen; women were made for his domination.

Her face gave no sign of disturbance; her voice spoke the words of welcome and he stepped backwards. Whether he had noticed her as a woman it was impossible for her to say. He had saluted her correctly; no more.

From his place Mortimer considered the Queen. He was not one to blind himself to a woman's beauty, nor yet to be blinded by it. A handsome enough piece; they didn't call her *the Fair* for nothing! Spirited, too, he judged well-versed in women. Passion in that small body . . . unsatisfied; a man could smell it! He'd like fine to put her to bed—were she not the Queen of England. Well, there were enough pretty women to go to bed with; no need to make trouble for himself on her account! A man's work came first, his career, his ambitions; women a long way after. But even were he disposed to make love with the Queen, there was no time; no time but for the business in hand—swearing obedience to the Council, taking his place, listening to its policies and taking his instructions—if he saw fit. These things done he and his uncle must hurry back to the Border; it needed constant vigilance—iron hand, iron heel.

Mortimer was gone. The Queen sighed, shrugged and forgot him. She was absorbed once more in the press of affairs; the need to watch, to guess, to wait, to choose the moment for the right word. There was, for instance, the stewardship of the King's Household; in that matter she had laughed too soon. Certainly Lancaster's toady had not been chosen; but then, neither had the King's. It was Pembroke that had his way in the affair; Pembroke! He had chosen Lord Badlesmere—unacceptable to both King and Queen; and his wife still more unacceptable—the loud-mouthed harridan. A mean and ill-bred pair. In this matter, at least, King and Queen thought alike.

The King's dignity disregarded, his personal desires ignored! For this neither he nor she had bargained; some show of respect, at least, they had expected. Of the two she was the more shaken. She had thought to gather the reins into her own hand. But it was Pembroke that had gathered them . . . *But not for long, I swear it! The King is weak as water—stir it and it closes again; no mark. But I am strong; this slight I shall remember; and for it Pembroke shall pay!*

She heard her thoughts clear as though she spoke with dead Margaret; but there was no voice to answer—nothing but the voice of her own ambition, her own loneliness.

Chapter Nineteen

The King is not the true King. They were saying it, everywhere, even within Westminster palace itself. *How can such a one be son to great Edward?* And there were times when Isabella herself wondered whether the virtuous Eleanor had not played harlot in her husband's bed. The King, if he heard the rumours, seemed not to mind them— the rumours that smeared not himself alone but his Queen and his children; the very crown itself.

She endured it till she could endure it no longer.

'Sir—' and she was passionate, 'there's a fellow goes about the streets of Oxford that claims to be the true King. Stolen from his cradle— that's his story; and you, that call yourself King, put in his place!'

'It is not worth a moment's thought!' He was in a lazy mood.

She could have struck him full in the handsome face. No wonder they doubted his royal blood! She bit upon her tongue lest she speak her disgust. She gave him no peace in the matter and he gave way at last; he cared little one way or the other.

When the man was brought before the King he neither unbonneted nor bent the knee. A comely fellow, he stood erect and told his tale as though he were, indeed, the King. He spoke well; an unfrocked priest, maybe. He was plainly crazed and one doesn't punish a crazy man—not this King at any rate.

It was the Queen that spoke, ash-pale with anger that shook her head-to-foot. 'Sir, under correction, may I speak?' and did not wait for his answer. 'He who smears the good name of the King is a traitor. This fellow is such a traitor; he deserves to die the death.'

The King fidgeted in his place. He preferred to let the fool go free. But she had spoken in open court; he saw agreement on every face. Now he must show himself King, speak the hateful words of a traitor's death.

First taste of blood shed at her word. Power. Power over life and death. The thought went to her head like strong liquor. 'You should have torn his tongue out—it is the punishment!' she said later. 'But you . . . *you!*' Anger choked her. 'Nothing moves you, neither right nor wrong; nothing but your whims and your passions!'

It was the first time she had dared speak so to him; he took it mildly enough—women were kittle-kattle. 'You must allow me my whims and my passions—a King's but human. Yet mark this! When I am angered I can be cruel enough to satisfy even you, God forgive me! Otherwise I am satisfied to deal kindly with my fellow-men.'

'A King has no fellow-men!'

'We are all equal under God!'

They looked at each other. He saw her—nostrils pinched, eyes narrowed, lips lifted above white, sharp teeth; it was as though he saw her for the first time. She saw him, as she always did—foolishly kind, foolishly smiling, lazy, insouciant. In him surprise was deepening to distrust; in her scorn was hardening to dislike.

In the north the people suffered even more cruelly from the Scots. And Lancaster, captain of the northern forces, did nothing.

Berwick had fallen, English Berwick; and still Lancaster did nothing.

Pembroke, once captain of those same forces, could endure it no longer; the King's honour must be redeemed, the Scots driven from the north, from Berwick and from every place where they had no right to be. Scotland must be made to acknowledge the lordship of England. Commons as well as barons demanded it.

The King of England was not greatly interested. Why plunge, once more, into the mess, the discomforts of war when one could sleep soft, could bide at one's ease? If men must pit themselves against each other, he preferred to watch his servants wrestle in the courtyard while he stood by to mark their points; he had no desire to see men expire in useless agony.

'Sir, England's honour is in the matter!' Isabella told him.

'They laugh at us; make songs about us—our clothes and our customs—the half-naked savages!'

'They are welcome—save that their poetry is vile!' He shrugged and smiled.

She sent him a long look out of her green-flecked eyes, staring with insolence at the handsome face, the head and beard golden and long-curling, the bright jewelled gown. There came to her the sudden memory of Mortimer—close-cropped head, strong naked chin, plain leather jerkin. A man! As for this King—useless. Useless!

Scotland must be taught its lesson. Parliament stood with Pembroke in this and called upon the barons to assemble each with his own men; not one to absent himself. June in the year of grace thirteen hundred and nineteen, five years since Bannockburn, the great army assembled at Newcastle, leading them that handsome figurehead Edward Plantagenet of England; at his either hand rode the Despensers able with sword as with tongue, no coward, either of them. At their heels rode the King's half-brothers, eager each to prove his worth. Hereford was there with Arundel, Richmond and their brother peers—not one absent. A little apart Thomas of Lancaster rode with his brother and heir, Henry of Derby. Lancaster looked upon Pembroke riding in friendship with de Warenne and at the sight of them his gorge rose. De Warenne he hated; but Pembroke even more. De Warenne had robbed him of his wife—a thing of little worth; Pembroke had robbed him of his own place—the highest; not only in the Council but in the army Pembroke led them all. In Lancaster bitterness rose, it tasted bitter on his tongue.

Berwick. Day after day the bitter siege. In the end it was the English that must withdraw, must surrender castle and town. And it was not because of defeat in arms. Traitor Lancaster had laid his plans. Himself he did not appear in the matter but he knew the man to act as go-between. Ten thousand Scottish pounds the Bruce paid; for the fall of Berwick, cheap enough. A simple plan . . . though it did not turn out exactly as Lancaster had planned.

The Queen walked in the garden this fine summer day. She fretted within the walls of Brotherton whither the King had commanded her with her children. She wondered how he carried himself; she prayed, without much hope, that he made a show, at least, of war-like behaviour. She longed to be at Berwick; longed for the sound of trumpet and the clash of arms.

'Madam!' She wheeled about.

It was my lord archbishop of York, Melton himself; he was covered with dust and pale as ash.

'Madam,' he said, 'you must come with me at once. We are for York. Send for the children. The Scots are upon us!'

She stared at that. The Scots so far south! She could not believe it.

'The Black Douglas leads—ten thousand at his heels. Madam, you have been betrayed!'

'Give me some proof. I'll not be a laughing-stock—the Queen that runs from her own shadow!'

'Madam, you waste time! My spies have seen them—we forever look to the Queen's safety. The Douglas hides in a wood some two hours' ride away. We must take the road; we go by water—I have a boat ready. Before he reaches Brotherton you will be safe in York. Now, Madam, will you send for the children?'

'Yes,' she said. 'The Queen must not be taken by pawns!' and smiled so that he marvelled she showed no sign of fear.

The wind was with them. In the nurse's arms the baby Eleanor leaped and crowed for joy in the sunshine; Edward, six-and-a-half and John just three, laughed, dabbling their hands in the cool water; and their mother laughed with them. The archbishop himself lent a hand to speed the boat. As they neared York they heard the bell ever louder, ever more demanding, summoning men to the town's defence—priests and farmers, burghers and craftsmen; and to captain this motley, valiant band, my lord archbishop himself!

Along the high road the Black Douglas came marching, ten thousand at his heels. Black he was, indeed, to find Brotherton empty, the birds all flown that were to win Scotland for the Scots. Had Lancaster played double traitor, warned the Queen? No matter! He'd take them at York if he had to sit down before the city for a year. And God damn His meddling priest!

God's meddling priest had no intention of letting the Scots anywhere near York. At Myton-in-Swaledale the two armies met—

the Douglas with his Scots, hard-disciplined men that had fought from their cradles; and the archbishop, man of peace, with his band undisciplined to war, untrained to arms.

Inch by inch, the valiant men of York gave way. They had lost the day; yet they had won it. They had done the thing they had set out to do—the Queen and her children were safe on their way to Westminster.

The Scots had no more use for York; now, by the Bruce's command, they were for Pontefract, Lancaster's stronghold. A master-stroke to bring Lancaster home at a run—home with his men behind him. And many a baron, fearing a like attack, followed Lancaster's example. Each man for himself!

Now the King of England must make what peace he could. An inglorious truce; immediate evacuation of Berwick town. England that had marched in such glory must return in shame.

The King was the worse for the Scottish venture—a man indifferent to everything, to loss and defeat in Scotland, indifferent to the disapproval of Parliament and Council alike; indifferent, Isabella thought sickened, to everything but his light pleasures. But she, herself, had gained. She knew it. She had proved to herself her own courage, her own strength.

A word from her and a man had gone to his death; his deserved death for slander of the King. She had faced that responsibility when the King had failed. She had washed her hands in a man's blood, and, so the cause be right, would not fear to do it again. She had faced dire danger—danger of being carried prisoner into Scotland; the threat of ignominy and shame. She had kept her courage and her head. Before fleeing with her children she had asked for proof, weighed that proof. She had not been the Queen that foolishly ran away.

Not to be afraid to command a man's just death; not to panic in the face of direst danger—these were her triumphs.

Chapter Twenty

Pembroke had lost face over the Scottish campaign—and for the second time. What now? Isabella considered the matter. She did not think he would easily regain it. Nor was Lancaster likely to come back to power; certainly not for the present. The man was unpopular, and his treachery, though not proven, suspected; the aura clung.

Edging into the seat of power—the Despensers.

No-one now to curb the King.

Isabella could not see the sun for the Despensers. Her hatred of them darkened her whole world. It seemed to her that, like spiders, they forever spun their web; were she not wary she, herself, must be caught therein. The King, that willing captive, had long been caught; they held him fast with sweet flatteries, they turned his head with their clever, lying arguments.

For they were clever; so much she must ruefully admit. They might have done the country some good—save that they sought no good but their own. They were liars, they were cheats, they were utterly untrustworthy. Some dishonesty one must expect in a statesman—that she knew, but those two went beyond all decency, all belief. Men that had done them no hurt they fleeced and cast into prison there to rot. They extorted unjust dues; they would seize upon everything a man had so that he must beg his bread or sell himself —a bond servant. They accused innocent men of such evils that the poor creatures were excommunicated or executed or both; robbed of body and soul alike.

And bewitched by his passion for the son, the King said nothing; not though the people cried aloud their hatred—and some of it for the King himself. The Despensers had no friends—least of all the Queen; and that they knew well. Beyond the poison of their tongues they could, at the moment, work her little harm—she was beloved by barons and common folk alike. But patience—they could afford to wait. Meanwhile they treated her with open insolence; and the King allowed it—as he allowed them everything.

'How long must I endure the poison of their spite?' Isabella, goaded, cried out to Madam de St. Pierre. 'Harsh, corrupt and cruel, both of them—and the son worse than the father! He's cast in a meaner mould; more vicious, more spiteful, even. Cruelty for its own sake—the man's not human—a wasp to sting because he must, to sting a victim to his death!'

'Madam, I think he's not a full man! That pink-and-white, those fair curled locks, that body rounded where it should not be. The waist so pinched, the hips so padded! He's neither man nor woman —a thing we must despise. Such men know it and it makes them spiteful!'

'His wife knows the truth of that, poor wretch! He has no use or women—the King's mignon!'

Even did the King desire it, he could not free himself from those two. They had lent him money; and though they had repaid themselves a hundredfold, the debt, it seemed, was unpaid still. But the King did not desire it; he loved his fetters. When Gaveston fell foul of the barons, those two had stood by the King, those two alone. When Gaveston died, young Despenser had truly wept—they had been palace boys together; that grief the King could never forget . . . not though the tears were quickly dried. So they went on, father and son piling fortune upon fortune—one made out of offices seized by themselves, one out of offices sold, a third the rake-off of the King's domestic expenses.

But if the King was a poor judge of men Pembroke was not. Why then had he admitted those two to his party, allowed them seats on the Council, appointed the son High Chamberlain? Why had he given them a chance to thrust great Pembroke from power?

When she asked him his answer was clear. 'Because I thought through them to win the King; I thought myself strong enough to keep them in check—as but for Berwick I should have done.'

'Liars and cheats! You are not overnice my lord.'

'In the game I play I use any piece to protect the King.'

'It is a lesson, sir, I shall remember; but I shall see to it that it's a piece I can handle; a lesson it would seem hard to learn. There's Badlesmere. You made him the King's Steward. His insolence to me is intolerable—and so I have told you. But still it continues. He's another piece you chose and cannot handle. He's no longer your man but my uncle of Lancaster's.'

'Enemies always! That they are friends now, I cannot believe.'

'It is a thing you may have to believe. That two men hate each other doesn't make either your friend.'

'Madam, you are a wiser teacher than I!' He bowed low but whether he spoke in jest or earnest she could not tell.

She had not bargained for this supreme elevation of the Despensers; with them she would have no truck, mutual hatred lay between them. Now she must consider the future once more. Their power hung upon the King; upon the King, alone. Let the barons press— and those two would end like Gaveston. Her future, then, it was clear, must lie with Pembroke or with Lancaster. Pembroke was the better man. But his defeat in Scotland had cost him too much; and his very moderation had led him to make too many mistakes. Lancaster? Not to be trusted . . . unless he saw her interests as his own. And that she could make him see; she was cleverer than he! Lancaster was her man.

Down Pembroke. Up Lancaster.

She was glad, now, that she had shown her uncle no coldness; now she must seek to win him with assurance of love; lure him from Pontefract where still he sulked, coax him back to Westminster. It would take time. He was a slow thinker and cautious with it. Dear God, let him not consider too long!

Lancaster rubbed the Kiss of Peace from his cheeks. He thanked Madam his niece for her kind thought of him; to Westminster he could not come . . . at present. Of Pembroke he made no mention —the man was clearly on the decline. He could not, he said, breathe

the same air as the Despensers. They ate up the country between them; and their insolence to Madam the Queen was such that flesh-and-blood could not tolerate. What he did not say she understood very well. *The Despensers ride too high for the moment. Give me time.*

Until that time he was sitting quiet in Pontefract. But he was busy; he was very busy. He was in constant communication with Badlesmere—a man of no importance save as a mischief-maker; and, kept sweet with Lancaster gold, he was making all the mischief he could. He spied on the King and the Despensers; he ran with his tales to the barons. He was playing his part in Lancaster's return.

Isabella passed through the Queen's apartments into her closet. In the anteroom her ladies, sitting over their work, rose to their curtsey. As she passed, the Queen noted without surprise—she had grown used to such slights—the jewel in Eleanor Despenser's coif. It had been her own; part of her father's wedding-gift. The King had taken it for Gaveston, and thereafter for his sweetheart the Despenser. But he, slighting the gift as not sufficiently fine, had thrown it to his despised wife. Jeanne Mortimer, too, the Queen noticed for her coif. It stood out from the bejewelled headgear of the others by its simplicity, its perfect freshness; there were some to think that a jewelled chaplet atoned for soiled linen.

Of all her women the Queen might have liked these two best. Eleanor with her high look, her elegance and her charm was a true Clare; she was so like young, dead Gloucester that, coming upon her unexpectedly, your heart turned over. Wed to another, she would have been the Queen's choice for friend and confidante . . . but she was Hugh Despenser's wife. Love him she did not—she had no cause; yet she gave him perfect loyalty. She told him everything—every word the Queen let fall, every gesture the Queen made. She had been set in her place as a spy; in the early days, when she had not sufficiently reported, the thing being repugnant, there had been bruises upon cheeks and wrists. Once she had been a laughing girl; now there was little to be read in the pale oval of her face. She walked in dignity aloof from life . . . a dead girl walking.

Sometimes the Queen would talk with Mortimer's wife; she would say nothing important, waiting to see how true this new lady might be, how discreet. The appointment of Jeanne had been a surprise; but the Queen had her reasons. It was because this new lady of hers was Mortimer's wife and in constant communication with him—a man like Mortimer, an ambitious man, needed to know what went on in court. Such a man, ambitious, knowledgeable, powerful, the Queen would know how to use! Between them Jeanne, born de Joinville, a house faithful to the Capets, was an essential bond. She was older than the others, with a clever monkey-face; that this plain yet not unattractive woman should be wife to the fascinating Mortimer was not surprising. Marriage is a matter of business; the Queen knew it better than most.

Now, passing, she called to Madam de St Pierre to dismiss the others and then to come bringing with her my lady Mortimer of Wigmore. When they were settled about their work in the Queen's closet, Théophania said, 'The lord Despenser's wife is not happy to be excluded. She will be punished for it no doubt, by her husband.'

'Would to God they were at the bottom of the sea—the Despensers! Not Despenser's wife; I must not trust her yet I wish her no harm. But the father and the son! They may yet plunge us into civil war!'

'My husband fears it too!' Jeanne said. 'The people will no longer endure to be sucked dry!' She bit off the end of silk with sharp, white teeth. Her husband hated the Despensers and she spoke like a good wife. 'All those lands and revenues, all those licenses to sell and to buy, all those dues from markets and fairs, they've got enough, wouldn't you think? And the son—he's got the best part of the Gloucester inheritance as well. And still he's not satisfied!'

'Gloucester's death was one of the tragedies of the Scottish war,' the Queen said. 'Not only because he was a man such as we can ill spare, but because he died without a child to inherit. The business of the Gloucester inheritance may yet drown the whole land in blood!'

'But that business was settled.' Théophania was puzzled. 'As I remember the land was divided among the three sisters. Despenser got the lion's share because his wife's the eldest.'

'He got the whole of Glamorgan to say nothing of half South Wales; and, because he's what he is, he's not satisfied,' Jeanne said. 'He wants the rest. He wants Newport—so my husband writes; and that belongs to Audley who married the second sister. And he wants Usk and that belongs to Damory through the youngest. He wants, in fact, the whole of the Gloucester property.'

'He wants more!' the Queen said, very slow! 'He wants to be— Gloucester!'

'It isn't possible; even he must know it!' Jeanne said. 'He's not born Clare!'

'Only too possible—if he press the King hard enough!' the Queen said. 'The title died with Gloucester; he's pressing the King to revive it. Gloucester's royal title to fall so low! By God's Face!' she spoke with sudden passion, 'I could love the man that puts a spoke in that wheel!'

'There's one man could do it!' Jeanne lifted a thoughtful face, 'and that's the lord my husband. He leads the marcher lords—and this concerns them. And he hates the Despensers—both. Yes, he could do it but it means bloodshed, as Madam the Queen says; civil war!'

'Send to him!' the Queen commanded quick and urgent. 'Bid him make an end of those two. For let us sit with folded hands and they'll make an end of England. Tell him he shall have the Queen's love.'

'I will tell him, Madam.' Mortimer's wife smiled, she took the Queen's hand and kissed it. *He shall have the Queen's love.* Later she was to remember the words; and then she did not smile.

Chapter Twenty-One

Earl of Gloucester. Hugh Despenser marched steadily towards his glorious goal. The Queen watched with anger and she watched with fear. Already he ruled in Glamorgan with rights more sovereign than ever royal Gloucester. He had forced Audley to give up Newport in exchange for poor land; he had got both hands on Lundy Island . . . and both eyes on the lordship of Gower. The old lord was failing; Mowbray the natural heir could go bury himself with his father-in-law! Bristol he meant to have also; Bristol that fine city with the rich estuary lands of the west.

And still Lancaster sat tight in Pontefract. Though he had estates in Wales that might also be threatened he made no move. This was Mortimer's affair: to challenge the leadership of the marcher lords would be foolish. When his time came he would need all the support he could get.

When will Mortimer move? The Queen asked herself night and day. But from Mortimer also—no sign.

'Despenser looks to make himself King of Wales!' she told the King and she was sharp and bitter.

'Why not?' He sent her his charming, lazy smile.

'Because'—and she forgot the need for caution in the surge of anger, 'because the people hate him!'

'You mean *you* hate him?' and he was smiling still.

'This could cost you your crown!' she told him, anger still driving.

'My crown?' And now his eyes were bitter above his smiling mouth. 'As long as my loyal wife seduces my Londoners and charms my barons, I'm safe enough. I can always hide beneath her skirts.'

'It is no laughing matter, sir!' she cried out, stung.

'If it were not I'd have you in the Tower. You speak sedition, my dear!' And for all the lightness of his tone there was warning behind the words.

Despenser's time had come. The old lord of Gower was dead; Mowbray his son-in-law sat in the old man's place.

'Ned,' the younger Despenser told the King, 'Gower is forfeit. Mowbray took possession without consent or homage.'

'Then we put it in more loyal hands. Gower, my sweet, is yours.'

'Now Mortimer must move; surely, he must move!' the Queen cried out.

Jeanne Mortimer lifted her troubled head. Certainly her husband must move to protect the rights of the marcher lords; he had no choice. But, move directly against the King! It was treason.

'The marcher lords will take it ill,' Jeanne said. 'They are not subject to this law. Mowbray takes possession through his wife; he has the right. The undoubted heir takes possession without the King's consent—it has been their privilege and they'll not let it go. They'll fight to the death.'

The marcher lords were gathering—Mortimer had sent a secret message to his wife. Now that civil war threatened the Queen lost some of her complacency. This could mean a torn and bleeding country. It could set father against son and son against father. It could mean hunger and sickness and poverty—utter devastation; and in that devastation all, all must suffer.

Should she speak to the King, warn him of the deep, stubborn anger of the marcher lords and the threat of civil war? Yet, surely he must understand this for himself! While she hesitated the King sent for her. Despenser's wife in the anteroom had caught here a word and there a word and had done her duty.

She found the King in his closet fondling his sweetheart.

'Madam,' he said unsmiling, 'do not presume to question my wisdom. And watch your tongue. I tell you once and for all—and you may spread the good news—Mowbray is at fault. Gower is Hugh's.'

'If he can take it!' she cried out and, too late, bit upon her tongue. To answer so was the act of a fool; but his rudeness, his stupidity, together with the Despenser's intolerable triumph, and above all fear of trouble to come, drove her beyond reason.

'Sir,' she said and ignored the insolent look Despenser cast upon her. 'Consider; I *beg* you to consider!' And held out her hands as though she prayed. 'Do not tread upon border privilege nor yet upon Welsh privilege. The pride of these lords you should know— you were Prince of Wales. Do not press that, in this, they are subject to English law!'

'They are subject!' Despenser broke in, insolent.

She ignored him. 'Sir, I beseech you, pause. It is wiser to hold by the spirit of the law than by the strict letter; and especially in this case. Mowbray is the natural heir; he inherits by right of his wife. Sir, this *friend* of yours . . .' and she cast a look of contempt upon Despenser triumphant and smiling, 'shall make great trouble for us all.'

'You talk like a fool!' the King said, contemptuous, forgetting that she and she alone had reconciled the barons at Leake. 'As for that other fool—Mortimer's wife—send her packing or it will be the worse for her! I've no doubt this nonsense of yours is of her making. Madam, I warn you again, guard your tongue!'

'Queens have found themselves in prison for less than this!' the Despenser said.

She deigned no answer; but the insolence drove the colour from her cheeks.

'He speaks truth; mark it well!' The King put back a lock of Despenser's hair; arm about his friend he went laughing from the room and left her standing there.

The marcher lords were mustering.

First and foremost Mowbray that Despenser sought to rob of his inheritance; and with him Audley and Damory robbed, also, of the best part of their possessions by those same hands. With them marched Humphrey de Bohun of Hereford, in fighting mood; his lands lay close to Glamorgan and he had no mind to wait the

Despensers' next move. All the barons of the March mustering, save Pembroke and Arundel that still stood by the King. And behind the marcher lords the lesser lords that had suffered from the greed and cruelty of the Despensers. And, leading them all, the Mortimers, uncle and nephew, closer than father and son; men of strength, of power, that did not mean old freedoms to be violated.

Now the Queen cast away the last of her doubts; now she knelt thanking God for the Mortimers, beseeching their victory, bribing Him, cozening Him, bargaining, bargaining, bargaining. These days she missed Jeanne Mortimer; yet she was glad to have her go lest the Despensers lay hands upon her to hold her for ransom. Isabella smiled, remembering the anger of the Despensers that Jeanne had escaped their hands. And, thinking of the wife, how could she but think of the husband, that strong, commanding man? She would find herself wondering, at times, how a woman must feel in bed with such a man? Herself she had known nothing ever but the fainéant King.

The Despensers forever burned that Mortimer's wife had gone free of them. The Queen had robbed them of their strongest weapon; and the Queen should pay for it. They vowed it and did not care who heard. Let her walk with care lest she find herself in the Tower! Now she must guard her every word, her every glance, her every breath, even. The King, she knew, would lift no finger on her behalf.

Against his rebel lords the King's anger was hot; but against Mortimer of Wigmore it had passed into hatred deep and personal. And it was not, the Queen thought, on account of his leadership alone. Mortimer of Chirk was equal leader. What was there in the younger man to arouse this almost mad resentment?

It was the King himself, that let fly the secret.

'By God's Soul he was always a thorn in my flesh; always, always!' It was to the young Despenser he spoke, not caring who might hear. 'I hated him from the moment he came to Westminster —one of the palace boys. He was put in Piers' charge; remember? And Piers did his duty by him; that and no more! Piers cared for me, for me only! But Mortimer, the fool, didn't understand. He was forever at our heels, Piers and mine. Short of kicking him out of the way—impossible to be rid of him! But Piers was too kind, forever too kind!' He kicked the stool at his feet as though he kicked the boy Mortimer. For whatever he might say, he must still remember that shoe had been upon the other foot. Piers had loved the boy above all others. He could see them now, those two. Piers, arm loving about the boy and both of them laughing at a shared jest, their prince left out in the cold, eaten with jealousy at the love between those two.

So that was it! Mortimer had been Piers' pupil and Piers had loved him best. And for that Mortimer must bear the King's undying hatred. The palace school had, it seemed, much to answer for.

The revolt was spreading. By January it had reached Herefordshire; by February Gloucestershire was in arms.

'And God knows, sir, where it will end if we do not move at once!' It was the elder Despenser that spoke, urgent, in the King's ear. 'We must march for Gloucester, show these Mortimers, these Bohuns and the rest of the pack'— and he spoke as though they were dirt, 'how we deal with traitors.

'But—February; it is not fit weather!' the King pouted into his sweetheart's face.

'We march within the week!' the elder Despenser said.

Where, Isabella wondered, did her uncle of Lancaster stand in this? Certainly not with the King and the hated Despensers. His place was with the rebels to protect his estates in Wales.

But still from Lancaster, no word. Still he sat within Pontefract watching the way things should go.

It was March when the armies set forth, Edward leading them upright on the great horse, the perfect picture of a King. But when they had left Westminster behind and came into open country and the march winds cut sharp as a sword through the furred houppelande, then the King let the older Despenser take the lead while he and his sweetheart took their ease in the charette; when they passed through a town of any size the King would lead again.

Within the second-best charette Isabella resentful but gratified sat with Madam de St. Pierre. She was gratified because the King had commanded her presence; he had remembered, it seemed, her good offices at Leake. She was resentful because she rode in the second-best charette. She was the more resentful because she was once more with child. The King, as usual, had made no pretence of affection; he had done what he was pleased to call his duty—to prove his manhood, she supposed. The more the better, he had said when she told him the news; that, and nothing else. All very well for him! He had not to carry a child within a swollen, tormented belly! 'By the blessed Virgin,' she burst out to Théophania, 'I'll *kill* him before he gets me with child again!' And looked as if, given the chance, she would carry out her threat. Théophania made her prayer for the unhappy Queen.

The King had been defeated; everywhere the citizens had refused to fight for him. Town after town, castle after castle had fallen to the rebels; they held all Glamorgan. Now they pressed steadily forward, driving the King ever backward.

Edward had been forced to accept their terms—and bitter they were! The Despensers must appear before the next Parliament; until that time he was sworn to keep them safe.

Behind a quiet face the Queen rejoiced. Though still she must endure them near her, fouling the air she breathed, though still she must endure their insolence, it could not be long. Parliament would deal with them!

Lancaster moved at last.

He had summoned the northern lords to Pontefract; and they had answered the call.

'For this I must thank God!' Isabella said. 'Before that same God I wish the lord King no harm; but the Despensers—I could tear them to pieces with my own hands!'

Théophania turned troubled eyes upon the Queen . . . The second time within a little she had spoken in hatred and spite. She had changed so much; a process so long, so slow one had scarce noticed it. Gentle she had never been nor patient; yet she had been loving. But she was no longer a child—twenty-seven; and one must expect change; and it was a change for the worse.

Yet who could blame her? Théophania's thoughts went back over the long story. Unloved, Isabella had loved her husband, and, patient, had tried to win him. She had endured—if not always in silence—more than most women; more, certainly, than could be expected from so passionate a nature. And chief cause of her humiliation—the Despensers! It was human, surely, to desire their punishment; yes, but punishment within reason. As long as the good Queen lived, Isabella, whatever she felt, had shown no spite. But beneath constant humiliation, constant unkindness, one must harden or break. Isabella was not one to break. She should be blossoming now, body and soul—a flowering tree. Her body flowered in beauty; but her spirit? Théophania made her prayer. God grant it be not cankered at the root.

Chapter Twenty-Two

Things between the King and Queen were going from bad to worse. Once he had been known for the mildness of his humours; true they had been marred, at times, by fits of rage, fits of cruelty, but so it had been with his father and grandfather—his Plantagenet inheritance. Now he had grown so irritable he could scarce look upon the Queen without anger; and the Despensers rubbed his anger raw. Sufficiently rude before, their insolence now to the Queen was almost unbelievable. And the King allowed it all. Soon his beloved friends must face Parliament; and Parliament meant the Piers business all over again! By God, it should not end so!

Meanwhile they insulted the Queen in every way; they turned their backs upon her in full court, they interrupted her without any show of courtesy when she spoke with the King. Themselves they spoke to her not at all save to admonish or deride. She never knew when she might be free of them. They would burst into her private apartments when the King was there and stay until he left with them. She had no doubt that, if they saw fit, they would accompany the King to her bed when he chose to visit her. Indeed, she doubted, at times, whether the child she carried was not of their counselling—to keep her in her place. Once, goaded, she cried out to the King, 'Since you take no pleasure from me in bed or out, why come to me at all?'

'Duty not pleasure brings me!' he told her. 'Two brothers died before me—and between us a gaggle of women. Had my father not continued in his duties—what then?'

He had saved us all much trouble! She bit back the words, loathing him as he stood there handsome and complacent; she prayed with passion she might never again feel his flesh upon her own.

The sight of her big with child was an added irritant. She offended

his taste; he must be rid of the sight of her. 'To the Tower you shall
go, treacherous as you are! For, hark you, to hate those that love
me is treachery, indeed. And, in the Tower you shall stay till it
please me you shall leave. And that, Madam, continue as you are,
may well be never! And when you are there, think of what lies
below the palace—the strongest prison in the world. And that, if
you do not mend your ways, you shall, by God's Face, see for
yourself!'

'Farewell, sir, till happier times!' She swept him her curtsey and
so was gone.

She was glad to go; glad to be free of him and his outbursts, of
the persecution of the Despensers and the insolence of the Badlesmeres. The Tower palace, if not so well-found as Westminster, had
its own attractions. The rooms were smaller but thick walls kept
them cool these summer days. She was comfortable enough with
Théophania and some half-dozen women. For Segrave the
Governor she did not much care—a man that for all his subservience
to Madam the Queen, she did not trust. With him she watched her
every word. With young Alspaye his lieutenant she was careful too,
though she liked the charming young man so taken with his Queen.
She would invite him, of an evening, to bring his board and his
ivory pieces and they would play at chess. He was no match for her;
but quite often she let him win and was clever enough not to let
him know it. Once she stretched out a hand to take a piece, and,
by no accident on her part, their fingers met. She felt his excitement
at the light touch; she sent him a smile so bewitching that he all-but
swooned. At that she gave him her whole hand and he kissed it
with a most respectful fervour. 'Madam,' he said, 'Madam . . . I am
now and till death your most faithful servant.'

She thanked him with yet another of her smiles and registered
his vow.

Here, in the Tower, she found the gardens gayer, the river busier
with trade, with the coming and going of people—a different sort
of people. At Westminster there was a coming and going of bishops
and barons, of ambassadors and foreign visitors, of poets and
craftsmen and clerks. Here she could watch the merchant ships
sailing out or coming into port. She could see the foreign sailors in

their strange bright clothes, loading and unloading; she would wave to them and they would smile back, white teeth splitting dark faces. She would walk in the river garden; and the Londoners passing in their boats, seeing her so fair, so rich with child—their taste being less fine than the King's—would call out a loving greeting. She had given the country three princes and was about to give it a fourth; she scanted nothing of her duty. So much could not be said of their King; she had a poor time of it with him! Their hearts went out to her; she was the most popular of Queens.

Now, with time on her hands, she asked leave to have her children for a while—the children she hardly knew. Young mother with children—it would endear her still further to the Londoners.

A reasonable request, the Despensers advised the King. She might—it was their secret hope—let fall some thoughtless word for a child to repeat; enough to keep her in the Tower for ever—though in less pleasing accommodation.

Edward she hardly recognised; a tall, strong boy, not handsome like his father—and she liked him the better for it—but pleasant to look at. A dark little boy with a good forehead and a firm chin; the image of his grandfather, great Edward, people said. An even-tempered child for the most part, with occasional flashes of the Plantagenet rage. He was, she was glad to see, conscious of his position; not yet nine he bore himself like a little King. He was quick in every way—quick in movement, quick in mind; quick to take a point, quick to learn, quick to decide and quick to act. His generosity, his willingness to forgive, she considered childish; those things she must check. She must teach him to discriminate—a thing his father had never learnt; she would not have him at the mercy of his enemies, still less of his friends. Like any child he was to be won with honeyed words; against such words she must warn him. More; she must teach him himself to speak such words, keeping his thoughts secret.

Such a child is not hard to teach. But, at times, these lessons in diplomacy were too much for his sturdy honesty; then there would be tears and punishments. The tears would be hers; the punishments his. She was clever. She gave no punishment; but worked upon the boy so that himself asked for punishment, chose his punishment—a punishment harder than she would have given—and endured it almost with contempt. He adored his mother; she was lovely and she was kind; and every word that dropped from her lips a pearl of truth and wisdom.

And loving and obedient she intended him to remain. Though in affairs of state he could, at his tender age, count for little, in a few years he must count for much. So she wooed the boy, rewarding him lavishly and punishing him—so it seemed—only at his own request. But she truly loved him, he was very lovable; though there were times when she found his honesty and the serious way he had with him tiresome.

John was going on for five, a pretty child that favoured his father in looks; it took away something of her appetite for him. A little boy passionate in his rages; then he was not to be controlled save by his brother; to all others, blind and deaf. Edward he followed blindly, trying to do whatever the nine-year-old could easily manage. And Edward was kind to the little boy; between them the bond of brotherhood was strong. No need for their mother to put herself out over John; whoever won Edward won John.

For her daughter she surprised within herself a passion. Eleanor was just three—a fat, plain little girl. But she was the plaything with which the child Isabella had never cared to play—a wooden baby could neither laugh nor cry. But the little Eleanor laughed or wept as her mother chose. One smile and the tears dried on the baby cheeks; one frown and the tears welled. Isabella, delighting in this power, found she preferred the little one to smile rather than cry. The plain little face would beam up at her and she would feel a rush of love and pity for this little one that would never be a beauty. She'll never put her mother's nose out of joint, the nurses said; and since this was clearly so she loved the child more.

In the first week of July, in the year of grace thirteen hundred and twenty-one, the Queen's fourth child was born. Labour was long and hard; the child, they said one to another, would be the death of her. Gritting her teeth upon the pain she vowed that never would she allow her husband to touch her again.

Another daughter, this little princess of the Tower, small and fair and fine. She'll be a rare beauty, fit to be a Queen like her mother, the midwife said. *Happier than her mother, pray God!* Isabella made her prayer. And yet, because she had not wanted this child, because the birth had been hard and because this morsel of flesh might one day challenge her mother's beauty, Isabella could not love her.

Life had been cruel to the Queen. That she could not love this child was the measure of that cruelty; her nature was hardening to bear her burden.

Of this birth the King took little notice. He was much concerned with his Despensers; Parliament was to meet next month and Lancaster, so long quiet, looked to be making trouble. At the news of the child's birth he rewarded the messenger; but to the Queen he sent no gift nor any wish for her speedy recovery. Nothing but the command to christen the child Joanna, after his dead sister— and to remain where she was.

Lancaster was clearly out to make trouble. Finished his solitary sulking. Now for the fight; the fight for power. Now or never. He had invited the princes of state and church to meet him at Sherburn-in-Elmut. And it was not the northern lords, only; it was the nobles of the south, together with knights, bannerets and simple gentlemen. To Sherburn, also, came my lord archbishop of York, my lords the bishops of Durham and Carlisle, and abbots and priors more than a man could count. One name the Queen noted with interest; from the Welsh marches came Mortimer of Wigmore. Of their business Lancaster made no secret. They were to discuss the King and his failures; his bad advisers and his worse friends. A rehearsal for next month's Parliament.

The rehearsal was over. Sixty of England's magnates—earls, barons, and prelates—had pledged themselves to destroy the Despensers. They had proclaimed Lancaster their leader; they had sworn to stand with him against the King.

The King leapt from his chair when he heard; teeth clenched upon shaking jaw, fists clenched upon shaking hands. The older Despenser thought, at any moment he will scream or weep.

'Lancaster's private Parliament!' the younger Despenser said mocking. 'Is Lancaster King to call his Parliament!'

Father sent son a warning look. This was no mere gathering; it had the look of a rising, a national rising. But the younger Hugh would not be warned. 'Lancaster overreaches himself!' he said. 'It is Lancaster and his friends, only! All the barons are not with him— the Percies are not there; nor Arundel, nor Pembroke, neither. Nor does he carry all the bishops with him; and certainly not Canterbury. He had best take care lest that ugly head of his part company with his uglier body!' the young man smoothed back the fair locks of his own shapely head.

The King stopped pacing; he was calmer now. 'You are right, Hugh, my dear! It *is* Lancaster and his faction—he and he only! But his voice is loud enough to drown all Parliament. Me they cannot hurt; but you, dearer to me than all the world, they are pledged to destroy!'

'I put my trust in the King.' The younger Despenser bent and kissed the King's lips; but the darkness did not lighten in his father's face.

July. The month Parliament was to meet. And the King had not yet set a date. Nor intended to. For at this Parliament he had sworn to produce the Despensers for judgment.

The date had been fixed. But not by the King. It was Lancaster that had set it, Lancaster and his friends assembled at Westminster.

'By God, Lancaster shall lose his head for this!' the King burst out. 'It is for the King to summon Parliament, the King and no other man. This is no Parliament. I will not go!'

I will not go! Parliament had met. The King was absent; so also were the Despensers. Pembroke, so long loyal, turned from the King; and with him many more besides. It looked more than ever like a national rising. In mid-August, the Despensers standing by, Pembroke, that patient man, had audience of the King.

'Lord King, you must meet your princes. Take heed of the danger that threatens you. Sir, for the good of the land you must free it of wicked men; and this you swore at your crowning.'

The King sat still as stone.

'Sir, if you will not listen to your princes,' and now Pembroke's words came battering like stones, 'then, sir, I think you will lose your crown. Sir, I entreat you, meet your Parliament.'

'Parliament!' The King's laugh, splitting that face of stone, was shocking in the silence. 'What Parliament? There *is* no Parliament unless the King call it. Pembroke, you and your friends speak treason. Go, warn them!'

Pembroke stood looking at the King. Then, in the silence, Pembroke bowed very low and walking backwards, as is seemly before the King, left those three alone.

'I will not go, I will not go, I will not go!' When he so repeated himself it was time for those that knew him to doubt his word. 'They'll not rest until they've robbed me, as they robbed me before, of the thing I love best in the world. Oh Hugh, Hugh—' and he took the young man's hand, 'what shall I do and whither shall I turn? Already they have judged you. I shall lose you both—my father and my brother. Oh Hugh, Hugh, what shall I do?'

He thinks not at all of us—our loss, our danger. It is of himself he thinks, himself alone. The thought was instant to both father and son.

They turned and left him; and, as they went, they heard him asking still, *What shall I do?* Asking and weeping.

I will not go. I will not go. But go he must. Let him go on refusing and his princes would act without him; they had sworn it. That they would put the Despensers from their place, and he powerless to stop them—he knew well. That they would put him, the King, from his place, he did not for a moment believe.

Parliament had spoken. The King's attendance had not carried a hair's weight; he might as well have stayed at home. Those two were banished men.

Hugh the elder left England at once; he had funds aplenty salted abroad.

'Whither he's gone no man knows and no man cares! He's gone. It is enough!' The Queen said, joyful.

'But where the son is no man knows, neither!' Théophania said. 'They say everywhere he hasn't left the country.'

'I fear the King will find a way to keep him near, a curse upon the land! Till he is gone I cannot breathe!' Isabella laid a hand upon her breast.

'If he stay, he must die. The barons have spoken.'

'They reckon without the King. I tremble lest he find a way—a way so devious none but he could think of it.'

Certainly she knew the King better than any other. He had found a way to keep his sweetheart safe; a way so ingenious none but he could have thought of it—a way cursed by merchants and sailors and by all that must cross the narrow seas.

The King had given him a fine ship well-found; if Hugh must not rest on English soil he should rest near it—nothing had been said as to that! The ship lay at anchor near the south-east coast and by the King's command the men of the Cinque Ports must guard her safety. For the King's sweetheart had turned pirate and no ship went free of him. Crews he attacked and killed, goods he took for himself . . . and left the King to pay the damage.

But still the barons had had their way. The King had bent to their power; the Despensers were not to be found on English soil. Now, surely now there would be peace.

The King had graciously allowed the Queen to leave the Tower. Now that the Despensers were not at his elbow to poison him with accusations against her he was disposed to be kind—he was a lonely man. And, indeed, he could scarce object. She was making a pilgrimage to Canterbury to give thanks for safe delivery from childbirth. She had other thanks to give too; but these she did not mention. She meant to make offering to God because the hated Despensers were gone at last; and because she was rid, also, of those other thorns in the flesh—the Badlesmeres. The husband had left the court, he was now openly Lancaster's man; and his wife had gone with him. Isabella wished the creature's household joy of her! Life, at last, looked to be supportable.

The first week in September the Queen's procession took its way through the golden countryside. A great procession as befits a Queen—ladies, knights and pages, men-at-arms and servants; horses, charettes and laden wagons. Within the charette the Queen sat at ease, Madam de St. Pierre with her and no other. Eleanor Despenser had gone no-one knew whither; no need to guard one's tongue.

The rich countryside flowed steadily past. Tomorrow they would reach Canterbury; she was glad of that, recent childbirth had left her easily tired. Last night they had lain at Rochester and she had not slept well; tonight they would lie at Leeds Castle, the Queen's Kentish house and very comfortable.

'Madam we shall soon be there!' Théophania gently touched her arm; and there were the castle towers black against the skyline.

It was growing towards dark when they stood before the walls; the castle had a closed and shuttered look. No sign of life; neither men-at-arms nor sound of trumpet. Between travellers and castle lay a ditch foul and deep.

The Queen stared unbelieving. She had made her intention known. Was this the way to receive the Queen; and into her own house? Anger began to rise. She was by now utterly weary; this last hour the shelter of her own house, a good supper and a comfortable bed had grown ever more needful. For this piece of carelessness someone should pay!

She bade a servant sound the horn. The clear demand rose in the quiet air and died; silence flowed back. Again the horn sounded and again. And always the silence returning and never an answer.

At long last a man appeared on the turrets; and at him the Queen stared in even greater amazement. She knew him by his shape; there was not another such in Christendom. A long. lanky fellow with a head like a pea set between unequal shoulders. None other than Colepepper, seneschal to Badlesmere. And now her anger was hot and high. At Westminster the fellow had copied his master's insolence as much as he'd dared. What did Badlesmere's seneschal do in the Queen's house?

She was to learn at once.

I cannot admit Madam the Queen.

Not admitted! Into her own house, not admitted!

The words fell upon incredulous ears. Now, her almoner came riding up. 'Madam, Lord Badlesmere—I have this moment heard it—is constable of the castle.'

'Constable. Of my own house! And I not know it!'

'You were absent from Westminster, Madam; I fancy it was the lord Lancaster's doing.'

Lancaster. He had been so long from court he could not know the injury he had done. She would let him know at once. Meanwhile the house was hers; she must get inside and send Colepepper packing. She stepped from the charette.

'This is the Queen's house!' she cried high and clear. 'I command you, let down the bridge!'

The figure on the turrets stood as though he had not heard. And now John de Fontenoy, clerk to the Queen's chapel, came riding up. 'Madam, the lord Badlesmere is away; he is with my lord of Lancaster. I heard it in the village as we came through. Since there's dispute between the King and the barons Badlesmere is not minded, so they say, to have the gates opened lest it be some raiding-party to take it by surprise.'

'I am no raiding-party. I am the Queen. And this house is mine. Who takes charge in Badlesmere's absence?'

To that she had her answer at once. For now the lady herself appeared upon the battlements, her bold figure black against the pale night sky. Cupping her jaw in both hands that her voice might carry she cried out, 'Madam, you must seek some other shelter. I can admit no-one, not even the Queen's self, without order from my lord!'

At this piece of insolence hands flew to swords—a useless gesture since the ditch lay between. Suddenly, before a man could take in his breath, from the castle walls flew a volley of arrows. Before the Queen was safe within the charette six of her escort lay dead in the dust.

Along the dark country road went the Queen's procession, her escort shocked and furious, her ladies shocked and frightened. Within the charette, where now light from the torches flickered through the horn panes, the Queen sat unmoving; in her white face the red paint of her lips and the dark circles beneath her eyes, the only colour. Her whiteness was not the whiteness of fear; it was the white heat of her rage.

Chapter Twenty-Three

For this insult the Badlesmeres should pay, husband and wife, both; the Queen vowed it. And the seneschal whose tongue had dared the message should have that tongue torn from his throat. But who should make them pay? Not Lancaster. He had offered no apology; nor given reproof to Badlesmere. He had need of every man; and Badlesmere had a respectable following.

'Insult to the Queen is insult to the King!' Edward said, forgetting the countless insults himself had condoned. 'The matter goes beyond the Badlesmeres. It lies between Lancaster and me!' Ever since he had been forced to bow to the barons in the matter of the Despensers, pride ate within him like verjuice. Now he would teach them —Lancaster and all those that sought to belittle the King's dignity! Now he would gather his forces and no man could deny the right, nor would deny his right—the Queen was well-loved.

'And, sir,' she said, gentle as a dove, 'when you have gathered your forces and punished this insult, who shall question what you do next? And if they do? The King in arms shall answer them.'

To his well-beloved peers the summons went forth. Isabella smiled; herself had drafted it.

We, Edward, lord of England, Ireland and Scotland duke of Aquitaine, lord of Ponthieu and Gascony, by reason of the contempt which our beloved consort, Isabella Queen of England, has been treated by the family of Bartholomew Badlesmere who insolently opposed her in her desire of entering Leeds Castle a general muster of all persons between the age of sixteen and sixty is called to attend the King in an expedition against Leeds Castle . .

Isabella had become London's darling. There was no man great or small that would tolerate insult to their Queen. Almost she loved lady Badlesmere whose insult had carried her still higher on the tide of the people's love.

Within Leeds Castle the lady laughed. 'We have food, we have water, we have firing aplenty. Does he think, the foolish King, that the barons will suffer him to take this castle? Let him try!'

The barons had no intention of supporting her insolence. Their quarrel was with the King; in the Queen they found no fault. Lancaster forbade his followers to march; and that was as well since many of them had already joined the King. Badlesmere, himself, that useful man, Lancaster kept safe in the north. Let his ill-mannered shrew stew in her own juice! So across the quiet Kentish country no man came riding to her aid; armed men aplenty came riding, but they were all the King's men.

On the last day of October the castle surrendered. Before those gates where he had refused entrance to the Queen, Colepepper was hanged and eleven men with him; and those eleven, robbers and murderers that had, at last, met their just fate. To the Tower went my lady to remain at the King's pleasure.

At this last Isabella found herself shaken by a storm of rage; herself she was surprised at the violence of her desire to punish. Why had the woman not shared the fate of her steward? He had obeyed the slut's orders!

'I shed no woman's blood,' Edward said. 'But when I get my hands on Badlesmere he shall pay for both!'

And with that she must make herself content. But she would not forget! Revenge was beginning to taste sweet in her mouth.

The insult was avenged; but the King did not disband his forces. *Make an end of the rebels.* Again and again Isabella urged him, sending out her will to strengthen his. For, it was clear from the barons she could hope little. Lancaster was in the ascendant—and he had done nothing to avenge the insult to the Queen. Nor in the ever-shifting loyalties of the barons themselves, their constant changeover from side to side, could she expect much. What then of the wayward, inconstant King? Him—the Despensers gone—she might influence; she could not count upon it. Her one hope was in herself. She saw, very clear, the pattern of her own behaviour. To watch each side, to balance one against the other, to stand at the fulcrum and hold things steady—if she could do that her power was assured.

For a woman and young, a big *if*. She knew it.

Make an end of the rebels. Shorn of his dignities the King made a poor showing; she found the sight offensive. The country must see him strengthened, honoured.

'Now that many remember their duty—Arundel, de Warenne and the others, the rest will follow. You have the army; you have but to march.'

'Yes, they will come; all of them will come!' He was all complacency so that she longed to strike him. That they had returned for love of herself never troubled his conceit. Yet she was shrewd enough not to count upon that love. Had they not been already weary of Lancaster they'd not have stirred on her behalf. Well, whatever the reason, here was the King at the head of an army well-found.

Through the grey November weather rode the King, the army at his heels. He was for Cirencester to keep an eye on the Welsh marches; he had commanded the Queen to join him to celebrate the Christmas festival. Robbed of the Despensers he was not unglad of her company; that he ever went to her for advice, much less took it, never entered his head. But one thing he did know—the King and Queen in good accord strengthened the goodwill of the people towards him.

On his way he made good use of the army. The castles of those that remained with Lancaster he attacked, their lords being for the most part absent. And those within he punished so harshly that, the word spreading, none dared resist the King.

And now it was Christmas; at Cirencester the Queen was waiting. It was a larger court than she had dared hope. Yet more of the rebels had returned. Richmond had come in; and the King's half-brothers, Thomas of Brotherton now Earl Marshal and Edmund earl of Kent. These last were a great asset—they were young, they were valiant, they were well-liked. And, best of all, Pembroke had returned. It was good to know that once more Pembroke stood with his King. Things were beginning to take a sweet turn, Isabella thought. And the King himself had shown courage and determination. Was the fainéant beginning to show himself a King? Respect for her husband, so long withered, threw out a small, green shoot.

The shoot barely green was dead.

The Despensers were back. Reynolds, unworthy archbishop, had declared their cause just, their excommunication void.

The Queen took in her breath when she heard it. She turned her back upon the King all joyful with his news and, like a blind woman, sought the refuge of her closet. She leaned against the door and stood looking at Madam de St. Pierre. She tried to speak and could not speak; her lips just moved. Théophania led her to a chair and there she sat, staring, it would seem, at nothing. When she could speak at last she said—and there was wonder in her voice, 'Have I not suffered enough? Does it begin again, the humiliation and the spite? I had hoped . . . dear God how I hoped! Yet still the King shows himself for what he is—the dog that returns to his vomit!'

Théophania said nothing; only her hand went to her mouth as if that gesture could silence the Queen.

'I'll not be silent!' Isabella cried out, passionate. 'Let the whole court hear! Let all Christendom hear! The King's a fool! When all's set fair, he must damn his own bright fortunes!' And she wrung her hands.

Grief, anger, dread of further insult had loosened her tongue. She could not, though she died of it, keep silent now.

'Fourteen years, fourteen hateful years! Yet I never forgot I was a Queen and I never forgot I was a wife—though by God's Face there's been plenty to make me forget both! This King and his sweethearts! Yet as a Queen I have carried myself; as a true wife no less. I have endured this King that was never a King, this husband that was never a husband—save when he used me to breed upon. Years of misery, years of insult! And now when there's hope of dignity, hope of peace, he must cast it all away!'

She stopped to take in her breath, her voice rose higher; nothing could stop her now. She must spew out this poison or die!

'Oh God that the rebels had stayed of one mind! They could have put him from the throne, this unworthy King that plays with his mignons, that breaks the sworn word, that listens to none but those two—wicked father and foul paramour!'

'Madam, Madam, I implore you!' And Théophania was on her knees before the Queen. 'Last time it was the Tower; but the palace, only. Next time—Madam you speak sedition—who can say?'

But still she would not, could not be stayed. Too long misery had eaten into her, the acid of her bitterness.

'Did I call the King a fool? I am the fool, I, *I*! The fool that bade him summon the barons. I should have closed my mouth upon the Badlesmeres' insult. I should have kept him dallying in London. But no! I must advise him to march against the rebels. Had I held my peace the barons would have marched united—Lancaster hates the King! And all, all alike hate the Despensers. And for that I love them all—be they rebels, be they what they may! They would have put the King from the throne, they would have crowned my son; they would have chosen me—Regent. Not Lancaster but me—*me* the Queen the people love. I would have held the reins and held them well. *Peacemaker* they call me; and peacemaker I have been. But peacemaker no more. Let the King dig his own grave!'

Madam de St. Pierre said nothing. But . . . *She is right, she has suffered too much. Now bitterness darkens the clear mind. Dear God, let it not destroy the good within her, or what shall be the end of this?*

January in the year of grace thirteen hundred and twenty-two, trumpets shrilling, banners flying, the King left Cirencester, a Despenser riding at either hand; at Shrewsbury he crossed the Severn. He must face them, the strong men, the once loyal men that had kept his marches safe. Now, because of those unjust gifts to the Despensers of Welsh land and marcher land, the dispossessed lords and those that feared dispossession, must stand against him—at their head, the Mortimers.

'I do not fear the outcome,' he had said, bidding the Queen Farewell. 'The best of my lords are with me. As for these marchers lords, they know what to expect. From Cirencester to Westminster I punished the rebels.'

'Yes,' she said, 'Yes.' *But they were not there to punish. It was the women and the children you punished, defenceless. . . .*

'All men fear my name.'

The Mortimers do not fear you. You will never defeat them! And it was of the younger Mortimer she thought.

At Cirencester she waited for the King's defeat. His spurt of courage could not last; she prayed it could not last. Once more he was in the hands of evil counsellors; and into those hands he would deliver her also. Wretched the wife that must pray for her husband's defeat! Yet if he should win she was ruined and all England with her.

Victory to the King.

She sat upright in her chair. Stone-faced she took the news; the unbelievable news.

Now I face a life of endless insult. For even should the paramour die —and why should he, being young and strong?—the King being the thing he is, there'll always be another till he lies in his grave.

Till he lies in his grave. The second time the thought, the thought unbidden. The first time she had considered his death as an event to be desired but an event in the nature of things, not to be reckoned a possibility as yet; and it had gone as soon as come. Now she considered it again. No hope of it. He was young, he was strong; and in battle he kept from danger. She put the thought from her without pleasure or regret.

Within a few days she had the whole story.

The marcher lords had submitted without a fight; they could do no other.

'And, Madam,' the messenger said, 'the lord Lancaster did not send the men he promised. The rebels had not the men and so they must submit. And now, since God gave the victory, the Mortimers are taken prisoner, they and the rest of the rebel lords.'

She sat very stiff, making her mouth to smile; she remembered to thank the messenger, even to reward him. When he had gone she set to pacing the room . . . up and down, up and down, as though she would never rest again. For the first time she thought not of herself, but of the Mortimers; of one Mortimer.

He was in prison—if not already dead. . . .

She stopped transfixed by a thought; it was as though an arrow had pierced her to the heart.

The fault is mine; as much as any man's, mine. I demanded punishment for the Badlesmeres—the thrice-damned Badlesmeres, forever pricked the King to my revenge. Through me the rebel lords returned. But for me he could not have fought, nor the Mortimers been taken. The fault is mine . . . mine . . .

The Mortimers were in the Tower.

The Queen nodded, indifferent, it would seem; but against the bony cavern of her skull the thoughts went beating. Almost she put up a hand to stop them.

The Tower; most dreadful of prisons. I sent him there. . . .

She longed with passion to save him. It was not love that drove her, nor even any affection for the man. To help him was her responsibility and her need. Such responsibility, such need, she had never known before. In this dangerous court, all need had been for herself. Now she must help another's need. How she did not know. She knew one thing, only. She must show no interest, ask no question.

No need for either. The messengers told her all—the black and stinking cell, the cold, the damp, the near starvation; the certainty of a shameful death—like the lowest felon hanged, drawn and quartered. Revenge was sweet to the King, so much was clear; revenge for that long-ago jealousy because of that love between the oldest and the youngest palace boy—Gaveston and Mortimer.

No longer did she pity herself alone; her pity was equal for him —for the proud, strong man shut from the light of day within a cruel prison. Death, so it were not shameful, she knew he could face; he was a soldier. But a death of shame following upon a sapping of strength of hope she did not think any man could endure. Pity and guilt bound her to him like a cord.

He was forever in her mind, forever in her dreams. She saw him clear as though he stood before her—thickset and strong; pale eyes wary and cold, mouth brutal, sensual. Sometimes, half-awake, she would wonder what it must be like to feel that mouth coming down upon her own and, so wondering, feel her body open to desire. Then, finally awake, she would remember that without her help, his mouth would never touch a woman again. Sleepless she would lie there scheming, planning, rejecting her plans, making others. And never once did she think of Mortimer's wife that had been her friend. The thing was between Mortimer and the Queen.

The King turned his back on Shrewsbury; he had punished it well. Through the winter weather he was marching; marching triumphant, for Hereford. Success to his arms, success everywhere. The fall of the Mortimers had struck fear into the hearts of rebels everywhere. Castles and towns had fallen to the King; and those that had held them he punished with death. Triumphant he put from their places sheriffs and judges he did not trust and set his friends in their stead.

He had publicly upbraided the bishop of Hereford, Adam Orleton.

The Queen permitted herself a small and secret smile.

Would he never learn discretion this foolish King; which man he might safely humiliate and which it was wise to let go in peace? This bishop was one to be handled with care. The King had been lenient to stop at words; wiser to have made an end of him altogether—the bishop was a Mortimer man, hand-in-glove with them. But to humiliate this proud bishop of unchristian spirit, to humiliate him before his own flock! It was a thing Orleton would never forgive, never forget!

Her mind took a sudden leap.

This bishop devoted to the house of Mortimer, shamed and full of rancour; a tool, a tool in my hand . . . if I can find the way to use him.

And still victory for the King, victory all the way. Every day brought more rebels in to his banner; and the Despensers, with every fault, were able men. The elder kept a careful eye upon men, upon arms, upon horses and provisions; the younger upon plans and strategies. Upon the King's success hung their lives.

And what of Lancaster? Back once more in Westminster the Queen must pray for his success; not for her own sake but for Mortimer's. Lancaster in arms could save him; Lancaster alone.

The King was once more on the march. Lancaster made no move. From him, shut in Pontefract, no sign.

Why? Why? It was not the Queen alone that asked.

'He cannot fight. He has lost the best part of his friends!' the older Despenser said.

'He has lost more than friends. He's lost his wits and his nerve!' And the younger Despenser laughed.

Let him move dear God before it is too late! the Queen prayed, desperate for Mortimer.

Lancaster was marching at last; at Burton-on-Trent he halted. His forces were small but sufficient to keep the bridge. The King should come no further!

The King had reached Burton. Hated Lancaster held the bridge. Before him flowed the wide, deep Trent. He could go no further. His men were many, Lancaster's few; but for all that, he could not force the Bridge. Again and again his men attempted the task. Some were shot and, swimming, threw up their arms and drowned, some in boats, weighed down by their gear, sank like stones; others that managed to reach the bridge fell twisting and spinning to their death.

Lancaster, triumphant, looked across the river pearl-pale in the early morning light. Most of the King's forces had withdrawn, those that were left were making no further attempt; it looked, indeed, as though they were striking camp.

'He has run away as usual, the brave King!' Lancaster said and laughed.

The King and the best part of his forces had indeed gone. Under cover of night they had slipped further down the bank where the river ran shallow and was easily forded.

Lancaster had laughed too soon. Even while he laughed the King was attacking from the north; and those apparently idle men were suddenly seen to be full-armed. Lancaster's men were surrounded, forced from the bridgehead. Where all had been calm confidence there was confusion and panic. When the men turned to their leader for orders, there was none to answer. Lancaster, great Lancaster had fled the field.

The Queen put out a hand to steady herself. Lancaster defeated. *Lancaster!* Now she must smile, offer public thanksgiving, grace the feast. She alone, in the midst of the rejoicings careful lest in some way she betray her grief.

At Pontefract Lancaster would have made a stand—so much of valour he had left; but yet more of his captains had deserted, confidence in him was gone. Northwards he fled, the remnant of his forces with him; and northwards followed the King's armies relentless in pursuit. It was March before they came up with him: at Boroughbridge he must turn and face them. Southward he could not go; young Kent and de Warenne that grim enemy, blocked the way. Northward he could not go—the King's northern armies cut him off.

A fierce and bloody battle. Lancaster's sparse forces suffered cruelly. Here young Hereford died and Clifford fell so severely wounded he could not drag himself to his knees. And now the very men refused; what use to fight against such odds? Lancaster, himself, would have fought to the death—a better death than he must suffer if taken; but his captains for the most part dead or taken, and the men refusing, he must ask for truce until morning.

Come morning-light the most part of his men had deserted. And there was the sheriff of York to take his prisoners—Lancaster, Mowbray, wounded Clifford and many others. And to Pontefract they were carried; to Pontefract, Lancaster's proud castle.

Again the Queen must take the news with a joyful face. Now she could hope no longer. The end for Lancaster. And, save for her own wits, the end for Mortimer.

The King had chosen Pontefract for judgment—a streak of cruelty, the Queen thought, a refinement of torture. He did not mean to spare Lancaster anything; long and long he had nursed his anger against the murderer of Gaveston.

There was no trial. The King himself recited the tale of treason. Lancaster wanted to speak—and was not allowed to speak; there was too much he might have said. The death sentence was spoken—and not one of the seven judges raised a voice to claim the prisoner's right to speak. You are condemned, he was told; the words of the condemned are of no profit.

Isabella heard the full story, the messenger kneeling before her; and sickened. Refinement of torture she had expected; but brutality crude and vulgar—that she had not expected of the King.

'The judgment was no sooner spoken, Madam, when they led him to his death; they feared he would still speak those things better not to hear. They set him upon a broken-down jade; white she was with age and the ribs sticking out beneath her skin, and so low she was the man's feet dragged in the dust . . .'

And when she rebuked him that he had omitted the great titles, the messenger said, 'Madam, it is forbidden. The lord King has sequestered titles and lands. And, Madam, as he sat, the crowd laughed . . .'

Laughed at great Lancaster! She was ashamed; ashamed for the King. He could have taken full payment without so shaming Lancaster, so shaming himself. He should have remembered that Lancaster was a great prince, his blood as royal as the King's own. He should have remembered that, in his time, Lancaster had done the King some service. She felt anger sharp as pain, bitter as poison.

'Madam, they came to the place of execution. He would have knelt to pray . . . but it was not allowed.'

Denying the dying man his last prayer! Of all vile things, this was surely the vilest! For the first time she was pricked with hatred for the King.

'*He has long and long enough to consider his sins!* the lord King cried out. And then the headsman—and God knows where he learned his trade!—made three false strokes or four and ended life and prayer together. And, Madam, as the axe fell, the lord King, so I am told, was heard to say, *The measure you yourself measure out shall be measured to you again.*'

Pray God it be so! Startled she heard her thought clear.

'What, Madam, did my father mean?' Young Edward plucked

at her sleeve. She had forgotten he was there; now he stood staring with wondering eyes.

'That, my son, is hard to say.'

'And so my uncle of Lancaster is dead.'

'He is; God rest his soul.'

'Was he a bad man?'

'Your father thinks so. But each must judge for himself. When you are older you, also, will judge.'

'All that offend against the King, must die!' he said.

She stared at him, so young and so certain. Years later she was to remember his words.

Chapter Twenty-Four

End of Thomas, royal Lancaster, earl of Lancaster, of Leicester, of Derby, of Lincoln and Salisbury. Dead in his middle years, honour and honours alike forfeit, his blood, only, saving him from the shameful rope.

The Queen wept; but not too much—he had failed her. Tears, were she one to weep, must be for herself condemned to enduring insult from the Despensers; tears, too, for Mortimer in the dark cell awaiting death. Lancaster's death was Mortimer's death; in the pressure of events she must keep her eyes clear of tears.

The Despensers were riding higher, higher; lords as well as commons heard the whistle of their whip. The King allowed it all—and not only because he was besotted with his sweetheart; those two gave him the flattery, the assurance he longed to hear. They would make him absolute—they swore it; but it was not the weak and wilful King they meant to make absolute.

Maytime, in the year of grace thirteen hundred and twenty-two. Lancaster had been dead six weeks and already the country regretted him. Forgetful of his sullen selfishness, they remembered only his hatred of the Despensers and the way he had stood out against the King. From all over England men and women—simple folk for the most part—were making pilgrimages to his burying-place. They were offering prayers before the high altar at Pontefract where the monks had hurriedly buried him before the King could stop them; prayers and thanksgiving. They were spreading the legend of miracles worked at the tomb. To simple folk Thomas of Lancaster bade fair to become a saint. The King, for all his anger, could not stop it; and in her chamber the Queen smiled her secret smile.

Uncle Thomas dead, looked to be more useful than Uncle Thomas alive. Alive he had stood out against the Despensers; he stood so still, with all the added moral force of the martyred dead. The people were discontented, discontented and disappointed. Had they hoped for anything? This new Parliament, she thought, must show how vain the hope . . . *It jumps to the crack of the Despensers' whip. No single reform, no single thought for the welfare of the people. Nothing but obedience to the demands of the King, which are the demands of the Despensers. . . .*

Herself, she had expected little enough, God knew! But even she could scarce believe that Parliament had repudiated the Ordinances.

All things ordained by the Lords Ordainers shall henceforth and forever cease. The laws and statutes made by our lord the King and his ancestors shall remain in force.

The Ordinances cast aside! The thing for which the barons had fought and bled and died. The safeguard of the people. *The King digs his own grave!* She heard the thought as clear as though she spoke aloud.

The King's death. Again the thought; for the third time the thought. It shocked her no longer. As long as he kept the Despensers about him, so long he built up hatred against himself. And where might not such hatred end?

It was not, at first, the repeal of the Ordinances that angered the people; such news takes time to be fully understood. It was the immediate shock of the gallows springing up all over the land, hung with foul fruit—fruit the people could see for themselves, smell for themselves—obscene orchards to feed their bitter anger. For the King had shown himself merciless. His rebel lords he had hanged— as many as he could lay hands upon. But they, at least, had been the leaders, and they had escaped the full sentence—the drawing of their entrails while yet they lived. Common folk that must obey their betters did not escape so lightly; everywhere from tree and gallows men hung gutless.

'Cruelty grows in the King like a sickness,' Isabella told Madam de St. Pierre. 'I sicken at the sight of men dangling. In one hanging alone I take my pleasure. Badlesmere dangles from his rope; would to God that his shrew dangled with him!'

Her own fierce demand for punishment of those that had offended against her, Théophania thought, should warn the Queen of that same cruelty like a sickness within herself.

'But God be praised, many have escaped to France!' and Isabella sighed to think of the prisoner that had not escaped. 'France where I would give much to be! Would God I might escape, awhile, from my own griefs and those of this unhappy land!'

And unhappy the land was! Cruel in punishment the King was madly lavish in reward; the Despensers, indeed, did not wait for reward—they rewarded themselves. Their estates and revenues were swollen with wealth sequestered from their victims; their strong rooms could not hold the half of their ever-growing treasure, nor their dungeons the half of their prisoners. The elder Despenser was my lord earl of Winchester now; but the younger, though he had honours enough, was not earl of Gloucester.

'The King covets the title for his paramour,' Isabella said; she spoke beneath her breath for Eleanor Despenser was back, forced upon an unwilling Queen. 'So far he has not dared. But there are no more Ordainers. Will he not dare it now? They'll not rest, those Despensers, until best part of England is in their hands. Already they've got Lancaster's stronghold of Denbigh, they've got Swansea, town and castle. They own between them, the whole of South Wales. They've got all the Bigod lands beyond the Severn. They've got the ransom of half-a-dozen kings salted down with foreign bankers and they know well where to put their hand on more. No money comes amiss, not though it be slippery with blood. Will there never be an end to their wickedness?

Their latest wickedness she had yet to learn.

They had sent a secret embassy to the Pope praying him to dissolve her marriage. It was not so secret but that my lord bishop of Hereford had got wind of it—that same bishop the King had publicly rebuked. Orleton had his friends in Rome; he knew that same embassy to urge the Queen's divorce, urged also his own removal. He did not believe the Pope would grant either petition—his friends had the Pope's ear. It did not make him love the King or the Despensers more. His own future, it was clear, lay with the Queen. She had shown him some kindness since that public reproval; a man smarting under humiliation and devoted to the house of Mortimer might prove useful. A devious man she found him; shrewd and discreet.

When he told her of the embassy, anger and fear battled with disbelief. For her husband she cared little; for her position and her honour, very much. The loss of her crown, disgrace and the smearing of her name, herself shut within a convent or worse; or else crawling back dishonoured to France! The frightful possibilities battered at her frightened heart. It could not be! Yet with glib tongues and sufficient bribes—who knew what might not happen?

'The charge, my lord bishop, the *charge?*'

'Their lies will serve them—so they think. But the lord Pope is no man's fool; he knows how to value these Despensers! Besides, Madam, I have my friends; they have his ear—and tongues to speak into that ear.'

She turned her lovely, troubled eyes upon him—even in this moment of fear she knew how to use them. 'If I am unhappy in all else, I am happy, my lord, in your friendship. Never in this world shall I forget it!' She bent and kissed the sapphire ring of his office. He was a man—she knew him—to feed upon praise, greedy for honours and place. Reminder of her sad state with promise of reward in happier condition was salutary.

She said, 'I must go at once to the King; I must demand the reason of his request.' She had no intention, subtle as she was, of any such thing; it was the bishop's own subtlety she tested.

'Madam, under your pardon, no! Much harm could come of it! Silence is best; ignorance in the matter your strong weapon. The lord King, of himself, is not willing; he fears to offend your brother of France. It is the Despensers that want it; and the lord Pope is no man's servant to obey an idle whim. The lord Pope knows—Madam, I have sent to tell him—the people of England would not endure it. It would cost the King his crown. The people love you, Madam—the Queen without fault. Say nothing; show no disquiet. You are safe leaving all to me.'

But for all that she trembled; it was long before she could calm herself; thereafter she set her set wits to work. This bishop was shrewd and cunning; he was a man of influence. He had the ear of the Pope, he had lost no time championing her cause. A cautious man that for all his anger had not criticised the King by so much as a lifted brow. What better helper could she find? This was a man to use!

Her mind gave a sudden leap so that for a moment she forgot her own troubles.

He hates the Despensers and he loves the Mortimers.

In that moment, without a shadow of reason Mortimer's fate became linked with her own. If he were free, the ugly threat of divorce would pass her by; if he died that unspeakable calamity would fall upon her. She must save him to save herself.

The Mortimers had been in the Tower six months. Mortimer of Chirk was no longer there. He was dead. The rigours of his prison had killed him as surely as axe or rope. The King laughed when he heard the news. 'He saves me some trouble! The other, though, shall die the traitor's death. That is a trouble I shall relish!'

The death of the elder Mortimer troubled the Queen little save as a pointer to prison conditions. Mortimer of Chirk had been hale enough; now he was dead. How long before the younger man followed him to the grave? Now Mortimer of Wigmore was forever in her thoughts; she was obsessed with desire to save him and the sense of her own guilt. Had she not urged the King to arms Mortimer would not be languishing in prison. The sense of guilt possessed her utterly, strengthening beyond any reason her certainty that upon his fate hung her own. They stood or fell together.

The country was growing ever more restless. Impossible to set foot out of doors without remembering the King's cruelty; every chance wind brough the stench of it. And, resenting their poverty that fed the bottomless greed of the favourites, men sickened yet more at the pitiless arrogance of the Despensers. And this resentment was sharpened further by rumours—set afoot by my lord bishop of Hereford—that those two urged the Queen's divorce; their good Queen!

But most of all they resented the casting-aside of the Ordinances; now they had had time to understand what it meant. The Ordinances had stood between then and the King's excesses; now between them and those excesses—nothing.

For the Despensers were ruling like Kings; no curbing them. Many of those that had worked for the Ordinances were dead or fled. Henry of Lancaster, had he been man enough, might have taken his brother's place—leader of the barons. But he had been granted Thomas's lesser titles—he was my lord earl of Leicester and Derby— and hoped for the rest; above all the great name of Lancaster. Moreover he remembered his brother's death and was not minded to die the same way; he was not likely to make much trouble. Pembroke, the one man to be trusted, had died in France; de Warenne no man was foolish enough to trust. Richmond was a foreigner and in the King's pocket. Thomas of Norfolk and Edmund of Kent were too young, and too-lately forgiven for their part in the later revolt.

No-one to stand between oppressor and oppressed.

In the north, the people were, as usual, in worse plight; besides the trouble they shared with the whole country, they had troubles of their own. Border-raids were savage and without respite; those that escaped slaughter by the Scots died more slowly by famine, poverty and pestilence. Worn with constant suffering, weary of a King that left them to their suffering, encouraged by their own archbishop of York, they declared their willingness to acknowledge the Bruce King of Scotland.

England, it was clear, could no longer hold Scotland. The Despensers, able men when not blinded by greed, advised the King to let it go.

Edward flew into a Plantagenet rage. 'Scotland is mine and I will keep it.'

'Move now—and you lose it forever. In our own good time when least he expects it, we shall take it again. You have nothing to do but sit quiet.'

The King nodded; he saw the point of that!

Peace on the border at last. And, for the first time in his life, the King of England free of the burden of the Scottish wars. But the country did not take the loss lightly. *We have lost Scotland,* men told each other puzzled and amazed. *Scotland is lost . . . we have lost it.* And cursed the Despensers that had made the truce.

'We have lost Scotland!' the Queen cried out and wrung her

hands. Shame she felt and anger; and it was not all patriotism. She could never endure to let go anything she considered her own. 'I am ashamed. I am a*shamed*.'

'Madam, under pardon, Despenser's wife is in the anteroom,' Théophania said. 'She is all ears!'

'Then let her hear; she can do me no more harm! They would have had my marriage dissolved, but God's Mouthpiece is not their mouthpiece to set a scandal on foot to shake all Christendom! Since he'll not serve their turn they set their spies to scavenge some tit-bit. Well, let them try! For all their spying they'll find no fault. My life is barren and desolate, God knows; but still they'll find no fault. Yet were I to take comfort from any man who should blame me? Who husbanded me, ever, who cherished me? The life I lead is bitter, bitter!'

The Despensers had promised to make the King free of Parliament. The only use of Parliament was to supply the King with money; money they knew where to get! Beneath renewed extortion the country bled.

The Queen saw it all with satisfaction. 'How much longer will the people endure it?' she asked Orleton; she had been seeing much of him of late. 'Surely they must see that this is worse, far worse, than the repeal of the Ordinances. To make the King free of Parliament—for them the worst betrayal of all!'

'Madam, the people suffer like animals; they are slow to act. But they pray. They forever make their pilgrimages to Pontefract. They wait for a voice to speak from Lancaster's grave. One day that voice will speak—or so they believe; and when it speaks they will follow!'

People were laying flowers beneath the gallows where corrupting bodies still offended eye and nose. Parliament besought the King for his own sake to take down these breeders of bitterness. He had, of himself, been willing enough; his resentments, as a rule, were not enduring. The older Despenser counselled him otherwise.

'Sir, it will be taken for weakness in you!'

And the younger, 'Sir, we have freed you from this Parliament. Pay it no heed. Let it not vex my King; for when my King is vexed I cannot sleep nor eat.'

And how should the King refuse his sweetheart, all troubled for his King? The bodies should hang until the last rag of flesh fell from the bones.

He had done better to listen to his Parliament. As the bodies rotted, so more surely the people's anger increased against the King. Now all their loyalty, all their affection, all their duty turned towards the Queen, the Queen alone. Men everywhere recounted her virtues and her wrongs. She had a heart to grieve for her people pressed beyond bearing. She felt the shame of Scotland lost. She was wise, she was good. She was persecuted by the Despensers. She was a wronged wife, a wronged Queen. And she was the mother of the heir.

She had become a symbol of justice, of mercy.

So dumb, so hidden this turning towards the Queen, none but the sensitive mind could register it. Isabella recognised it, Orleton recognised it. The Despensers recognised it.

Ridden more than ever by the belief that her luck rose and fell with Mortimer, she dared risk that luck no longer. Fail him now and God would perhaps fail her; change His mind about her divorce and say so through His Mouthpiece; or he might turn the people's heart from her. Her plan had long been ready; she waited only to be sure of her accomplice. She had been weighing up Orleton— his caution against his courage; his ambition against his honesty. In him these qualities balanced—more or less; she could have wished him more courage. But let her wait till kingdom come she'd find none better for her purpose. But for the unrest throughout the land Mortimer must already have come to his death. That he was unwell she had heard from Orleton. 'Madam, his strength grows daily less. I fear he will die of his weakness.'

She must move—and at once lest death find him first.

Chapter Twenty-Five

The King had declared his intention of putting an end to Mortimer.
A public execution; a warning to traitors.

The Queen sent for Orleton; she came to the point at once.

'The lord Mortimer will not die of his weakness; he's to die by
the rope!'

'Madam, I fear it. But—the *rope*!' He looked at her out of a
sick face.

She nodded. 'The day is not yet named; but it will be soon.
Neither insult nor torment will be spared.'

'It is a man not afraid to die—though he will live as long
as he can. But—a shameful death; it will break heart and pride
together!'

'Then—' and she looked him full in the face, 'we must see he
does not come to such a death. My lord, we can do it!'

'How, Madam?' He lifted a shocked face. 'It is the strongest
prison in England—triple walls, many towers, a great keep and a
deep ditch. How can a prisoner escape thence? And, if he could?
Then he must cross the river in full sight of the guards. The thing's
impossible!'

'Not impossible; difficult, difficult, only!'

My lord bishop of Hereford spread long, fine hands. 'Madam,
man's wit cannot encompass it. The Tower. It has stood above
two hundred and fifty years and no man has ever broken free.'

'There's always a first time. And if man's wit cannot encompass
it then a woman's can. Tell me where he lies, who are his gaolers
and what men have access to him.'

He looked at her; he was deeply troubled. He knew her—the
quick wits, the single-mindedness, the strength of will; but this
was beyond even her powers. As for himself, he dare not move in

this; he was answerable to the Pope himself, and already the King had complained of him to Rome.

And still she pressed him.

'The cell; where?'

'Beneath the White Tower—the bottom-most dungeon; hard by the great sewer. A man could die of the stench.'

'Good!' she said, surprising him. 'Now! Let us consider. First of all, Segrave. He's a fool. Never in my life would I make him Constable of the Tower. Well, for his foolishness, God be praised!'

'Then, Madam, there's young Alspaye his lieutenant. He cannot help us—though his will is good. He hates Segrave for a drunken brute and a cruel one; endlessly cruel to the poor wretches he has in care. *Care,* God save the mark!'

'Goodwill is somewhat!'

'Not enough. He can do nothing. He complains that Segrave treats him as a child; will not allow him to handle keys nor even to know where they are kept. The gaolers have their own keys— but only to the cells; keys to the outer gates they never see. To find these keys, much less use them—impossible! There'd be an instant hue and cry; and before a man could take in his breath, young Alspaye would be hanging. He'd not face it were much to be gained; but when nothing's to be gained save a hateful death for himself—! Madam, you cannot expect it!'

'Yet I do expect it. I know young Alspaye; we were friends when I lodged in the Tower.' She smiled remembering the young man's infatuation. 'And many a game of chess we had together!' She smiled again remembering that sometimes she had let him win. Now it was the Queen's turn to win. 'With Alspaye I can deal. Now for the turnkey; what of him?'

'Only this; he, too, would suffer death were he discovered—and discovered he must be!'

'Who else has access to the prisoner?'

'Myself, Madam; but only upon special occasion. And Ogle the barber; he goes in once a week to shave such prisoners as desire it; and also those about to die.'

'I know him. He shaved my servants in the Tower.'

'A man, Madam, without compassion. To save a child, even, he'd not lift a finger without reward.'

'We must see he has his reward. So then there's Ogle and Alspaye. And there's you, my lord bishop. You will, I take it, hear his last confession; where is the gaoler then?'

'He must wait without; in view but not in hearing. Confession is between a man and his God.'

'One last question. Is it allowed to take the prisoner some small comfort . . . white bread, perhaps, or a bottle of wine?'

'It is not allowed this prisoner. Yet—a last confession and thereafter the man to die! It could be managed.'

'Now, my lord bishop, leave me. I have to think awhile.'

'Madam!' And again he spread his hands so that the ring flashed and glittered. 'You cannot help him. I beseech you do not meddle in the affair. I have great love for the lord Mortimer—but even more for my Queen!'

And most of all for yourself! Well she could not blame him. He was a cautious man and already high in the King's displeasure. But once he gave his word he would stand by it.

She said, gentle and devout, 'My lord, this is God's work. He will help us. If I did not know that, I would not dare put my hand to it; much less bring another into danger—and especially one I revere as my father in God.' She knelt and pressed her lips to the ring; hand upon the bent head he blessed her. But he had not, as yet, vowed himself to the work.

When my lord bishop came to her again she said, 'Mortimer dies on Saturday—if we allow it. Well, we do not allow it! The plan is perfect and complete.'

When she had laid it before him he shook his head.

'Madam, it is not possible; the thing's too involved, too complicated.'

'Not so, my lord. Take it step by step—and it is simple.'

'Madam, you must allow for chance. The slightest thing untoward—!' He shrugged. 'I cannot think luck will be with us!'

'Fie, my lord. There's no such thing as luck—must I remind you? God either smiles or He frowns. In this matter I do not think He will frown! And if He should; who's the worse? Not Mortimer.

If we do nothing, he must die. To die without at least a bid for freedom—and such a death! Can you think he'd hesitate? And for ourselves; we are safe enough. I cannot see how suspicion should fall on you or me—God's bishop and the Queen! Well?' she held him with her strange compelling eyes.

He made no answer; and still she held him with that gaze.

'So be it!' When he spoke at last it was without his own will.

'Now for the first step. I have slept ill of late. The lord King sent me a physician; he gave me a sleeping-draught. I did not take it. The Despensers—' and it was as though she spat, 'would give much to find me so sound asleep they could do with me what they would. This—' and she drew from the bosom of her gown a packet wrapped in silk, 'will put the gaoler to sleep.'

He searched her face. . . . Beautiful, clever, and for all her talk of God, he judged unscrupulous.

'It is distilled from the poppy and harmless; the physician told me. Before God I'd not offend Him with any man's death.'

That was good sense; he must believe her. He took the package wishing himself well out of this.

'Now!' she said. 'On Friday morning you hear Mortimer's confession. Later Ogle will go shave him; he will take with him a bottle of wine. Why not? The prisoner's to die in the morning. You'll need to pay Ogle well—he'll have to get out of the country!' She put a purse into his hand. He emptied the silver and handed it back. 'The Queen's purse could have a long tongue!' he told her. He handed back also, the one gold piece. 'Gold is for princes, not barbers!' he said. 'This could betray us all!'

She smiled; until this last moment she had been testing his discretion. 'You are wise, my lord! Now here is your part; it is simple enough—to hear a confession and to bribe a barber. Alspaye's part in this he knows and will perform it. I have his promise. When you have heard the confession you have nothing to do but wait until Mortimer has crossed the river.'

'That, Madam, I fear he'll never do'.

'Then, my lord, you are saved some trouble! But I believe he will; and you must be ready. Once he leaves his cell comes the hardest part. Ten paces to the left there's a shaft; Alspaye told me. The shaft—from two privies I regret to say—opens upon the drain that carries the filth into the ditch. The drain that has caused him such discomfort shall bring him the greatest comfort of all— freedom. The shaft is wide enough to take a man; up this shaft he must climb—he's nimble as a cat, I hear. The shaft runs as far 'as the Queen's lodgings. He must climb until the shaft branches— and a long climb it will be! That branch he must not take—it leads to Segrave's lodgings. He must climb until he reaches the second branch and that is the one he must take. The second shaft —mark it! It leads to the Queen's privy. From the privy he may come into the Queen's closet and there a short staircase leads to the leads. How often I have used it to take the air! There Alspaye will leave a rope.'

'One question, Madame; what of Segrave?'

'One Friday night he sups with me. It is a courtesy long overdue; he was, in some sort, my host when I lodged within the Tower. Mortimer's road to freedom is not salubrious; but it offers life. The rest—when he reaches the Southwark side—my lord bishop I leave to you!'

The lord Mortimer of Wigmore was sunk in melancholy. To- morrow he must die; a tormented, hideous death. A clean death he could face. But the shameful rope; and being cut down half hanged, the entrails torn from his bleeding body while yet he lived! He all-but vomited. And thereafter—no Christian burial; his mutilated body quartered, his head fixed high upon the Bridge— a warning to traitors! He was no traitor, not he! He'd done an honest man's best against a dishonest King. Had Lancaster played his promised part, he'd not be lying here with a filthy death coming hourly nearer. He had grieved to see his uncle die, reduced within a few short months, from sturdy middle manhood to frail old age. Now he wished passionately that he might die likewise, sinking into merciful sleep. No hope of it. Weakened he was; but strong enough to face tomorrow.

Tomorrow . . .

Round and round the thoughts beating through his head, rats in a cage running round and round.

He heard the grind of bolts, heard the key turn; saw the pale light creep, lie along the filthy floor, heard the scamper of vermin away from the light.

The gaoler had brought his food—stale crust, stale water, salted meat.

'Sir,' the fellow said, 'your priest sends word he will confess you; and you may have the barber, also—the rope slides sweeter for a shave.' He laughed and was a little annoyed that the prisoner did not join in the joke. A dull dog, this lord Mortimer! He set down the food; the door clanged, the light went with him.

The prisoner fingered the loathsome food; his belly craved it, yet rose at the smell of it. He put a piece of bread in his mouth; it tasted of mould.

Tomorrow . . . tomorrow . . . tomorrow. How long till tomorrow? Was it—the sickness came up into his throat—already tomorrow? In this dark place one lost track of time. It could not be tomorrow; Orleton had not come, nor yet the barber. . . .

He dozed and woke and dozed again.

Once more the grating of locks, the grinding of bolts.

He awoke in sick terror. They had come to take him to his death!

The gaoler set down the lantern; Orleton came in. He was dressed as a simple monk, his face half-hidden in the cowl; he was carrying the Sacrament. He bade the fellow go. 'Stand where you may see; but on peril of your soul, where you can hear no word. A dying man's confession is between himself and his God. Overhear one word, one word, only, and your soul shall burn in Hell.'

When the fellow had withdrawn, securing lock and bolt, Orleton prepared for Extreme Unction; Mortimer knelt to confession; but it was Orleton that spoke. When all was finished he gathered up the holy vessels, blessed the prisoner and was gone; and the gaoler with him.

Mortimer waited until their footsteps had died away. Slowly, painfully, he struggled to his feet. Amazed he heard no clanking of chains, felt no weight dragging at his legs. The fellow had unlocked the fetters that the prisoner might kneel more seemly and forgotten to fasten them again. Supporting himself against the wall the painful blood forced its way through vein and artery so that he could have cried out with the pain, he yet remembered to thank God for this blessed piece of luck. Presently he sat down in the straw, rubbing his legs to help the circulation. He looked to be the same man as before—gaunt, unshaven, dirty, utterly forlorn; but within him hope screamed like a mad thing. He brought both hands to his mouth to forbid the sound.

Now, now he could eat; *must* eat. But still he could not force himself to the food. Excitement tightened his throat and the food stank. But he needed it to strengthen himself. God had given him his chance—he must not throw it away. Tomorrow he might be free . . . At the thought tears rained down his face.

He sat in the stinking straw and weighed his chances. He was grim, he was determined; he was scarce hopeful. No man had ever escaped the Tower. He stiffened his spirit. Then he would be the first. He was Mortimer of Wigmore and Chirk and he had good friends. And luck was with him—the matter of the fetters had made that clear. But suppose luck had not smiled; suppose it mocked, merely? Suppose they took him on his way to freedom? Of one thing he was certain—there'd be no traitor's death for him! He'd dash his head against a stone wall; or send himself spinning from the top of the keep—if he got so far. He preferred it to spinning on the hangman's rope. Excitement and foul food were making him sick; he thrust down the vomit and waited.

He lay in the dark considering each step in the escape; over and over again. What time was it? Time crept so that he could not tell whether hour after hour passed or minute after minute. He awaited the barber as he waited salvation. Yet how he had hated the fellow with his dirty water and the stinking hands and the blunt razor that took skin as well as beard. Even now there was a nasty place where dirt had caused an open cut to fester. But today . . . today! Let the fellow do his worst—he'd be as welcome as a saint from heaven!

Time unmoving, time eternal.

Sudden, violent in the silence—grinding of bolts, creaking of key. He had expected the moment, longed for the moment; yet the sudden noise shocked his heart into wild beating.

The gaoler put his lantern down in the straw where it gave a faint gleam. 'Master Barber's here, my lord. He's late. But better late than never! Were he much later, though, for you it would be never; come tomorrow there'll be no need to shave!'

The prisoner made a shift to laugh, laughter stuck in his throat like a bone.

'It's good to hear you laugh, sir; now you shall laugh heartier still. Master Ogle has brought you a bottle of wine—a friend sent it. And since tomorrow's the Day—we'll stretch a point as well as a neck!' And he laughed again. 'It's a large bottle. And my lord—' he made a grotesque bow, 'would not wish to go drunk to . . . wherever he's bound; that would never do! So let's drink turn and turn about!'

Ogle, pouring the wine, stumbled in the fitful light; the lantern fell upon its side and went out. Cursing the clumsiness, the gaoler felt for his flint; by the time the lantern was lit and the light steady, wine stood in three mugs. Before the others had set lip to mug, the gaoler's was empty and held out for more.

'Good wine.' He smacked his lips. 'Some body to it!' He held his mug for a third filling. 'Now here's a funny thing! Beer has head and wine has body and man has both . . . till it comes his turn for the axe. But that don't trouble you, my lord!' And again that grotesque bow, unsteady now. 'You keep your head—even if the neck's stretched a bit!' And laughed at his own wit.

Laughing, belching, hiccoughing, the fellow was enjoying himself. In the middle of a lewd joke directed at the prisoner his head nodded; he fell upon the straw.

Mortimer bent to take the keys from the fallen hand. Again he blessed his luck in the matter of the fetters; it had given him extra minutes of time and the blood flowed sweetly in his veins. Luck had played its part; the rest was up to himself.

Ogle stepped from the cell carrying the lantern; alone in the cell, darker now than ever, Mortimer heard his footsteps grow fainter; heard him call a cheerful Goodnight to the guard, heard the answered greeting.

It was the signal. And the moment.

He stepped from darkness into darkness; the man's drugged snores followed him. He locked the door behind him carrying the keys.

To the left. Ten paces Orleton had said. He'd know the direction by the ever-worsening stink. His foot struck against something hard and jagged so that he all but stumbled into the filth of the drain. It was the heavy stone weighting the dangling rope Alspaye had left. A not salubrious climb Orleton had said; he had, Mortimer thought grim, understated the case. But nothing was likely to be cast into the privy tonight; the royal apartments were empty and Segrave out for the night. That, at least, was a blessing!

He cast the key into the drain; let them search for it there! He put his head into the shaft and brought it back at once; it was an instinctive movement of disgust. He took in his breath and began to climb.

He was weaker than he had thought. Hand over slow hand up the slimy alley of the stinking shaft. Time stood still. Soon, grown used to the stink and the darkness, he climbed more quickly. He seemed to be climbing for ever; it seemed as if forever he must climb. How long before he reached the branching of the shaft?

Before ever he reached the first branching he found himself uncertain, confused by excitement, by the long climb and the stink. Two branches Orleton had said; one some ten feet above the other . . . the one led to Segrave's lodgings, the other to the privy of the Queen's apartments. But which?

Which? Which?

He couldn't remember . . . he couldn't remember! Suppose he chose wrong? Suppose he came out in the Governor's lodgings? The odds were that some servant about his business or a man-at-arms would give the alarm. But even if luck held and he met no-one at all, how in the darkness would he find the waiting rope? The directions would be useless . . .

For the moment he felt like weeping. A man could take great

risks, put forth all his courage, all his strength and then! *Which?* On so small a thing his life could hang . . . and hang, indeed!

Climbing fearfully he came upon the first branch. And now he that since childhood had relied upon himself, his own strength, his own wits, breathed the name of God.

That steadied him. And now he remembered. Three steps up from the Queen's bedchamber you came upon the leads. Three steps . . . and then the leads. It was the upper branch.

The short distance seemed endless so that he feared lest in the darkness he had missed the branch. But he came upon it at last. It was narrower than the main shaft and he must force his way through He thanked God for the poor food that had reduced not only his strength but his girth.

A faint light rewarded him; it was the rushlight Alspaye had left. He dragged himself through the mouth of the shaft and up the privy basin. Twenty paces—and he was through the Queen's chamber and up the three stone stairs and out upon the battlements.

For the briefest moment he was lost in wonder at the wide sky and the multitude of stars; a miracle he had never considered before. Moon there was none; he remembered to thank God for this before he leant upon the battlements and vomited. He felt better now though weak and wet through with sweat. He put back the hair from his forehead and one hand upon the coping, walked, counting his steps. At twenty he stopped as he had been told. For the moment he saw nothing and once more could have cried like a child with weakness and disappointment. Then he saw it; the rope well-secured and dangling in the shadow of a buttress. He put out a hand; he could not see the end of it in the darkness, but it felt taut in his hand. It was well-secured below. Alspaye had taken some trouble.

This, this was the supreme test—the downward climb—and be not seen nor heard. But the night was blessedly dark and Alspaye had chosen the place well. Within the deep shadow of the buttress a careful man might well move unseen.

He took the rope in his hand. He stepped over the coping.

He knew the moment's blind panic as he took off. The river,

faint-gleaming in starlight seemed no more than a thread, an immeasurable distance below.

He began the downward climb.

Slowly . . . slowly! It was agony to check his frantic desire to go down quickly and make an end of it . . . and an end, indeed! A swift-moving object could not fail to challenge attention.

The rope slid slowly through his hands; he felt the palms grow hot, swell, blister.

Down . . . down.

The blisters were rubbing raw; the smell of his own stench came up to him. But now he did not care for either. The ground was coming nearer. The worst was over. Soon, soon please God he would be free!

He stood upon blessed ground; almost he could bend to kiss it. Behind him the grim walls went up to the sky; behind him lay the Keep and below it the prison. Before him lay the moat. It was wide, it was deep and it stank; well, to that last he was well-inured.

He slipped into the moat. With slow and silent strokes he made for the other side.

And still the silence held, the blessed silence.

He climbed his careful way out of the moat. He stood upon the strand; before him lay the river . . . the wide river flowing between him and safety.

He turned to the right, he counted a hundred paces. Hidden within the creek he found the boat and within it Alspaye and Ogle.

He had come to the end of his strength. His legs all but gave way. Alspaye put out a hand.

With long, steady strokes, Alspaye and Ogle sent the skiff across to the south bank. The night was still blessedly dark, the muffled oars made no sound. Crouched low, shivering with cold and utter exhaustion, Mortimer could not, even yet, believe his luck.

On the Southwark bank six horsemen were waiting—his own men to be trusted to the death; Orleton, too, had done his part well. Through the night, keeping ever south and west, they galloped; when day broadened they lay hid, at night they rode again. Refreshed and cleansed, good bread-and-meat inside him, Mortimer was his own man again.

And so to Southampton and there a ship was waiting. John de Gisors and Richard de Bettoyne, silk merchants of London, had arranged it all; they owed the lords Despensers a grudge for unjust lightening of their pockets. Across the narrow channel towards the Isle of Wight; let them go seeking Mortimer there! Half-way across they changed course to a ship anchored at the Needles.

And so to France and safety!

Part Three

The Queen and Mortimer
Check to the King

Chapter Twenty-Six

The King, as always, took his bad news badly; first with disbelief and then with a fury that must, until better times, satisfy itself in words. 'We shall comb the country inch by inch—and especially the west and the marches. Louse that he is, he'll not escape my combing!' And anger was the greater that there was no-one to punish. Segrave could not be held responsible; that night he had supped with the Queen—a royal command. Alspaye and the barber were nowhere to be found; true, the wretched turnkey had been well-flogged—and lucky to be alive! But there was little satisfaction in that.

From the first the Despensers suspected the Queen—without reason, as they themselves must admit. She had never set eyes on Mortimer save for that one brief moment he had come to kiss hands; she had never shown the slightest interest in him. Yet Segrave had been commanded from the Tower that particular night—surely cause for suspicion here! But how could a woman carry out such a plan from her closet, a woman alone? It was clearly impossible. And alone she had been! According to Eleanor Despenser she had not walked abroad, had seen no-one for weeks, no-one save . . . her confessor.

Orleton. Orleton again! No friend to the King that one, nor ever had been! They were certain, father and son alike, that the Queen and the bishop knew more than a little of the matter. They could prove nothing . . . at present; but for proof they would not cease to look.

These days Isabella walked with care. She showed concern that the King's enemy had escaped; that all their searching had come to nothing. No flaw in her behaviour. The Despensers suspected her yet more strongly; her subtlety they had long recognised. They must content themselves, for the time being, with a second petition to Rome praying for the dissolution of the King's marriage and the unseating of Orleton of Hereford.

Mortimer was in Paris. Charles le Bel, Isabella's brother, made much of him—as indeed he might. Mortimer, famous captain, was pledged to serve the French King, to fight for him at need. Alspaye, too, was in France where his pleasant manners were already serving him better than in London. Ogle was another to find Paris to his taste. He had set himself up as a barber, gotten himself a wife and turned respectable citizen.

Suspicion that could not be proved deepened the Despensers' hatred against the Queen. One day . . . one day they would have her head! Until that happy time they made her life unendurable—and not with insult alone. Now it was clear persecution. By their advice her lands—lands of the Queen's dower—were sequestered; her income pared to the bone. At times she was hard put to it to order a new pair of shoes. Worse than robbing her of her money, they robbed her of the last of her friends. Everyone she trusted was removed; even Madam de St. Pierre, dear, comfortable friend, sent back to France—a mischief-maker, the King said. Despenser toadies were set in their place; and, chief of her ladies—Eleanor Despenser. Now the Queen was all alone; in her household not a single soul her friend.

But for all that her courage was high. She had proved herself to herself. No man save Mortimer had ever escaped the Tower; but then no man before had a Queen to be his saviour! It was she that had planned every step in this dangerous enterprise; she that had persuaded from their duty a prince of the church and an officer of the Tower. For all the persecution, all the humiliation she must endure, hope rose in her like a flower from the bud. Mortimer was safe and she would triumph; the mystic bond held them still.

And hope she needed. Eleanor Despenser had not sweetened with the years. Embittered by neglect, harshly used if she did not bring sufficient information she now did her once-unwilling work with zest; and when there was nothing to report, she still had a tale to carry to her master. Eleanor, once scrupulous and fine, was her husband's victim no less than the Queen.

The Pope had refused both requests. There were no grounds for dissolving the marriage, none for unseating the bishop. For both these things the Queen thanked God on her knees; but still she prayed that her life might be less penurious, less circumscribed, less humiliating, less dangerous. For this wretchedness she must blame her husband; he was too weak of will to say *No* to his friends, too over-loving to see through them, too little-loving to protect his wife. When she thought of him her anger rose strong as poison. She was turned thirty; she was a woman and no nun. She was weary of loneliness and of her empty bed; weary of penury, weary of watching herself in every word and deed. Would there never be an end? She saw no hope but in a miracle.

And suddenly there was an end; the miracle had happened— such a miracle as she had not admitted to her wildest dreams. God had remembered her.

She was for France; for France with the King's goodwill. For France, dear land of her birth; for France and her brother—little Charles with whom she had once played and now, unbelievably King of France. And best of all Théophania, dear comfortable Théophania. To Mortimer she gave no more than a passing thought. Him she did not expect to see; he had been sent with an army into Gascony. These days she could think of nothing save her journey into France—France where she need not watch every word, where she would be esteemed as a Queen and as a woman. She would tell her brother of the way she had been treated—her lands, her incomes sequestered, of the humiliations and the insults—and he would see her righted. He was King of France and her husband's overlord in right of Gascony, Aquitaine and Ponthieu.

And that was the key to the miracle.

Edward had paid no homage for his French possessions since her father's death; and some excuse there had been. Her eldest brother had come to the throne and then her second; they had reigned so short a time; death had excused Edward from his homage.

Now there was no excuse. Her youngest brother wore the crown—and there'd been time and time enough. But, as always, Edward was unwilling so to affront his pride. Now, unless homage were paid and at once, Charles threatened to take Gascony, Aquitaine and Ponthieu back to himself. That Mortimer was already in Gascony with an armed force showed it to be no idle threat.

To Isabella it seemed as though fate forever set Mortimer against her husband. Did he know of her part in his escape? She thought not; she had ordered Alspaye and Orleton to hold their tongue—though that they would have done without her command; the affair was dangerous. Whether he knew or not mattered little—she was not likely to see him; yet she would have liked to see him—the man her own wits had saved.

She brought her thoughts back to the matter in hand.

Edward had sent an embassy to Paris, but it wasn't having much success. Nor could it. It was trying to pacify Charles—and no promise of homage. And then from the Pope, from the Pope himself the request. Let Madam the Queen go to France; already she had proved herself a peace-maker. Let her make peace between brother and husband. She must, she supposed, thank Orleton for that! From France the unsuccessful envoys welcomed the Pope's request and the King's Council supported it. To her joyful surprise the Despensers made no objection—they were glad to be rid of her. They believed she would fail in her mission. She would return discredited . . . if she returned at all. Either way would please them.

All the time the matter was being discussed she, herself, had said no word. When, at last, the King made his will known she said, neither eyes nor mouth betraying her overwhelming joy. 'Sir, in this, as in all things, I am the King's obedient servant.'

Now preparations were on hand. Had there ever been difficulty about the Queen's expenses? Now the master of her gowns was summoned together with her tailors and her silk merchants. Now she was to be dressed as befitted a Queen. Had arms and throat and head gone bare of jewels? Now there was no lack; her casket overflowed. Never let it be seen in France that she was treated unqueenly.

It was a gay company that set forth—the Despensers and their spies left behind. In Dover harbour lay the royal ship fresh-painted, fresh gilt, standards flying and her seamen all in new clothes. On the ninth of March in the year of grace thirteen hundred and twenty-five the Queen sailed.

And what was to become of that sailing no man could foresee nor the Queen herself imagine.

She leaned upon the bulwarks; she saw the cliffs of Dover fall away on the skyline; she felt the sad years fall away with them. How had she so long endured her life in bitter England?

And now, quite suddenly, the death of her father and of her brothers that, in England, had seemed to touch her little, broke upon her afresh. She was filled with grief, as though going home to the new-dead. There was surprise in her grief and some pleasure. She had thought her heart withered in England.

Charles received her with joy; a pleasant young man, very handsome, the little boy still lurking on his pouting mouth. He had ridden to Calais with a great train to do her honour. Now he begged her to excuse his Queen; she was pregnant once more and the physician had ordered her into the country until the child should be born. Already she had lost two children in pregnancy and Charles was troubled about the succession. Isabella murmured her regrets and wishes for mother and child. She was not sorry Jeanne was not to be in Paris; Jeanne of Evreux was a noted beauty, Isabella preferred to shine alone.

Now from Calais through the countryside of home the procession rode where peasants flocked with blessings to greet their long lost princess; and out came the seigneurs riding to kneel in homage, to bring her with love into their castles.

Paris at last; Paris with its walls and towers and churches; with its numberless bridges crossing the river bright as a riband; the smell of the Seine, the almost forgotten stench, came up to her sweet as roses.

In the great hall of St. Pol she sat to receive homage and greetings. She looked—gold head to foot and hung with jewels—like an image; no Christian image Madam de St. Pierre thought, but like some heathen idol. Gracious and smiling she received them all—relatives and old friends; the unsuccessful envoys, and Englishmen exiled or discontented. Madam de St. Pierre, unable to take her eyes from this beloved child, saw the long jewelled fingers stiffen upon the golden gown.

The lord Mortimer of Wigmore had come to kiss his Queen's hand.

Save for the stiffening of that hand—the only sign of her whole body braced against the shock—Isabella sat motionless. The heavy gold of her gown hid the panic pulses of her heart. It was as though he laid his hand upon her naked breast. She felt it leap like a wild, frightened thing beneath the hunter's hand. And all the time she asked herself *Why?* Why this tumult in all her blood? But even in this moment she remembered to guard her eyes. She glanced at him; no more. But in that brief glance she saw how he stood out from all the rest, for all their fine clothes; stood out even above her handsome brother—this sturdy, stocky man in the leather jerkin and plain cloak. His eyes were unchanged—grey and cold and wary. He wore a little beard that, she thought, became him vastly; the reddish hair he still wore cropped showing the handsome shape of his head—the one handsome thing about him.

He dropped upon his knee; he saluted her hand no more nor less than was proper. Yet when his lips came down cold and heavy upon her hand, arrows of sweet pain pierced her through and through, pierced through heart and breasts, drove into the very womb. She was faint with such desire she had never known. Beneath the ecstasy she sat rigid; ecstasy . . . and fear; fear of the thing that had fallen upon her. And all the time the clamour of the flesh deafened her to reason, to duty. *I starve and only he can feed me. I saved him once; now let him save me. Sweet Mary let him know the passion and the bond* . . . and did not know she blasphemed.

He lifted his head; she saw the cold eyes pricked with desire that was not love. Well, so he fed her now she would be content.

Through all the day's high ceremonies she was obsessed by him. Lust alone moved him—she did not deceive herself; lust and lust alone. But that lust she knew well how to play upon, to sweeten with ambition; a Queen's power to give more than love to an ambitious man. And she cared not at all about Jeanne that loved him and had borne his children—Mortimer's wife that had been her friend. As a wolf obeying its nature thirsts for blood, so she for the body of this man.

Chapter Twenty-Seven

Mortimer had wasted no time. That first night of their meeting he had come to her bed. And it was all unexpectedly easy; Charles, in sentimental mood, had given her the apartments they had shared as children; a wing at St. Pol where an outer stairway ran direct to the ruelle of her bedchamber.

That first night, when they had made love and she lay beside him longing to be taken again, she said, seeking to rouse him once more, When you saw me first—at Westminster, what did you think of me?'

'Nothing. You were the Queen and not in my sights.'

'And when you saw me today?'

'A handsome piece and a hot one; the way I like a woman.'

'Did you not think Here's a Queen for my bed?' she asked piqued.

'A Queen's like any other woman in bed; no better than she proves herself!'

'Do I prove myself?'

He looked at her naked and lovely and all soft with desire. 'You do well enough!' And he'd give no woman the advantage.

She stretched herself against him; he smelt the scent of vanilla. She was sweeter in her habits, he thought, than most!

'You do well enough,' he told her again; and now, desire swelling, said, 'Or so I think. Come, let's try again!'

She loved him because he made no flowery speeches; he was forthright, simple in his lovemaking; but more because he satisfied her yet left her desirous still.

When they lay back waiting till desire should take them again, he said, 'You are better than all women—and not because you are a Queen. You are wild as a gypsy and fresh as a virgin!' he slid his hand between her thighs.

A little later she asked him if he had known it was she that had saved him from the Tower.

'I did not know. I marvelled whose wits had planned it, whose tongue persuaded others into so dangerous an enterprise. I might have guessed it was a woman—a woman in love.'

'I was not in love—not then. I did not know you.'

'No woman—and certainly no Queen—risks what you risked save for love. Certainly you were in love—and, I fancy, you knew it!'

'It was not love. It was fear . . . fear for us both. I felt our luck rose and fell together. But now it is love; love for ever!'

'For ever's a long time,' he said and took her again; it could not happen too often for her pleasure.

She lifted herself upon an elbow and looked down with doting love upon the closed eyes that, in the act of love, stared amused into her own. She doted upon every wrinkle in the strong, brutal face, every thread in the greying hair. The Tower had taken toll of his youth, but of his manhood, nothing. She doted upon the strong body, upon the arms and legs that, like steel, clipped her close. She delighted in his maleness; the smell of his sweat and of his love-making intoxicated her. After they had made love it was her habit to lie watching him willing him to take her again. Nor did repetition lessen pleasure; rather it deepened delight. Now, in pretended sleep, he knew how her eyes devoured his nakedness. He opened an amused eye, grinned and stretched out a hand.

She lay beneath him delighting in the vicious thrusting of his body. She thought of her husband's indolent, insolent performance —love-making she could not call it—with anger, with disgust. She was thirty-one, she had been married full seventeen years; and only now had she been satisfied. She had come at last into her woman's inheritance. For this she gave him not passion alone but an almost servile gratitude.

What must become of this she could not think. That she could part from him so lately, so wonderfully found, she could not accept. He was here now, within her, part of her own body. That he should come to England could not be; his life was forfeit. She must not think of the future; still less of the past when she had lain shamed by her husband's indolence. She must think of the present, only—that she lay with her lover in her own land of France. She must live in the present; she must make the present stretch as far as possible.

Charles spared no honour, no pleasure, for his sister. There were hunting-parties and tournaments, there were feasts and games, there was music and dancing. When Mortimer saluted her Queen of Love and Beauty she was happier than when they had crowned her Queen of England, happier, even, than when she had borne the heir to the crown; that last had brought her added consequence, yet like all her child-bearing had been a duty still. Now she understood a woman's need to bear a child to the man she loves. She wished with all her passionate blood that she might bear Mortimer a child; for this she would welcome the discomforts of pregnancy, the dangers of labour. But—she reckoned the time since the King had come to her bed—she dared not.

These days she was beautiful enough to make a man catch his breath. She was all a flame; she that had been quiet and pale—an unlit lamp—was now lit with the joy that burned within her. The amber-green eyes glowed like a cat's in the dark, her mouth showed ardent, red and full. Madam de St. Pierre watched, troubled. How to keep back the gossip whispered upon all tongues? And when would that whisper become a shout to be heard across the sea, to give the Despensers the longed-for grounds to set the Queen aside?

But she, once so subtle, had lost herself in love. It was as though she believed that in the sea that flowed between England and France all scandal must be drowned. Théophania tried to make clear to the Queen the danger she courted.

'Madam, you are a Queen and an honoured guest; and here, in Paris, we take kindness between . . . friends, lightly. But in England it is another matter. Who would make light of kindness between the King's wife and the King's enemy? Certainly not the Despensers. They would—and could—make it matter enough to dissolve your marriage. Then—forgive me, Madam, if I put it plain, I speak with the tongue of love—you would no longer be welcome here in France. We French are a shrewd people; we know how to jump with the times.'

The Queen said nothing. Only her eyes narrowed; there was about her an almost greedy look.

Théophania watched deeply troubled. It was hard to blame the Queen; her life had been loveless and harsh, her young womanhood run to waste. Yet there would be plenty to blame her—and not only her enemies. Censure would spread throughout Christendom. Then, however unwilling, the Pope must speak. Let her look to her marriage and her crown!

Théophania's words had served as a warning of another kind— the shortness of time; the need to waste no moment. Now the hours of night were not enough; now Isabella must make her chances, stealing away from feast or hunt, drawing Mortimer with her to take their pleasure when and where they would. She was growing thin, her beauty fine drawn; she was burning herself up with passion. That Mortimer's passion was neither deep nor true, nor yet lasting, she knew well; she had caught him by his lust and his ambition. This was her first experience of love; it was by no means his. He had taken women wherever he found them; not only in his own marches but all the way from Paris to Gascony and back again. He had told her so, not boasting but mentioning it lightly—his male right. She would tell herself she did not care— other women were so much cattle; never before had he won a Queen to his bed. Besides herself all women must pale. But for all that she was, at times, eaten with jealousy of those unknown women. But it was nothing like the jealousy that tormented her on account of the woman she did know. Now she remembered Jeanne was his wife, the mother of his children; to whom he owed an affection, a loyalty that must hold him for life. All other women, the Queen included—were but women; his wife was his wife. When Isabella thought of Jeanne she was eaten as by a canker.

At times jealousy drove her to excite him with lewd words, to touch him with erotic fingers; and then, though she herself fainted with longing, to hold him off. It was always she that surrendered first, yet not until she had roused him to brutality, a brutality she savoured with delight, crying out with joy in the pain.

Brutal she could make him but never tender, never loving; always he was cold, half-amused. Sometimes in the crisis of their love-making he would abruptly stop—it was a game two could play—telling her that she burned herself out with passion; that within a few years there'd be nothing worth any man's taking. They knew, both of them, that he played upon her secret fear; it made her love him ever more slavishly. She was sick with dread of losing him. He gave her no cause for jealousy. He was not yet tired of her; she was beautiful, she was passionate, and in spite of all disclaimer, there was pride in having for his mistress a Queen.

Gossip was growing louder. Isabella did not care. This was not England; this was France where such things were better understood. Meanwhile there was the business on which she had been sent. Charles was willing enough to be reasonable—he was not a quarrelsome young man; but that would settle the affair far too soon to please his sister. 'The King of England is bound to pay homage for his French lands,' she told him. 'If of your courtesy you spare him this, how shall it go with the other lords great and small that hold land of you?'

Yes, he saw the wisdom of that! To England went his letter.

The King of France, your suzerain, agrees that all your possessions in France . . . shall be restored to you as soon as you, yourself, come to pay homage. Until that homage be paid, the King of France holds them in charge. Out of love for our very dear sister we grant you until the first day of the eighth month of this year, thirteen hundred and twenty five.

Four months; four months to enjoy her love. In four months much could happen!

Edward, they heard, had fallen into a fine Plantagenet rage. And the Despensers encouraged him. *If the King of England cross into France his armies shall pay homage for him!* they declared.

'Oh,' Isabella said and she was laughing—she laughed easily

these days, 'men he may collect and ships make ready—and there they'll stay, his side of the Channel. Fighting; he loathes it. And even had he a mind to it the Despensers would not trust him out of their sight. Stay in England without the King? They dare not. Without his protection they'd not live a day. The barons would see to it. And let the barons delay, the mob would tear them in pieces. I tell you he'll not come!'

She was right. The Despensers spoke They would not again permit the King to leave England. And more; any man that should advise him to cross into France they would hang—a traitor.

'Is my brother of England so weak as to allow it?' Charles asked. 'Has he no shame in the eyes of Christendom?'

'He'll find the way to save his face!'

August. And the King of England ill; too ill to cross the sea.

She had expected it; she knew her man. Her plan was ready; a plan simple, reasonable, excellent.

'Brother,' she said, 'the King of England is ill. But, well or ill, you'd get no good of him. His word's not worth the breath with which he speaks. But . . . suppose he agree to send my son in his place? Suppose he send the Prince of Wales? Ned's a boy; but he stands to his word like a man!' And waited, breath indrawn, for the answer.

'Only the man that holds the land can pay homage,' Charles said. She had known the answer; the only answer. She was ready.

'Suppose my lord husband agree that you grant the lands not to him, but to my son; would that suffice?'

'It would suffice.'

She had won. With wile and guile she had won. Her body could scarce contain its triumph. She knew well that whatever her husband might feel about letting these lands pass to his son, the Despensers would force him to it. They would move heaven and earth to keep their protector in England . . . they had not forgotten the fate of Gaveston!

Chapter Twenty-Eight

The Prince should come; her husband had agreed.

'We shall have the prince in our hands!' she told Mortimer. 'Now we shall make our own terms with my lord husband!' And she made of those last words an insult. 'God has been good, my love! He sent me back to France, He gave us to each other; and now He sends me my son that we may set the King and his accursed friends dancing to our tune.'

Mortimer's lips lifted in a grin; it gave him the wolfish look that excited her. 'It is like a woman to besmirch her husband's honour, to enjoy her love—and then to proclaim it from God! It is like a woman to plot with her lover to dispose of her husband—and thank God for it.'

'Dispose of the King! I have never said it!' Nor, indeed, had she. By making terms she had meant little but staying in France and enjoying her paramour; or, at most, bringing him back pardoned that she might enjoy him still.

'Do you play innocent?' Mortimer cried out. Rough with disappointment that ambition had leapt too far, he pulled her down upon the bed. She gave herself up with ecstasy—an ecstasy forever tinged with melancholy—he was a man soon to tire; the longer she could satisfy his ambition, the longer he would satisfy her body. That ambition she must feed little by little; for ambition satisfied he'd make no bones about leaving her. She was more than ever aware, that let him be never so deep in love—which was not likely—he would never lose sight of the claims of wife and family. He was of great family and that family, in the end, must come first. But she? For love of him she would sacrifice husband and children. *But not the crown; not the crown.* Even in her moments of ecstasy she knew it; that was a treachery her royal blood could not allow.

The Prince's first journey from home. The King was concerned as to how the boy would bear himself; he gave his instructions and his warnings. The Prince listened with respect; but when the younger Despenser sought to add his lessons, the boy turned away with scant ceremony.

He was thirteen. He did not perfectly understand the relations between those two, he fancied, though, it might not stand to his father's credit. But he knew perfectly well what all England knew— that the Despensers, father and son, commanded the King; and for that he hated them. He loved his father; as a little boy he had delighted in the presents—the hound, the horse, the little ship carved by the King's own hand. Now, at thirteen, he loved his father still—the handsome man, generous and loving to his children, skilled in every sport, kindly to all, save when his Plantagenet rage took hold of him—a failing the boy knew he must look to in himself. But most of all he hated the Despensers because they had insulted his mother; they had caused her great unhappiness, they had made a division between her and his father. He loved his parents equally; and that love the Despensers had tried to corrupt. With them, as far as was in his power, he'd have nothing to do!

He was overjoyed to be journeying into France; he had never left home before and he was, besides, half a Frenchman. He had heard from his mother of the glories of France, the gaiety of the court; and above all he longed to see his mother again. And he wanted to see Mortimer—there was a hero if you like! Mortimer had escaped the Tower—*how* nobody knew; that would be a tale worth hearing! He was Prince of Wales and heir to the throne; but he was only thirteen and ready as any boy to hero-worship.

He was to sail on the twelfth day of September; Stapledon, good bishop of Exeter and one of the few men the King could trust, should have him in charge.

Isabella pulled a face when she heard that last. 'This Stapledon the prim-prude—he never liked me! When I think of the tales he could carry back, I tremble.'

'He may not live to carry them!' Mortimer said, amiable.

'God is good; but not, I doubt, *so* good!'

'Then we must help Him a little.' At her surprised look his lips lifted in that wolfish grin.

The Prince had arrived at Boulogne. He had been met by his mother and a great retinue; now he was on his way to Paris and his uncle. He was charming everyone with his young courtesy, his grave bearing; and then, suddenly, by his boyish pleasure, his clear young laughter. He had not the handsome look of the Capets nor yet of his father; but he was so fresh, so honest, so ready to please and be pleased. Isabella presented her charming well-mannered boy to her brother with pride. Young, honest and innocent; gossip lowered its voice as he went by.

He was surprised to find that he did not like Mortimer; he had come prepared to hero-worship; and he smarted with disappointment. He no longer wanted to hear of the wonderful escape; unlike his mother he was not taken by that wolfish grin. He was surprised, also, to find the man so often in private conversation with her. Nor did he like the way Mortimer carried himself towards his mother, Madam the Queen of England. The man had a way of touching her—shoulder or hand; and once it was her breast. That she did not countenance such behaviour was clear in the quick flush of her cheek and the sharp glance of her eye. She bore with it, the boy supposed, out of her courtesy. But—could she not see it? —Mortimer was, in his way, no less disrespectful than the Despensers themselves.

'I do not like this Mortimer,' he told Stapledon, 'neither the man nor his manners. I would to God he were still fast-locked within the Tower!'

'You must make some allowance for the manners of France!' He tried to calm the boy; but for all that the good bishop was troubled. The Queen of England's behaviour did not, to say the least of it, consort with the dignity of the throne; he must indeed condemn it—a mortal sin.

Young and guileless the boy might be, but he was no fool. He had caught a scrap of conversation between his mother and Mortimer and, puzzled though he was, knew how to put two-and-two together.

'My lord bishop,' he said, and was careful how he chose his words, 'I think you are . . . perhaps . . . safer in England.'

Stapledon looked up sharply. The King's friend, he had been looked upon sourly by Madam Queen Isabella. 'You know something, sir?'

'I know nothing; but I fear much. You should leave France, my lord, as soon as you may. Would to God I might go with you!' Walter Stapledon asked no more question; he would put no further strain upon the boy's loyalty. He, himself, had felt some malice —and the boy was neither a mischiefmaker nor a fool. Stapledon was not one to waste time. Leaving his retinue behind he travelled post haste through the night. By daylight he had reached the coast and found, by good fortune, a ship on the point of departure.

The King of England listened to my lord bishop with dismay.

That the Queen had cuckolded him with Mortimer he did not for a moment believe. Royal pride forbade such belief! But that she had been indiscreet was only too clear; foolish, she had smeared her honour and his own. For the first time he began to question whether there had not been something between those two—his enemy and his Queen? The Despensers had thought so; he remembered their suspicions. Had her hand, after all, been in the fellow's escape? He could not forbear mentioning it to Hugh the Younger, asking his question and himself answering it. 'No, no! It could not be! And why should it be? They have set eyes upon each other once and once only!'

'Once is enough for mischief between men and women!' Despenser said.

Despenser had planted the barb; and the King could not withdraw it. The Queen was a snake, a serpent. She must not be left where she could work her mischief. She must be commanded home at once.

Twenty-first day of September, in the year of grace thirteen hundred and twenty-five, the Prince of Wales, handsomely attended, went in procession to Bois-le-Vincennes to pay homage for Gascony. Proud, yet somehow humble, high upon the great white horse, he made a gallant showing; and as he went, there were cheers and blessings for the boy from England, so courteous and so debonair.

Isabella's pleasure in the longed-for event was spoilt. This homage, this peace was of her making; others had failed but she and she alone had brought it about. And now, the weak-willed fool her husband that had not lifted a finger in the matter, had dared summon her home; home to the insults—and worse maybe, that the Despensers chose to put upon her. He had commanded her to leave this court where she was treated with all a Queen's dignity, where she was happy; this court and her lover.

'Sir,' she told her brother when, somewhat unwilling, he reminded her of her wifely duties, 'I am not truly married; nor any way a wife. Marriage is a joining together of man and woman—a sharing of flesh and spirit. These wicked men, these Despensers have come between my lord and me. It is they, not I, that break the bond. The father sows his discord so that my husband is divorced from me in spirit; as for the flesh, I am banished my husband's bed. Shame it is to say it, yet the thing must be said—the son takes my place therein. They have made me a widow, flesh and spirit.'

Something of this he had known, and had shown her the more kindness. Now, when he questioned her she said, 'Brother, I fear the Despensers; I fear them for my life. Since they could not break my marriage one way, they mean to do it another. They have it in mind to put me to death; and they will do it, too. They hate me because I would stand between them and the King to protect him.'

Edward wrote courteously requesting the return of his wife; Charles made a reluctant stand.

The Queen came here of her own will and may freely return if she chooses. But, if she choose to remain, she is my sister and I refuse to send her away.

And, Edward writing more urgently, Charles replied,

I cannot permit her to return to you unless she is guaranteed from evil that is meditated against her by the Despensers . . .

Isabella awaited the next move. What she had told her brother was true. She did fear the Despensers—and with good cause. But what she had not told him was equally true. Were the impossible to happen; were Edward to dismiss the Despensers and seek his wife again, she'd have none of him. 'Share his crown, I would!' She told Théophania, breast heaving, eyes aflame 'Share his board—that also if I must. But share his bed—never!'

No need to say it. Théophania understood perfectly. The Queen belonged to Mortimer. She was a woman in love for the first time; and, Théophania would swear, for the last. One could grieve at such folly, such fall from grace; one could disapprove. But one could not blame. Her husband despised her, her lover lusted after her, both alike insulting her womanhood. Between husband and herself—a gulf no woman could cross. Between lover and herself some human warmth, a giving and a taking. For so long spirit had starved with flesh. Was it not possible that, satisfying flesh, she might feed spirit also; through mortal sin to come at last to some excellence of soul? Théophania sighed. The matter was beyond her.

Isabella explained to her son why she dared not return home. She must, she knew, be careful what she said; he disliked Mortimer and made no secret of it.

'It is the Despensers; accursed father, accursed son. Let me return and nothing would save me from death! Your father promises me safety; but in his heart he sees no need of such a promise. A foolish woman's whim he thinks it. Well I cannot blame him; a man must trust his friends!' And she was too clever to belittle father to son. 'But let him turn his back a moment, let him but close his eyes—and goodbye Queen!'

He saw that she was shivering a little and put a comforting hand upon hers. 'I hate them, also. When I am older—let my father do what he will—I will make an end of them for you. And Madam, dear mother, till there's no more danger stay in France, I beseech you; come home no more.'

Edward was bewildered by his wife's accusations. Danger to her life! What nonsense; none but a foolish woman could have thought of it. She had been angry with his two Hughs—and, perhaps, not unnaturally. But beyond sequestering her lands and cutting down her incomes—and both dictated by needful economy—they had done nothing to her hurt. All this he must make clear to his brother of France.

. . . You have been told, dearest brother, that our companion the Queen of England, dare not return to us, being in peril of her life from Hugh le Despenser. Certainly, dearest brother, she cannot have fear of him, or any other person in our realm. By God, if Hugh or any other man alive in our dominions would wish to do her ill and it came to our knowledge, we would chastise him in such a manner that it would be an example to all others . . .

'But it would not come to his knowledge,' Isabella told her brother. 'They would see it did not; they are sly and secret as the grave.'

Charles nodded. He went on reading.

We beseech you, dearly beloved brother, that you will be pleased for your honour and ours and more especially for that of our consort, to return her to us with all speed, for certainly we have been ill at ease for want of her company in which we have such delight . . .

'Such delight!' she cried out. 'By God he is forsworn!'

. . . And if our surety is not enough . . .

'It is not enough!' she cried out.

. . . then let her come on pledge of your good faith in me . . .

'There is no faith. Brother, be warned. There's no pledge can stand against the lies of the Despensers!' And she wrung her hands.

'My brother of England asks also for his son; with that you can have no quarrel. Listen.

. . . and we pray you suffer him to come to us with all speed for we have often sent for him and have great need of his counsel . . .'

'His counsel—and he but thirteen!' And now she was openly mocking both writer and letter. 'Need of a hostage; more like, a hostage to bring me back! I take this to be further proof—if proof were needed—of Despenser perfidy and his own great foolishness.'

Letters. Letters. Letters.

Autumn gave way to winter, yet still there was no respite. Isabella had come to dread the arrival of the messengers; she wondered how long her brother would endure the perpetual bombardment.

And still it went on.

Edward, King of England, to Isabella Queen and consort.

Lady we have often informed you of our great desire to have you with us; and of our grief at your long absence. You do us great mischief by this. Therefore we will that you come to us with all speed and without further excuses. Before the homage was performed you made that your excuse. Now you will not come for fear of the Despensers . . .

Again, again the Despensers! Again the protestations that never had they shown her aught but honour. *Aught but honour!* And they daring their reproof in the King's own presence; and all the time Edward sitting there and nodding and smiling. Had either of those two lifted a hand to strike her, still he would have gone on smiling. What safety if she were fool enough to return? She struck upon the letter with the flat of her hand. *What safety?*

And now it was the Prince's turn.

From Edward King of England to Edward Prince of Wales.

Very dear son, as you are young and of tender age we remind you of that with which we charged you at your departure. You answered then, as you know, with goodwill, that you would not disobey any one of our injunctions at any point, for anyone. Since your homage has been received by our dearest brother the King of France, be pleased to take your leave of him and return to us with all speed in company of your mother. If she will not come then come *you without further delay.* Stay not for your mother nor for anyone else on our blessing.

Given at Westminster on the second day of December, in the year of grace thirteen hundred and twenty-five.

Letters. Letters. Letters.

Letters written in anger and in anger received. And all the time the French court abuzz; sly words and laughter behind hands. *The Queen of England does her husband wrong; like any strumpet she'll not leave her lover nor return to that honest good man her husband.* So quickly does the weather-cock of regard turn with every wind!

The young Edward knew not what to do. His mother must not return to the anger of his father, to the hatred of the Despensers. But himself? His father had charged him to delay no longer. A son must obey his father, a prince his King; too long already he had disobeyed. But a son must protect his mother, a prince his Queen . . . and her enemies sought to make of him a hostage. He could not believe his father would use a son to injure his mother. But the Despensers might! He saw that very plain.

The gossip had reached his ear at last and he knew not what to think. *She is not to blame.* It was his first thought; she was his mother and he loved her, his Queen, and he honoured her. True he had often found those two alone . . . and the air uneasy for his coming. He had seen for himself the man's familiarity; but in his mother nothing save a gentle dignity. He did not blame her now, not even after last night, when, troubled by this last letter from his father, he had gone somewhat late to ask her advice. He had heard voices from within; and a fellow wearing the Mortimer livery had suggested, with deep respect, that the lord Prince wait until morning. It was late and Madam the Queen at her prayers. Did God then, answer in a man's voice familiar with the ring of the west country? And why did Mortimer's men guard the Queen's door?

He had pushed the fellow aside. He had found his mother rising from her knees; she was, he noticed, naked beneath her bedgown which was not usual this winter weather. She was flushed; she had not the look of a praying woman; and the bed had a tumbled look, as if rising to pray she had hastily smoothed the covers. He

THE QUEEN AND MORTIMER 237

had felt himself an intruder; he had turned and gone without a word.

Now, all day, he had been wondering whether the fellow at the door had not raised his voice in warning . . . there was an outer staircase behind her bedhead and there had, he remembered now, been a slight draught as though someone leaving hastily had left the door ajar.

The voice, the tumbled bed, the draught of wind . . .

He was taken with anger against his mother for so belittling her dignity as to receive the owner of that voice alone. He dared not listen to his own inner voice that whispered something worse of her; he was still very young. It was Mortimer that received the full measure of his hatred; Mortimer that cared so little for her good name that he gave scandal yet more to feed upon. Now she must be made to return at once, to give the lie to foul gossip. Once safe at home he would breathe no word about last night for fear of his father, for fear of the Despensers. No great harm had been done; when she was gone the talk would soon die. Yes, he would carry her at once to England where Mortimer could never come.

Chapter Twenty-Nine

Edward of England was angry. It was not the quick Plantagenet rage but a deep slow-burning anger that spoiled his sleep and ruined his pleasure. The year had moved to Spring; more than a twelve-month since she had gone, this wife of his that thumbed her nose so that all Christendom laughed. He had no use for a wife, they said.

'She stays in Paris enjoying her paramour and seeking to blind me with excuses!' he told the younger Hugh. 'That she fears you I don't for a moment believe—she has no cause. She went into France to make peace and peace she has made. But if she doesn't return and soon, that peace shall be broken; and it is we, we ourselves, that shall break it!' He looked up at the young man, wondering how the Queen could pretend to fear so loving a creature; he missed, as always, the coldness of those eyes.

'Sir,' Hugh told him, 'there's news from France. There's talk, that Madam the Queen—' and he was careful to speak with respect, 'is arranging a French marriage for the lord Prince of Wales.'

He had the satisfaction of seeing the King leap from his chair.

'I do not believe it. She knows that we negotiate a match with Spain! No, I cannot believe it, double-dealer though she be!'

He set to pacing backwards and forwards.

'She knows that matters are advanced for betrothal with Castile; that already we have asked the Pope's dispensation. Can she be ready to offer this insult to Spain! Instead of the hand of friendship we shall have the hand of war!'

Backwards and forwards driven by his anger.

'Always she sets herself against me; against my friends, my advisers and my heart's desires. Play me false in this! Never! I tell you, never! I charged my son upon my blessing, to enter into no marriage-contract without my consent . . .'

He paused trying to calm himself. 'I must write; I must write at once, put an end to her mischief before she does yet more harm. I must charge my son . . .' He took his head in his hands. 'I cannot think . . . I cannot think! Find me the words.'

Despenser hid the smile. Every letter, temperate or angry, he had dictated to the King. He began now, in his clear high voice.

Edward, fair son, remember well the charge we gave you not to contract marriage nor suffer it to be contracted for you without our knowledge and consent. Remember, also, at your departure from Dover you said it would be your pleasure to obey our commands, as far as you could, all your days. Fair son, if you have done this you have done well; if not, then you cannot avoid the wrath of God, the reproach of men and our own indignation. For no other thing you could do would cause greater injury and pain of heart to me . . .

You seem to say you cannot return because of your mother. It causes me great uneasiness of heart that you are not allowed to do what is your natural duty, the neglect of which must lead to great mischief.

Despenser's voice came slow, and slower. So far the King had allowed no slur upon the Queen to be made to her son; might not this be the time? Voice gentle, he continued.

You know how dearly she would have been loved and cherished if she had come timely according to her duty . . .

Edward looked up and smiled; how well Hugh understood.

Despenser took in his breath; he knew well how to play upon the King. Now was the time to accuse the Queen!

We have knowledge of her evil doings to our sorrow. We know how she devises pretences for absenting herself from us, saying it is on account of our faithful Hugh . . .

Yes, the King was writing it, every word, save that he had added *dear* to *faithful*.

. . . our dear and faithful Hugh who has always so well and truly served us, while you . . .

And now was the moment to test his power over the King, to make an end of the ridiculous courtesy towards this hateful, dangerous woman.

> . . . Fair son, you—and all the world with you—have seen how openly, notoriously, and knowing it to be contrary to her duty, and against the welfare of our crown, she has attracted to herself and retains in her company Mortimer, our traitor and mortal foe, proved, attainted and adjudged. And him she accompanies in the house and abroad . . .

The King nodded, mournful; another man had stolen the thing that was his own. Want her he did not; need her he did. He needed her to ride by his side, be seen with him, seen by all at his side. He needed a Queen; and he needed *this* Queen, that the people so unaccountably loved. Remaining from him she lessened him in the eyes of his people. She did him great injury.

Despenser's voice drove him on.

> And worse than this she has done—if worse could be! She has allowed you to herd with our said enemy in the eyes of the world, thus doing very great dishonour to yourself and to us and to the crown itself.

Despenser stopped. The King had allowed it, allowed the word *herd* with all it suggested. Now his voice came hard, deliberate.

> Therefore, sweet son, desist from a part which is so shameful and may be dangerous to you in many ways. We are not pleased with you. Your mother has written to us that, if you wish to return she will not prevent it. Do not then delay to come to us. Our commands are for your good and honour. Come then at once without further evasion.

And, when the King would have signed, Despenser added a further threat.

> Trespass not against our commands, for we hear much you have done that you should not. . . .

And now it was finished. And the King, having signed, Despenser added,

Given at Lichfield the 18th day of March this year of grace 1326.

Two other letters Despenser dictated—one to the Queen of England the other to the King of France.

Isabella tossed her letter aside. Let her fool of a husband send her a hundred such she would not stir; it could not be expected, she told her son; she was in fear of her life! Young Edward was sullen and sad. He wanted desperately to please his father, his gentle good father. True his mother said he was free to go; how could he return —a hostage, she swore it, to bring her back to punishment; maybe to death itself? The truth in his father's accusations he knew; it had grown upon him since that night he had gone to her chamber. And still she sought to blind him to her passion for Mortimer! He was ashamed of her; yet, for his own sake, he was relieved to have the decision taken out of his hands; fear of his father lay heavy upon him. *We are not pleased with you.* Fear for his mother, fear for himself inhibited him—he was not yet fourteen.

Charles was weary of the incessant letters, weary of the constant complaints of husband and wife, weary of replying, weary of the sly laughter of his court and the shocked faces of the ambassadors. And to crown it all, his wife new-returned to court, disliked his sister.

And now this last letter had settled the matter; a very proper letter reminding him that the Queen of England had been in France above a year and that her work there was finished. Besides, he recognised her bad behaviour. As long as it had gone unremarked he had been content to let it pass—himself was not so virtuous! Now he could let it pass no longer. He did not mean to embroil himself with his brother of England—a quarrel that might well go deeper than the question of homage. Still less did he mean to embroil himself with Spain; already her ambassadors were casting sour looks, were threatening to return home.

Isabella must leave France at once; if not by her own will, then by force. He was the King.

'Sir, brother!' She lifted green-gold eyes aswim with tears. 'By God's Face I fear these Despensers—so besotted is my husband, so full of deceit are they! And, if I feared them before, now my fear is greater still. I have accused them of infamy; and for that they will murder me. Brother, if you send me to England now, you send me to my death!'

He looked at her with distaste. She was the cause of all his embarrassments; her behaviour allowed no shadow of excuse.

'Sir—' and now she was kneeling, holding him ridiculously by the knees so that he dared not move for fear of stumbling, 'Sir, give me a little time, I beseech you, for the love of God. The people of England love me. They know of my wrongs; the lies of my enemies do not deceive them. Nothing can injure the love they bear me.'

'Then—' and with care he withdrew from those clutching hands, 'you have nothing to fear!'

'Have I not, brother? When has the love of the people kept a man from his death?'

'Then how shall time profit you?'

'My lords the barons will intercede for me. They will see to it that the Despensers do me no wrong.'

'So be it!' and angry with himself he turned away. 'But I'll not give you long. We are in the third week of March; by the third week in April you must be gone!'

She took his hand and covered it with kisses.

A month; a little month! Still, with luck it would do! If not, she'd stay until it pleased her to go! *My lords the barons will intercede for me.* And so they would; but not in the way she had given her brother to understand. He knew nothing of the secret news forever passing between Orleton and herself; nothing of the ever-growing band of England's rebellious princes. Finished their attempts to counsel the foolish King; ready, the most part of them, to march with the Queen, to take her for leader. Had he understood the half of it, he would, she knew, have put her under guard and despatched her home at once. King does not countenance treachery against King, especially treachery from a wife!

'Good news from England and every day growing better! Orleton does his work well!' Isabella told Mortimer. 'My lord and husband—' and, as always, she made of the words an insult, 'steps every day into hotter water. The whole country's aboil—and can you wonder? The army goes unpaid; soldiers savage town and country. Empty bellies make desperate deeds. And everywhere, the gallows thicker than ever before. You'd think, God save us, the country was an orchard heavy with foul harvest. The barons stand ready to fight for us, the bishops to bless us. If we muster a thousand men, they'll do the rest.'

'A thousand! There's several hundred English here who've either fled justice or cannot stomach the Despensers. But—a thousand! They don't grow on blackberry bushes!'

She smiled. She knew well how to charm men to her cause. She was a woman beautiful and unfortunate. She was a Queen beautiful and unfortunate. And she had a shrewdness to weigh men and a honey-sweet tongue; she knew well how to promise each man the thing he most desired . . . when she should come into her own. She had drawn to her not only refugees that longed for home and soldiers of fortune that looked for reward but many a chivalrous young heart; and of these, the chief, Sir John of Hainault.

'I think I know where to put my hand on fighting-men!' she said.

'You mean your young fool of Hainault?'

'He and his friends are dying to die for me! But such things take time. Thank God for a month!'

'News from England grows better and better!' Isabella lifted a face of triumph from the letter before her. 'My uncle Henry of Derby—Lancaster if he had his rights—has joined us. The foolish King withholds the best part of his inheritance. I promised him full rights if he would come in to us. And I promised him more. Thomas of Lancaster died a traitor's death; I have sworn the word *traitor* shall be cut from the records. It was that, I think, finally won him.

He's a good man to have; honest and far from rash. People trust him; he'll bring many in to our cause.'

She went on reading.

She lifted a face of triumph. 'Orleton keeps best for last. This I have prayed for, longed for . . . and with little hope. The King's brothers have joined us—Edmund and Thomas, both! By God's Face this strengthens us! We've but to set foot on English soil, to raise my standard—and we bring the King to heel!'

'And if he'll not lick the hand that holds the whip!' He was sour lest, in such royal company, great Mortimer shine less bright.

'He shall lick it. You will see!'

'Very well for him! But what of me?'

'You and I are one.' And when he did not appear wholly satisfied, she said, 'The Queen's lover may well become her husband—and at no great distance of time. The King must make at least a show of fighting; and in that fighting who knows how or when death may come?'

She had spoken idly to placate the man. For young, strong, and avoiding danger, how should the King die? And, besides, Mortimer was married! She had forgotten the thought almost before she had finished speaking. Not so he. *The Queen's lover may become her husband.* Why not? His wife had been ailing lately; she was far from strong. And the King? Who knew how or when his death might not come? *The Queen's lover may become her husband.* Until her husband was dead he was to know no peace.

She had been commanded to leave by the third week in April; now it was May and she showed no sign of going. Charles was finding his position intolerable. It was not only the upbraiding of the injured husband, it was not only the reproaches of his own wife; now there were admonitions from the Pope himself to countenance her no longer. Yet short of force there seemed no way of getting rid of her.

May passed into June. And still the King of England troubled his brother of France with bitter complaint, still Madam the Queen of France reproached her husband; but now the Pope's admonition had become command. If Madam the Queen of England were not sent out of France at once, the King of France should find himself cut off from God and man. Excommunication.

'Two weeks, two little weeks—it's all we need!' Isabella laughed. 'So much time my brother will surely allow me. He'll never turn me from his door!'

'Will he not?' Mortimer asked, grim. 'Will he lose his soul's salvation for you? How loving has he been of late? How long since you've as much as set eyes on him?'

A knock fell upon the door. Sir John of Hainault came in and knelt before her; it was as though he knelt to the Madonna.

'Madam, I bring you ill news. The lord King has made a proclamation. Whoever shall assist Madam the Queen of England, or speak a word on her behalf, shall forfeit all possessions and be forever banished!'

She cried out at that, one hand at her heart. Mortimer laughed; his laugh was sour. 'There's no Frenchman will follow you now! All those protestations of love and service—you may kiss them Goodbye!'

'My love and service still stands!' Sir John said at once. 'I am a Hainaulter, I have little here to lose. But were it a thousandfold, I am still, Madam, your loving and obedient servant.'

She said no word; she bent forward and kissed him full on the mouth.

'How long does my brother give me?'

'A fortnight, Madam.' He lifted his dazzled eyes; it was as though he had drunk from the grail.

'Then all is well,' she said.

'Thank God my brother's a fool!' she cried out to Mortimer when the young man was gone. 'There will go with us, if not the thousand we'd hoped, at least five hundred English. Certainly we shall return to England—but in a way the King of France doesn't expect; no, nor the King of England, neither!'

Charles was not the fool his sister thought.

Two nights later they were awakened by a low knocking upon her door. Isabella, cheeks white as her naked breast, started up; Mortimer, instinct warning him, stood already by the door, sword in hand.

'Let them come in!' he said. 'For enter they will with our *yea* or without.'

Sir John of Hainault came in.

'Madam—' and he was all breathless with his haste. 'The King your brother plays you false. He says nothing; but I think he knows our plans. In the dark of the morning you are to be taken, all three of you—yourself, Madam, the lord here, and the lord Prince. You shall be put upon a ship, it lies already in harbour. You are to be carried into England by force!'

She was whiter now—if whiter could be. She stared at him with great golden-green eyes.

'Madam,' he said, 'fear nothing. I am your good knight.'

Even in that moment she managed a smile so sweet, so piteous, so trusting, it ravished the young man. That he had all-but found Mortimer in her bed troubled him little—save that he could wish himself in that same place. He had expected to find the man there; the whole court knew they slept together. He had no blame for her; she could do no wrong. She was his chosen lady and an injured wife; in every tale of chivalry the most worthy knight bore away the prize.

'Madam the Queen,' he said, 'will it please you rise and dress?' To Mortimer no need to speak; already he was drawing on his hose. 'I have sent to summon the prince. I will take you, all three, to a safe place. The horses are waiting.'

'What place?' Mortimer asked, sharp. If he could have trusted any man it would have been this one; but he trusted none.

'Hainult. My brother, the count, shall give you good welcome.'

'I bless you for that!' Isabella said. 'His wife is my own cousin.'

Robert of Artois came in with the Prince; the boy was pale and only half-awake. At the sight of Mortimer dressing himself there in his mother's bedchamber, a sullen look closed down upon his face. That Mortimer slept in his mother's bed he knew by now, but to have the knowledge thrust before his eyes! He was resentful, he was mortified.

Down the narrow staircase that led from the ruelle and across the garden, and out through a postern where the horses waited. At the gate, the sleepy watchman hearing the password let them through. And so out into the summer night—the Queen of England, her paramour and young son; and with them Robert de Artois and John of Hainault and no other—not so much as a tiring-woman, the Queen must manage as best she could. Edward sat his horse, swaying a little with sleep; dragged from his bed, clothes bundled upon him, he'd had not time to ask what was afoot.

'Where do you take me?' he asked now, half-resentful, half-fearful.

'To a place that will please you well,' Sir John said.

'Home?' And it was plain that home he had no wish to go. He should have gone these many months; he feared his father's anger.

'Not yet, sir. Soon; when we have made your peace with your father,' Sir John said and believed it. That the Queen had any plan more serious he did not know. Half-asleep the Prince was glad to be persuaded.

Riding, riding through the quiet night the sound of their horses muffled in the dirt of the road. And now they were fording the Seine, the horses picking their careful way through the river. And so to Compiègne and a long rest in sanctuary; and in the evening on again, through Amiens, through Gerberoi and into Cambray. And now they were over the border and safe. Now they could sleep at night and ride by day, and rest where they chose. At Ostrevant they halted; and there a poor knight, one Eustace of Amréticourt rode out to meet them, to bring them into his own house and give them of his meagre best.

Chapter Thirty

William count of Hainault was not willing to receive Madam the Queen of England. Overmuch scandal for his sober taste had gathered about her name. But his wife, the Queen's cousin Jehanne of Valois, spoke gently to him. 'Who can trust the tongue of scandal? Only too often the innocent have been smeared. Welcome her and judge for yourself whether scandal speaks truth or lies.'

He was still unwilling; the more so because of his four young daughters; but Madam Jehanne, like a good mother, was interested in the boy who would one day be King of England . . . and would most certainly need a wife. So still she laid out her arguments until Sir John went spurring back to Ostrevant to bring his lady back into Valenciennes.

She knew by his face that he had brought good news. Sitting in the dark and shabby house while twilight fell upon the flat land, her spirits had sunk low indeed. Mortimer was riding for Ghent and she missed him intolerably. But if she hoped for help here in Hainault she must keep him at a distance; she must not offend the good count and his virtuous wife. *Good, virtuous;* the words were sour to the Queen's mind.

The young man knelt before his saint. 'Madam, it is time to leave this poor place. My brother and the lady his wife are waiting to welcome you; the little girls, my nieces, long to see so beautiful, so royal a lady.'

'Sir,' she said, 'words are poor things, but all I have to give at this time. But when I come into my own, be sure your goodness will not be forgotten.'

'I am your knight,' he reminded her. 'To die for you at need is enough reward.'

'Sir—' and she was all honey and salt tears, 'live for me and my cause.' And wondered how long they must continue in this exalted strain. In the morning, Sir Eustace standing humble at her stirrup, she bade him Farewell, thanking him with a sweet grace and the promise of good to come.

Some three miles from Valenciennes the procession rode out to meet them—Count William and his wife, together with knights and ladies; and the burghers, also, very rich and sombre in velvet and furs. Garlands and flowers there were none; this was no triumphal procession; but there was kindliness and the promise of help.

For eight days Isabella and her son contented themselves as best they might while Sir John busied himself about help for his distressed Queen. He was forever riding the countryside, calling upon his friends to up and arm; he was forever dictating letters, assessing with his clerks the number of promised knights, of men-at-arms, of horses and weapons, of ships to carry all into England.

The young Edward was subdued and moody. It was not only that he feared to face his father; he was increasingly troubled by this mustering of arms.

'What need of soldiers; of foreign soldiers? We are going *home*?' he said.

Isabella looked at him, green-flecked eyes wide and candid.

'It is not your father, we fight; God forbid such a thing! It is the Despensers—the country's enemy and ours, yours and mine; and most of all your father's enemy—did he but know it! Your father is a most loving man—' and her mouth twisted remembering his love for the younger Hugh. 'Where he loves he sees no fault. It is for us, his true friends—to save him.'

Like many older than himself he was taken by her subtlety, so that he doubted not only his own wisdom but the wisdom of his father.

She had quieted him for the present. Now she must keep him at arm's length; she wanted no more discussions with him. It was vital that he did not understand before sailing that this mustering of forces would not stop at pulling the Despensers down; it meant civil war. She was, besides, deeply occupied with letters from England, welcome letters with unexpected offers of help—and these required careful consideration. Henry of Derby, his slow anger steady against the King, had written again offering love, offering loyalty, offering every resource he could command. There were letters, also, from the King's brothers welcoming her return, and letters from Orleton listing all those sworn to her cause. A very great number, more than she had dared hope . . . and the less young Edward knew of her affairs the better! He needed to be managed, this son of hers with his boy's ideas of truth and loyalty; he could be obstinate and troublesome. She had sufficient difficulties already without any of his making. He needed careful handling, and she had not the time.

These days she felt herself isolated: as though, she thought rueful, she sat in the centre of her web and spun her threads. In all the vast responsibility of this enterprise there was no-one here whose mind marched with hers, in whose companionship she could rest. The solid virtues of the count and his wife oppressed her; and she was more than a little weary of Sir John. Without doubt he was mustering forces; but he was forever striking poses, forever making speeches to which she must respond in kind. She knew the rules of the game. To him it was no game but a way of life; to her a piece of nonsense and a waste of time.

Her longing for Mortimer grew daily, longing that was a pain to rack her, body and soul. He played no games, uttered no flowery speeches. She thirsted for his plain speech whether in love or in war; and most of all she thirsted for the man—his body . . . *his naked body, his naked truth*. The words were her prayer, her talisman.

The day of her departure was fixed; she waited only for Sir John to bring in his troops. She knew exactly how many to expect from him and how many she might expect in England. She knew exactly where to land, which princes, on landing, to receive, what promises to make to them as a body, what rewards confirm to each man. *Death to the Despensers,* her battle-cry; the country's first wish and her own. But what of the King? How did she stand in that? As a King she would treat with him, make her terms; as a husband—never, between husband and wife there could be no terms.

On this last thought every doubt, every hesitation, suddenly crystallised into clear fact. All this time she had deceived herself, deceived others. She was going into England to drive the parasites away, to free the King of their indignities, the people of their greed. So she had told herself, told Orleton, told those princes of church and state that had offered loyalty, told the young Sir John ... above all told her son. And for that—save for the boy whom she had blinded to the full implications—they had been willing to bring upon the country the curse of civil war. Now she understood that this was was but half the story; she meant to drive the matter to the ultimate, the only possible end. She meant to rid herself of Edward altogether—not as husband only but as King. She meant to put young Edward on the throne, herself the Regent. And she meant to keep her lover; the Regent could outface them all.

The first thing then, was to win her son from his coldness on Mortimer's account, to bind him to her with love and gratitude. She must find out what the boy most ardently wanted; and that thing, however wild, she would promise.

Edward had been whiling his time away with the other boys. He hunted, he practised at the target, he played matches at the ball. Swift, sure of hand and eye, amiable in manner, he was well-liked and great things promised for him. At nights there was singing after supper, there were games and dancing. But even a boy cannot be on the move forever; there were times when he was content to sit and talk with his cousins. Margaret already past fifteen seemed to him a full woman; Jehanne at twelve was too young and Isabel a baby. Philippa, younger than he by some months was his best companion. Sometimes, skirts lifted, long fair hair flying, pink cheeks pinker, blue eyes bright with laughter, she seemed much younger. Yet she could be gentle and understanding; a listening heart, he thought, and then she seemed older than himself. She knew when he was troubled; she listened when he wanted to talk, or if she thought it wiser, would turn his mind to happier things. She knew that, at times, he longed to talk of his mother; she knew, also, that she must not listen. Having once spoken, embarrassment might drive him to avoid her. He found her utterly honest, utterly trustworthy— to him no small thing; he loved her for her honesty; even more for her gentleness. Gentleness became her, he thought, gave promise of the woman she would be—a woman as unlike his mother as possible. That this buxom pink-and-white girl was not the world's beauty; and as like her sisters as peas in a pod, he would not have believed. This was the one girl in all Christendom. To her a man could come weary, heartbroken and she would make him whole again. And, indeed, she had a rare beauty of spirit his boyish eyes had been permitted to see.

Isabella encouraged the friendship; Her chief anxiety lay still with her son. Suppose, with his love for his father and his belief in the sanctity of kingship, he would have nothing to do with her accomplished plan? Suppose he refused to accept the crown? Or—and it was a thought to shrivel the heart —suppose having accepted it, he tried to send Mortimer away? It was a thing she dared not risk. She saw the way to win her boy.

Now, however engrossing her plans, she found time to be pleasant with her young cousins; but Philippa she singled out for special kindness, giving her now a riband, now some other trifle with loving words. She could, she thought, give herself a worse daughter-in-law than this gentle, unremarkable girl. No rival here! Indeed, winning this simple girl she could strongly influence her son. Her own integrity lost, she missed the integrity of the girl's whole nature. And certainly, apart for the boyish affection for which she cared not a fig, the match would be for her son's good, also. Philippa's young comeliness would hold him awhile; and he would never know the moment's unease on her account. As she grew older, bore her children, she'd thicken the way these Hainaulters did; he need never be afraid to wear the horns. In addition, there was the little matter of a dowry; her father's wealth was known to all Christendom. To give his daughter a crown he'd be willing to dive deep into those gold-lined pockets of his!

Now she spoke often of the girl with great kindness . . . Philippa was so gentle, so kind, so honest, so pretty. *Yes,* he said, *Yes,* his heart warm again because she praised his beautiful, his perfect Philippa.

But there were other things besides integrity Isabella had missed.

This was a girl with a sturdy commonsense, a clear-seeing that, at times, came near to genius. Edward had already discovered it. Of late they had talked of their two countries.

'Yours is so rich and mine, alas, so poor! The Despensers eat us out of house and home; and then, like rats, they pick our bones.'

'Then you must drive them out! And that the lady your mother has sworn to do. But that won't make you rich. You may fatten a little; but rich you'll never be! A country grows rich on trade. *Gold on the sheep's back,* my father says. *The old tale of the golden fleece with a difference.* So it is with us. We are rich because we make cloth and sell it. And where do we get the best part of our wool? From you; from England. Why don't you set up your own looms; we cannot handle half the wool here. You could make your country very rich!'

Trade! Trade to build up a country's wealth! Such an idea had never entered his head—a prince bred to the arts of war. Gold on a sheep's back for the taking! Yes, he saw how it might be. Money saved carrying the wool across the sea, money saved on dyeing, on weaving, on the finished cloth, money saved shipping it back again . . . the golden fleece!

'When all the fighting's done—' he said suddenly and stopped. He had meant to say this thing but not now, not like this! Yet now was the moment . . . and the way. He said—and he dared not look at her, 'Could you come . . . one day . . . and help me set up such a piece of work?'

'How could I? What could I do? You should speak with my father, ask his advice. He might lend you some craftsmen . . .'

'Yes,' he said. 'Yes . . . but would *you* come?'

'I don't *know* anything!' Suddenly she understood. He was offering her the crown of England's future Queen.

She said knowing more than he of the coming-and-going of such a business—the policies, the endowments, the conditions, 'It is not in our hands. We are not old enough.'

'*I* am old enough; and one day I shall be King. But that's too long to wait . . . for me at least. Could *you* wait so long?'

'It is not for you or me to say. I cannot say it.'

'But if were proper for you to say *Yes*; would it please you to say it?'

She looked at him with her true eyes. 'It would please me. But I entreat you, I do entreat you, say nothing now. You are young and I am young and nothing is smooth. When the time comes, speak; and, for my part, you may be sure of me!'

He kissed her hand; it was not a boy's kiss nor a courtier's kiss. It was a lover's kiss. No word of love had passed between them; yet all had been said . . . said and pledged. They knew it, both of them.

Isabella's sharp eyes saw exactly how things were with those two. Now was the time to drop the word to trouble the boy, to make him fear for his love, to bring him openly out upon his mother's side.

'For me it is easy to go home,' Isabella said. 'I shall make my peace with your father. I shall live my life as best I may; happiness I do not expect. But for you; for you it is different.'

'How so, Madam? You have promised my father shall forgive me.'

'Yes, forgive you he will. But I cannot promise he will change his mind on other matters.'

'What matters, Madam?'

'He is set upon your marriage with the Infanta of Spain.'

The angry red flew into his cheeks. 'I had not heard it.'

'You would not,' she said, very smooth. 'The Despensers have seen to it. And I would not grieve you until I must. But you remember—surely you must remember—when you parted with your father you promised not to betroth yourself without his permission! Why did he do that do you think? Because already the Spanish match was in his mind; already negotiations begun, the Pope petitioned for dispensation. The bride is Eleanor of Castile . . .'

'No!' he cried out. 'No!'

'But yes—if the Despensers have their way. And why not? The match is good enough. This Eleanor is very rich; and, as I hear, not ill-looking. A slight squint; but what is that to you? Not ungraceful they say—if she shed some of her fat; *if*, it's a big word, her family

runs to fat. A will of her own, so I hear; somewhat hasty in judgment, and in her judgments obstinate. There's a cruel streak in
these women of Castile. But let these things not trouble you.
You'll be her husband; I'd not think much of you if you couldn't
keep her in her place!'

'Her husband I'll never be!' he cried out, passionate.

'You have no choice—if the Despensers have their way; already
they've dipped their hands in Spanish gold. We must be rid of
them; but before that time there's a weary way to go. Yet of this
be sure. I fight the Despensers not for myself but for us all—for the
barons that they may be free to cast away new bad laws and bring
back the old good ones; for the people that they may be free to
live under those laws; for your father that he may be free of the
Despensers and win the heart of the people again; for you that you
may be free to choose your bride when the time comes!'

She said no more. Let him weigh well her words.

Chapter Thirty-One

Point of departure; the longed-for day. Young Sir John had gathered forces from Hainault, from Brabant, from Bohemia. In England Orleton and Henry of Derby had done their work; barons and bishops held themselves ready. And it was not only England's princes; the common people heard of her coming and blessed her. Sick to death, everyone, of the Despensers and the weak-willed King, of the crippling taxes, the cruel extortions, the hateful punishments. And the loss of Scotland forever rankled.

Isabella had warned her son against a show of grief in parting with his sweetheart. The promise of betrothal had been made and a great part of the dowry already paid; a matter of further congratulation to Isabella who needed the money for her troops. But no contract had been signed. They had yet to win his father's consent; until then the matter must be secret as the grave—an open show of grief might yet mar all!

Now, bending to Philippa's hand, the boy was careful to salute it no longer than those of her sisters; but his mother, noting the dejected eye, the pale cheek, smiled. She was sure of him now. And for his sake, too, she was glad—those two were in love. Once she would not have reckoned that part of the bargain; now, herself in love, she valued it . . . but not too much.

They were on the road to Dordrecht; Sir John rode beside his Queen. And, *Madam*, he said *Madam*, continually plucking at her thoughts. 'Madam, God Himself, filled me with this enterprise. You, Madam, after God, are my whole life. Madam . . . Madam . . .'

She was weary to death of him. He had done his work—now let him leave her to her thoughts; there was very much upon her heart. Soon Mortimer should take the burden from her—her captain and her love. Soon she would see him again; soon! At the thought of their meeting she was shaken body and soul.

That night they lay at Mons Castle. For all her long riding, Isabella could not sleep. She was oppressed by the weight, the nearness of the enterprise. Lying open-eyed in the darkness, she ached for her lover, flesh and spirit. The hours of parting already endured, the hours yet to be endured, gathered now like a monstrous wave to drown her in anguish. That she should see him tomorrow was no comfort now; what comfort of water tomorrow to him that dies in the desert of thirst? The summer day was still dark when she rose hollow-eyed to busy herself about unguents, her lotions and her paints. Let the whole world fall, this day she must be fair to meet her love.

He sat his horse filling his eyes with the sight of her; of late he had grown used to her charms—he was not one to enslave himself to any woman. And, unlike her, he had not since their parting gone empty of love. But not then or ever had he found a woman like her. It was less her beauty than the passion that he sensed palpable as perfume; it kindled him afresh. He was down from the saddle; almost he leaped upon her to lift her from her horse. She lay in his arms her whole body crying out *Take me, Take me!* But time pressed and they must content themselves with touching; they could not keep their hands from each other and cared not at all who might see, not though it was her young son himself.

But at night, lying by his side, filled with love yet thirsting still, she asked herself, would she be satisfied to give up all for him; to go to some quiet place where they might live together? *No!* Her answer came at once. Keep him from his ambitions—if that were possible—and he would come to hate her. As for herself—deep her love, but ambition deeper; in that they were equal. Crownless she would be less than herself, crippled with the loss of some vital part. With such a loss she could not hope to keep him. There was but one way to hold him. Together they would fight, together succeed, together hold power in their hands. To her husband she gave scarce a thought; his part she had already decided. He must give up the throne, go to some far place—across the sea, or bury himself in some monastery; she cared not which. From her son she need fear nothing; she had bound him to her by his love for a girl.

On the evening of the third day they embarked. The sky was dark and the wind high. The sky was restless with coming storm; and she with coming events. Her future shone in glory as in joy; her marriage-bed cleared of trash, her lover by her side, her son obedient, the Despensers dead and rotting. She was filled with her destiny.

The wind rose higher, the threatening storm rose to a tempest. Between heaving sky and heaving sea the ships lifted, dropped, lifted again, drifted helpless upon the tumult of the waters. The very sailors sick, the ship lost course; fighting-men lay low, groaning as never on the field of battle. The Queen herself, love and glory forgotten, lay and retched upon her pallet. But Mortimer, erect and grim, stood by the captain to fight the storm.

Dawn broke barely perceptible in the sullen sky; daylight came, nebulous as the dawn. And still Mortimer stood at his post to bring the Queen's ship safe to land. And, grounded at last, though they knew not where, nor even in what country—they carried the Queen ashore and made a rude shelter of branches and kindled a fire with such buoys as had been cast upon the beach, and so left her to take what rest she might. But rest she could not. She knew not where they were—whether in England or Spain, or driven back to France? What had become of the other ships? How different had been her picture of this first day of her return?

And now, ship by ship the rest of the fleet, wind-driven and battered, came limping to land. And now, also, scouts that had been sent out came back with news to cheer the heart. For this was England; and not so far from Orwell where they had meant to land; they were but a few miles from Walton-on-the Naze. And now, though it was late in the day, the Queen gave orders to march. So they left their cold harbour, and cold it was, for in spite of the summer afternoon the sharp wind blew from the sea to chill them to the bone. They were glad, indeed, to come into Walton where the good monks welcomed them with food and lodgings. The next day they were on the march; through Bury St. Edmunds to

Cambridge where, according to plan, the Queen's supporters were to gather. Here the troops should take a needed rest; the Queen, herself, and Mortimer lay at Barnwell Priory where the monks could not enough honour their Queen and the gallant captain that had come to set all wrongs to rights.

˒ Now came the gentry of the neighbourhood and beyond, their men behind them, to kneel and offer their loyalty; and simple folk, with hearts no less loyal, came also to offer their lives to her service.

The Queen's forces, being idle, were foraging the country-side; they were taking by force food and whatever else they fancied. The Queen cried out in anger when she heard it. 'Such behaviour we leave to the Despensers! Every man that so offends again shall be punished. Let it be known! And let it be known, also, that whosoever has complaint on this same score shall be paid the full worth of what he has lost.'

'To pillage is the way of soldiers,' Mortimer told her, laughing and teasing. 'If you are to be a soldier you must learn our ways!'

'We come not as enemies but as friends; I am not one to pay where I may take, but this payment I must afford. To lose one heart—that I cannot afford!'

The Queen was for London. So far the King had done nothing— he and his Despensers had not thought it worth their while. Now she heard that the Tower had been fortified, that orders had gone out to fortify castles throughout the land, and soldiers sent to guard the coast. At that last she laughed. 'How like him to lock the stable-door when the mare is gone!' At Dunstable, some thirty miles from London, they halted. And now came Thomas of Norfolk and Edmund of Kent, their men at their heels. This was great comfort, for now the people could see for themselves that even the King's own brothers had turned from him to stand by her cause. 'Dear sister, the Londoners long for the sight of you,' Thomas told her. 'They are with you, everyone. They await you with men and arms and most loyal hearts.'

Henry of Derby came with all his forces; and upon him she bestowed, at once, the great title of Lancaster with all its lands and honours. He smarted still that his name had not been cleared; and that his brother lay still in a traitor's grave. *A nest of traitors these Lancasters* the King had said. Once more she gave her royal word that the name should shine forth in clear honour.

And now came Richmond and Beaumont the King's own friends to offer their service; and a host of other lords already sworn to her cause. And Orleton came, too; and with him my lords the bishops of Winchester and of Norwich . . . and more to follow, Orleton said; Orleton that had served her well both in the matter of Mortimer's escape and in drumming up men for her forces.

'Now we are strong, indeed!' Mortimer said. 'We have Madam the Queen and the lord Prince of Wales; we have the King's brothers and the chiefest lords of church and state.'

'And best of all—you, my captain!' The Queen flung both arms about his neck and cared not at all that Orleton stood by.

He disentangled himself. 'There's no victory but a man must fight for it!'

'We must pray God for his continuing kindness,' Orleton told her, displeased by her wanton show of affection. 'And for that kindness we must make ourselves fit.'

She sent him a side-long look, gold-flecked eyes narrowed. How far could she trust him? Only as long as his ambition marched with her own; no further. For all his talk of God, ambition and revenge, not righteousness drove him to destroy the King.

For that was what he had meant from the beginning; the King was to pay dear for that public reproof. Long before the idea had entered her own head he had meant to put down the King. Very like he had guided her thoughts in that direction. But she must watch him, this man of God, so secret, subtle and revengeful; she needed him . . . but she did not trust him.

Through the countryside wound the Queen's armies—fife and trumpet, banners flying; foreign knights with unknown arms, English lords, all of them in glittering armour. And before them the robed bishops, jewelled croziers lifted. Who could doubt the rightness of her cause? And whenever she halted, beautiful and gracious, she received her people, promising them the things they longed to hear, so that it seemed with her the good times must come again. They fell in to march beneath her banner, gentle and simple alike.

The Queen's wrongs were the people's wrongs. The King had deserted his wife for his playboy—as he had deserted his people. He had robbed her of her possessions, he had left her all but penniless —as he had left his people. There was some gossip that the strong man riding by her side was her lover! Malice, merely, put about by the Despensers. None could believe it! Else why did the bishops make nothing of the matter; nor the King's own brother riding by her side; nor the good, quiet man, her uncle of Lancaster? Good luck to the gallant Queen and her gallant captain!

The King was riding through London to rally the citizens to his cause and riding too late. Sullen they admitted him; sullen they stood while he rode their streets, his soldiers at his heels, a Despenser at either hand. In deadly silence he rode; it was as though he rode through a city of the dead. He had been told that where she rode, false Queen, there had been cheers and blessings.

Arrived at the Tower he gave himself up to bitter thought. Her he dared not—if he could—touch; the people's love was too great. But with her followers he would deal—traitors all! Traitors to die a traitor's death—unless they returned at once to their allegiance. And so he would proclaim it. Promise of pardon—and she'd soon find her fine army melting away. And that promise he'd keep—for the most part; he couldn't afford to kill off the bulk of his lords. But Orleton he'd not pardon; the sly bishop should meet an accidental death—one couldn't afford to anger the Pope. But Mortimer—nothing accidental about *his* death; the traitor and seducer that had vilely dishonoured the King's bed should be punished as no man ever before. He could not wait to get his hands upon the man!

For Mortimer he offered a thousand pounds in gold. One thousand golden pounds! It would not be long before his hands closed upon his enemy.

That's a hare he'll never catch! Men grinned, remembering the miraculous escape from the Tower.

They were right. The King offered more; he went on raising the sum. By September it stood at a King's ransom. Mortimer laughed aloud. 'I am held in high esteem by King and Queen alike!' and fondled her neck.

But not by the Prince. She bit back the words. In spite of all her efforts still he hated Mortimer; nor, though she had coaxed the boy with the bait of Philippa, did he entirely trust his mother.

London had turned bitter against the King. At first it had merely withheld help; now the people were like dogs, teeth bared. He turned his back upon his capital and did not dream he was never to see it again. With the few supporters he could muster, the Despensers, Arundel and de Warenne for captains and Baldock bishop of London to give them blessing, he marched for the west . . . *fled's* the better word, the Queen told Mortimer.

And now with love and high welcome all London prepared for the Queen. That she rode in company with her paramour, outlaw and traitor, that she had brought foreigners to spill English blood, that she was bringing civil war—of all wars the most cruel—mattered not at all. She had proclaimed her reasons and God Himself could not fault them. She had come to release a free people from their cruel bonds, she had come to punish those that bound them . . . and above all she had come to punish the Despensers. And, as the King's price for the head of Mortimer rose, she doubled it—twice a King's ransom, thrice a King's ransom for either Despenser alive or dead.

Mid-October; and everywhere the Queen's position strengthened. Orleton played his part well—a good orator this bishop that knew how to stir up trouble. And stir it he did—more than even he had dared hope. His words were carried throughout the country like flame before wind. The Queen—he said it boldly—was the King's declared enemy; England's princes knew it. Beneath her banner marched barons, and bishops to bless her cause. The bad times had come to an end. He so inflamed the people that, let a man, anywhere say a good word for the King and he was savagely attacked so that he was like to rue it for the rest of his days—if he lived at all!

London went mad. Upon excitement, excitement fed. Londoners

went about in gangs to punish any that spoke against the Queen, or who might have spoken, or who could possibly speak. There were lynchings and hangings—murder of the innocents. Nor did a man's cloth save him. Walter Stapledon, good bishop of Exeter, riding with two priests, was set upon with cries of *traitor*. And no reason save that he was trying for peace between King and Queen. At Paul's Cross the mob closed in upon them all three, holy, good men that asked nothing but to serve God and man. Urging their horses that they might find sanctuary within the church they were pulled to the ground. There, in the churchyard, in the very shadow of the church, beneath a butcher's knife, they met their death.

In the west country Edward wept for Stapledon, 'Good man, good priest that sought to heal this poor country.' To the Queen went the bloody head. She looked upon it unmoved—so it seemed 'So let it be with all traitors,' she said.

It was her first look upon murder in her cause; murder of an innocent man, a priest . . . and she did not condemn it. It was her baptism in blood.

So let it be with all traitors. She had actually praised the deed. Her praise added violence to violence. Now London was given over to violence, to slaughter. Foreigners of all nations were stripped of their wealth—and lucky if they got off with their lives! For was it not the cursed Italian bankers that had supplied the King with money, that had helped to make him free of Parliament? And Londoners that were only suspect suffered worse; their homes were burnt and themselves roasted in the flames.

Mad with success the mob stormed the Tower. They forced the Constable to give up the little prince John of Eltham; him they would keep—a hostage. They demanded the children of Mortimer whom the King had seized for hostage; them they would keep in some safe place. They set free what prisoners they would. And all these—even the little boy, the King's own son—were forced to swear to forsake the King and to stand with the Londoners, to die with them at need. And that done, they seized upon all priests they could lay hands upon and justices and officers of the city and forced them to that same oath.

And now, fearing punishment—for the mayor and chief citizens had looked askance at their doings—they sent to the Queen craving permission to put the mayor from his place. She sent her gracious greetings, her praise for their loyalty and herself named the mayor— that same de Bettoyne that had helped Mortimer in his escape and who now looked for reward. And she appointed also a new Constable of the Tower—John de Gisors that had worked with de Bettoyne and also looked for reward.

Mortimer's friends in key positions in London! So far, so good, so very good!

And now the Queen must press westward in relentless pursuit of the King.

Chapter Thirty-Two

The Queen pressed on to Bristol; Bristol she must have. Within the castle the King sheltered with his sweetheart; the older Despenser and such friends as the King had left, kept the town.

And now for, the first time, she was joined by the barons of the north, the Percies at their head. And, as she moved further west, the barons came from the Welsh marches to do her service. At this last she lifted a face of love to Mortimer. 'It is for you they come; for you!'

'For us both. All Christendom loves a brave man and pities a wronged woman!' As always he put himself first.

A national rising.

Within Bristol castle the King and the younger Hugh sat and trembled.

'Have no fear,' the King said, talking above his own fear to comfort his friend, 'your father and Arundel command the city. It is well-garrisoned and there's food and firing aplenty! Your father will know how to deal with this Queen and her traitors!'

The elder Despenser had no chance to deal with the traitors— they outnumbered him ten to one; it was they that dealt with him. Bristol was for the Queen. Without a blow the city surrendered; the city but not the castle.

On the twenty-seventh of October in the year of grace thirteen hundred and twenty-six, Edward, Prince of Wales, unwilling and distressed, was proclaimed Keeper of the Realm.

'And that means you, dear love; you and me!' the Queen told Mortimer. 'Now, now we are on our way!'

'But not yet arrived. We have still to deal with the King.'

She shrugged at that. 'We'll send him to some far place where he can make no mischief.'

'He will always make mischief so long as he lives!'

'Then we must see to it that he cannot!'

He sent her a sharp glance. Did she mean . . .?

'Keep him fast!' she said. 'Some pleasant place, castle or monastery, I care not which, so long as it be far enough, secure enough!'

She had not meant the thing he saw clearly must be done! Her mind did not march with his in this matter; not yet. She must come to it; of that he was certain.

That same day the older Despenser was brought before the Queen; Lancaster, Mortimer and the King's two brothers—these and these alone, stood by to pronounce sentence. Without trial nor any pretence of one, he was sentenced to death. It was Lancaster that spoke for them all; Henry of Lancaster speaking each word with satisfaction. At last, at last, revenge for the smear upon his name and his brother's dishonoured death.

'Sir Hugh—' and he would grant no greater title, 'this court denies you the right of answer; for you, yourself, made a law that a man could be condemned without right of answer. This law now applies to you.

'You are an attainted traitor; and, as a traitor, you were judged and banished by consent of the King and all the barons. And never has that sentence been revoked. Against the law of the land you have taken to yourself royal power. You have counselled the King to disinherit his lieges, most notably Thomas of Lancaster whom you put to death for no cause. By your cruelty you have robbed this land, wherefore all the people cry vengeance against you. You have advised the King to the hurt of Holy Church and treacherously taken from her her liberties.

'Therefore the court decrees that you be drawn, hanged and beheaded. And that your head be sent to Winchester of which place—against law and reason—you were made earl. And because you have dishonoured the order of chivalry, you are to be hanged in a surtout quartered with your arms and thereafter those arms shall be destroyed for ever.'

Ignoble in his living, he was yet noble in his dying.

'Madam—' he said and he ignored Lancaster, 'would that God had granted me an upright judge and a just sentence. Well, if we cannot find justice in this world, we shall find it in the next.'

'Such justice would chain you forever in Hell.' she said.

So they took him away and, in full armour hanged him and thereupon cut him down that he might suffer the full rigours of the bitter sentence. And that it might be the more bitter, they hanged him in full sight of the King and his own son.

'They should have shown more courtesy,' the King said, hand across his eyes that he might not see. 'An old man . . . nigh upon ninety years. They might, at least, have let him say Goodbye to us that loved him.'

The Hugh that was left turned his sick face. 'That woman . . . no mercy in her. A she-wolf . . . and leads the pack.'

There was a long silence. Then the King said, 'I had not dreamed it would come to this! I had thought, at worst, to parley with them, to come to terms.' The sight of his sick and shaking friend brought him sudden understanding of what those that had so barbarously used the father might do to the son. There was, as yet, no thought of what they might do to himself.

'We must get from here!' he cried out. 'We came here of our own free will; we are not prisoners . . .'

'. . . not yet!' Hugh covered his face with his hands and wept.

'Not now; nor ever! God be thanked I have a boat. We make for Chepstow and Wales. The Welsh will shelter us, the Welsh will fight for us. I am Edward of Carnarvon, their own prince!'

'Why should they help you? What love have you ever shown them? No! There's no help but in ourselves. We must make for Lundy, my own island and my own castle.'

'Yes, yes! And thence to Ireland. Ireland and safety. We are King of Ireland; in Ireland we shall gather our forces! By God's Face the woman shall pay for this!'

'Do you think the Irish will welcome you? Or that they will cross the sea to fight for you? Or that England will receive you again? By God you have built your house upon shifting sand!'

But still the King looked lovingly upon his friend and bade him be of good cheer. For he was still King of England and Ireland and Wales, yes and Scotland, also. It would go hard, indeed, if he could not muster enough loyal hearts to put the traitors down!

'It will go hard, indeed!' Despenser said and would not be comforted.

They had left the castle and embarked—the King, his sweetheart, Baldock the chancellor and Sir Thomas Blount the King's steward.

'Throw Blount overboard,' Despenser spoke low in the King's ear. 'I do not trust him.'

'You are jealous—and no cause!' The King took his friend by the hand. Despenser pulled it away. This fool of a King that lived in his own dream world! Did he suppose so poor a thing as jealousy—or so low a thing as Blount—would trouble a man flying for his life?

A small boat upon a wide sea; but the water was calm and the wind favouring. God has us in charge, the King said and watched the outline of Lundy grow darker. Despenser said nothing. He knew his channel and its sudden changes of wind.

They were so near Lundy now, a man could count the men-at-arms upon the turrets. A few hundred yards from shore the boat began to turn; nor could all their efforts bring her round again. They took in the sails, they bent to the oars, the King himself taking a hand. The wind blew yet more strong. Between island and boat the water forever broadened: the clear outline dimmed. Now came the rain. Lundy island was lost . . . forever lost.

The rain stopped. The sun shone from a clear sky. But the wind drove them still. Now the coastline shone clear. They saw the mountains of Wales.

'God knows best. And still He has us in charge!' the King said.

Men on the run. Hiding breast-high in wet bracken by day, travelling footsore by night.

Day after day; night after night.

Full fifteen days running before the hunters. By the second week in November they were in Neath Abbey, thankful to shelter from the driving rain. Here the monks made them welcome; here they might rest. This was sanctuary.

It was not until supper that they found Blount missing.

'He will come,' the King said, cheering the troubled Hugh. 'I blame myself that we did not miss him before. He could not keep up with us I suppose; he has more flesh to carry than the rest of us. Still he will surely come; he knows where we're to be found.'

One day and the next; three and four days . . . and still Blount did not come.

'Still he will come!' the King said.

And come he did. And Lancaster with him.

The King was walking in the garden with Despenser. Out of sanctuary, both!

'You are my prisoner,' Lancaster told Despenser. 'You are for Gloucester!'

For Gloucester and the Queen. Despenser's doom had been spoken.

And now it was the parting between those two. The King threw his arms about his friend as though to protect him still; but the soldiers pulled them apart and closed in about the prisoner. The King stood and watched them go; he shivered so that the teeth rattled in his head . . . and it was not the chill of the November morning; it was the shock of parting with his heart's love. He stood until his eyes could see them no longer; then he turned about weeping for his friend. What would they do to Hugh? For himself he had no fears. He was the King.

Lancaster broke in upon his weeping. 'Sir, we are for Kenilworth. It is for your safety. You shall be my guest.'

Through Monmouth, through Ledworth to Kenilworth rode the King. Fresh-clad, well-horsed, Lancaster attentive by his side, he might, indeed, have been an honoured guest . . . save that he rode under guard. And, as they went, he might have seen for himself that it was not London, alone, that had turned against him; for through every town and village he rode in silence, silence broken now and then by hisses and foul words. But he noticed nothing; he was in bitter grief for his friend.

Kenilworth at last, where Lancaster saw to it that his charge was comfortably lodged and courteously served. But though he allowed the King all bodily comfort, Lancaster granted him no peace of mind; for he spared the King no detail of Despenser's last, dreadful journey.

Despenser had been taken to Gloucester, to join the Queen's train. They had chained him hand and foot; and strapped him upon a sorry nag so low that the man's legs scraped the ground.

So they did with Piers. It all came back to the King clear as yesterday. He remembered the end of Piers .To that Hugh should never come; weeping, he swore it.

To taunt Despenser still further they had put upon him a tabard emblazoned with the arms of Gloucester—reversed; a taunt upon his hope of that earldom, he that had no blood of the Clares. And to jeers, foul words and filthy missiles, he that had sat so high went upon his last journey.

That this could be the last journey the King, deceiving himself as was his way, would not admit. 'When I am in London,' he told Lancaster, 'I shall set him high again!'

'We shall set him higher still!' Lancaster promised. And even now, it did not occur to the King that he, himself, stood in some danger.

Trumpet and drum and banners flying, the Queen left for London. Before her, alone, as though he were a leper, rode the prisoner—first object of all eyes; before Mortimer, before the Queen, before her even. Eyes closed against the hatred of the mob, its hatred yet reached him; his ears he could not close to their screams of fury, of derision. He heard, too, as he passed, cheers for Mortimer and blessings upon the Queen that together had rid the country of his father and himself.

Day after day the dreadful journey. Mercifully a man may endure so much—and no more. As they neared Hereford, though still the crowds cried their insults, pelting him with filth, the prisoner knew nothing. He lay slumped across the nag and would have fallen save for the straps that held him. Since he had been taken he had eaten nothing; now he let the nag carry him and did not stir from his dreaming. When it rained he did not know it; nor that his bare feet—his shoes cut to pieces dragging upon the road—bled. Outside noises filtered through his dreaming. . . . He was riding with the King; the crowd must cheer whether it would or no.

He was all but senseless when at Hereford they took him down and thrust him into a cell.

'He will die before we reach London,' Mortimer told the Queen. 'If we are to taste the full sweetness of his death we must hang him at once!'

She hesitated. She was a woman and there was mercy in her. The man was suffering most bitter punishment. If he died beneath it —though he died senseless—she was satisfied. She had no further desire for revenge. She said, 'He is beneath contempt.' And since Mortimer was a soldier and within his rights, added, 'Do with him what you will!'

On the twenty-fourth day of November, Hugh Despenser stood before his judges that already had judged him. Some wag had crowned him with nettle that stung whenever he moved his head. But so dimmed he was with fear, with fatigue and with hunger, he felt no pain nor understood much of what they said to him. The long list of his crimes flowed over his all but senseless head.

'We'll bring him to his senses soon enough!' Mortimer promised. Isabella's eyelids flickered. Revenge might be sweet; but of revenge she had had enough. She looked with distaste upon the poor broken thing that had been Hugh Despenser; she was weary of the whole affair.

'The sentence is just,' Mortimer reminded her. 'And you must be present to see it carried out.'

She wanted to cry out *No!* This death the man deserved; but from the sight of so hideous a dying she should be protected. But, let her falter now and she lost Mortimer's respect; and with it his love for ever.

She nodded.

The gallows, forty feet high and the greatest ever seen, stood waiting. Naked the prisoner was led forth; and still he moved as in a dream. But soon—as Mortimer had promised—he was brought back to his senses. The traitor's death was enlivened by little tricks of Mortimer's devising. Despenser had been the King's lover; now his member was torn from him. The air was rent with his screaming.

'Now he comes to his senses!' Mortimer said. Isabella sent him a side-long look; he was clearly well-satisfied. She bit upon her lip to thrust down the sickness. She held it back while the screams came fainter and then died. She was thankful the man was dead before the disembowelling; thankful for her own sake rather than for his.

She held back her sickness until she reached her closet; and there the vomit burst forth. She drew the bolt upon the door and sponged her hands and face; her women must not see a chicken-hearted Queen.

She was herself when she faced Mortimer again. She was more than herself. She had not shirked one moment of that hideous dying; she was stronger now than ever before . . . stronger and more woman. And so Mortimer found her when he came to her that night. A new lust stirred in her blood.

Chapter Thirty-Three

The King wept for his love and would not be comforted. As always his grief flowed into words. 'She shall pay for it! By God's Face she shall pay! A woman present at his death—and such a dying! From such a dying God preserve all good men.' He crossed himself. 'A woman? *No woman but a wolf—he* said that, Hugh. And he said right. Wolf she is and those that trust in her shall rue it. She . . . she . . .'

The words died in his throat. He stood there, his body shaken with long shuddering sighs, his face purple with the congestion of blood. Lancaster thought he would take a fit—and could not but wish that he would. Better the King fall senseless never knowing the thing they purposed against him.

'She . . . she . . .' The hot wrath of the Plantagenets burst through, drying his tears. 'By God I'll make an end of her! If I have no knife I'll tear her with my teeth!'

'Sir, leave such talk. Should it reach the ears of Madam the Queen, it could do you no good!'

'Good? What good from her, she-wolf that she is! And what evil can she do me now? She has murdered my only friends. Hugh was a father to me—more loving than my own father, that man of stone. And his son was a brother to me—truer than my own false brothers. He was both brother and son; a better son than my eldest that stands with his mother to betray me! Now I am alone, alone. Well—' and in his grief he screamed aloud, 'what more evil can she do me, what?'

It was clear he had no notion of the evil intended—the taking of his crown.

'Comfort yourself, sir,' Lancaster said. He had come to some unwilling pity; the man was, after all, his cousin and his King. He treated the King with kindness, allowing him every freedom he might. Though guards were posted on wall and gate the King might walk in the gardens at his will; he dined with his host and, when the royal mood allowed, they played chess together. A pleasant enough prison . . . but still it was prison; it was prison.

Feverishly the King waited for news; but for him it was always bad. Those that had followed their King had come, all of them, to a traitor's death.

'They stood by their allegiance; to follow his King is a man's bounden duty!' the King cried out. 'And yet they died as traitors—and no trial; no word allowed in their defence. It is against the law!'

'It is the law; the Despensers made it!' Lancaster said and thought of his brother.

It is against the law. It was not the King alone that cried out upon these executions; everywhere men were saying the same thing. Those that loved the Queen said, *It is Mortimer! Mortimer rules the armies and gives his orders—Mortimer and not the Queen!* And those that feared lest the future be worse than the past said, *Shall King Mortimer reign over us? And shall he be more merciful than the Despensers? Have we exchanged a hard yoke for a harder?*

Shut within Kenilworth the King had time to think. The whole country, it seemed, hated him. Why? What had he done?

Lancaster told him.

'Cousin, it was your friends. You did not protect us from the Despensers, their cruelty, their greed; you did not see to it that the people, high or low, had simple justice. Why should they love you?'

'But hate. Such hatred! They murdered my good Stapledon for no reason but that he was my friend. And for that London shall suffer, the whole city. I'll forgive them, never!'

And he doesn't understand, Lancaster thought half-pitying, half-angered, that London wants no forgiveness from the King, nor any truck with him. Finished. Finished with him for ever!

The slow months went by. Autumn was golden in the land. The leaves fell and cold winds blew. Soon it would be winter.

Anger against Mortimer was growing; his arrogance, his harshness, his greed a continual exacerbation. He openly played King, yes, even in the Queen's bed. Opinion in that matter was changing also; he befouled her name. Even in London some remembered with regret the imprisoned King. In himself he had been well enough—an easy goodnatured fellow for the most part; a kind way with simple folk. The Despensers dead, he might, with good counsel, yet do well. Surely he had learned his bitter lesson.

No-one quicker than Isabella to catch the slightest changing of the wind.

'The King must not be allowed to make his peace with London!' she told Mortimer. 'Be very sure his first condition would be your death!' She closed her eyes against the thought of that beloved head rotting upon London Bridge. 'We must summon Parliament at once. It must depose him—the useless King, and put my son in his place!'

Walter Reynolds, primate of England and tool to whatever man sat in power, had already given the matter some thought.

'Madam, without the King's assent you can do nothing. So long as he lives he is still King; and, unless he give his consent, cannot be deposed. You must send to him, Madam, on behalf of the whole realm, to summon Parliament, and himself attend it. Of deposition —no word! Say merely that it is needful for him to discuss and dispose of . . . certain difficulties.'

Let him ride the countryside! Let him show his handsome face in London. With the ever-growing anger against Mortimer who knew what might not happen? She was too clever to speak her fear; he too clever not to guess it.

'Madam, he'll not come,' Reynolds told her. 'I know him well! He'll not come; but we must *send*: and those we send must speak for the whole country—barons and bishops and citizens from every shire.'

The archbishop had prophesied truly. The King refused to summon Parliament—much less attend it. 'I have no truck with traitors!' he said.

Back it came, the grand representative embassy. 'The King is filled with that same evil purpose as in the past!' they reported;

and nipped the tender buds of affection beginning to unfold towards the King.

The Queen smiled, and herself called Parliament. Early in the new year of grace thirteen hundred and twenty-seven Parliament met.

Anger had turned once more against the King; anger more deep, more bitter and more lasting than before. He had refused to meet his Parliament, he had denounced the country's embassy as traitors! Now every man that entered London, were it but for an hour, was made to swear upon holy relics to take his stand with the Queen.

De Bettoyne, Mayor of London, put into high office by the Queen herself, petitioned barons, bishops and citizens throughout the land to beseech Parliament depose the King and set the Prince of Wales upon the throne.

Things were moving . . . moving.

January the thirteenth. The princes of church and state riding to Guildhall to hear my lord bishop of Winchester make public accusation against the King. The good bishop had been one of the embassy to Kenilworth and smarted still.

The King's offence lost nothing in the telling. Ugly the tale and cunningly he played upon his listeners. With one voice they swore to support the Queen and her son; to fight for them to the death. One by one they came forward to pledge their faith—bishops, barons and knights; judges, mayors, sheriffs and chief citizens. And, the news spreading, people came posting in from the country so that the swearing-in took three whole days.

That first day, Orleton, striking while the iron was hot, preached against the King on Tower Hill to a congregation of humbler folk —a congregation larger than ever a church could hold. He took as his text, *A foolish King shall ruin the people.* Every foolishness, every weakness was held up to hatred; of any real kindliness, any real goodness—nothing! An eloquent preacher this Orleton, that knew well how to stir the people! And stir them he did so that they cried out in hatred *Away with the King!*

The second day Winchester, also, preached on Tower Hill. He took as his text *My head is sick.* 'When the head of a kingdom is sick beyond curing, then that head must be taken off!' The crowd roared its delight.

The third day of the swearing, my lord the primate of England preached in the great hall of Westminster; his audience consisted, for the first time, of all three estates—the church, the peers, and, represented by their members in Parliament, the commons. He took as his text *Vox populi vox dei* flattering them that the voice of the people was indeed the voice of God. 'And now that voice has declared that the King must be put from the throne never to rule again. Therefore, in the name of the people, we, bishops, princes and commons do renounce our homage. And, in that same name, are agreed together that his first-born son shall wear the crown in his stead.'

And with one voice the congregation roared its assent.

They had reckoned without the boy—the Prince of Wales. He hated Mortimer, he did not wholly trust his mother . . . and he loved his father. The outcry against the Despensers he perfectly understood. But they were dead, they had paid for their sins. His father, he knew, was not a wise King nor even a wise man; but he was, for the most part, kindly; and, if he heeded his council could make a good enough King. Any way you looked at it he was a better person than Mortimer; and *he was the King*, the King crowned and sanctified.

'I am not willing to step into my father's shoes while he still wears them,' he told his mother. 'I am not old enough! The crown is too heavy; the throne too high . . . too hard.'

She held herself in to patience. 'The voice of the people is the voice of God; the archbishop has said it!' she told him.

He lifted his troubled face. 'The voice of the people is the voice of wild beasts. I have heard it!'

'Then it is wise not to offend them. Please them while they are willing to be pleased. The country is done with your father. Whatever you say, whatever you do, they'll have no more of him. If you are not willing they'll find another to step into his shoes.'

She saw him start as though stung. *Another to step into the King's place, and that other not myself; not the Prince of Wales!*

She nodded. 'And believe me, they'll not have far to seek!'

Someone . . . not far to seek! Can she mean Mortimer?

She said nothing; but from her sly and secret smiling he thought that she did.

He said, and he could scarce speak for anger and dismay, 'Madam, you must give me time to think!'

The more he thought about it, the less he liked it. He could see no way out. He could not thrust his father from the throne. Nor could he, by refusing, give up his own right to anyone on earth, not even to his brother. As for Mortimer—Mortimer that slept in the King's bed—so long as there remained a son of the blood royal, the people would never accept him as King. And, if there were no such son, still they would not accept him—already they were likening him to the Despensers. Let his mother say what she would there was no question of King Mortimer. But suppose he himself went on refusing? Suppose they offered the crown to his young brother? Then Mortimer would be King in all but name; John would never stand up to him. No! Whenever their father gave up the crown—whether by death or his own act—then the Prince of Wales must step into his rightful place.

But still he could not endure the thought of uncrowning a King —and that King his father.

Isabella sent Orleton to him, the subtle bishop.

'Sir,' Orleton said, 'be certain that the people will no longer endure your father as their King. And for him it would be better too. He would, believe it, be happy to put aside the cares of state; but happy, only, if he might put the crown into your hands, see his first-born son upon the throne. Kingship has taken overmuch of his leisure. He would be free to hunt, to sail his boats, to match his skills against others; free to choose whatever friends he please. . . .' Orleton paused that the boy might reckon for himself his father's lack of kingship, his father's light pleasures.

'If he were no longer King, freedom, leisure and respect would all be his. But only if *you* were King. But, if you are not King . . . *if you are not King* . . . it could be a 1other story. Sir, I pray you consider the matter.'

For the first time it came to h m that they had his father entirely in their hands; that they might make him suffer more than he had suffered already. If he himself were King he would see to it that his father's life was royal still. But, if he were not King? If he let them crown his brother?

The thought of how his father might fare in Mortimer's hands sent him running to his mother's closet.

'Madam,' he said, 'if I must be King, so let it be! But I'll not be led into this blindfold. If my father is willing I should have the crown, I'll take it. But not otherwise. Before God, not otherwise!'

'That is right and proper. Have you seen the articles of Deposition?' And when he shook his head, not having heard of such articles and never believing it would come to that, she said smiling, 'I think you should! Parliament wills that you should marry . . .'

She saw him take in his breath.

'Not Spain's daughter,' she said very smooth, reminding him that his father would have betrothed him against his will, 'but to a daughter of—whom do you think? The count of Hainault—no less! There's no mention of *which* daughter; it is not seemly that already you make your own choice. For here England marries Hainault, not Edward, Philippa. But for all that your choice stands.'

And when for every surprise and joy he could not speak she said, 'It is what I promised; I am one to keep my word, always.' She dropped a light kiss upon his forehead and went softly away.

Philippa. Philippa. Philippa. He found himself saying her name with a longing that brought him to the edge of tears.

He stiffened himself. Not even to make her a Queen would he accept the crown against his father's will; not though it meant losing her altogether. Nor would he agree to the littlest thing to his father's hurt; nor would she wish it, neither.

He cast his eye upon the document. It was very long; disturbed as he was he had not patience to read it through. His mother had marked the clause concerning his betrothal and upon that his eye lit and lingered . . . *and we will that our lord the King shall wed a daughter of the count of Hainault.* . . . It was enough; he would read the rest tomorrow.

And so he missed the clause that followed . . . *and because of the anguish she has suffered our lady the Queen shall continue to reign all her life.*

Chapter Thirty-Four

In the comfort of Kenilworth and the courtesy of his host, Edward could not believe that his people were finished with him; not though he had heard of Parliament's decision.

'It is no Parliament. I did not call it. I do not recognise it.'

'But the people recognise it. The whole country is set against you, cousin—' and Lancaster no longer called him *Sir*. 'Soon the embassy will be here to tell you so.'

'I'll not receive it. I sent the last one away with a flea in its ear.'

'Had you received it with courtesy things might be better for you now. Now they will bring you a heavier message; and it will not be a request; it will be a demand!'

'No demand can separate me from the crown. No man can take it from me. The sacrament was sealed into my flesh with holy oils. This embassy shall fare no better than the first, I promise you!'

Wandering the winter walks of Kenilworth he thought that, after all, he would receive the embassy—and receive it with courtesy. He must, perhaps, bargain with them a little; accept a Council of their choosing if there was no other way—though God knew he'd had enough of their Ordainers!

But what had they got against him? They said he lived a life of pleasure.

Pleasure? What pleasure? Self-pitying—and not without cause— he took himself back over his life.

Save for those two friends of his heart—a loveless life. For the boy the rod; for the young man humiliation upon humiliation. And always those he loved torn from him. From this place where now he lived, a prisoner, Thomas of Lancaster, liar and traitor, had dragged Piers out to die. An old story .... but the heart, remembering, ached still.

They blamed him for the loss of Scotland; Scotland that, for all his glory, his father had never won. Scotland was never lost because never won! They blamed him for extravagance. Extravagant—with what? His father had left the country bogged down with debt. Whatever he himself had spent upon his friends was nothing but a fleabite to what his father has squandered upon his useless wars.

They blamed him for preferring men to women; well, who could blame him? Women were not to be trusted. Look at his wife—lustful, deceitful, cruel and wanton; and hard, hard with her ambition . . . through her Hugh had come to a cruel death.

Well, what was done was done; no sense in weeping. He'd receive the embassy and come to terms. He'd call a fresh Parliament and choose a Council strong enough to keep it down. But first of all he'd deal with *that bitch*—the Queen!

At the thought of her his mouth drew to a bitter line. Had a Queen's head ever rotted upon the Bridge! If not hers should be the first!

The embassy had reached Kenilworth. The King had worked himself into cheerfulness; he received them with courtesy. That these men making their humble salutations meant to take away his crown he could not believe. But when, at their request, he had withdrawn into his closet with my lord bishop of Winchester, no friend of his, and with Orleton of Hereford, still less a friend, he was forced to believe it.

'Sir,' Orleton said and minced no word, 'the country will have no more of you. We are willing to put the lord Prince of Wales in your place. If you consent, so it shall be. But if you do not consent—we must choose some other.'

'My lords,' he told them, 'I cannot think my son will take the throne without my goodwill.'

'Sir, it is so. He asks your blessing; and you would be wise to give it. For, if the natural heir refuse, then our choice is wide. We may choose a King not of your house!' He let that sink in. 'The lord Prince John is very young; and why should we take a child when we can take a strong man? Yet the lord Prince of Wales promises well; with him we should be content. The choice is yours.'

A strong man. Who but Mortimer? Courage fell from him like a rag.

He had no choice; no choice. But, for all that, he could not force the bitter words upon his tongue. Dumb as an ox he nodded.

Without further word the two bishops returned to the great hall to beckon Lancaster; and those three led the King back to face them all.

There they stood—priests and nobles and common people. All, all inexorable, unpitying.

It was the end. Even he knew it.

He staggered and must have fallen save for the arms that upheld him. Tears pouring down his cheeks washed away the last remnants of his kingship. Voice strangled in his throat he spoke the words from which there was no going back.

'For my many sins I am punished; therefore I beseech your pity in this my fall. My people hate me; and for that I must grieve. Yet I am glad my eldest son finds grace in your sight. I give thanks to God and to you, for choosing him to be King.'

He was all-but swooning; and they carried him from the room.

Next day, eyes sunk deep within an ashen face and all in black, the King met his lieges for the last time.

It was Sir William Trussell that spoke the words to free England from its allegiance. He spoke them with pleasure; his life and lands had been declared forfeit for his part at Boroughbridge and he hated the King.

'I, William Trussell, proctor of the earls, the barons and all these others, having full and sufficient power, do give back to you, Edward, once King of England, the homage and fealty of the people of this land. Hereafter they will account you as a private person without any manner of royal dignity.'

And now Orleton, unpitying, presented the regalia they had brought with them; and with his own hands Edward of Carnarvon took the crown and the sceptre, took the orb and the spurs resplendent upon their cushion and placed them within those hands that had worked for his fall.

Last step of all. Sir Thomas Blount, Steward of the King's household, traitor that had betrayed his King in Wales, did the thing which is done only upon the death of a King. He broke his staff across.

A King no more he let them lead him away.

The new King's peace had been proclaimed; the Council of Regency chosen.

Isabella tapped with a jewelled finger upon the parchment.

'The Council for my son's minority,' she told Mortimer. 'The names for me to refuse or accept as I choose. I can, it seems, do no wrong!'

'Then we have them all—Council and people—fast in our hands!'

'Only if we're careful; only if we're wise. For that reason I'll take no place upon the Council!'

He stared at that. Had she gone crazy to refuse herself place of power . . . *the* place of power; head of the Council, her right as Queen?

She laughed in his face. 'Oh Mortimer, Mortimer, *consider*! The country's unsettled, restless. Some turning of the tide there's bound to be—pity for a fallen King, blame for those that put him from the throne. Ebb and flow; it is the way of men! Let this Council prove never so wise, some offence it's bound to give. If anger rises, *when* it rises let the Council take the blame; they, not us!'

'Well enough for you! But what of me? A man must speak for himself!'

'There'll be plenty to speak for you—trust me for that! You're a soldier; the best in England. Keep that image bright. But, state affairs! Let the Council bear all. In its shadow we two shall rule!'

'It sounds well enough!' And he was doubtful. 'Before I agree let's hear the names of our friends.'

'There's Orleton for one. I name him Treasurer—and a useful treasurer we two shall find him! His devotion to your house and especially to you has long been proved; and besides, he carries great weight. There's Hotham of Ely—we'll make him Chancellor; he'll carry out our wishes, the good bishop . . .'

She went through the list, adding or striking out as it seemed to them good.

'I am content,' he said at last. 'Save for Lancaster. Him I do not trust!'

'Nor I; but it makes no matter. With all our friends he'll be out-voted; It is right and proper he should rule the Council; his kinship to the King and to me demands it. It will reassure the people. And when aught goes wrong, he'll take the blame. The people's patience is not eternal. It'll not be long before Uncle Henry follow Uncle Thomas to a traitor's death!' Her lips lifted to a smile.

She was indeed the Queen that could do no wrong; and certainly in the shadow of the Council she and Mortimer closed their hands upon the power. And certainly Orleton was to them the best of Treasurers; the Council saw to it that the Queen's dower was restored and her incomes trebled.

'It is not enough,' Mortimer said. 'Not near enough.'

'It is not enough,' she agreed, 'seeing that I have gone short for years. But patience; there'll be more . . . and more.'

In January the jewels, the plate, the tapestries and all the furniture of the younger Despenser were granted to the Queen—a treasure beyond price. She delighted in their immense value—she had been poor so long. It gave her an exquisite joy to wear those jewels her bitter enemy had worn, to eat from the plates he had used. She would remember the cold eyes, the contemptuous mouth; already the crows had taken them from the head that rotted yet upon the Bridge. She would whip herself into a very madness of joy fingering the treasures of the dead man. Nothing of his, she vowed, should escape her. She bade her Wardrobe Clerk search the inven-tories to seek out the least of Despenser's goods. It was the first sign of the greed that was to fasten upon her; it showed itself now less as greed than as triumph of revenge.

She proved to Mortimer the value of friends on the Council, himself absent. Parliament, urged by this same Council, made him the tremendous gift of Glamorgan and the lordship of Denbigh —all Despenser land.

'I never thought to sleep with the lord of Glamorgan and Den-bigh!' she said and laughed.

'I must have Gloucester lands and Gloucester's title!' he told her. 'I'll not rest until I'm earl of Gloucester!'

'Have care, my love. There's an old tale of the tinker that, for a good deed, might name his reward. And so he did. He asked and kept on asking; and got it, too. Until he asked too much . . .'

'I am no tinker. I am Mortimer. And Gloucester's title I mean to have!'

She sighed. She said no more.

The Queen could do no wrong; she ruled the country. Parliament and Council bowed to her bidding. The young King she kept beneath her eye; she chose his bodyguard. Wherever he went there went a bishop, an earl and two barons; they obscured his judgment with their specious arguments, they curbed his freedom, they reported upon his every word. So bound, so blinded, so deafened there could be little trouble from him.

The Queen and Mortimer in control.

In Kenilworth Edward of Carnarvon gave himself to alternate despair and hope. When he heard that his cousin Lancaster, his kindly gaoler, led the Council, his heart lifted; when he heard the names of those that sat with him, his heart sank—too many were Mortimer's friends. When he heard that both the Queen and Mortimer had no place, up went his heart once more; when he heard that Orleton was not only of the Council but had been advanced to Treasurer, down it went again.

But nothing could keep that hopeful spirit down. When the sun shone in the winter garden where every twig sparkled like jewels in his lost crown how could he help but be cheerful? 'I am not finished yet; by God's Face not finished!' he told Lancaster, 'I have friends. I have friends, yet!'

'Sir, I beseech you, put away such thoughts,' Lancaster said. 'The country has cast off its allegiance. Consider! You are a prisoner; but nothing's so bad it couldn't be worse! Here you are honourably treated; here you may walk freely and receive your friends. None but myself would, or could, allow it. This talk of winning back your crown could lead to much evil for you. A little patience and you shall fare better still—the lord your son has told me. Then you shall go free as the best gentleman in the land.'

'I am the King! Kingship is sealed into my flesh and only with the flesh can it be dissolved.'

'Is the prisoner comfortable at Kenilworth?' the Queen asked. Neither King nor husband would she call him ever again.

'Too much so!' Mortimer said, gloomy.

'So long as he's kept fast I am content.'

'Lancaster's a fool!' Mortimer said, spiteful. It irked him that Edward who had so rigorously confined him in the Tower should, in his own prison, find such comfort.

'The man was my husband and a King. I'd not have him too harshly confined.'

'And if Lancaster prove too much of a fool? If there should be danger of escape?'

'Then it is upon the prisoner's own head.'

Chapter Thirty-Five

On the first day of February, in the year of grace thirteen hundred and twenty-seven, the young King went to his crowning. He was scarce three months above his fourteenth birthday.

Walking beneath the blue velvet canopy his young face was troubled. Was it right to put a King from his place, a King anointed before God? It was a question he still must ask himself, and one new question he'd been forced to ask. It was last night in the Tower where he had lain to make his progress through London today. 'If a King may be so easily cast from the throne, how might it go with me?'

'It shall go very well, sir—if you will work with your princes and not against them,' Lancaster had said.

Well, it was an answer; but it was not the whole answer. His father had lost his crown because he'd not been strong enough to keep it. Unsleeping, the boy had made his oath, beseeching God to help him keep it. *I will be strong. From these princes I shall learn the craft of Kingship. Thereafter I shall rule with a sceptre not of gold but of iron . . . the iron rod.* And, so vowing, he had fallen asleep.

It had not been a happy sleep. For his father that had lain in this very bed the night before his crowning, stood before him. *I cannot find the crown,* his father said, tears pouring down his face. *I will help you.* He wanted to say it, but the words choked in his throat. He had woken . . . and the tears on his father's cheeks were the tears upon his own. It was long before he slept again for pity of his father. Tomorrow he would be crowned. Tomorrow, or the next day, he would take his father from prison and set him up with all royal state as befitted the father of the King. Tomorrow . . .

Now, walking, his brother with his cousins carrying the great mantle high above the frost-slippery cobbles, monks before him chanting and swinging censers, bishops and barons behind, each in his degree, he remembered his vow . . . *a sceptre not of gold but of iron*. He walked between Lancaster and Mortimer; each held a hand lest, in his great robes, he slip upon the cobbles. Dislike for Mortimer rose strong in the boy; it was as much as he could do not to pull his hand away. He had wanted to keep the man from the crowning, but Lancaster had counselled a still tongue. 'To question the man's presence would arouse Madam the Queen's displeasure: Even a King at his crowning might find that a bitter burden.' Well, he must wait. Today the sceptre of gold; tomorrow the rod of iron.

Across Palace Yard went the great procession while, forgetful of the bitter cold, the people stood and cheered. *So they cheered my father; yet they had put him from the throne. But they'll not put me, so gracious and obedient . . . till it be time for the rod of iron.*

He went through the long ceremony; he carried himself well. He knew exactly what he must do; his cousin of Lancaster had rehearsed it with him.

He had shown himself to the people and heard their joyful acclaim. He had sworn the oath his father had sworn, that same oath, word for word in the French tongue; the oath they now held against his father saying he had not been faithful. Now, taking the words upon his own lips, he felt himself exalted. This oath he would keep because it was a right oath; he wanted to keep it.

They were unrobing him; he felt upon the head and breast the sacred oils. They were leading him to the high altar. Lying there, offering himself to God, he felt exalted and strong; but he felt humble, too. And now the archbishop took him by the hand and led him back to the throne that they might robe him in the square mantle of majesty. It was heavy with gold and his young shoulders ached beneath the weight; but he carried himself upright. They brought the Sword of Mercy and the Rod of Peace; and they put upon his finger the ring that married him to his people.

And now they brought him the sceptre of gold. He saw it—his rod of iron—and grasped it until the knuckles showed white.

And now the supreme moment.

He felt the crown heavy upon his head and held himself rigid lest it slip. Exaltation fell from him. He knew himself young and weak and lonely. The crown was too heavy, and his robes were too heavy . . . and he wanted his father.

He sat at supper beneath the canopy of estate—the highest place of all. On one side sat his mother, on the other the archbishop that had crowned him this day. Behind his chair, stood, as was proper, his brother John; behind his mother stood, as was not proper, hated Mortimer, usurping Lancaster's place of honour. Sitting there, he sensed the lust between those two—his mother and Mortimer— rising high; and, above that lust, triumph in today's business not for his sake but for their own. They meant to use him for their own advantage and he must submit; for a while. Well, let them wait; wait for the rod of iron!

He was too young to understand that he who wields the rod of iron is loneliest of all.

Knights knelt offering him this and that; he scarce saw them. He was weighed down with fear—the burden of being a King. He was not ready; not yet. He was still a boy, a boy only. And like any boy he wanted his father; he wanted peace and goodwill between his father and mother. But what he wanted most and couldn't have and never had had, he wanted a home.

Quite suddenly he remembered Philippa and was comforted. His thoughts came gentler now. He was the King and there was no going back. He would learn to be not only a strong King but a good one. It was as though she had whispered in his ear.

Philippa. She was his haven and his home; she was his conscience and his truth. His mother, he knew, thought little of his betrothed. Once, to serve her own ends, she could not enough praise Philippa; now, those ends gained, she did not trouble to hide her opinion that the girl had not an overflowing measure of beauty, nor the quickness to leap to a judgment. Maybe! Philippa considered a matter with her good heart and her good head. She was not quick to punish; there was mercy in her. And where there is no real goodness beauty grows weary to the eye. But Philippa's face he loved; it would carry its own beauty ever fresh and new. That those two, Mortimer and his mother belittled Philippa he would remember; one more item in the long account!

In Kenilworth Edward did not cease to hope. He made use of his limited freedon to talk with all manner of men—with merchants and soldiers, with craftsmen and farmers; he knew the gossip of the outside world.

Hatred of Mortimer, growing doubt of the Queen were resulting in some turning towards the one-time King; a movement as yet unanchored and frail. But there were some that, come within the circle of his charm and wishful to comfort him, said more of the matter than they knew; or even believed.

'Plans are afoot. Soon I shall sit in Westminster again; the people will see to it,' he told Lancaster.

'Cousin, Cousin!' And would the fool never learn? 'They have crowned the King; he sits upon the throne. You know it well.'

'It is not his place; I am not dead. Nor would he keep it against my will—his father and his King; he has said it. He will himself step down and yield me my place.'

'Your princes would not allow it!'

'The common people turn to me.'

'Never count upon them; they have no leader. And if they had? Against the sword of the barons and the cross of the bishops they could not stand.'

Edward paid no heed, how could he help but hope? Even here, in his prison, he had friends sworn to his cause; and chief among them he counted the Dunhevid brothers. Despenser men both; on that account Stephen the elder had lost his lands and would move heaven and earth to get them back. The younger, Thomas, a Dominican friar, had the gift of words to move the passions of men . . . foolish men. Upon the King, the King alone, depended not good fortune alone but their very lives.

'Do not trust them, cousin,' Lancaster said. 'Yes, I have heard of their nonsense—tattlers and prattler both; their deeds do not match their words. And they are scoundrels, besides! But were they never so secret, never so brave, Kenilworth is strong to keep its prisoners. I tell you, again, there's no hope in them!'

But still the prisoner could not leave his hoping.

And now he had much to make him hopeful. Day by day the people's anger grew, and the more their anger, the more

Mortimer pressed with cruel thumb. The Council could not stay his hand—he had too many sycophants there; and the infatuated Queen gave him his head. Still he searched out any that had stood by the King—combing them out, he said, like lice upon a comb. Once the King had used those words of him; now it pleased him to fling back the words; revenge worked like a madness in the blood. All those he so much as suspected he hanged with every obscenity of a traitor's death—good loyal men. And any that, tongue slipping, ventured a good word for the King, was hanged likewise. Again the country was sown thick with gallows. Nor was this all. Among the Queen's very followers dissension had spread. Come to know her better, some sickened of her rule, others thought they should be better rewarded. Nor was the country quite so pleased now with the good Queen. It was unbecoming that she should take a lover, more unbecoming her shameless flaunting of him, most unbecoming of all that he should be Mortimer the oppressor. Dissatisfaction grew daily; willing ears were bent to the stirring words of the irresponsible friar.

And the common people—Lancaster knew it well—did, indeed, pity Edward of Carnarvon. Now it was remembered how once he had sought out humble folk, delighting in their company, preferring them to his princes; for which reason his princes were angered against him!

Talk of rescue for Edward grew daily louder. Such plots must, in the end, come to nothing. They were planned by those with no knowledge, no resources and no leader. But they unsettled the country; they could bring death to plotters and innocent, alike. To the prisoner such plots must bring greater misery . . . if nothing worse.

Lancaster was not minded to shoulder responsibility any longer. He besought Mortimer to relieve him.

Nothing could please Mortimer more. Now it was not revenge alone that drove him; ambition forever pricked with wounding spur. Edward of Carnarvon dead, the Queen was free to take a husband. And who that husband but the man she so infatuatedly loved? And why not? Mortimer blood was as royal as her own, blood of the great Arthur himself. His wife? She was neither young

nor strong . . . ailing they said. She'd not long stand in his way!
The young King? Let him show himself obedient and he could keep
his empty crown. If not; one could deal with him—and gladly.
When everything pointed to one glorious end, how should so
small a thing as a prisoner's death stand in the way?

'I shall remove the prisoner from Kenilworth,' he informed the
Queen. 'I shall put him in charge of two watchdogs. If there's
any more nonsense, they'll not hesitate to show their teeth—and
use them, too!'

'I'll not have him hurt,' she said; and meant it. As long as he
made no trouble surely he was harmless enough! Even now her
thoughts had not reached to his death.

'They'll not bite unless they must.'

To that she could make no objection; it was reasonable enough.

'Where do you take him?'

'To Berkeley.'

'And the watchdogs?'

'My son-in-law for one—naturally!'

She nodded. Thomas of Berkeley owned the place. He was
much beholden to Mortimer and would happily oblige him in the
matter of the prisoner.

'Somewhat harsh?' she asked, a little troubled.

'Let your husband, my dear, taste his own physic!'

At the word *husband* she winced, remembering, as was meant,
the miseries she had suffered at his hands.

'And watchdog, number two?'

'Maltravers.'

'You keep it in the family!' Maltravers was his brother-in-law;
him she knew, also. He had fought against the King at Boroughbridge; but he'd been one of the lucky ones. He'd escaped to France
and he'd been one of the first exiles to join her cause. But even
then she hadn't liked him . . . and she didn't like him now. A hard
man and sour; even to the Queen ungracious. Well, so much the
better gaoler! But for all that she sighed. She disliked the thought
of the prisoner helpless in the hands of Mortimer's kin. But passion
for Mortimer was greater than any compassion, greater than any
good within herself, greater than her fear of God.

'And the arrangements for his keep?' And there, at least, she might a little sweeten the prisoner's confinement.

'Five pounds a day.'

The exact sum the King had allowed his Queen for the upkeep of her royal state when the Despensers had filched her lands and incomes.

'It is enough,' she said.

'It is more than enough! More than he deserves; much, much more!' His brow darkened, remembering how, in The Tower, his uncle had starved to death; and how, he himself, for all his youth had scarce the strength to escape with his life.

'I had rather he were left with Lancaster.' She was still troubled.

'Then, my dear, you're a fool. Lancaster's too soft. There's overmuch talk in Warwickshire of rescuing your husband. No, my dear, I mean to keep my prisoner safe, and for that be thankful. You had a husband that took no thought for you; be glad you have a lover that does!'

It was only afterwards that she remembered the word he had used . . . had a husband. *Had.*

Chapter Thirty-Six

'Cousin, you must up and dress!' Thomas of Lancaster spoke in the dark night.

The prisoner sat up in bed, shielding his eyes against the lantern-light. Half-asleep, he was hunting still. Piers rode on one side, Hugh on the other; he could feel the wind lifting hair and beard.

'Up? At this hour?' And the wind in his hair was the draught that lifted the curtains at his door. His heart began to beat in his throat. Could this be, he wondered, even now not full-awake, the first step in his escape? Had Lancaster come into the business after all? One look at Lancaster killed the hope, brought him back to cold commonsense.

'It is the order of Parliament,' Lancaster said.

Dressing hastily in the flickering light, Lancaster handing him his clothes, Edward could not rid himself of his dear hope. This was the rescue—though Lancaster did not know it.

He followed Lancaster out into the courtyard. One look at the escort that waited—and his heart sank. The grimness of their bearing, the lack of respect that allowed him to stand unsaluted, the unwillingness to meet his eye told him the truth.

'It would need an army to take you out of their hands!' Lancaster said, pitying the man. 'I warned you; but you'd not be warned. Now you are taken from my care. Pray God things go not too hard with you, Cousin. Farewell.' He bent and unexpectedly, even to himself, kissed the prisoner on both cheeks.

A hard journey, little stop for food and less for rest. Hard for any man on the rough tracks they followed instead of roads; for the prisoner that had not set foot in the stirrup for five months, bitter hard; and, though he swayed in the stirrup, there was no respite.

Riding for the most part at night, hurried through such towns as they could not by-pass, the face of the prisoner was scarce seen. And, if it was? A man hurried to his doom was no new sight.

Journey to break the heart. But even so there were compensations. He felt the free wind on his cheek, was aware of rising sap and the life of growing things; and, in those brief snatches of daylight, saw the willow golden by clear-running water and the new leaves tender and bright.

On Palm Sunday they reached Gloucester and Llantony Abbey, where the monks, hiding their pity, served the prisoner with a loving respect. For them he was still the King; but for them only. Always half-a-dozen of the escort went with him, even into his bedchamber; and there they sat dicing and drinking, swearing, spitting, urinating, caring not at all that they disturbed the prisoner's restless sleep.

The next day saw them at Berkeley, its single tower thrusting upwards into the sweet sky like a finger of doom.

An outer staircase led them to a doorway midway up the Tower, and there, in the guardroom, Sir Thomas Berkeley was waiting. He did not rise to greet his King nor speak a word of welcome; he motioned with a surly head and the gaoler led the prisoner away.

When he saw his lodgings he could not, at first, believe his eyes and refused to enter, so small it was, so dark with its slit of a window set high in the stonework. But there was no help for it; enter he must and the gaoler locked the heavy door behind him. Soon, as was his way, his spirits began to rise. It was not damp and it was not so very dark; the narrow window let in more light than one would have thought. The rushes upon the floor were clean; the pallet, too, was clean and the blankets, though thin, were fresh. There was a stool and a table, also, with quills and ink—an encouraging sign; a bucket stood in a corner so dark that a man had his privacy.

A prison cell; but a cell for an important prisoner, its furnishings not much worse that he'd endured many a time on the march. It was not a dungeon—and for that he was devoutly thankful; the dungeons, he reckoned, must lie beneath his cell. It would do well enough; he'd not be here long. He had seen Stephen Dunhevid along the road; Dunhevid had made a sign.

And soon he had further cause for hope. The gaoler was a Gloucester man and friendly. He knew nothing of politics; a simple fellow whose loyalties must shift with circumstances. Now, like many another, he was taken by the handsome looks, by the gentle charm the prisoner knew how to exercise. And the prisoner was the King; and a King forever carries about him the glory of kingship. And more. There were plans on hand to set him free, rumours everywhere. If a poor man played his part, if only to show some kindness, what reward might he not look for?

It was only too easy to find cause for kindness. But for him the prisoner must have gone hungry—the food was scant; the five pounds a day went to a worthier cause, in Berkeley's opinion, than the well-being of the man that once been King. Often the gaoler brought him food from his own table, coarse but grateful to an empty belly; and sometimes there would be a little wine, thin and sour—but still wine. And he would bring a blanket, ragged but clean, so that the prisoner might lie warmer at night. In spite of Mortimer he was not ill-treated; Berkeley and Maltravers had other things to do than sit at home and watch the prisoner; they must ride the wide countryside watchful for signs of revolt. By July they had Dorset under the whip with Hereford, Wiltshire, Hampshire and Somerset besides.

But for all that the conspiracy was growing.

'And it isn't only one place, lord King,' the gaoler told him. 'There's Gloucestermen and Warwickmen and there's men from Worcester and Stafford, aye, and from Oxenford, too. And it isn't only poor men like me want to see you back where you belong. There's lords and there's knights and there's priests. And, best of all, there's friars that move quick about the country; they're the ones to spread the news. All, all, lord King set to put you on the throne again!'

'Friend, when that time comes I'll not forget you. By God's Face I swear it!'

With such a gaoler the room seemed ever less small, less dark. Through the high window he could see the summer sky, and through the bars the sunlight slanted in upon the rushes turning them to gold. And sometimes the gaoler would let him walk in the garden where he would lift up his eyes to the bright hills and feel the wind on his face. But for lack of exercise he tired quickly and then the small, bare room beckoned like home. And, best of all, the gaoler brought him news so that his fingers seemed to touch not freedom, only, but the very crown. Yet news was not always good; he must learn the hard way of patience, and, harder still, to control his passionate Plantagenet pride.

Stephen Dunhevid had been arrested; Berkeley had put him to a hateful death. Berkeley himself, making occasion to visit the prisoner, had spared him no cruel detail.

'Lord King do not grieve overmuch, there's others aplenty to take his place!' The kindly gaoler sought to comfort him; but he could take no comfort, grieving not only for plans gone awry but for the death of his friend—and so hideous a death! He prayed long for the souls of those that, worthless though men called them, had yet died for him. Thereafter he prayed for himself. *Oh God release me from this place that I may prove a worthier King. But if it be Your will that I shall reign no more, then help me to be a worthier man. I do repent me of my sins and follies and long only to serve You as You best wish.* And he remembered Llantony quiet among the Gloucester hills and the clean, simple lives of the monks; and he thought he might be well-content to live among them serving God until he died. But at other times he longed, unendurably, to sit once more upon the throne, to feel the crown once more upon his head. Kingship is not lightly put off. It is sealed into the flesh with holy oils.

It was night; what hour the prisoner could not tell. Unsleeping in the darkness he heard the noise—the shouts, the clash of steel, the unmistakable, sharp explosion of gunstones. Red flare from torches painted the high window, stole beneath the door; the cell was rosy with light. He heard footsteps; they were coming louder, coming nearer. He leaped from the mattress all-but suffocated by the mad beat of his heart. Was this the rescue; the rescue at last?

The key turned in the lock.

Friendly faces, God be thanked! No time for salutations. Hasty hands brought him his clothes, threw a cloak about him, drew on the riding-boots.

He was free.

He was riding in the night air, a good horse beneath him; a score of riders, friends, every one, closed about him. Beneath the good cloak his clothes were thin, were shabby; but much he cared for that! He rode free, free with his friends; nothing else mattered. Riding, he thanked God, muttering in his greying beard.

Edward of Carnarvon was free. Mortimer cursed when they brought him the news; cursed Berkeley for a fool that had left the castle to be pillaged and the prisoner taken from beneath his nose, cursed Maltravers and, most of all, cursed Edward himself. Isabella took the news grey-faced. And all the time a voice spoke clear in her head. *He must be found! Neither of us can permit the other to live.*

He must die. Her conscious mind refused the thought; her unconscious mind received it, accepted it.

First terror passed, she addressed herself to God, promising gifts and alms without stint; for a King's death a King's ransom. But God helps those that help themselves; and, quieter now, she considered the matter. Two things she must do at once—calm Mortimer and reassure her son.

High-painted, in full beauty, no whit troubled it would seem, she sought Mortimer. 'These friends of his!' And her scorn was high. 'Already, be sure, they're quarrelling over the prize. Well, they'll not keep him long; soon we shall have him in our hands again!'

'At which time,' he cried out, harsh, 'I trust you'll not be so tender of his comfort.'

'So you catch him and hold him fast, do with him what you will!'

And to her son, the new young King, seeing him shaken and

uncertain in his duty, she said, 'Your duty is clear—to stand by the oath you swore at your crowning. Those that work upon your father to revolt are guilty of treason against you, the King they have chosen. And, would God I might not say it, the greatest treason is his that gave away the crown declaring his will it should pass to you. Do not think to give it back; for that you cannot do! You have been chosen and consecrated. You are the King. Two Kings there cannot be. It would mean war; no less! Civil war—there's no war so bloody. For let which side win the country must bleed. We must find your father and keep him safe till all is quiet again. We must do it for his sake and for the country's sake.'

Torn with grief for his father, shaken by his own guilt, unable to trust her whom above all he should be able to trust, he made no answer. Time. He must have time.

She made her last effort. 'Sir . . . my son. When all is quiet again, your father shall live in honour and dignity. He shall have every-thing he asks, everything he can desire—'

'Save his freedom. Save his crown!'

When she would have answered to that he said—and there was a new authority in him, 'Madam leave me! I must consider the matter.'

Alone once more, in her closet the sweet reason she had shown to her lover and to her son fell from her. It was more than a rabble that marched with Edward of Carnarvon; and more, she guessed, would join him every day. The people were disappointed; and, like all disappointed people, angry. They'd expected, the Despensers gone, to find the land suddenly awash with milk and honey—the fools! Discontent—she'd call it nothing worse—was flowing to-wards herself and Mortimer. As yet there was no danger, but *send Mortimer away*. More than once Lancaster's veiled words had suggested it. Scarce troubling to hide her anger those words she had disregarded. Send Mortimer away! A confession of weakness. To keep him by her side was a confession of greater weakness—subtle as she was, that she did not understand. Without Mortimer she could not live.

Edward of Carnarvon's following was increasing; in every town and village men fell in to march beside him. The cold light of reason told her that there was little to fear; for lack of arms, of money, of leaders it must all come to nothing. But the cold shadow of fear was stronger. Lying sleepless by her lover she would ask herself how it would all end? How could she forget her husband's words that, no weapon being at hand, he would tear her with his teeth? And now could she forget how the younger Despenser had died—his member torn from him? What punishment then for him that had given that command; that had sinfully loved the Queen?

No need for fear. Mortimer knew the risks as well as she. Even while she besought her son, he had acted. His armies were combing the countryside; everywhere in market-place and on church door a reward was posted—a King's ransom for the man that had been King, dead or alive. With all her heart Isabella hoped it would be dead. There was neither spite nor revenge in the hope; merely the simple knowledge that it would be best for him, best for them all.

The revolt was at an end; the ringleaders secured, the King taken.

'He goes where there can be no escape!' Mortimer said.

Isabella nodded. Until now she had been glad to spare the prisoner the worst rigours of confinement; so she had assuaged the guilt that, in spite of reason, at times assailed her. Now, remembering her night-time terrors, she was not minded to suffer them again. As before she said, 'Do with him what you will!' And this time she added. 'I shall not enquire of him.'

Young Edward had had time to consider the matter. He had listened to Henry of Lancaster and to Orleton; the one twice-bound to his father by ties of blood, and leader of the Council; the other prince and priest of God. Those two had made things clear. His father had played both son and country false. He had delivered up the crown to his son; now he would snatch it back again. He would give the country over to the sword and the horrors of civil war. Such a war must be averted.

To step down from the throne stripped of his crown that though heavy was yet glorious, to be no more a King! It was a humiliation his spirit could not brook. This he would not, could not admit to himself. No. He must keep the crown because the people had chosen him; and because he must keep the oath sworn to them and to God.

Chapter Thirty-Seven

The King's dark journey had begun.

Where he was no man knew. Hustled from prison to prison—and each worse than the one before—he never saw sweet daylight now; scarce knew when summer ended or winter began. Always the bitter journey by night that he be not recognised and again rescued.

Riding; riding in the dark and the cold, the wind making nothing of his garments threadbare and in holes—those same garment in which he had been taken. Why give him better? If he died of the cold it would save himself and everyone else a good deal of trouble. They had shaved him—a further precaution against any man knowing the King; they had taken filthy water from the nearest ditch. His face, denuded of its beard, had a weak, womanish look; where they had cut him with the dirty razor, his face festered. Thin, grey, the once-clear skin scabbed and running; little fear of any man knowing the King!

Berkeley to Corfe, Corfe to Bristol, Bristol to a destination unknown; thence back to Berkeley. When he saw again that grim tower blocked against the sky his poor heart rejoiced. His own small room waited to welcome him, more dear than any palace; the kindly gaoler waited, more dear than son or daughter. He was coming home.

But it was a different gaoler. And it was a different cell . . . a dungeon cell.

Of all the cruelties he had been made to bear and had stoically endured, this was the most cruel. When they thrust him into the dark he sat upon the wet and filthy straw and wept.

Time was endless in the dark cell where he lay by the world forgotten. His eyes—the bright hunter's eyes—were growing dim with darkness and with tears. One privilege he was allowed; he might write to his wife and to his son—but to none other. The gaoler, stone-faced, unfriendly, with no mind to follow his predecessor into the grave for kindness to the prisoner, would bring him candle, paper, quills and inkhorn. Crouched upon the low stool, writing upon his knees, weak eyes peering close in the dim light, he would pour out his heart.

Whether they had received his piteous appeals he did not know; from neither of them an answer. He must wait, wait, wait, wear his heart out with waiting; but never an answer.

That he had never heard from his son was not to be wondered at. The young Edward had never received his letters; could not even discover where his father lay. As for his wife—it was no wonder, either; she never answered. To put herself into any sort of relationship with him was physically impossible; revulsion and guilt alike, forbade it. But she sent him gifts—as it might be to a beggar, linen and a woollen cloak lined with fur, not too good a fur; and was glad to be thus easily free of her duty. He never got her gifts. Sir Thomas Gurney, now in charge of the prisoner, took them for himself. Too good by far for the poor wretch in the cell! With the cloak she forced herself to send a few false words. She would have visited him long ere this but Parliament had forbidden; yet she would come soon. Her message he did not get, either, which was as well; she did not mean to set eyes again on that weak and handsome face. When she told Mortimer so, he laughed. If what Gurney wrote was true, that face was anything but handsome now! She heard it without pity; she had neither pity nor anger for him now, nor any desire for revenge. Nothing but a most deadly repulsion. She would die—or he should—before ever she endured the sight of him again.

He had stopped writing his letters; his last hope he knew to be hopeless. But since speak he must, he was pouring his heart out in a poem—lament for a life ruined, for friends false, for a wife faithless and cruel. A long poem; he had much to say and time was endless. Through the long unsleeping nights he thought upon it, through the long unending days he worked upon it. Searching his heart for the truth, he moved slowly from bitterness to acceptance; acceptance, first agonising step in his long calvary. Step by painful step he came from acceptance to prayer for forgiveness. So he came at last, to affirmation of his belief in God and His goodness. For always beneath his frivolities and vices he had held fast to his religion; and for that reason the monks at Neath and at Llantony had forgiven him much. Now, alone in the dark cell, his faith centred upon God. He spent his waking hours praying and writing; and both were his solace in the endless hours.

The Song of King Edward son of King Edward, that he himself made.

So he called it, defying those that had declared him not great Edward's true-born son. He wrote it in French, a tongue he held to be the true language of poetry—the tongue of his childhood, his innocence.

The first lines came easily; he wrote them, the tears pouring down his grey scabbed cheeks.

> My winter has come; only sorrow I see.
> Too often, too cruel, Fortune has spoken.
> Blow after blow she rains upon me,
> Heart, hope and courage, all, all she has broken.
> Be a man fair or be a man wise,
> Perfect in courtesy, honoured in name,
> If Fortune forsake him, if his luck flies,
> To the blast he stands naked—a fool come to shame.

Of Isabel and her part in this, he found, anger driving, only too easy to write.

> The greatest grief my heart must bear,
> The chiefest sorrow of my state
> Springs from Isabeau the Fair,
> She that I loved but now must hate.
> I held her true, now faithless she;
> Steeped in deceit, my deadly foe
> Brings naught but black despair to me,
> And all my joy she turns to woe.

And he forgot that he had never loved her, that he had neglected her for his mignons, shamed her with his mignons. He remembered only that a wife should be loving and true; and that she was unloving and false.

And since there was no hope in man he must turn himself to God and to sweet Jesus.

> To Him I turn my contrite heart,
> Who suffered for me on the cross.
> Jesus, forgive my baser part,
> Bend thou to me in my dire loss.
> For all my sins and treacherous deeds. . . .

Treacherous deeds. The words had written themselves; he stared at them astonished. Treacherous—he, so betrayed? His many sins he had, at last, faced; but treachery—never. Now, for the first time he must search his heart in the matter; and come to his bitter conclusion. Treachery, treachery was the word. He had forsworn the oath of his crowning, betraying his people and God Himself. His enemies had done less; far less. He had betrayed the King of Heaven; they but their earthly King. As he hoped for forgiveness he must learn to forgive them.

But it was hard, hard. His punishment was dire, was bitter, was never-ending; and he was but a man, and a weak one. There were backslidings when he cried aloud cursing them all—false wife, false friends. Then he must force his mind from their cruelty to thoughts of his young son, the boy that sat in his father's place; and he would remember that Ned had refused that place until his father should consent. Then, tenderly, he would pray, beseeching Jesus to keep the boy against all traitors, that all his enemies be brought to shame; and the boy himself grow wise and strong to shine bright in the chivalry of Christendom. Then he would pray for his son until his strength gave way and he lay prone in the filth of the floor.

Day by day searching his soul, agonising for the truth, reshaping his verses, polishing. But for all that it was not a good poem; yet it was the stuff of true poetry since his soul's agony reached out to move the hearts of those who should read it; even the heart of Isabella . . . some day.

And so he came to the last lines, asking the prayers of all men, wise and simple, entreating the ear of Mary, Mother of Mercies,

> That she beseech the child she bore,
> The Son that on her knee she sat,
> His tender grace on me to pour,
> And grant me mercy yet.

Gurney had received his orders. The Queen knew nothing of them; she desired to know no more of the affair. The prisoner's life grew ever more bitter. Such captivity was not fit for a savage beast let alone a man—and a man that had been a King. From his dungeon, than which he had imagined nothing worse, he was removed to a cell above a cesspool; the stink was so foul that never for a moment, could he forget it. He tasted it in his food so that, racked with hunger, he must turn from his meat in loathing; it followed him into his sleep so that he awoke retching upon an empty belly. When he tried to pray it came between himself and God. The stink fastened upon himself—it was in his body, in his hair, it had become the breath of his nostrils; it had become himself. The last cell had been dark and cold; here darkness was so dense, the cold so bitter, that though it was high summer without, with him it was forever black winter. And, since they no longer allowed him to write, no candle-light ever penetrated the darkness. Damp straw his body had grown used to; but the straw on which he now lay was no longer damp; it was wet from the cesspool and his own urine. It soaked through his rags, through the flesh to the very bones; he was racked with a swelling in his joints. He could not sleep for pain; and let him fall, for a moment into uneasy dreaming, he was awakened by vermin. Rats rustled in the straw, lice fed upon the once-fair hair, the once-bright cheeks of Edward of Carnarvon.

His mind began to play him tricks. For long stretches of time there was no clear understanding of where he was or what had happened. Now he was a child, now a man, now a King to rule, now a boy to be punished. His father came, the great tall man with the old, cold face. His mother never came; it did not surprise him—he had never truly known her. But Madam Queen Margaret came and sat with him and held his hand; she loved him and he loved her and when she went away he cried like the child he had become.

He had a lot of sisters; how many he didn't know. Elizabeth he remembered and Joanna because they came often. Elizabeth laughed a lot, even in this strange, dark place she laughed; her yellow hair lit the dark like a summer day. Joanna was loving and lovely. You mustn't be afraid, Joanna said. Aren't you afraid? he asked. She shook her bright head. Not even of our father? Well yes, she said; a little. But I hide it; when you're afraid nobody must know.

His mind gave a leap, brought him back to the black and stinking cell.

He wasn't young any more. He was a man and his eyes were dim with darkness and with tears. There was no more father, no more Madam Margaret, no more Elizabeth nor Joanna. There was only the woman his wife, that flaunted herself—the Queen; that ruled for the young King, that slept with her paramour; lecherous and treacherous she dwelt in a world of her own making—a heaven of power, a heaven of lust.

He lifted his arm in one of his old, sudden angers, to strike; it fell upon the fur covering worn to the skin brittle, heavy with grease. He thought he struck with power; the blow fell light as a withered leaf. Yet for all that it was a blow of power; for with it vanished his last will to violence against her and her paramour, the last of his anger. He had no anger against anyone, not any more. He no longer wanted his crown nor his place of power. All he wanted was to be free. Freedom, clean air, a crust of bread so it were not mouldy, fresh water; and most of all his head bare to the wide sky.

Three people were anxious about the fate of Edward of Carnarvon.

The young King was anxious for news of his father. More than once he had spoken to his mother on the matter; and each time, 'Soon he will be free!' she had promised. 'Until then he is well, and lodged as befits a King!' And when he asked that, with his own eyes, he might see his father, 'Soon,' she said. 'He's best not disturbed until he's free.'

Isabella was deeply troubled. Would to God the man was free of his prison—but not in the way she would have the boy believe. Yet she would lift no finger to take away his life. She had believed the rigours of his prison would do that work for her; but nothing seemed to put an end to this hateful man to whom she was bound. And she was the more troubled by ever-growing rumours of plots to set him free. His weakness and his vices forgotten in the bitter discontent, favour was turning ever more strongly towards the deposed King. And now it was not the common, the ignorant alone that favoured him. She knew the heavy anger of the barons, of the church. How long before the storm broke? It was a question she did not care to face.

Most troubled of all was Mortimer—and his anxiety was all for himself. He had played a leader's part in driving the King from the throne. He had treated his prisoner with the utmost cruelty. He had defiled the King's bed. He had put to death, in circumstances of horror, the King's sweetheart. If ever Edward of Carnarvon came back to the throne he would see to it that for all these things Mortimer paid in full, in his own flesh to suffer the torment he had put upon dying Despenser.

'The man must die; and at once,' Mortimer said.

Isabella lifted a white, shocked face. She longed for his death, prayed for his death . . . if it might be natural. But in his murder she wanted no part. Let her lift no finger, let her have but knowledge, knowledge, only, of that death, then she was more bound to the murdered man than if he were alive and in her very bed. He would take possession of her thoughts, possess her very life. Never in this world would she go free of him. And in the next? Of the next she dared not think.

'Why in the name of God will he not die?' she cried out and wrung her hands.

'We have driven him from pillar to post,' he said, sombre. 'We have starved him, we have given him over to the cold, the darkness, the nauseous stinks. We have so dealt with him that even his own son would not know him. But still the man lives! And there are plots aplenty to bring him back. And this last plot we must take account of. For now the rabble has found a leader. It is my old enemy Rhys ap Gruffyd. He plans to restore your husband and to take his own revenge upon me—two birds with one stone. We can wait no longer. It is time; time to make an end altogether!'

And still she made no answer. Many things she had done that people would call evil—but murder was not one of them. She had never in her life consented to murder. Yet—and she could not but remember it—murder once committed, she had accepted it; she had even rewarded the murderers. Yet for all that she was guiltless of blood. But this! This was murder planned; and the man to die—her husband. She had no mind to be linked with a ghost all her life—and such a ghost. *No! No! No!* The word screamed through her mind; but still she did not say it.

'The man must die for all our sakes!' Mortimer said. 'For your son's sake, for the country's sake lest the throne rock and all England with it. And for your sake he must die . . .'

And still she said nothing, staring at him out of her white face.

'Let the man return,' Mortimer told her, 'and one of two things must happen. He will forgive you; or he will not. In the latter case you will spend your days in prison; in the former—pledge of his good faith and reconciliation—you'll spend the nights in his bed!'

She put up a hand to stay the sickness in her throat; but still she could not say the word of consent.

'Well if you are content . . . !' he shrugged. 'I do not say think of me; but I beg you, remember the Despensers!'

At that she swallowed in her throat. 'Do as you think fit,' she said.

'By God, no! Not as *I* think but as *we* think; we two together. For, if we are not in this together, then we are best apart—in all things and forever!'

She held out her shaking hands as though for mercy; her strange, wild eyes were desperate. He would leave her, not a doubt of it! He was her whole woman's life; of his man's life she was but a part. He had his wife, his children, his ambitions. His ambitions! By his lust for place, for power, for wealth—there, at least, she held him.

But even now she could not say the word.

He stood there implacable; the full strength of his male virility came to her—an aphrodisiac. For all her handsome looks she was in her mid-thirties—and the marks of a hard life upon her. She could not help but know it; he had told her often enough. She had never in her life loved any man but this. Him she must keep for her body's need—love or lust, call it what you would. Without him she would dwindle to her death.

'He must die,' she said. 'I will it!'

But, for all that, she was greatly troubled. The thing was forever in her mind. At night it was worse. She could not sleep; not though she pressed close in the darkness, seeking courage from her lover. She could not rest for the fear of it.

At last, she said, greatly daring lest she anger him, 'Leave this thing alone. It will bring ill-luck to us both. Die he must and soon. You have but to increase the rigours of his prison.'

'There can be no more rigours!'

'Then in such conditions a man must die. So still I beseech you let this thing alone.' And still she would not call it murder. 'Death by violence must leave its mark . . . and to whom shall those marks point but you?' And in this moment she had no thought for the man that was to die; her fear was all for his murderer.

'I do not mean to die for Edward of Carnarvon!' He was contemptuous. 'He shall die—and never a mark upon him!'

'It is not possible. The cup or the dagger; the cord or a man's bare hand—each must tell a tale.'

'Trust me, I know the way—simple and secret. Listen.'

'No!' She covered her ears with both hands so that the jewels at her wrist and finger glittered like small, wicked eyes.

•But still you should know! Why should I take the blame of this to carry it alone?'

'I am a woman. If I am sick or cry out in sleep. . . .'

'There's reason in that! But the man must die; and die the way I choose. On that we are agreed?'

She made no answer. But still he held her eyes, pressing down upon her with his will.

'We are agreed!' she said and let out a great sigh. She had done her best. She dare no more in the matter.

Part Four

Mortimer and the Queen
Checkmate

Chapter Thirty-Eight

Edward of Carnarvon was dead.

The twenty-second day of September, in the year of grace thirteen hundred and twenty-seven—a year to the day of the Queen's landing—he had been found dead in his cell.

The young King lifted a shocked face. His mother had promised all would be well with his father; she had *promised*.

'He is truly well now. God Himself has set him free!' she said and her eyes were full of tears; strangely the tears were real—tears for opportunities wasted, for graces cast away. She was remembering Edward so handsome and herself so young . . . so very young. She had been ready to love him; had, indeed, for a little while loved him. He need never have come to this. Or perhaps he must; within himself the flaw inherent.

Weeping like any boy that has suddenly, shockingly lost his father, Edward's grief broke in upon her thoughts.

'It is better so,' she said gentle. 'To wear his life away in prison. He should have been free as a bird. I longed to set him free, I prayed for the day. But I dared not; dared not give the country again to bloodshed. There were revolts enough as it was, God knows! He encouraged them and who could blame him? How could he content himself lacking the crown?'

'I should never have taken it!' he cried out guilty, desolate. 'But you told me he wished it; you *told* me!'

'I did tell you; and it was true. Your cousin of Lancaster heard him and all those that went to Kenilworth. The crown was his no longer; by the will of the people, forfeit. If it had not come to you, then it must have come to another!'

'Would God that it had—so he put Mortimer down! But for

Mortimer my father would not have died, I know it! Madam, you must send him away; the man offends me!'

'Sir; my son. Let not grief carry you too far. You owe very much to the lord Mortimer. See to it you do not offend him!'

'Mortimer! Mortimer!' He struck fist upon palm; it was the very action of his grandfather, great Edward. 'But for this same Mortimer my father would be alive and wearing his crown. Now he is dead, but Mortimer is alive and you are alive . . .'

'Would you have me dead, too?' she cried out, stung.

'Not you,' he said. 'Not *you*!' She was his mother; and if she had taken his father's crown she had safeguarded his own. 'Forgive me, Madam, I am not myself.' He lifted her hand and kissed it; but it was a courtier's kiss, not a son's. He turned and left her.

How did the King die? It was a question on every tongue. He had been a healthy man, very strong; yet within a few short months —dead. *Murder*. There arose the usual cry; but this time, it seemed, with reason.

'Murder?' The King lifted a shocked young face, the word whispering from his throat.

'The parrot-cry whenever a prince dies!' Isabella shrugged. 'It was always so; and so it will always be!'

'But he was so strong; above all men strong!'

'When Death puts his hand upon us the strength of man is of no avail.'

He said no more; young as he was he detected the insincerity.

Now he was utterly forlorn. He had so hoped to see his father again, hear his voice, touch his hand . . . and now his father was dead! Against the mother he did not trust and the man he hated, how could he stand; and who would help him?

The news brought Orleton hurrying.

'But murder; *murder*, Madam!' He spread his hands. 'How is that possible? What man would—or could? What opportunity?'

She shrugged. 'He had enemies everywhere. Those the Despensers did not make for him he made with his own tongue. Even you, my lord, had little cause to love him.' And she pricked him gently with that long-ago reproof.

'They suspect . . .?' And he winced at the prick.

'Everyone. Even you, my lord, may find yourself not exempt!' She smiled into his face and he knew, for certain, that her hand had been in the matter; he knew that smile.

'But of course,' she said, 'he was not murdered at all. There's no sign of violence on the body.'

How did she know that? She read his quick suspicious look.

'Oh my lord,' and she was all gentle reproach. 'That is the first thing I would enquire?'

'If there's no mark,' he said thoughtful, 'if you are sure there's no mark, you must show the body to the people. It is the one way to scotch rumour!'

To Berkeley went the order. The King's body to lie in state; all that so desired might pay their last respects.

In the great hall the King's body lay beneath a royal mantle; the poor body that but yesterday had known naught but rags. The head was crowned, the face uncovered. No sign of violence. But the face! Frozen in so terrible a mask of pain—unrecognisable. So comely he had been, comely beyond all men! If this was, indeed, the King and he had not come to a sudden, violent death, he had been cruelly murdered inch by slow inch.

Showing the dead King to the people had done little to scotch rumour.

By command of Parliament and by the wish of the young King, the body was carried in state to Gloucester, to the minster Edward of Carnarvon had loved and where his name was cherished. The slow procession wound along the Autumn roads; a great pageant such as the dead man, himself, must have loved. Upon high-stepping horses, black and harnessed in black, the golden leopards emblazoned, rode the knights all in black and gold. Now came the hearse hung with black taffetas; in each corner stood a great gilded lion carrying a gilded saint. By the side of the saintly riders pretty boys, dressed as angels, swung their censers. Upon the coffin, itself, draped with black velvet, emblazoned with the King's arms in gold, lay the carved and painted image of the dead man in all the pride of his handsome manhood. It was clothed kingly, and royally crowned so that all men wept with pity. Immediately following the hearse, in a charette all hung with black, came the Queen pale in her mourning weeds, grief-stricken, beautiful. Beside the charette walked the King, his young face drawn with sorrow; behind him Lancaster and the young John led the princes of the state, archbishop Reynolds the princes of the church.

And now it was all over. Now Edward of Carnarvon was dead and out of the way for ever.

Now the Queen and her lover could breathe freely.

All quiet . . . for the present.

'My son-in-law sends in his bill. He's a clever fellow!' Mortimer chuckled. 'He took care to be absent from home the day Ogle called at Berkeley—there's none to point a finger at him.'

'The bill?' she interrupted, impatient.

'Five pounds a day for the custody of the body, five pounds likewise for dyeing the silk upon hearse and coffin. He sets down, also, the cost of carrying the body to Gloucester. And, your son, it seems, ordered the bishop of Llandaff together with five knights to guard the body until after the funeral; the cost. . . .'

'The *total*?' She had a growing dislike for paying her debts.

'For the funeral items alone three hundred pounds.'

'I'll not pay it! You may tell him so!'

'Would Madam the Queen haggle over the price of her husband's funeral!' Mortimer asked, sour. He made a sudden, irritable movement; a silver-stoppered vase upon a shelf went tumbling.

'Pick him up. It's Edward; his heart!' Her laughter held a note of hysteria. 'They sent it from Gloucester in the pious belief I'd cherish it. Hide it away, Mortimer; thrust it where I may never see it again! As for the bills, I'll not haggle, though Berkeley makes us pay through the nose. Such a funeral must put an end to gossip; for that alone it's worth the money!'

The splendid funeral had not stopped tongues. Everywhere the questions. *How was it that the King, that strong man, met a death so soon and so sudden? Why had Berkeley been absent from home at the time of the death? Why was he never questioned; nor Gurney the steward that ordered all things at the castle; nor Maltravers? Why, above all, is Maltravers raised to a great position—High Steward to the royal household—no less?*

To all these questions—one answer. *Murder!*

Edward of Carnarvon is not dead. New rumours, even more disturbing to the Queen and her lover; to the young King infinitely distressing. *Edward of Carnarvon is not dead.* Unable to set his mind upon any other matter he went about half-hoping, wholly disbelieving—for had he not, with his own eyes, seen his father buried?

And then the first bald rumour tricked out with details.

The Welsh rescued him; they keep him safe until good time. The tale of his death—a lie, put about by those that should have better guarded him. The body that lay in state; who recognised the face? The funeral; a mockery. Whose body lies in the royal tomb? Some poor wretch that died; or was murdered to cover the King's escape . . . For escape he did.

Edward of Carnarvon is not dead. . . .

'Your father is dead!' Isabella told him. 'And fools must forever make false tales for their own amusement. But—a King! It behoves a King to put away childish nonsense and vain hopes. A King must face the truth however hard.'

And when he made no answer said, 'Think, my son. Were he alive should I not know it . . . here.' And touched her breast. 'I was his wife.'

'You *should* know!' he said; that and no more. And what, she wondered, did he mean by that?

Edward of Carnarvon could not, it seemed, lie quiet in his grave . . . if it were, indeed his grave. There began to spread tales of wonders performed at the tomb of the dead man; tales of sickness healed, of lost things found, of prayers answered. Surely the late King lay in his tomb, he and no other! And, as surely, he had been murdered. Martyrdom had made of him a saint; Gloucester became a place of pilgrimage.

Isabella said, 'Your father was no saint; and would be the last to make such a claim! If we should make a saint of every man that comes to a sudden death the country would be crawling with saints as a peasant's shift with lice. No. Simple folk look for signs and wonders; how else shall they endure their hard days? Now we must give them new events, new loyalties. We must give the people cause for other talk, joyful talk. I think, perhaps, my son, you understand my meaning.'

The rush of colour to the young cheeks showed that he did.

Mortimer came into the Queen's bedchamber; he wore a dissatisfied air. He said, 'Gloucester's title; Parliament will not give it me!'

She was not surprised; not though she and his friends on the Council had worked for it. Gloucester lands and Gloucester wealth he had; the Gloucester title he had not nor could look to have. It was a royal title; that Despenser had dared aspire to it had been remembered with mockery at his hanging.

'But—' and she was puzzled, 'nothing? Nothing at all?'

'They've made me earl of March. Well it must do for the present,' he said ungracious and grudging still. 'They must do better when I marry my Queen.'

The winged brows flew upwards.

'My wife's taken of a consumption, my steward writes me; she'll not outlive the winter.'

Even she, knowing him as she did, was chilled by his unconcern. She felt the moment's grief for Jeanne that had once been her friend. She felt the moment's grief for herself. She could never marry him; he must know it as well as she. Her son would not allow it, nor Parliament sanction it. As for the people—she would lose the last of their waning love. Even to consider such a piece of folly would cost her dear; him, dearer still.

'I must content myself till then!' he said. 'But what does not content me, is your son. You must speak to him, Madam. He carries himself towards me in a way I'll not tolerate.' And he spoke as a man that having put down one King might easily put down another.

'You must win him: you have not tried.'

'Win . . . *him!*' The contempt in his voice pricked her on account of her son.

'He is the King; it is not wise to ignore him. Young he is; but his memory, believe it, is long!'

'I won him his crown; I. Now it seems he cannot forgive me the gift. He suspects me of some part in his father's death; And no reason; he knows nothing.'

'Instinct speaks louder than reason; but, indeed there's reason enough! The more need then to win him.'

'I'll not truckle to any man, still less to a boy; not though he be a King—a King I made.'

'But still you must win him.'

'Your own efforts have not been crowned with success.'

She flushed at the taunt. 'Then I must make a greater effort; and you must help me. We must turn his coldness to affection; there's a simple way. He pines for his Hainaulter. Let him have her! Give him the girl—and we win his favour.'

Chapter Thirty-Nine

The young King was restless. The rumours had not stopped. *Murder.* An ugly word; and when one's own father is named victim, the mind sinks beneath the weight of horror. And still there were tales of miracles performed at the tomb; miracles that pointed steadily towards martyrdom. And what is martyrdom but murder by torment? Yet he might have come to terms even with that but for those other rumours flying the length and breadth of the country. *Edward of Carnarvon is not dead. He has been seen in Gloucester, seen in York, seen in Avignon, seen in Rome . . . not his ghost but his very self.* It drove the boy to a frenzy of restlessness. Seesawing between despair and hope, he knew no peace. His restlessness, his misery, deepened his resentment against his mother and her lover. He could not bring himself to enter her closet lest he find Mortimer lounging in a state of undress.

The King has been seen in Wales. This last rumour forced him to seek her out. And there the fellow was, paring his nails with a small dagger and making no attempt to hide his nakedness beneath a bedgown carelessly fastened and stiff with gold. Speak of his father to these two! The man, at least, knew more than somewhat of the matter! By God he longed to make him speak, to force the truth out of that lying, laughing throat. Sickened he turned upon his heel. Mortimer's amused laughter followed him.

On his way back to his own lodgings he saw his cousin of Lancaster and beckoned him. In the anteroom his attendants waited —the bishops, the earls, the barons the Council had forced upon him; he had given them the slip by escaping through the ruelle. Now, ignoring them, he went into the inner room taking Lancaster with him. He was about to speak, anger so fierce in eye and mouth that Lancaster shook a warning head; Lancaster opened the door to the anteroom and dismissed those that waited. They went unwilling. Never to leave the King—the Council had given its orders. But Lancaster led the Council and Lancaster must answer for this!

Edward, said choking in his throat, 'That man . . . Mortimer! His insolence grows beyond bearing. I cannot nor I will not endure him!'

Lancaster said, 'Sir, have patience, yet a little.'

'Patience! Always it is patience, patience, patience! I am the King; yet always my will must wait upon others!'

'It is part of the business of being a King . . . a young King. When you have learned to curb your will yet keeping your purpose firm; when you have learned patience until your hand closes upon the thing you mean to have—then you will, indeed, be a King; maybe a great King!'

'And meanwhile that man has the laugh of me!'

'Let him laugh while he may; he'll not laugh long. Once your council was packed with his friends; the same men sit there—but they are no longer his friends. They refused him the Gloucester title; once they had not dared. True they created a new title; a so much lesser title. That's the writing on the wall! Myself, you know well, I never liked the man; your uncles Kent and Norfolk have already withdrawn from him. Orleton stands in Mortimer's black books. And the offence? Orleton accepted the see of Winchester and paid no fee to Mortimer. Orleton's right; Mortimer's wrong. The see is in the Pope's gift, not Mortimer's. Soon it must come to open quarrel—Mortimer's a fool and for his foolishness must pay! Without Orleton he must fall; he needs the bishop both within and without the Council. In the Council Orleton carries the greatest possible weight—wise, knowledgeable and discreet as he is! And in private he's Mortimer's counsellor—wise, faithful and devoted. Soon Mortimer must go lacking that influence on the Council; must lack still more that shrewd advice. He quarrels with his last friend—the rest of us don't forget the way he behaved at Salisbury, how he came storming in to Parliament, his private army at his back, defying us to oppose his wishes on pain of death. No King ever dared so much!'

'I do not forget, neither; nor yet the way he spits upon my royal dignities. He sits in my presence; he *dares*! Nor does he rise till I rise first. We sit and sit, each hoping to outsit the other. In the end I can endure it no more. It is *I* that must rise, I the King! When I walk, he comes up with me and walks step-by-step, cheek-by-cheek. And, if the path should narrow so that one of us must go first, it is he . . . *he*!' The boy choked in his throat.

'I have seen it; we have all seen it. He shall pay for it, never fear!'

'But when? *When*? Who shall stand against him, my mother at his right hand, the army at his back?'

'A while ago you might have added, *the Council beneath his thumb*! But that, for your comfort, is no longer true. Your princes are offended, the church displeased, the common people bitter. And who can wonder? He keeps such state no prince in Christendom can afford, nor King nor Emperor; no, not the Pope himself! His troops of knights, his private armies, his hordes of servants. He holds his tournaments more glorious than any yet seen. He has his Round Table—no less!'

'He claims King Arthur as his forebear!' the King cried out, scornful of such foolishness.

'To keep up such state he drains the country dry; he's greedier than both Despensers put together. When he rides abroad the people stand and gape; his train is richer, finer, greater than your own.'

'I know it; he sees that I do! He's so rich and I'm so poor. Cousin, do I set my heart upon a horse or a hound, I must go without . . . or take it a gift from his hand. And that I'll never do. Rather I'd go naked in my shirt!' The boy's voice rose high; he was near to tears.

'Once he was the country's saviour,' Lancaster said, 'come to bring freedom and prosperity to us all. For that freedom, for that prosperity, we wait still. Well, he has lost best part of his worshippers. Once when he rode through London the streets rang with cheers; now he rides in silence. There's no favourite, ever, but he comes to a bad end! Wait, Ned—' and at the little name the boy softened, 'wait yet a little and you will see!'

'My son is restless,' Isabella said.

Mortimer shrugged. He cared nothing for the restlessness of any fifteen-year-old!

'He is no longer a child,' she said. 'We must look to his future . . . . and our own.'

'Who may plan for the future? Who knows what it may bring? Did your husband? Did Gaveston? Did the Despensers?'

'Fools; fools all! But we are wise; we make our own future, shape it as we will . . . but only if we win my son. I have said it before, but you would not listen. Now you must listen; it is more than time. We have promised him his bride; but we have done nothing. We must busy ourselves about the affair. For, mark you, with this marriage we win not my son alone, but the girl . . .'

'The Queen,' he reminded her. '*The Queen*. Once she is here you take second place, I cannot think that will please you!'

'You may leave that to me!' Her mouth lifted to a smile.

She should be careful, he thought, how she smiled. Read that smile—and you read her character. Implacable; despising the wisdom of others. To herself, indulgent; to him also . . . as long as he was faithful; but only so long. Besides, smiling no longer became her; she had lost a tooth. As long as she kept her mouth shut she was a handsome enough piece still.

'Yes,' she said again, 'you may safely leave it to me! That she —the plain and plodding creature from Hainault—should put *me* from my place!' She could not forbear to laugh.

'Put you from your place, Isabella the Fair! Isabella the subtle! She'd have to change her face and her wits both!' He laughed also.

The joke was good; it was hard to control their laughter.

When next the Council met, the Queen raised the subject of her son's marriage.

'It was agreed by you that the lord King should marry a daughter of the count of Hainault. It is a marriage for this country's greatest good. It will bring us great prosperity. The most part of the wool-trade is in Hainault's hands; from it, indeed, comes the best part of Hainault's great wealth. This trade has already brought us some measure of prosperity; marriage between our two countries will bring us wealth beyond counting.

'And with the bride, herself, the dowry will be great.' And she omitted to mention that the greater part had been paid; and spent. 'All the daughters of the count of Hainault are young, healthy and virtuous. Any one of them would bring sons and daughters to strengthen our royal house.'

She had won them all. Lancaster alone asked his question, he did not trust his niece. 'How says the lord King?'

'He is content.'

'He is old enough to speak for himself. How say you, sir?'

'Kings marry where they must. I am content.' He gave no sign of the joy within him; a King must hide his innermost heart.

'The lord Pope must first grant dispensation,' Lancaster reminded them. 'Madam Queen Isabella and Madam the Countess are near in blood.'

To the lord Pope went the request, with gifts, that his Holiness be pleased to grant dispensation; and, that being granted, Orleton that once worked evil for the father, now worked good for the son. Mortimer, angered still, had refused, at first, to send him; but the Queen, remembering the bishop's good faith and subtlety, and hoping still for friendship between those two, had prevailed. 'Sir,' Orleton told the King, 'I go to Hainault to choose your bride. But have no fear; my choice shall march with your own!'

The bishop approved the King's choice; he understood very well why the boy had set his heart on this girl. As like to her sisters as peas in a pod the Queen had said. And it was true; but it was not the whole truth. It was the steady look in those clear eyes, the bright intelligence of the brow, the sweetness of the mouth and the strength of chin that had caught the King's heart and held it.

'Sirs,' Orleton told Parliament, 'amongst so much virtue, so much beauty it was hard to choose. After much prayer I chose the lady most fitted in age to wed the lord King—the lady Philippa.'

The wedding treaty was signed, the bridal garments being sewn, jewels and equipages chosen. It was left to my lord bishop of Coventry to complete the arrangements. Orleton had, at last, fallen. He had failed to wring further gold from Hainault.

Now all is finished between them. The first nail in Mortimer's coffin,' Lancaster told his King.

'God send it,' the King said.

'I am married!' Edward said, awestruck. 'I have not seen Madam Philippa since Hainault. She is as she was, and I am as I was; nothing is altered . . . yet everything is altered. I am her husband and she is my wife.'

'Marriage by proxy—a wedding but no bedding!' At Isabella's laugh the boy's face took fire. 'Soon you shall wed her in your own person—wed her and bed her. But duty comes first. We are for the north!'

The colour died in the young King's face; the news had come with no warning.

'Until you have punished the Scots, my son, your face will not shine bright in the north; nor in the south, neither.'

'Madam the Queen is right in this,' Lancaster told him later. 'She is to put it to the Council; and the Council will agree; must, indeed, agree. The Scots have broken the truce; broken it again and again. No end to the burning, the thieving, the raping. There's misery in the north; and the south watches with growing unease. And who can wonder? We've been patient too long. We must make an end; And you, sir, must march at the head of the armies.'

Being a King, the boy thought, was more kicks than pence!

To Bartholomew Burghersh, Constable of Dover, went the King's command.

We desire and command that you receive into the Kingdom the nobleman William Count of Hainault, with the illustrious damsel Philippa and the familiars of the said count and damsel . . .

And to every town through which the young Queen must pass,

We will that all and singular, my nobility and the people of the counties through which the count and his daughter must pass with their familiars, do them honour and give them needful aid . . .

He could do no more save march to the north and pray to be
home again.

The Scots war was not going well. Queen Isabella—and no longer
might she be called *the Queen*—and Mortimer were making no
move to face the enemy. Content, it seemed, with delaying tactics
they made no attempt to cross the Border. The young King fretted;
he had his grandfather's warlike spirit. He had come to fight; and
to get back to his bride as soon as he could.

'Why do we not move to meet the Scots?' he kept asking; and
always the same answer.

'It is not yet time!'

'When will it be time?' he cried out in an agony of frustration.
'The Scots over-run Northumberland; they're marching southwards burning, raping and we do nothing!'

'You'll make a fine soldier . . . one day, my son!' Isabella told
him. 'But every man must learn his trade. You're lucky to learn
yours from my lord of March.'

'I'll learn nothing from Mortimer; nothing that's good!' And
he'd not grant the man his new and glittering title.

'Beware, sir, how you offend him!'

'Let him beware how he offend me!'

How long did they intend to keep him here idle in the north;
how long keep him from his bride? He was weary of their cunning
and their lies; he longed for Philippa. She was not only his wife and
his love; she was his companion and his need. Need for her was a
constant longing, a small sharp pain.

The Scots were pushing ever southwards. Mortimer, in spite of
greater numbers, was not willing to fight—and with some reason.
Had he been able to meet the Scots in battle-order, he had been
willing enough; but the Scots were not so foolish. They had no
intention of facing greater numbers all heavily armed. They had
their own manner of fighting. Lightly armed they would make their
sudden darting raids on small, swift horses. They could sit in the
saddle daylong without food or rest; they needed no food but the
bag of oatmeal each man carried at his saddle. Hardy and daring,

these Scots, swift and unexpected. Mortimer felt unable to cope with them. He ordered a withdrawal to Newcastle.

'You have shamed me and all England this day!' Edward said cold and bitter—his fighting grandfather come again.

'You are wrong. But you are young; you will learn!' Mortimer spoke in the slighting tone that never failed to anger the boy. 'We have not come to open battle because the Scots will not meet us!'

'Then we must go hunt them out!'

'We are not hunting-dogs,' Isabella said. 'We are good watch-dogs. Let them venture too near the house and we bite! It is they that do the running! Let them run until they're weary; soon they will be suing for peace.'

She had spoken some truth. If they had not hunted down the enemy, certainly they had kept them on the run. But she had not spoken all the truth—she was sick of the war. She had marched to win approval from the people whose love did not shine so bright as once; of such approval there was little sign. Now she'd had enough of this barbarous north and its discomforts. More; she did not care or dare, to stay longer from Westminster: she and Mortimer had too many enemies. Surely a firm peace was better than the border misery! And, besides, she knew a better use for money than pouring it away in the Scottish wars. She was ready for peace at any price.

Old, tired, eaten with leprosy, the Bruce was not unwilling for peace; peace upon his own terms.

'Never!' Edward cried out. 'Scotland is ours. If we grant peace, then the terms must be ours.'

'They shall be ours,' Isabella promised.

'A pity if we can't get the better of a sick old fool!' Mortimer said, brutal.

Edward swallowed his disgust. Argument was useless; Mortimer led the forces. One must do one's uttermost to defeat the enemy; but one could admire him—and the sick old man had shown himself a hero.

In Edinburgh Castle the Bruce laid out his terms. They were simple enough; nothing more nor less than Scotland itself. Edward listened appalled, anger and sickness rose together in his throat. They

had lied to him, his mother and Mortimer, both. Sullen he gave
his consent; but only if Parliament would consent, also. Till then
he would sign nothing. If Parliament agreed, Scotland no longer
belonged to England.

For this his grandfather had fought and won his glory! And his
father, though men slighted him, had fought, also. He had fought;
and because he had failed, it had been a complaint against him . . . a
step towards his death.

Plantagenet rage shook him; frustration curdled like poison within him.

Even so he had not heard half of the peace-terms! His little sister
Joan was to marry David Bruce—the bride seven, the groom four.
A prince does not marry for his own pleasure—he knew it well. But
he was in love and fate had been kind. That his little sister was to
be married off at so tender an age—and never a chance for fate to
show kindness—struck him as sad; sad and wrong.

England was to receive twenty thousand pounds on the signing
of the treaty. Twenty thousand pounds! It would not begin to
pay for the damage to the north. Twenty thousand pounds; a
wretched sum for the sale of Scotland—and his little sister thrown
into the bargain. She was to be sent at once into that barbarous
country.

'Never grieve, my son, we have done well. Be satisfied. The north
will prosper because of this. Peace and prosperity! Now we are for
York to meet Parliament and put the treaty before it. Your bride,
I hear, has reached London. She's to join us at York!'

'Why was I not told?' he burst out. Even in this thing so personal
to himself, so close to his heart, he knew nothing until they chose
to speak. Another item in the long account against those two!

With every step that took him nearer York his anger against them
grew. And with anger, his resolve. He'd take counsel with his
cousin of Lancaster and with his uncles of Norfolk and Kent.
Between them they'd find the way to rid England of Mortimer
and to restrain his mother. Millstones both about the neck of a
free King.

Chapter Forty

Philippa had landed at Dover. Two days before Christmas it was, and, in spite of a sprinkling of snow and a sharp wind blowing from the sea, crowds had gathered to greet the new Queen, and to stare all amazed at the glittering retinue. The much talked of wealth of Hainault was proved no myth; everyone down to the smallest page clad in velvets and fine flemish wool, in vair and sable. Through the narrow streets and out across the country to Canterbury went the high-stepping horses harnessed in spanish leather, went the great charettes decorated with pure gold leaf, went the bright pennants, the jewelled crosses and the swords of state.

And in the midst the young girl serene with all the promise of goodness in herself, and in the good she would bring to a sad country that had allowed itself—it was beginning to believe—to be hoodwinked by a bad woman. Through town and village, high upon a white horse, rode Philippa, at her right hand John of Hainault—her father at his last moment prevented by sickness. Chanting priests walked before; bishops, nobles and an array of knights, Hainaulters all, rode behind. And, wherever she passed, blessings rose to the skies, gifts were tendered on bended knee; and were the gift precious or but a few eggs in a basket she received it with equal grace. Goodness shines in her face, the people said.

On Christmas Day she entered London; a day of good omen the Londoners thought. Beyond the city gates, as far as open country, came the Mayor to greet her with his aldermen all in scarlet and sable; came the guild-masters splendid in the rich attire of their mistery, came the journey-men and apprentices gay in holiday dress. Over the garlanded bridge she rode, the young girl, wise with the wisdom of her own good heart. At the Guildhall the Mayor presented her with London's wedding-gift—a rich service of gold plate; no Queen had ever the like before. And there were more blessings for the young Queen and prayers that this marriage should heal all scars; and rejoicings for the prosperity this alliance should bring.

London went mad about the new Queen. Fountains of wine ran in the streets; there were pageants glorious to behold, a great tournament on the Bridge and a water-spectacle on the river. She could not, alas, stay to grace the proceedings; the King waited at York. She longed for wings to fly; she was more than a sweetheart riding to her lover, more than a bride riding to her young husband, she was a friend riding towards her heart's friend.

She set out in the dark of a December morning; but with her it was all Spring. Now there rode in her train John de Bohun, earl of Hereford, lord Constable of England—her husband's cousin and now her own, together with many an English nobleman and knight. New Year's Day brought them to Peterborough; and here, as everywhere, the sweetness of her young face and the happiness that shone from her won every heart.

In York Edward waited with a most loving impatience. He was wild to leave York, to ride with her through his English countryside. Madam Queen Isabella restrained him. 'Do not spoil her triumph by sharing it. Let it be hers and hers alone!' The reason seemed good to him and he set it down to her kindness. Only herself and Mortimer knew that her heart burned because henceforth it must be Edward and Philippa—the King and the Queen. She would put off the evil moment of seeing them together as long as she could; her own power she would never relinquish. *Because of the anguish she has suffered, our lady the Queen shall continue to reign all her life.* So it had been promised and so it should be!

Messengers rode daily with news of the young Queen's triumphant progress.

'A dull, good child!' Isabella told Mortimer.

'Madam the Queen is no child!' and he flicked her with the title. 'Young, yes; a child no! Nor, I think, can she be dull. Dullness doesn't call forth love; but goodness—that's another story. When next you meet take a good long look at her! You'll find, I don't doubt, a spirit to match your own.'

She sent him a quick sharp look. He had changed his tune. Had he learned something new, received some warning? She thought not; he could know nothing that she, already, did not know.

It was his way to fling words where they would hurt most.

'For my part,' he said, lust rising in him, 'I like my ladies well-spiced with wickedness . . . and for such a lady I am in the mood!' He sent her the look that never yet had failed to stir her blood. For once her lust did not rise to meet his own. She said, 'Have I been wise to bring such a paragon into the country?' And in spite of her mockery she was clearly troubled. 'Will the people love me less?'

'That they cannot do!' He was brutal because she delayed his satisfaction. 'And it isn't because of the girl. It's because of yourself. They say you sold Scotland for a song and put the gold in your own pocket—and that's true enough! They say you made peace for your own ends!'

'They are fools! The war with the Scots has never been won and never can be won. We cannot afford to lose good fighting-men nor cast away gold in a lost cause. The peace is for the good of the whole country; and if I gain somewhat, peace is none the worse for that!'

'It's not the peace they quarrel with, it's you! You, yourself are the worse for it!' And he was weary of the whole matter. It was over and done with. But a man's lust for woman is never over and done with—unless he be no longer a man. He said with the lewdness that worked in her blood like fever, 'If you'll not come to bed I'll take you where you stand!'

She went with him at his bidding. But, even as he took her, her mind was upon her problem. This girl with her goodness! Does she hope to outshine me, me they called the good Queen? And with reason! Who rescued the country from the Despensers? From the weak and wilful King? Who made peace between him and his barons? Between England and France? Between England and Scotland? But people forget; a new toy takes their fancy. So I must use this toy of theirs, win her for friend—already she's beholden to me for her husband. Treat her with a show of love. If she recognise her duty—to keep her husband obedient to his mother—well and good. But let her try to make her mischief, to set son against mother! Let her try!

'I like your attention, my dear, as well as your body!' Mortimer said; she cried out at the sudden, vicious thrust.

York was to celebrate the King's wedding. And such a wedding! A wedding to bring happiness to the country, wealth and peace—and the young couple head over heels in love! Never a city so gay. Ribands, tapestries, laurels, garlands, and everyone in his best clothes. Streets crowded; scarce room to move nor a lodging to be had. For it was not only the wedding-guests come from every corner of the land, come from Flanders and France, but one hundred Scots knights come, also, to seal the peace made in Edinburgh. England would prefer not to be reminded of that; and in the general rejoicing, it might, for the moment, be forgotten.

The young Queen was within a mile of the gates; out went the King to meet her with a great company—Madam Queen Isabella and the late King's two young brothers; Parliament and the Council; princes of church and state; knights, English and Scots together, with the Mayor and chief citizens of the town. Such a company had not been seen in York within memory of man. From the narrow streets rose joyful acclaim so that the January sky, clear as crystal, must, it seemed, like a crystal bowl shatter and fall. But the sky remained serene, the fountains ran with wine; ribands, garlands, tapestries and pennants floated free; and over the joyful notes of pipe and tabor and the clear call of trumpets, rose the sound of the people's joy.

Riding by her side, the King dared not trust himself to look at his bride, lest, unkingly, he wear his heart on his sleeve. He loved her face; she was, he was ready to swear, the beauty of the world. He loved the way she held her head, and the frank look in her eyes, and the gentleness of her mouth. He loved the hands firm upon the reins, he loved every line, every movement of her young body. She was his other self; his better, his perfect self. Lacking her, for all he was crowned, he was nothing; with her his life was crowned, indeed.

January twenty-fourth, in the year of grace thirteen hundred and twenty-eight, in York minster, the third Edward espoused Philippa of Hainault, to the great blessing of himself and of all England.

Wedded and bedded. Frolics and lewd songs. Naked in the nuptial bed the young couple, whose combined years numbered scarce thirty, endured it with dignity. Beneath his quiet face Edward hid dislike of the jests. It was customary, he knew, but he needed neither jest nor song to prick his desires—he had not been alone with Philippa since they had parted in Hainault. Philippa, come from the staidest court in Christendom, yet bore it with grace. This custom—usual, as she knew, everywhere though frowned upon at her father's court—she endured with a young and touching dignity; there was about her an inviolate modesty. Jealous of that untouched innocence, fearful for her own threatened power, and above all envious of the love and trust that shone clear between them, Isabella longed to strike the girl. He would come to his wife for comfort and he would find it. He would never doubt her nor she deceive him with another man. And good reason—she hadn't the looks! Nor would she lie to him ever, in great things or small—she hadn't the wit! A compulsive truth teller at bed and board—she wished her son joy of his bride!

And now the nuptial wine was brought; fingers entwined about the heavy cup, the bridal pair drank. And, the blessing pronounced by my lord archbishop, the bedcurtains were drawn, the company departed. And now they were free to turn to each other. Gentle, a little fearful, he took her; as gentle, but nothing fearful, she gave herself.

Now he knew the meaning of marriage; no less than the delight—the sacrament. And now he better understood the thing his mother had done. In dishonour she had given herself; in dishonour Mortimer had taken her. If ever she had thought the tenderness of marriage might soften him, she was wrong. More clearly than ever he saw that she had betrayed his father, tarnished her husband's honour as well as her own. Of the wrongs that husband had forced upon her he was too little experienced to understand. He knew one thing only; she had betrayed the sacrament of marriage.

They stayed in York for Parliament's assent to the Scots treaty, and thence to Northampton for the signing. As the procession rode the countryside there were cheers and blessings for the new-wed couple; and for my lords the late King's brothers, and for Lancaster there were cheers, also. But where Isabella rode and Mortimer—silence. It offended her vanity, rubbed raw her resentment against her son's wife; but, *our lady the Queen shall continue to reign all her life.* If they did not kiss her hand they should kiss the rod.

The court spent Easter at Northampton; thereafter the King and Queen rode for London. Isabella and her paramour with the Scottish knights were for Berwick where the little princess awaited her marriage with David Bruce.

'A pretty pair of babes!' Sir Geoffrey Scrope told the King; he'd been sent on a special commission from Edward much concerned with the happiness of this small sister. 'Sir, you need have no fear. The lady princess Joan is happy. She has her familiars about her, and chief of them her good nurse. And more; now she has a playmate to command—and that, I fancy, she will always do! She would have parted with Madam Queen Isabella with no more than a formal curtsey but that the good nurse bent to whisper. At that the little one raised herself on tiptoe to salute her mother's cheeks and then turned again to her playmate. So they parted, mother and child—and never a tear, either side!'

The young King looked at his wife. Were he and she forced to part with a young child they would grieve, all three. He supposed he should grieve for his mother, unloving as she was! Her love for Mortimer he was too young, too new to love, too prejudiced to admit. With her it was lust; lust only; greed and the itch to power.

The late lord King was done to death; and in that business his wife's hands not clean!

Yet another rumour to lend new horror to an old tale. Upon so foul a slander the young King turned a deaf ear; but, as it grew ever louder, he found himself forced to listen. Was this why the people had let her ride in silence? Could there be any truth in the rumour, any slightest foundation? He did not know what to think. He was beginning to believe that, although of herself she would have had no part in so appalling a wickedness, under Mortimer's influence she was capable of any crime. And then, having in his heart accused her, he must believe her innocent. How should one believe any rumour; any rumour whatsoever? For now that other rumour cried louder than before, *Edward of Carnarvon is not dead.* Even now, he held in his hand a letter from an unknown priest, written from some place unknown.

The priest had heard the dying confession of a man who knew, beyond all doubt, that Edward of Carnarvon lived and another buried in his place. The dying man had been the gaoler privy to the King's eascape. For proof the priest sent papers written by the King in prison—writings that had been put into the man's hand by the King himself, with the request that they be taken to the lord King his son. The good man had fallen sick of the plague but the papers delivered, according to his promise to the young King.

It was a poem; in his father's well-known hand and written in the French tongue he had loved so well. And, for further proof the title. *The song of King Edward, son of King Edward that he himself made.* . . .

> My winter has come; only sorrow I see.
> Too often, too cruel, Fortune has spoken.
> Blow after blow she rains upon me,
> Heart, hope and courage, all, all she has broken . . .

Reading it, grief rose like a sickness within him. This, this his father had suffered!

When he came to the lines concerning his mother—*a faithful wife turned to deceit*—he bit upon his lip to keep back anger and grief. That, at least, was true; he knew it for himself. Reading of his father's humiliations and his acceptance, he felt his own heart break. But when he came to the prayer for himself,

> Keep him Jesu, son of Mary
> From traitors. . . .

and the prayer that the young King should shine in honour, then the tears ran down his cheeks and would not be stayed. And though the heart was broken within him, there was pride in him that, in such bitterness of grief, his father had thought for his son, prayed for his son. To weep for such a father was right and proper. . . . a boy's heart is not made of stone.

Tears dried at long last, he strode into his mother's room to find, as usual, Mortimer carelessly lounging. He thrust both letter and poem at her; Mortimer he ignored. 'Read it, Madam!' Her brows went up at his air of command; she judged it best to humour him. Her eye went quickly over the papers. Of the priest's letter she said, shrugging, 'Some madman or jester!' Of the poem, 'This is not your father's work. He was no poet—not even a poor one. He could scarce put two words together!' It was a lie. He still had his father's letters commanding him home from France; and she, herself, had received letters more than enough!

'My father could write very well . . .' he began.

'Even so!' Mortimer's coarse laughter lifted in the room. 'How could he write—unless like the blind he wrote in the dark? And with what would he write? His finger dipped in his heart's blood? There's no blood here! He never wrote this stuff!' He flicked it away with a contemptuous hand. 'Be sure he was allowed neither light nor paper nor pens nor ink!'

It was out; out at last, the appalling cruelty of his father's prison. They had lied. All the time they had lied. Liars, liars both. He felt the sickness come into his throat; the gay colour of his mother's chamber swung in dizzy arcs, himself swung with them, swinging, swinging. He put out a hand to steady himself. He turned and all-but ran from the room lest he vomit there, in their presence.

When he was sufficiently recovered he sent for Lancaster.

'Shut in the dark. Like a felon, a madman, a wild beast! My father. A crowned King and my father. And all the time the lies about the comforts he enjoyed. Comforts! Deprived of light, of pen and ink. Deprived of what else, God alone knows! Deprived of life, also, maybe! That's not so hard to believe. Yes, yes it follows. They murdered him those two, Mortimer—and God pity us all—she, my mother!'

'I have believed it this long while!' Lancaster said. 'Your father was strong; how should he die in so short a time? And yet . . . *murder*. There was no mark upon him.'

'Is it possible he lives still?' The boy's heart was torn for the pitiful prisoner, violated at the horror he had conjured against his mother.

'I cannot think it. This verse proves nothing. We do not know when it was written. It need not have been at Berkeley. It could have been at Corfe or Bristol or Kenilworth, even!'

'Not Kenilworth; there he lived like a King . . .'

'Save that he was not free. Sir, to the prisoner all light is dark, all comfort bitter. I cannot think he's still alive! Your uncles Kent and Norfolk are hopeful in the matter; myself I have no hope!'

'By God's Face we must search into the matter, no clue unfollowed, no stone unturned. While there's still doubt I cannot endure the sight of my mother's face. As for the crown—I have no heart for it; the way it came . . . too soon. I need time, cousin. I am too young, too little-wise to be a King.'

Lancaster was a troubled man. The second Edward, with every fault, had not wrought so much evil as those two that once the country had hailed as saviours. These days he sat with the Council, watchful and withdrawn. He had no mind to associate himself with its policies. For Mortimer, though he had lost goodwill, had still a tyrant's power. Before one could strip him of that power one must deal with Madam Queen Isabella. From such a bitter farce as the Council Lancaster had wished to withdraw. He was growing old and his eyes troubled him. 'Yet stay, cousin,' the young King besought him, 'I must have one heart faithful to my service.'

Kent and Norfolk were yet more troubled. Not only did they grieve deeply for the country's plight; conscience smote them to the heart. For this bad Queen they had taken arms against their brother and King. Greedy, lascivious, she let nothing stand in the way of her shameless pleasures. She cared nothing for the welfare of the people. She had put down the Despensers to set an even bloodier tyrant in their place. And now this new rumour—that her hand had been in the murder; a rumour her behaviour made only too likely! Now they must ask themselves whether they were not fratricides and regicides. Now they must remember that Edward had been a most kind brother and to their mother a devoted son. From a lean purse he had made offerings for joy of their birth—so she had told them. And now they had, in all likelihood, helped to kill him. Edmund—more heart than head—was the more affected. Until he had found out the truth of the matter his wits were in danger of being overthrown. If Edward still lived, if that sacred blood were not upon his own head, he would wear his knees to the bone in thanksgiving. But, if Edward had been murdered, then the murderers, whoever they might be, should pay the penalty!

Chapter Forty-One

'I believed in her,' the young King said. 'When I was a child I believed in her as in a saint. When I grew older I knew no saint walked the earth—not even you, my darling!' He took Philippa's hand and laid it against his cheek. 'But still I believed her the best of women. Even the things she said against my father, I believed. I loved him; but still I believed her. When I went to France I believed her still . . . until I found out about her and *that man*! I believed my father was cruel, I believed that he robbed her, I believed she stood in danger of her life. *She*—from *him!*' His laugh was bitter.

Philippa said, 'The things she told you were not all lies. Her life was never easy, nor your father always kind. And he did keep her poor; when she came to us in Hainault, I doubt she had a silver piece in her pocket.'

'She soon found the way to fill it! Where's the dowry your father gave you? We should have it to ease us now—God knows we're poor enough! And where's your English dower—the Queen of England's due? Where the rents, the incomes, the jewels and the lands? She has them all. Nothing left; not even to pay for your crowning—and that grieves me most of all.'

She said, gentle, 'You must learn to weigh and to reason. Once you thought no word could tell your mother's goodness; now you think there's none too bad. And the truth, I fancy, must lie somewhere between the two. That your father came to a violent end, I do fear is all too true. But that your mother had a hand in so foul a thing I cannot believe.'

'You are too good, too innocent.'

'Neither the one nor the other. Nor yet a fool, neither.'

'Her greed, at least, you cannot deny. I am the poorest King in Christendom.'

'We have enough for our needs.' And she would not let him know how she must pinch and pare and was yet behind with her debts; nor how come from the richest court in Christendom, she longed for some allevation of her poverty. 'The rest will come.'

'I'll not wait for that. It is time you were crowned; time and time enough. I'll speak to Lancaster.'

Lancaster raised the matter in Council and then in Parliament. Madam Queen Isabella heard of it with anger; Mortimer added it to the score of his hatred against Lancaster.

Lancaster's protest did not go unheard. Parliament knew well the wrongs the young Queen had suffered. Fifteen thousand pounds a year had been promised in the marriage contract; it was little enough for a Queen of England. Yet not one penny of it had she seen. Expenses of the Scots war had been high, already taxes were heavy; there was little money about and the extortions of Isabella and Mortimer had made that little, less. As for the lands and incomes due to the Queen, Isabella held them fast; not one yard nor one penny would she let go.

'If Madam Queen Isabella would content herself with less of what is not truly hers, then Madam the Queen would have more of her rightful dues!' Lancaster said so plainly in Parliament.

'She to have more—the chit; and I less!' Isabella's eyes were jade-hard beneath the winged brows.

'I'll not forget this,' Mortimer's teeth gritted jaw on jaw, 'any more than I'll forget it was Lancaster that set himself against me in the matter of the Gloucester title. I've had enough of your precious uncle, my dear! I mean to force him to his knees, teach him a lesson he'll not soon forget!'

'He's not worth your anger. He's old; older than his years. And he's near-blind. He'll not live long to plague you. The first strong wind will carry him away—so much rubbish. Patience, a little patience . . .'

'Patience is a vice of the old—you are overpatient, my dear!'

She swallowed in her throat. He forever pricked her with fear of growing old. She needed no prick from him on that score; her mirror spoke plain enough of lines that marred her beauty; lines that came not from time alone. A woman cannot fight to the edge of endurance but the mark of the struggle is left. Still less can she breathe the very air of murder—though herself innocent—without it leave its mark. But Mortimer was a man and his conscience not over-fine, success had added to his looks, put a gloss upon the man; he was handsomer than he had ever been. It did not make him easier to live with; his kindness was ever harder to come by. He had never much tenderness for women; for her now it was less than ever. And, for all she loved him to the point of idolatry, still she must face it—gratitude was not in him. But for all his gibes he still enjoyed her body; yet were he refused it, he'd soon enough find consolation; nothing would be hurt save his pride. And there, at least, she had him! When her body no longer attracted him she could still keep him by his pride, his ambition; an uneasy way . . . the only way.

From her troubles there seemed no respite. It was not only Mortimer's fading desire nor Lancaster's interference; nor was it the open enmity of Kent and Norfolk, and the common people's clear dislike that weighed her down. All these; and more. Rumour tossed her from one horn of her dilemma to the other—the rumour that branded her with murder; the rumour that her husband still lived. To that later rumour details were constantly added so that she sickened lest, in the killing, an error had been made, and he would come back. He had been seen, they said; actually *seen*. Archbishop Melton of York that had known him from boyhood had recognised him in a monk's habit at Gloucester. Gravesend, bishop of London that knew the King's face as well as he knew his own, had also recognised him beneath a monk's hood.

It is not true; nor it cannot be true. Sweet Christ, let it not be true! She prayed, all unaware of blasphemy.

Archbishop and bishop summoned by Mortimer denied the tale. 'But my lord,' the archbishop said, 'I tell you plain, times are not good and there are many to wish the old days back!'

And the bishop. 'It is the friars. The late King favoured them; they grow impudent! They go about the country spreading their lies. It puts dripping on their bread and, with luck, a piece of meat!'

'It is those two themselves that spread the mischief!' Mortimer said when they had bowed themselves out. 'Give me time and I'll deal with them. But first we deal with Kent; he's the heart of the trouble, prime mischief-maker of them all. He swears his brother's alive; swears he's actually seen him. He never had the best of wits; he doesn't see the net he's spreading for his own feet.'

'He's honest enough, the fool!' Isabella said. 'And there lies the danger. He believes this tale because he must. He took arms against his brother; if that brother still lives—why Kent washes away best part of his guilt! To believe his brother lives—that's no crime.'

'Not yet.'

She looked up startled. Yet more bloodshed? She was weary of it. Shed blood if she must; shed needless blood—no!

He read her more easily than a book; he was no scholar—save in women. He cast a look upon her so that she was conscious once more of yellow cheeks and wrinkles beneath the high paint. He stretched himself that she might more admire the body she doted upon.

She tried to cover up her weak moment. 'Kent could do more harm dead than alive. He's well-liked. Shew him no mercy and we may regret it!'

'Only fools shows mercy to fools! Strange that great Edward should beget fools! Your husband was one and paid for it. Kent's another and he, too, must pay. To the wicked you may, if it suit your book, show leniency; to the fool, never—and especially the honest fool. He must be put down before he bring the world crashing upon our heads!'

'My brother is alive. I have seen him!' Edmund of Kent said, as he had said half-a-dozen times before.

Henry of Lancaster shook a weary head. 'He's dead, for him all is finished. And for you, if you persist in this, all will be finished, too!'

'I'll not close my eyes upon the truth. If you cannot believe me, then ask the friar Dunhevid; he knew my brother well!'

'A man you'd be a fool to trust!'

'A true man; he tried to rescue my brother from prison.'

'Had he minded his own business your brother would be living now.'

'He *does* live I tell you!' Kent's handsome face flushed with excitement. 'I've seen him with my own eyes; seen my brother!'

'A piece of deception; trickery—if nothing worse.'

'I saw him. I tell you, I saw him. I went with Maltravers.'

'Cousin, what have you done? Maltravers is Mortimer's man.'

'No longer. He's my man; my brother's man.'

Lancaster peered at him with pitying eyes. Kent went happily on. 'Maltravers told me that Edward was alive. Shut up in Corfe castle; I could see him for myself. It wouldn't be easy he said, but he'd manage it. And so he did. We went to Corfe together, he and I. And it was not easy. But see my brother I did. Through a window. There he was, as I've often seen him, the bright hair falling about his cheeks; he was writing—his very self!'

'Oh cousin, how are you misled! His hair was grey, *grey*. It began to turn the day they took Despenser; already at Kenilworth it was grey. Believe me, Kent it was not your brother!'

'I know my brother's face.'

'Did you see him close?'

'Close enough!'

'The time of day?'

'Twilight.'

'Light failing. They meant to mislead you—and they did!'

'It was light enough; light enough for me to know him. How should I not know my own brother? We are going to raise his standard, Maltravers and I, drum up an army, take him from prison, Maltravers has promised it.'

'Cousin, cousin. Maltravers is Mortimer's brother-in-law! Mortimer puts a rope about your neck; pray God your own hands haven't tightened it. Fly. Fly the country at once; take passage for France. Edward lies in his grave. Fly lest you go down to your own. Forget what you think you saw. You can help no-one now; none but yourself.'

'Forget? Run away? Finished? It is beginning, I tell you; beginning! And your advice comes too late. I have written . . .'

'To *whom* have you written?' Lancaster's voice was the voice of doom.

'To Maltravers. I sent him a letter for my brother, telling him . . .'

'Telling him—*what*?'

'That I shall rouse all England to set him free. That I shall hang Mortimer higher than ever man hanged yet; higher than he himself hanged the Despensers.'

'You have hanged yourself!' Lancaster said.

'He has hanged himself!' Mortimer pulled at his finger joints; stiffness brought on by his sojourn in the Tower was beginning to trouble him. He pulled a paper from his pocket. 'Kent's letter to—whom do you think? To Maltravers—no less! Here—' he tapped upon it with a jewelled hand, 'is enough to hang a dozen men!'

Kent had been taken at Winchester; now he must face Parliament there assembled; and the charge—high treason. He was not unduly troubled. Treason? To seek to release a brother wrongfully imprisoned; to restore a King driven from his throne? How could this be treason?

The young King did not understand it, either.

'Treason?' he asked Lancaster. 'How treason to release my father from unlawful prison? Treason against—*whom*? Against me? None! He is my father and I his dutiful son. Against his wish I would not keep the crown. Against Mortimer then? Mortimer is not King; treason against a subject—there's no such thing!'

'Yet still it is treason. Your father is dead!' Lancaster told him.

Kent stood before his peers gathered in judgment. He tried to explain, to make them understand a man's duty to his brother, to his King. They listened with respect and they listened with grief—he was well-liked; but, for all that, his letters spoke the mischief he had not understood. He had sought to disrupt the state, to being about civil war, to put the freely-elected King from the throne. That he had not known all this was no justification. He was condemned to die.

The trial had ended late; when Parliament rose at last Mortimer offered to carry the news to the King.

'Keep this from your son, Madam,' he told Isabella, 'until it's too late for him to interfere. We'll run no risk of pardon. Before he wakes—Kent will be dead!'

Lancaster tried to see the King—the boy must surely need some comfort: but, being told that he had gone to his bed, must leave the matter until morning.

So it was that the King did not hear the news until next day; did not even know the trial had ended until Lancaster told him. It sent him hot-foot to his mother.

'No!' he cried out in horror. 'No! What has my uncle done but show love for his brother and his King?'

'Not his King. *You* are the King!' she reminded him. 'The King he pretends to serve is dead and he knows it. No! He meant to make trouble; trouble for you. He meant to put you from the throne and put himself in your place!'

'I'll not believe it. I'll not allow him to die. I shall go to Parliament at once.'

'Parliament's dissolved; the most part of it gone home.'

'I did not dissolve it.'

'Your Council did.'

'It had no right.'

'It had the right. The Council may act without the King at need. There was need. You are young and your heart easily moved. The Council would not put so great a burden upon you.'

'I will call the Council, set aside the judgment.'

'Have you not learned what happens to Kings that flout Parliament and Council? Be satisfied that you can do nothing—the Council, also, has dispersed. But take this for your comfort; your uncle shall have an honourable death!'

He saw his uncle's handsome head bared to the axe—the handsome head so like his father's. It was as if his father came again to his death.

'I'll not have him die. I'll not have it!' He struck palm against fist—the very gesture of great Edward.

'Well, sir,' she lied, 'if you feel so deep in the matter you must have your way. When all's said, you are the King. You may command both Council and Parliament. We ride for London later in the day.'

'We start at once.'

'It cannot be done. There's much business before we leave. Nor is there need for haste; there's time aplenty!'

All day she kept him within doors beneath her eye lest he catch some whisper of what was toward. There was this document to sign and that; that matter and this for his consideration. He worked feverishly that he might be free to deal with the matter that lay upon his heart.

And all that day Kent waited upon the scaffold. They had led him in the early morning to die. The scaffold stood ready but save for the man to die—empty. The executioner was not to be found; for what had the condemned man done but what any good man must do . . . if he have the courage.?

Morning gave way to noon, noon to evening. The March wind moved in the young leaves, moved in the young prisoner's hair. It was hard to die when springtime stirred in the blood; to die for a crime that was no crime. Yet, patient he waited; patient and proud. And those that had come to see him die wept for him—so like the late King in his handsome looks, so fine, so noble. As the long minutes passed, it came to the prisoner sitting there that, let him speak the word and these people would rise and rescue him. In his slow mind he considered the matter. Speak he must not. He had been judged and by that judgment must abide. At last, night all-but fallen it came to him that to die for no wickedness was the act of a fool. He was about to speak to them that watched with him and wept, when he heard a hissing from the crowd; he lifted his eyes to the executioner. A prisoner, a base murderer had offered for the work on promise of release.

Butcher's work. The handsome Plantagenet head held high amid the groans of the people.

Edmund of Kent noble in his dying that might so easily have saved himself. Great courage—and less commonsense. It was his tragedy.

Chapter Forty-Two

Isabella, that subtle woman, had been foolish, indeed. Her lies on the day of Kent s death had set her son forever against her. His last lingering affection was gone; he would trust her never again. But the wound went deeper than his own personal hurt. The death of Kent—the haste and like manner of it—had been an insult to the throne. In this Lancaster and the King were of one accord; and Lancaster, alone, knew how grievous the hurt.

The speed with which the prisoner had been hurried to his death—royal Kent—shocked the whole country. High and low grieved for him, waited with fear and anger for the Queen's next move. For in this it was the Queen, the Queen to blame; she held the power. She had but to say the word to delay the execution, to enquire further into the matter. That word she had not said.

The tide was rising steadily against Madam Queen Isabella and her lover.

Murder. The cry rose louder, louder, louder. Edward of Carnarvon was dead; that they must believe. Lancaster, that honest man and leader of the Council, had proclaimed it. But . . . *how* had he died? And by whose hand? She that had hurried her husband's brother to his death, good young Kent, was likely to make short work of her husband—she and her paramour! It had not been a natural death. it had been a martyr's death; witness the unending miracles from the dead King's tomb.

'A saint—he!' Isabella laughed; but her laughter had an uneasy ring. 'If ever he got into heaven he'd corrupt the angels.!'

'They'd not interest him; they have not the where-withal!' Mortimer said, gloomy. 'By God your husband's more nuisance dead than alive! No end to his *miracles*. For look you, a saint's as potent as the philosopher's stone to turn base metal to gold. And this the damned abbot at Gloucester knows better than most. He'll not be in a hurry to lose his saint!'

Certainly the good abbot knew how to turn his new saint into gold. From every part of England came the lame and the halt. And why not? A blind man had seen the dead King in a blaze of light and the light had forever cured his darkness. A housewife had lost a silver piece; a voice from the tomb had told her where it might be found. A dead child had stirred in its coffin, had risen and walked. No miracle too great or too small.

Gloucester had become a place of pilgrimage; any man with a room or a bed or even a place upon the bare floor could command his price. The town grew in prosperity, the cathedral in wealth and beauty.

Edward more useful dead than alive.

'We must make out own pilgrimage,' Mortimer said, sour. 'It would look ill if we did not.'

'Before God, no!' she crossed herself. 'I've not forgot the funeral. I expected, every moment, the effigy to bleed at the sight of us. I'll not risk a second time. My son has commanded a fine tomb. Let that suffice.'

'By God, your son takes too much upon himself! He asked no leave.'

'He needs none. He is the King. And, besides, who would question such piety? Mortimer, Mortimer, my son grows in stature; old men and women say he grows like his grandfather, that indomitable man! When I consider the future, I am troubled; I am troubled, dear love—and chiefly because of you. Show him some respect; it shall serve us well!'

'Respect! the boy's scarce dry behind the ears. You make an old woman of yourself—you and your fears!'

He saw the flush spread under the paint; and, since she still held power, said quickly, 'But for all that there's none can hold a candle to you!' He flung out his arms in a yawn, 'Come love to bed!' And saw the raddled face brighten.

The young King felt his manhood strong within him. He was not only a King; he was to be a father. To hand on the crown strong and secure, was his plain duty. Eighteen. It was young, Lancaster thought, but not too young. The boy had a strength within him. It was true what they said—he was less his father's son than grandson to great Edward.

The tide that had been steadily rising came in with a rush. And now it was not only the common people, it was the princes of England, church and state, it was Parliament; but for all that they must speak in whispers, work in secret. Madam Queen Isabella and Mortimer, already uneasy, would be tigers to defend their ill-got power. Kent had been hurried to his death; why should they spare any other—Lancaster or Norfolk, or indeed Edward himself? They had thrust one King down into the grave, why not another?

The first step was to crown the King's wife, to set her image in the public eye, equal at least, in dignity to the King's mother.

'Sirs', Lancaster told Parliament, 'soon by God's grace the King's son shall be born. It is not fitting his mother should go uncrowned; already the matter has been too-long delayed.'

It was a crowning long due, Parliament agreed. But where was the money to be found?

'There's money found for all else!' And they knew to whose extravagance Lancaster referred. 'There must be money found for this, also!'

The last day in February, in the year of grace thirteen hundred and thirty the King's summons went out; it commanded his well-loved princes and prelates,

to appear to do their customary duties in the coronation of our dearest Queen Philippa, which takes place, if God be willing, the Sunday next to the feast of St Peter in the cathedral of Westminster.

It was not a magnificent affair. There was little in the Treasury and less in the Wardrobe. They were so poor, the young King and Queen, they had scarce enough to meet the modest demands of their daily life. Isabella was not ill-pleased at the meagreness of the crowning; everything that took from the dignity of the young Queen must add to her own.

She had reckoned without the girl herself—Philippa, great with England's heir, and her own incomparable dignity. So young, so moving in her pregnancy, there was a joyousness about her, a sweetness, a patience. Her known kindness, her clear honesty gave hope for the future; England had suffered too much under a bad Queen!

Isabella, handsomely gowned, ablaze with jewels, high-painted into beauty must yet take second place. She longed to weep; to weep for grief, for anger, for the injustice of this eclipsing of her glory. Once she had knelt in that very place where now her son's wife knelt, sat upon that very throne, bent her head to that same diadem. She, too, had made her vows; vows as good as those of the clumsy young creature kneeling now. Twenty-one years. In a flash . . . gone.

She shut her eyes against the young Queen.. Bitter, bitter beyond enduring to see another in her own place.

The words of the great ceremony fell upon deaf ears; she listened, instead to the words of her own thoughts.

. . . *She sits in my place; she has everything. She has the crown. She has a proper man for husband—more than ever I had! She is great with England's heir. Yet she's not half the woman I was . . . or am; or am! Where's the wit, the ambition, the daring? Where the beauty? Honest she may be; kindly and trustworthy—these things one looks for in a servant! For all her breeding a peasant! Yet my son looks at her as though that body of hers held the beauty of all women . . .*

It came to her with bitterness that, for all her own beauty, no man had ever looked at her like that. Her husband had insulted her womanhood. To her young knight of Hainault she had not been a woman of flesh and-blood; she had been his lady, some disembodied spirit of chivalry. She had for her lover the most magnificent man in England; but it was she that had made him magnificent . . . and he was an unkind lover.

Her eye came back to the girl on the throne . . . *the peasant!* She longed to shake her, shake her, shake her; to send the crown ridiculously toppling over her nose, to show her up for the figure-of-fun she was with her fat face and her heavy breasts, and the swollen belly. Yet the girl, she must admit it, was a dutiful daughter-in-law. There had been that large dowry, now regrettably spent. The girl might well have complained; but not a word. Not a word, either, about the Queen's dues kept in her mother-in-law's hands. And she behaved well whenever they met—courtesy from son's wife to his mother. But there was little warmth in it; her son's wife did not seek her company. As she grew older—and not so much older either—the creature would grow heavier, duller, lose what looks she had. Let her look to it that her husband's eyes did not stray—the Plantagenets were not known for their virtue, the Capets still less. Yet she would take it all as it came; shrug off his lapses—not in weakness but with her peasant's strength. Year by year she would produce his children. Always he would come back to her. Her respect would strengthen him, her affection steady him; commonplace, she would be his mainstay, his way of life.

She sighed, in spite of her contempt envying Philippa.

A simple crowning, a simple feast; and then to Woodstock to await the birth of the child. Here Parliament followed them; and here the King talked often and secretly with his cousin of Lancaster. The time was almost ripe; discontent festered throughout the land. But, for all that, they must wait until the Queen was safe-delivered; the King would not have her disturbed though the plot worked in him like yeast. His first thought was for her. He walked with her, talked with her, plucked her summer posies with his own hand; he offered up masses that the child might be a son; he gave alms, he prayed night and day for her safe delivery.

The child was born at Woodstock in mid-June. It was the longed for boy, handsome and well-made. 'We shall call him Edward— the fourth Edward!' the King said. But no man may foresee the future; this child was to die in young manhood, die before his father.

'She feeds him at her own breast!' Isabella told Mortimer, winged brows lifted in disgust. 'A Queen to behave like an animal!'

'All women are animals—queens and peasants alike!'

'It is you men make us so!' she said quick and angry.

'I've seen no unwillingness in you!' he smiled into her face.

Madam Queen Isabella might think a Queen too fine for such work but the country adored the young mother. Humble women suckling their babes felt kinship with the Queen. Painters chose her for their Madonna; her serene face smiled down in many a church.

When he looked upon his son the King was more than ever aware of his manhood. Now when he sat with Lancaster, the Queen made a third in their secret talk; this quiet girl, Lancaster found, wielded power over her passionate impatient husband. Their plans were maturing; peers and bishops in ever-growing number came in to the King. Lancaster's spies reported that the country waited for the word. To lull any suspicion on the part of an uneasy Isabella and Mortimer, the King proclaimed a great tournament to honour the Queen upon the birth of his son—an opportunity to gather, without undue suspicion, knights-in-arms; to assess their virtue in the field and the strength of their following. At Chepeside stands were erected, tier upon tier, with an enclosure for the Queen and her ladies.

It was long since Londoners had seen offered so fine a sight; the country was so poor, so sick at heart. Long, too, since they had set eyes on their young Queen; not, indeed, since she had gone into the country for the birth of her child. All this time there had been no court and no Parliament, now both were to return; trade would prosper once more in London. Now London was to see its Queen again—the Queen that had given the country its prince. After the hardships endured at the hands of the bad Queen and her lover, she brought hope of better times. It was said of her that, poor as she was—because of those accursed two—no poor man ever went empty from her presence. No wonder the King treasured her as the apple of his eye. It was said also—whispered very low—that he'd not put up much longer with the state of affairs. With such a King and such a Queen the bad times must surely come to an end.

The tourney was set to begin, every seat taken; yet more and more folk thrust their way through the tiers fighting, pushing, being in turn pushed and fought; the seats creaked beneath a weight they had never been built to hold.

With a flourish of trumpets the King and Queen entered. The summoning notes, the sight of the young couple they had not seen for so long, stirred the crowd to madness. They stood upon their seats screaming and stamping; the stamping was the last straw. With a crash the scaffolding gave way. Amid a litter of broken wood folk lay upon the ground groaning, shrieking, struggling ro rise. Some would never rise again; for over their bodies, frantic to escape, crowds surged in all directions. Amid flying timber, men and women fought with fists and feet, with sticks and pieces of jagged wood.

The King, arm about the Queen, saw it coming, the heavy beam. Even as he pulled her away, the jagged end crashed; down she went like a stone. He lifted her in his arms; he saw the white coif take the red stain. Himself, maddened, he fought his way treading upon those that blocked his path.

She lay senseless in his arms. She was dead, he knew it. Such happiness as his could not last long. Now, with her, his life had come to an end.

Her lids fluttered, she stirred in his arms.

She was not dead. God be thanked she was not dead! A terrible joy took him, thereafter a terrible rage.

She was not dead. But she might have been . . . *she might have been*. Men shrank from his face as he passed carrying his burden—the fixed jaw, the unseeing eye, the face of stone. In his anger terrible; those that had never seen his grandfather saw him now.

They had brought a litter; he walked, his hand upon it. He could trust none but himself to watch over her, lest still she slip from life. He and he alone could keep her safe.

She was lying in the Queen's lodgings in the Tower. He could not enough look at her, could not enough thank God. But, for all that, he had lost none of his anger; he was sick and shaken with anger. He would have the lives of those responsible for this—foremen and labourers that had not sufficiently tested their work.

'They shall hang, every mother's son!' he cried out looking upon her he had so nearly lost.

Every mother's son . . . She had so lately borne a son; the words played havoc in her heart. She raised her gentle head. 'There's no harm done!' she said.

'You might be lying dead,' he said and shook at the thought.

'But I am alive. It was an accident; a thing no man could foresee.'

'It *should* have been foreseen. Carelessness, bad work—it's no excuse. It might have killed you!'

'God shows His mercy. But, if yourself show none, how shall we deserve it of God?'

He turned his face from her. He loved her; and how nearly he had lost her! Those responsible must answer; he would not remit their just punishment.

A little unsteady she rose from the bed. A bruise marked the white skin of her forehead. Freed of the coif, her hair flowed free, her pretty brown hair. She looked little more than a child.

And she might have died, trampled beneath those brutish feet! He could not listen to her prayer.

She went down upon her knees; like any suppliant she knelt. She said no word. She took his hand and kissed it.

'I can refuse you nothing!' he said from a grim mouth.

Chapter Forty-Three

Henry of Lancaster heard the tale; the King himself told it, shame-faced that he had not meted out deserved punishment. The Queen's mercy, Lancaster thought, should add to her image. He told the tale everywhere. Londoners heard it and blessed the Queen; and blessed the King that had not turned his ear from mercy. The tale spread throughout the land; minstrels sang the ballad of the good Queen.

Isabella heard the tale and shrugged. 'Do you, for one moment, believe it was compassion with her? No, Mortimer, no! A show . . . a show only. I begin to wonder whether she isn't cleverer than I think!'

'You my dear, are not as clever as you think! You do not know real goodness when you meet it. To make a show of compassion —that's your way and my way and the way of most of us. But it is not her way; hers is the way of true goodness! It is her strength and you must reckon with it!'

'Goodness! Goodness!' she cried out goaded. 'If you admire it so much maybe you'd like to sleep with it!'

'It would be a change!' As always he lost no chance to flick her on the raw. 'But—' and now he applied the unguent, 'I didn't say I admired it; goodness bores me. But I do say it must be reckoned with!'

'It is not goodness!' she said again, obstinate. 'It's a slyness in her. She plays her game to win the people from me; to make an end of us both. Let her try! Clever she may be; but you and I, together, cleverer still!'

The King was in France. He had gone, all unwilling, to pay homage as peer of France to the new King. He had been bitterly set against it. Why should he pay homage for part of France when the whole of France was rightly his; yes, the throne of France, itself! For King Charles was dead and his cousin Philip of Valois ruled in his stead. But Edward's claim was greater—the only direct descendant through his mother.

'To pay homage is to deny my right!' he had cried out in anger.

'To refuse it is to assert your right—and we are in no state for war!' Madam Queen Isabella said. 'When we are stronger we will push your claim!' And in that she was wise, though it was not England she thought of, but herself. She had lost the trust of the whole country; let her declare war and the barons might well refuse to follow her. Thus defied and without an army at her back, what became of Mortimer, what of herself?

To her he would not have listened.

'We are in no state for war.' Lancaster said, repeating her very words. 'You have first to win England. Pay your homage now; when you truly rule here, we shall see about France!'

To Lancaster the King must listen. He had left England, bitter for France lost. But some comfort he had. His affairs he had left in safe hands; Lancaster and Philippa worked together in his cause.

'Madam,' Lancaster told her, 'our time is coming soon; very soon. While the King's in France all suspicion is lulled; when he returns, all will be ready. The lord Pope approves; he sent us, by secret messenger, his blessing. That, when we make it known, will put courage into all—priests, princes and common folk alike. Meanwhile all goes better than we planned. The good bishop of Durham has the privy seal and will hold if for the King. Salisbury has long worked in our cause and many a baron he has brought in to us. Burghersh has brought over the barons of the Cinque Ports and with them all the harbours. And, best of all, Parliament is for us. There's scarce a man in Parliament, earl or baron or simple knight, that will not lift his sword at the signal.'

'And the Council; what of the Council?'

'There Mortimer has not a friend left. Some make a show to stand by him now, because they must; but let danger threaten him and you'll see how many will be faithful. As for the common people—the galled shoulder will no longer bear the yoke. Save in his own marches there's not a man but longs to be rid of the tyrant. And he knows it. He grows uneasy; he shows it in his crazy arrogance. Men bow before him; behind his back they laugh at him . . . It is not a pleasant laughter. Soon the King will be home; we heat the iron against his coming. The hand that strikes upon that anvil is strong; a King's hand.'

'You make it sound too easy,' she said. 'Mortimer's a proved captain; and in all England there's no man so rich to bribe, so powerful to have his way. How if those that flatter him are afraid to leave their flattery . . . how if the iron, for all our heating, grow cold?'

'I have a plan to strike at white heat. A simple plan. I think it cannot fail.'

He went softly to the door of the closet; in the ante-room her women, Hainaulters for the most part, sat industrious at the needle. Guileless they looked and faithful they were, but for all that, he drew the heavy curtains that hung upon the door; he brought his stool close and whispered in the Queen's ear.

'A clever plan,' she said, 'simple and subtle; but it hangs overmuch on the honesty, the discretion of one man.'

'I know my man. He's for the King body and soul. I am not one for rash action; I'm tired and near-blind, but yet I hold life too sweet to throw it away.'

'But still,' she said, 'I cannot like your plan!' And out came her true objection! 'To persuade the lord King to lift his hand against his mother—I cannot do it.'

'Not against his mother; against Mortimer, archtraitor and murderer of his King. His hand directed that murder; how long —let him go unpunished—before he lift it once more against his King?'

At that she trembled and he went on, 'With Mortimer, Parliament shall deal; with his mother the King shall do as he chooses.'

And when still she hesitated, he said, 'Free Madam Queen Isabella from this wicked man and you may save her soul.'

'We cannot free her; she loves him.'

'She is entangled by lust as in a web. There's but one hope to save her soul—to cut her free.'

There was silence between them. Then, knowing her so well he said. 'Not for the sake of the country, nor for the King and your child; but for the sake of a woman who otherwise must burn in Hell, I implore you, Madam, advise the King in this matter.'

'I will think upon it.'

The King was home again; he burned with two separate angers and both of them against his mother.

He had done homage according to her command. He had placed his hands between those of Philip of Valois. He had been asked, *Will you become liegeman of the King of France as duke of Guienne and peer of France?* And voice strangled in his throat, *I will do it,* he had said.

And this anger was fed by that other, older anger, fuelled afresh by the new facts he had learned in France. The scandal concerning his mother and Mortimer he had long known. What he had not known was the way she had lied to her brother and to the whole court, making now a monster of his father, now a clown. He had not known that by the Pope's command she had been turned out of France. He had thought the old scandal no longer news; to find it very much alive, to hear the new tales, to find tongues bawdy about his mother, raised him to a pitch of madness against her. He was more than ready to listen to Lancaster.

Mortimer was growing uneasy. A man that thrusts himself into so high a place must, if he is to keep that place, be sensitive to every slightest wind that blows. He was watchful, he was irritable, he trusted no-one; and he carried himself more arrogantly than ever. Isabella wondered why still her heart was set upon him; why she endured his boorishness and not seldom his insults. But one look from those cold eyes, one touch of that unloving hand and she would risk her hope of heaven—a slight enough hope and therefore the more precious.

The Great Council—not the King's private advisers—was to meet in Nottingham. Frowning, Mortimer scrutinised the names.

'They call themselves friends; but which of them is to be trusted?'

'Those we pay best!' Madam Queen Isabella said. 'Unless, indeed, Lancaster pay more!'

He shrugged. 'I doubt Lancaster is much interested. He hates us, yes; but he's too old, too blind. His own affairs take all his time. It's as much as he can do to go on living.'

'You don't understand Lancaster,' she said. 'You never did. A stubborn man . . . a stubborn house. His business is the King's business—and to that he'll hold till the last breath's out of his body. And those half-blind eyes of his! They see more than many a man with clear sight.' *More than you, my love; more than you!* 'We should have sent him to join his brother long ago and so I told my son. But he'd not listen. He was all for "justice!" We must render to Lancaster all that is Lancaster's, he said; lands, honours, unstained name. Unstained name—traitor Thomas! Well, my son had his way and now we must deal with brother Henry . . . and that will be hard, and hard, indeed! Look at it how you will, he's no traitor.'

'There's more than one opinion about that! Meanwhile, Madam, your son is too close to Lancaster; it could spell danger to us.'

She looked at him with still-beautiful eyes. She was tempted to lie to him, to assure him that the King would obey his mother—but he was eighteen now and a father. To lie in this spelt danger to them both.

She said, 'He is restless beneath my hand. He took the peace with Scotland hard; harder still his homage to my cousin of France —nor can I wonder! It is my son that should sit upon the French throne. Of all claims in Christendom his is the best—grandson to my father in the direct line. Still I dissuaded him and I was right. Peace brings more prosperity than fighting about a crown however just the cause.'

'Peace! Prosperity!' His laugh was like a fox's bark. 'It's glory he's after, my dear! He snuffs at glory like a dog at a juicy bone. Keep him from Lancaster at all costs; Lancaster aids and abets him —the man's our enemy, so is the virtuous Philippa! But I fear our greatest enemy is your son, himself!'

'I told you to win him, I begged, I prayed, but you'd not listen.

Now that unlucky visit to France has rubbed his anger raw. He hates me; but more than me, he hates you!'

'I did not force you to my bed; you were willing enough!'

She flared into sudden anger. 'It isn't only that! It's you, yourself —the ambition that's an itch in the blood. The way you carry yourself prouder than a King; and the way you live, finer than any King in Christendom—you with your Round Table and your knights and your private tournaments! And the way you claim to be descended from King Arthur—King Arthur himself! What's the *use* of it . . . unless you mean to claim the crown!' She laughed at the thought; saw with some surprise he did not join the laughter.

She said, a little fearful, 'That's a great nonsense—I did but jest. But Mortimer, dear Mortimer, be a little careful. Watch how you anger my son. The old trick of making him rise first—it's played out. It is for him to sit, for you to rise. And still, all uninvited, you walk close to him; upon occasion—in front, leaving him to follow. You catch him by the arm, interrupt him when he speaks. You are unwise to scant his dignities; you anger not my son alone but our princes. Earls and barons, bishops and abbots—all are incensed. Show yourself a little humble. . . .'

'Humble? To him? That boy!' He could scarce speak for spleen.

'Boy no more; it's a man you must reckon with; a husband, a father and a King. Make light of all three if you can! A husband— that can scarce move you; your wife had little joy of you. A father'; she shrugged. 'A child is easy begot. But the crown! the crown's another matter. Even great Mortimer cannot afford to slight it. Young my son is; but a King with whom you must reckon. His grandfather all over again. The same courage, the same integrity . . . the same rages, the same fits of cruelty. I saw the old man once when I was a child in France. I've never forgot him. A frightening man; yes, even for you. Watch, watch yourself; give the King his due. Soon he goes to Nottingham; it is our duty to be there. Treat him with all courtesy; and God send it be not too late!'

He said with that arrogance that, like a cancer, had fastened upon him to bring him to his death, 'I humble myself to no man—not King nor Emperor nor Pope himself!'

Useless to urge him further. She could but hope that some

shrewdness as yet uncorrupted, might save him still. She hoped; she dared not count upon it.

Before ever the King could arrive Mortimer had taken possession of Nottingham Castle; the King and his officers must find lodgings elsewhere. 'Make what excuses you choose,' he told Isabella, 'I'll not have my enemies within these gates.'

'We have no right to refuse the King admittance into his own castle; nor any man he choose to bring with him. The gates are his—not yours.'

'And still I say again—I'll not have him here—him and his men!'

The King must find lodgings elsewhere. Madam Queen Isabella did not put it like that. The castle, she sent word, was old and cold; was damp, was rat-infested—unfit for the lord King, unfit for old Lancaster; for herself, it was well enough. And well enough it was, with great fires blazing and all the braziers flaming and warm hangings to keep out the October mists rising from the river at its foot.

In the fortnight before the King's coming she wasted no moment. Letters went out to all she believed she could trust. To Hereford she wrote twice; he had always been her supporter. The first time he sent his excuses; he was, alas, ill. Must she, she wondered, take this—a warning? She wrote again putting aside his excuses, demanding his presence; it was his duty to the King and Council. She sweetened the letter with promise of profit to himself. Profit. It was with her a word to speak louder than honour!

Hereford she must have. High Constable of England; a man of great influence and many friends. Let him show himself staunch and her cause would be safe. Yet much depended upon Mortimer. Dear God, let him carry himself more pleasant towards men; let him not anger his equals with self-destroying arrogance! No man might now address him save by his great title; when he walked abroad, he walked in greater glory than the King—the King whose treasure he wasted. Wherever he walked, my lord earl of March, a magnificent procession followed at his heels; friends, you might think—save that friends he had none. The gorgeous surtout hid cold steel.

The King was in Nottingham; his train was not so great nor so magnificent as Mortimer's, but friends, friends all. And like Mortimer, each man's surtout hid cold steel.

He had no intention of lodging within the castle. Shut himself in with those two and their armed men! Such a lodging was not to his taste; nor did it suit his plans. When he heard that they had shut the castle against him he laughed aloud; but for all that, he vowed Mortimer should pay dear for the insult. Meanwhile he was comfortably housed in the city with Lancaster and his friends— among them his cousin of Hereford; Hereford that knew which way the wind blew, had seen duty and profit go hand-in-hand. Armed forces were lodged near by at need; the King hoped there would be no need.

Isabella knew, as well as her son, the gross impropriety of denying the King entrance. Too late now to regret it; but still they could make some show of respect.

'You have walked your own way so far, now walk a little in mine. I beseech you, Mortimer. It is for your good; for you alone!'

The blackness of his brow did not deter her. She remembered her own rage, her own humiliation being shut out from Leeds Castle, and the bloodshed it had brought. Though all seemed quiet enough she knew in her blood the urgency to placate her son.

'You cause much anger by your bearing towards the King. They call you *the King's Master*; and truly it is as though you stood over him with a whip!'

'God's pity I cannot use it! Your son must be brought to obedience.'

'You talk of the King,' she reminded him. 'To be called *the King's Master* may flatter you; but they call you something else— *the Destroyer of the King's blood* . . . That cannot give you so much satisfaction. But like it or not, the names are dangerous, both!'

'Slander, it seems, is in the fashion; and you, my dear, have caught the sickness! But look to yourself!' And now he was plainly spiteful, 'They give you a name, also. You may hear it everywhere. *She-wolf of France.* I trust you like it!'

She stared at him in disbelief. This she had not heard. Her spies were everywhere; but this they had not repeated.

'It is not true, nor it cannot be true!' she cried out.

'It is true. Once you were *the good Queen, the beloved Queen*; now you are neither. Your son's wife with her bread-and-butter virtue has eclipsed you.'

'But *she-wolf*!' And now there was pain in the cry.

'She-wolf!' he said again, nodding and smiling.

In France we hunt wolves with dogs. Her own words to Gaveston, long-forgotten, were sudden in her ears. For the first time she knew the taste of fear. She spat it from her. 'Whoever speaks so of me shall hang from the nearest tree!'

'You cannot hang all England, my dear! And *she-wolf*!' he shrugged. 'It is no bad name. A she-wolf is strong and fierce; she follows after her prey with a most dogged purpose. She has a nose to follow that prey, eyes and feet to come up with it. She has a heart that fears not to kill, a heart that is faithful to its mate. She-wolf; it suits you well!'

Almost he saw her standing there, blood upon her mouth, blood upon her hands. It quickened his dying lust. His hands were on her tearing at her clothes. By God, if she didn't hurry the blood upon her should be her own!

She took in a breath of ecstasy. Let them call her she-wolf, were-wolf, what they would! So it quickened his failing desire she was content.

Chapter Forty-Four

'I cannot, Sir William, admit you!' Sir Robert Holland said, 'and you must tell my lord of Lancaster so!'

'You are the governor.'

'But still I cannot admit you; Madam Queen Isabella keeps the keys.'

'And sleeps with them under her pillow, so I'm told. It argues a guilty conscience.'

'Not so, sir; it argues fear—a very natural fear. All this scandal! I've seen her, poor lady, look sharp over her shoulder as though she expects . . .'

'A ghost, maybe!' Montague said, grim. 'Ghost of a murdered man.'

'A vile slander against the Queen . . .'

'She is not *the* Queen!' Montague reminded him very sharp. 'Too many beside herself forget it.'

'A vile slander,' Holland began again. 'Shame upon you, sir, to believe it! If murder there was—which God forbid—her hand was not in it. On that I'll stake my soul!'

'Beware lest the devil take you up on that! As for Madam Isabella, I see she still has power to charm. But not the people; not them any more. You know the name they give her now? *She-wolf.* She doesn't get that for nothing!'

'The tongue of scandal lies; it wags too loud, too cruel! So good a lady, so gracious . . .'

'No-one ever called her a fool!' Montague's voice was dry. 'Heed my warning, Holland! I know her better than ever you could do and I tell you this. As long as she and her paramour—and he is her paramour; that, at least, you'll not deny!'

Holland shrugged. He'd admit nothing against Madam Queen Isabella.

'As long as those two hold power there's no hope for the country. Between them they wring her dry. Inch by inch the rich lands of England come into their hands and good folk starve. If you wish well to the country, if you wish well to the King, you must stand with us!'

And when still Holland did not answer, Montague said, 'We could command you; we prefer your good will. Think on it, Sir Robert . . . and do not think too long!'

Lancaster summoned Holland; he took up the matter where Montague had left it.

'We command you, in the name of the King; we would rather your good will. We need every man; his heart as well as his right hand. Look you!' And he led Holland to a window. The young King walked below in the garden; he looked very young, very vulnerable.

'If we should fail,' Lancaster said, 'it's odds but the boy will go the way of his father—sudden death, of which no man knows the truth. Do not doubt it. Let the King grow in years and power! Mortimer would never dare. If you deny me now—though you should hold yourself innocent, your hands will be stained with blood; the King's blood.'

'And what of Madam Queen Isabella? She trusts me. Shall I betray that trust!'

'The man or woman who asks your help gainst your King is a traitor. Holland, you run grave risk of a traitor's death.'

And while still Holland hesitated, Lancaster said, 'Do you set yourself against the lord Pope? He has blessed our cause. I swear it by the blood of Christ and my own hope of salvation.'

'My lord, you must give me time.' And now Holland was shaken at the heart.

'There is no time. Come now, the keys.'

'I cannot give them. Every night I must put them in Madam Queen Isabella's hands. Nor would keys help you. The castle swarms with Mortimer's men. At the first alarum they'd be in their places to pick you off as you come up the hill. And if you

took us in the end—which I doubt—your losses would be too
great. But . . .' he paused; he said slow, unwilling, 'There's another
way. If you swear by Christ's blood it is truly to serve the King,
then you shall take it. But, by God, I am not willing!'

'I swear it!' Lancaster said.

'You could be upon Mortimer before he knew it!' Holland said.
'There's a secret passage; it leads from the water-meadows south
of the town. It follows the Leen; the river's cut a channel hid by
undergrowth. Some two hundred yards, before you get to the
castle rock, the path goes underground and then tunnels up into
the rock itself. It was made when the castle was built; the Normans
knew how to build! The path's a secret that's been well-kept; it's
handed on from governor to governor—and every governor
sworn to secrecy. Folk hereabout know it as a tale only.'

'And as a tale I heard it,' Lancaster said. 'That it should be true
—such a piece of luck I never dreamed!'

'It's hard to find—all overgrown with bramble; harder still to
follow. Myself, I know it well; it's every governor's duty to know
that path in time of need.'

'There is need, now!'

'The path, I must warn you, is dark; it's slimy with water-weed
and worn with the flow of water. When it reaches the rock—and
that's some eight hundred feet high—the rise is steep; in some
places one in three. Underfoot the stones are loose and the roof's
none too safe. A man may easily slip to his death or bring a boulder
down on his head. But it takes you into the castle itself, right into
the royal lodgings. There's a sliding panel leads into the anteroom;
the Queen herself—poor lady—does not know it!'

'There's but one Queen—and that Madam Philippa! How shall
we know you tell the truth? You are over-tender of Madam Isabella!'

'More tender yet of my young King. I'd not have his blood
upon my hands. And of Mortimer I am not tender at all!'

'You go with us to point the way?'

Holland nodded. 'By God's Face, I grieve for Madam Isabella.
I would serve her, if in all honour I could. But my first duty is to
my King!'

Mortimer had not heeded Isabella's warning; he carried himself to all—and especially to the King—so that every heart burned against him. The King said nothing. Between himself and Mortimer all had been said. He went his way, attending the Great Council, treating Mortimer with courtesy. He was grave and quiet; no-one, save the wife he had not brought for this bloody occasion, could have guessed at the sickness beneath that quiet face, the warring of heart and mind. At the thought of confronting those two—and both of them, very like, naked in bed together—he was all but overthrown. That he knew perfectly the nature of their association did not help; to know is one thing, to see with one's own eyes, another. And there was danger in it too—danger as well as disgust. Mortimer was accounted the best swordsman in England; and Mortimer, when anger took him, cared for no man, not though it were the King himself. But it was a thing he could not shirk; he must see the matter through to the end.

Mid-October and midnight. A cold, wet night; moon and stars hidden. A good night for such a piece of work. Through flat water-meadows the little Leen crept dark and slow. Wet earth sucked at their boots as they went bent double lest they miss the path. When the path went underground they lit their lanterns and, crouching still for fear of the low roof, planted their careful feet. But for all their care they went slithering in the mud; the clang of their weapons rang so loud in that enclosed place they feared lest the watch must hear and sound the alarum. But the low roof that made a sounding board within, muffled all sound without.

Slow-going; to them time seemed endless.

Holland's lantern suddenly lifted, showed them rough steps hewn in the rock steep and running with water. Immediately behind Holland went Lancaster, to his failing sight the lantern a hindrance rather than a help, at his heels Montague and some dozen gentlemen; in their midst—heart threatening to choke him with its wild beating—the King. He shook but not with fear—almost he wished it were; a horrifying repulsion shook him like a sickness.

The steps, rising sheer in the dark tunnel, seemed to have no end;

breath short in their lungs they climbed steadily. At last a glimmer or light broke the darkness. Holland put out the lantern.

The tunnel had come to an abrupt end. The glimmer was now seen to outline in the darkness before them, a square of some handsbreadths. Holland's fingers felt for the spring. With a tantalising care he slid the panel to one side. He stepped into the room; Lancaster followed him.

Hugh Turpington and John Neville were spending the long hours on guard wining and dicing; they were arguing the last toss, their voices loud enough to cover the stealthy movements on the other side of the panel. They had no more time than to turn about before cold steel took them.

It was over with them before the last of the party stepped into the room. The King, face to the wall, fought down his sickness; it was the first time he had seen a man slain before his eyes.

The King at his heels, Lancaster burst into the Queen's bedchamber.

Warned by his soldier's sense of danger, Mortimer had leaped from the bed and stood to his defence—naked body, naked steel. Isabella, eyes dark holes with fear, sat upright, pale as the sheets she clutched to her breast to hide her nakedness.

Montague secured the door.

Lancaster said, 'Your sword, sir; unless you would prefer to die under the eyes of the lady, here!'

Mortimer's sword went clattering. Lancaster said, 'You are the King's prisoner. Make yourself decent, unless you'd be taken through the streets naked.'

They watched while he threw on some clothes. He was quiet and composed; no sign of fear; only the red sparking of the eye, as of a rat cornered, betrayed him. When he was dressed they bound him with the Queen's girdle—a fitting cord since she had brought him to this, and led him away. He moved obedient to their hands; he moved as a man stricken. For the woman that loved him he had no word of Farewell. That he should go thus to his death, taken from a woman's bed and bound with her girdle, he, a soldier, kept him dumb lest he turn about and curse her.

And all the time she cried out, her voice high and thin with terror

—and that terror not for herself, *Pity, pity!* And it was not for herself she asked. And when no answer came she reached out an arm so that her breast and thigh shone white and naked, and caught at the King's cloak and cried to him, *Fair son, pity; pity for gentle Mortimer!* And when for very sickness he could not speak but must pull himself away, she cried out to Holland that had been her friend, *Do no hurt to Mortimer . . . no hurt no hurt. . . .*

There was no answer. They turned upon their heel. Her voice followed them fainter, thinner, as they took the prisoner away.

She looked about the room, the silent room that so short a time ago had been loud with the feet of men; the empty room . . . empty of her love. His cloak lay yet upon the stool where he had cast it last night in his haste for bed; his fine bonnet lay battered upon the floor, soiled with the trampling of their feet. She bent down and brought it into bed, cradling it against her naked breast to comfort it for its fallen state . . . to comfort herself with something that was his. And all the time the question, *What will they do with him?*

Beneath the question's torment, she could no longer lie in the bed. In the guttering candlelight she rose, and in the disordered room dressed herself as best she might. She was not used to such work; nor was she helped by her shaking hands, nor by the tears that, blinding her, fell upon her cheeks and into her mouth. And now it was not for him alone she wept but for herself, also; herself, desolate. Without him how should she endure to live?

What will they do to him? Again she remembered what he had done to the Despensers . . . and especially to the younger Despenser and bit upon her tongue to keep back the cry. *Not that, sweet Christ, not that!* Suddenly she remembered something else; the words they had written into the Articles of Deposition—*the Queen shall rule as long as she shall live.* She began to laugh, a little crazy laugh. They could not touch him without her word; and that word she would never give.

In the midst of her laughter, her son's face as she had seen it last, rose before her— the rigid jaw clamped down upon bitterness; in his eyes the sickness, the disgust. He had all the intemperate passion of his house, all the cruelties. Suppose she were too late? Suppose he saw to it that she was too late? All their promises would not help her then?

She flew to the door; the hasp would not lift. She tried until her hands were bruised, crying aloud the while. There was no answer. She called again, called and called; her own voice, hoarse with calling, was the only sound. She went across to the window. Surely someone would see, someone would hear. . . .

She looked down into the courtyard with some surprise.

It was morning; already it was morning and she had not known it. In the thin light servants were astir; behind her the candle flickered and went out. A man was sweeping; she heard plainly the drag of his broom on the cobbles. But when she wanted to call out to him the wind took her voice away. He went on sweeping.

Now other sounds split into the quiet. Dogs barked, horses neighed and stamped in the chill Autumn air, voices commanded; waggons came rumbling laden with furnishings, baggage was being carried out, baskets strapped upon sumpters . . . food for a journey.

Then she heard it; a quite different noise, stealing in upon the clatter of departure; a low noise, sustained . . . a sort of growling; the noise by which a crowd shows its anger. The noise rose, rose. . . .

When she understood the cause she put out both hands to save herself from falling.

It was for Mortimer, the noise of their hatred. They were leading him out. The breath stopped in her lungs; she thought she must die. She could not look; yet look she must, see him before they took him from her sight.

They had bound his two hands together and a fellow led him as though he were a dancing bear. They were thrusting him upon a beast of some sort . . . a mule? a donkey? She could not, for the blinding of her eyes, be sure; she could see only that it was a sorry sort of beast. They were strapping him upon the creature, they were handling him roughly. The animal was too low; his rider's feet scraped upon the cobbles. And now a fellow went before holding the reins.

A long, low moan escaped her. To this he was come—Mortimer,

the King's master, the Queen's paragon, proudest of men! Well, but he was proud still! He held his head high; proud he was and debonair. It was they that looked mean and shabby—not only those that so rudely handled him but Lancaster and Salisbury come to watch the fun. They, and all that had had a hand in this, her son even, should rue this day! On her own soul she swore it.

She saw the armed guard move to close him in; heard the grating of the portcullis raised, the drawbridge shut down. And worse, worse; she heard the growl of anger swell to a roar . . . all Nottingham gathered to spit upon great Mortimer brought low.

The courtyard was empty again; impossible to believe she had seen the hateful happening. But she had seen it . . . she had seen it! She turned back into the room, flung herself upon the disordered bed that held still the imprint of his body, the very smell of him; she laid her head upon the pillow where his head had lain. Now she was alone, forever alone! How should she endure them, the dreary procession of days lacking him?

By God she'd not endure them! She had forgotten herself— Madam Queen Isabella that ruled England.

She stopped weeping. She must be about her business! She crossed again to the door; this time the hasp lifted. In the anteroom a solitary waiting-woman lifted a pale, scared face; a page stared still through the narrow window though the show was over. He swung about as she came in and she bade him open the outer door. It was not locked; but a man stood either side, halberds crossed. She bade the boy run for the governor; run, run, *run*! For him the halberds dropped. She saw him go running.

How long before Holland comes? How long? How long? Every moment counts, every smallest moment . . . and the moments are flying, flying, the precious moments!

She beat her two hands together. Where were they taking him? Holland must tell her; she must be ready to follow on the instant. It came to her that, if she were to ride abroad, she must show herself unfrightened, debonair. She called to the tiring-woman. The woman laced her, brushed the long, tangled hair, brought water and towels, brought the paint, the unguents. When she asked for her looking-glass the woman hesitated; it was already packed she said.

She let it pass. No time to hunt among the baggage now! No doubt she looked well enough—the woman knew her work. The woman pinned the coif, brought the hooded cloak, the gloves . . . and still Holland did not come. Why? *Why?* Every moment was precious and he knew it. And there was her answer! He meant to make sure she was too late!

She went to the outer door. Behind the crossed halberds she called his name; and when still he did not come, screamed it aloud, screamed and screamed. They were to say afterwards that the taking of Mortimer from her very bed had crazed her wits.

When Holland stood, at last, before her she saw he could not meet her eyes. She didn't wonder at it—the traitor! Rage boiled within her; she hated him with a hatred violent as birthpangs. But long dissimulation instructed her to speak him fair; afterwards she would deal with him.

'Sir Robert,' she said, 'I hold you blameless. That you are still my friend I make no doubt!' *Judas, Judas!* 'Where does the King ride? Does he take my lord earl of March with him?'

'The lord King's for London, Madam; and the earl, also. And you, Madam, are to follow later.' And still he could not meet her eye.

'At once!' she commanded; and, at the refusal in his face, besought him. 'At once; I implore you!'

He shook a regretful head. 'I have the lord King's commands. You must await the appointed hour. You are to travel, Madam, by charette, the curtains drawn!'

She took in her breath at that. Why? Did her son fear that her sorrowful state would arouse the people's pity; turn their hearts to her again?

'You shall have honourable escort.' His cold lips touched her hand. 'Madam, Madam, forgive me,' he cried out. 'Would to God I had no hand in this!'

'By that same God, Holland, you shall have cause to wish it; and soon!'

He bowed and turned upon his heel.

She sat within the charette, curtains drawn. Men-at-arms enclosed about her, Montague rode in charge. *Honourable escort!* It was all of a piece with Holland's lying. As she took her slow way, news of her coming went before. That day, and every day, crowds gathered to hiss, to shout their insults. Now she knew why her son had commanded the charette, the drawn curtains. *They hate me.* The knowledge fell with all the shock of surprise. Their diminished love she had known, but *hatred!* That she had not dreamed. Well hate her or not, still she was Isabella the Queen; and Mortimer she would save.

That first night they lay at a monastery. When the tiring-woman had removed the coif and brushed out her hair, Isabella asked for her looking-glass. Again there was hesitation, again excuses; this time she would take none.

She stared into the looking-glass; she did not know the strange face. She could not believe it was her own; her hand went up to rub the mirror clear. And still the strange face stared back. And now she saw, with horror, it was her own . . . and the hair was grey, quite, quite grey. Dead hair. She wanted to cry out in pity for her hair as though it were some treasure, separate from herself, some lovely, lost thing. . . . Mortimer had loved it once. It has its own life, he used to say; it lives, it moves, it changes with every changing light. Those early days in France he would shift the lamp this way and that watching her hair move from green-gold to ripe corn. Now it would never change again. Dead hair. That her face was yellow, the eyes staring from bruised sockets, she held of little account; it would pass. But her hair, her hair. . . .

Terror on Mortimer's account was, for the moment, diverted to herself. What value in life to a woman that has no beauty to offer her lover? Though ambition drove Mortimer to her bed, some beauty he did demand—pride in his manhood required it. And, for all he pricked her with her age, when they lay together her beauty stirred him still. In the net of her golden hair she had taken him, held him. And now? What had love, passion, lust—call it what you would—to do with old, dead hair? Mortimer would come no more to her bed; and without him she did not want to live. But we are not free to choose; nor would she dare to die, her sins upon her. She was but thirty-five; and the years stretched ahead, the empty years.

She put her hands to her face and wept like a child.

It was the tiring-woman that brought her from the worst of her grief. 'Madam I have a brew; I had it from my grandmother, a noted wise woman. Soon Madam Queen Isabella will look herself again!' The promise restored her courage. The years ahead were good years. First of all she would save Mortimer; then she would gather her friends, plan fresh victories.

But, for all that, she did not sleep that night nor any night of this tormenting journey. If, for a little, she drifted into sleep she would awaken herself with weeping . . . Mortimer's body swung before her; and sometimes it lay headless in the black pool of his own blood.

The slowness of the journey maddened her; she was in a fever to reach London. She commanded Montague to halt nowhere, to ride through the night. He informed her that, by the King's orders, they were to travel by easy stages to save Madam Queen Isabella the fatigues of hasty travel. He was the perfection of courtesy, but it was clear that her wishes did not count. She knew now with anguish and desolation that the King meant to have Mortimer executed without the nuisance of her tears. She had comforted herself that without trial they could not judge him, without her signature dared not kill him. But could they not, dare they not? Dare they, indeed, allow him to live?

She forced herself to sit quiet in her place, to thank Montague for his courtesy; for all his dislike he must admire her. This slow, hopeless journey was a most cruel punishment; that the punishment was inevitable, the natural consequence of her own ill deeds, did not make it less cruel.

Through the Autumn weather went the slow, tormenting procession; on either hand lay the golden harvest. It should, she thought, be her own harvest-time; she should be gathering her own golden fruits. It came to her with appalling desolation that, if they killed Mortimer it must be winter with her now and for ever.

Chapter Forty-Five

London at last. After the week of torment she saw its walls and towers black against the pale night sky. As she neared the northern gate she was taken, without reason, by a fit of shivering. The gates opened to let her through; the streets were all-but empty. She was glad of that; demonstrations along the road had not been pleasant. Had her son commanded so late an entry to spare her the ignominy of a hostile crowd? If he had she might expect grace from such gentleness.

He had, indeed, commanded it and for that reason. But the gentleness was Philippa's; there could be no grace from him.

Some few citizens were taking the evening air. The riders, the men-at-arms challenged attention; the royal charette was recognised. Suddenly the street was black with people, the air menacing with noise. Two sounds repeated over and over, sharp, ugly, scarce to be recognised as words. But all the same she recognised them. Spiteful as flung stones, heavy as blows, blows upon the heart.

She-wolf! She-wolf!

Pale, Montague rode up to take his place by the charette; God alone knew how long the mob would content itself with insult! She showed no fear; only the curled lip, the pinched nostril showed her disgust; for what were they but barking dogs? And she forgot that once she had courted their favour, enjoyed their love; she forgot, also, it is in the nature of dogs to bite.

She said, 'I care *this* for them!' And snapped her fingers. 'I am blind to them, deaf to them; their stink, however, I cannot escape!' 'But *fear* them?' She pulled the curtains wide; and since she could not be well seen through the horn of the window, rose and flung upon the doors.

She stood there, the lines of grief, of fatigue, of ill-living washed from her face by the gentle dusk. Unflinching, royal and most beautiful she dared them all; and the crowd that had gathered to do her injury fell silent. And in that silence she passed. It was, perhaps, the greatest single triumph of her life.

Through London, between crowds silent and hostile she passed —an image dedicated to her own Queenship. The Tower, its walls and keep rose before her. In this place Mortimer had languished and she had contrived his escape. Could she save him once again? Had he already come to the block; and did the ravens already pick at his bones? Or did he hang upon the gallows, her son refusing him the nobler death? She remembered the king's face as she had seen it last. She was not hopeful.

Why were they bringing her to the Tower? Did they intend to imprison her—Madam Queen Isabella? Or even to quiet her for ever? If it suited their book they'd put an end to her here and now; afterwards they would make all good with fair words. *Put her to death!* Her son would not allow it. But Lancaster would allow it; would, taking a leaf out of her own book, hurry the business on. Her son would know nothing until the thing was done. Her heart was down; but her head was high as the procession halted.

At the royal entrance the governor stood to receive her. She was to enter as a Queen; that, at least, was reassuring. All was as usual. Yet it was not quite as usual. There was neither smile nor any sign of welcome; above due courtesy his face was blank as an egg. But for all that the Queen's lodgings were ready and waiting. A good fire burned; there was bread-and-meat on the table, there was a flagon of wine and a dish of apples. Not lavish entertainment for a Queen but it would do. In the inner chamber the bed stood ready, the linen fresh and smooth; when the woman turned back the sheets the bed was warm with heated bricks.

Eat she could not; she longed for the waiting bed but restlessness forbade her; restlessness and disquiet. The woman dismissed, Isabella knelt upon the window-seat. Little enough to see; all-but bare branches against the night-dark sky, dark mass of wall and tower and the gleam of the river heavy and oily beyond. There was little sound either beyond the creaking of boughs, the footsteps of the watch, the password demanded and given. The very ravens slept, gorged, no doubt, with flesh . . . *whose* flesh? She shuddered. And now breaking upon the small noises, the long roar of the lions within their cages. For the first time she pitied them, the royal beasts caged and confined. Like them, too, she was caged and confined. And she remembered that, from this very room, Mortimer had escaped to freedom; but though the door opened at her touch, for her there was no escape unless her son chose to set her free!

She tried to laugh away her fears. . . . She tormented herself to no purpose. She had done no wrong—nothing that could be proved against her. And who should dare to do her hurt—royal blood of France, Isabella the King's mother, *the good Queen*? But all the time memory uncomfortably pricked. Royal blood had not saved her husband, the King himself, from death within prison walls. She strained her eyes into the darkness searching for the first sign of dawn; she longed unspeakably for morning. Darkness made familiar things strange; daylight brought back their familiarity, sent unreasonable fears flying. And morning must surely bring her son. She would speak to him, bring him back to the obedience he owed his mother to whom he was beholden for crown and so-loved wife.

All night she knelt by the window. Sometimes she prayed, telling God her requirements; sometimes she rehearsed the words she would say to her son—strong words but not too strong, loving words but not too loving. Now and then she would rise to ease her cramped limbs, then back she would go to her kneeling. Once she took a piece of bread from the table, and, hunger driving, could scarce eat it fast enough though it had gone dry with waiting; she eased it down with wine. But when she tried the meat her stomach rose and she all-but vomited. Back she went to the window and there, the bread-and-wine comforting her, fell into uneasy sleep.

She opened her eyes upon grey morning. Mortimer. He was her instant thought. Where was he? Did he still live? How many days since she had seen him last? She had lost count; but many . . . too many to hope that he still lived. But when the October sun burst through the mist, when the river sparkled and came alive, then courage rose in her again. She could not believe him dead on such a day. Maybe in this very Tower he watched the sun and thought of her. But—she knew the way of princes, none better—if still he lived he would be shut away in some dark place where he could not see the sun. And, if he thought of her at all, it would be to wonder if she could save him, or to curse their association; nothing more. Love between them had never been equal; such as he had for her would never stand against strain.

The bright day clouded; morning passed into afternoon and still she waited for her son; waited in anger and in some fear, rehearsing the words she would say.

It was late in the evening when the King came.

She rose and made to bend the knee. He did not, as always, raise her before she touched the ground. He let her kneel; and when, at last, he gave her the nod to rise, let her stumble to her feet unaided.

'Madam,' and he called her neither Queen nor mother; nor did he sit nor invite her to sit, 'you are for Windsor to stay there during my pleasure—though pleasure is scarce the word! You are free to go where you will within the Queen's lodgings and to walk in the King's private garden but in no other place!'

She brushed his words aside. There was one thing she must know yet dared not ask. It was not fear of the boy her son; it was fear of what she might learn of a deed already done.

'Mortimer?' she said at last and there was no sound in her throat.

'Dead, Madam. What did you expect?' His young face was stone, the boyish look for ever gone.

'How?' She could say no more; the things she had planned to say were useless now. But if they'd granted him an honourable death she'd ask no more of God!

'What did you expect?' he asked again; she thought he had prepared his speech, so level the voice so scant the words.

Suddenly his anger broke through; she saw the havoc within. She saw it and did not care; did not care how he suffered so that the news he gave was not the thing she dreaded.

'A traitor's death. Need I speak it?'

And when she stood there, hand at her throat, eyes darkened in her head, he said, 'Hanged and drawn, Madam. Go out by the north gate until you reach the Tyburn—a small river but you'll not miss it, nor the place we call the Elms . . .!'

The Elms at Tyburn where they hanged the lowest of the low . . . and there *his* body hung! Now she knew why, last night, she had shuddered as they came near the north gate. Her eye had not seen; but her blood had known.

'You must have missed it by night. Go there by daylight, Madam; you'll see your lover once again. A pity to miss him while yet he's all of a piece; today we take him down to deal with his body—the traitor that murdered his King and defiled his Queen. We'll stick his head upon the Bridge—his insolent, wicked head. I advise you to make all haste to Windsor that you may escape the sight; it is not pretty. The lips you've kissed so often—I doubt you'll want to kiss them now!'

At the sight of her stricken face, he cried out, 'Are you so delicate, Madam, that you cannot speak of the things you two did together and did not hide your shame? No, rather you flaunted your sin! The man's death was just—fair judgment by his peers; a traitor's death for a traitor; not more nor less. Be thankful, Madam, we spared him the torment he put upon my father. Fair judgment and time to repent his sins—these things my father never had. We have been merciful, indeed; too merciful. We might have torn him with pincers as he tore the Despensers—for the one defiled his King, the other his Queen!'

And while she went on staring at this terrible stranger that wore the face of her son, he cried out, 'He confessed; your paramour confessed, there in the cell, before they took him out to hang. And it was not fear of what man might do; he was no coward, that much I give him! It was fear of God loosened his tongue. No need to tell you the things he said—what they were you know already.'

And now she saw what she had seen before but had not truly grasped. He was all in black; not only doublet, hose and cloak, but shoes, chaperon, and gloves, even. All black. A figure of doom.

Again her hands went to her throat. Now, now she understood the meaning. He mourned—and meant her to know it—as though, this very day, his father had died. What new thing had he learned?

What had Mortimer to confess beyond what all Christendom knew—that he had been the Queen's lover? That his hand had been in her husband's death? True it was—but let them prove it! Confession dragged from a man in the agony of torment! Let her son swear there'd been none—she'd not believe it! Confession heard —if ever it had been made—by one priest alone. Who could give credence to it?

But there *was* something more; something of which she knew nothing.

He said, 'I know now how my father came to his death.' And his face was sickening to behold—like a little animal, she thought, with a life of its own, writhing and twisting. What, she wondered, had stamped that anguish in his face, marks he must bear for ever?

'I know nothing!' she cried out, 'nothing but what they told me —that your father died suddenly.'

'Is that all, Madam?' And his smile was dreadful.

'That is all. What more? *Is* there more? Mortimer never told me, never *said* . . . not the smallest word. Sir . . . sweet son, for the love of Christ, believe it!'

'There *is* more. And what that is I know, and you know! So anything I have forgot you shall tell me!'

The white face framed in the black chaperon was stone now; face of the dead, incapable of love or pity. She felt his will upon her, his black will . . . like a great bird, she thought, fearful; one of the ravens flown in to sit upon her heart. But what did he want of her? What could she tell him? There came to her mind some words Mortimer had uttered in sleep.

She said, 'That night . . . the night he died, they gave him a good supper. . . .'

'Is that a thing to be remembered—that once the King of England had enough to eat? Did they starve him then, my poor father, and then cram him full before his death like a bird that's to be killed?' His face began to work again.

'A good supper; do you quarrel with that? A good supper and a good bed.'

'A good bed! Had he lain then upon the earth—the King of England? And the bed; *how* good?'

She said, desperate, since she knew so little, 'Good enough, I must suppose. A soft bed, clean. . . .'

'How clean? When they had finished with him—*how clean?*'

'I don't know; I don't *know*. *How* should I know?'

'Then let me help you, Madam. They cast him upon the bed; they threw him upon his face . . . and then?'

She tried to escape those eyes that held her prisoner. How could she tell him what she did not know? The eyes, relentless, held her fast. *The bed . . . the bed. . . .*

'They smothered him with pillows, Christ save us!' She hazarded her guess; how else could the thing be done?

'Not so clean a death nor yet so merciful. There was no mark upon him—remember? It was agreed between you!'

She could neither nod nor shake her head; she stood there, neck held stiff, eyes sunk deep into their sockets.

'And then, Madam?' he asked again. 'What next?'

And now she did manage to shake her head; stiff head upon stiff neck.

'Then I must help you. They took the table from the trestles. They laid it across his shoulders and across his back; the upper part of his back only—Madam, mark it! So there he lay helpless at the mercy of them that had no mercy. Must I help you, further?'

She stared fascinated, fearful of what must come; the horror she could not imagine, much less name.

'They took down his breeches like a child that's to be whipped . . . your husband and your King; the Majesty of England. They had a horn, a small neat horn . . . exactly shaped; you know what that was for!' And it was not a question.

And still she stood staring. She could not speak with her dried-up tongue, could not shake her stiff head. Because quite suddenly she knew . . . she *knew*. Mortimer's mumbled words clashed like cymbals. They had made no sense . . . no sense. Now they did make sense, beat out a pattern . . . a crime so appalling the brain blistered and bled; inside her head she felt the bleeding.

Let him not speak. Sweet Christ, let him not speak!

He went on speaking.

'They had lit a fire, Madam. He must have said his thanks for that. He was courteous and he'd been so cold. Into the fire they thrust the poker; it glowed red-hot. They took the horn, the small neat horn; they seized him, they held him fast. They thrust the horn—Madam, you know *where*! Where but between the buttocks! Do you whiten, Madam? These things you know. They were done; should they not be said? They took the red-hot iron and thrust it through the horn. Christ that a son should speak these things, that a woman give such orders, a man suffer such agony!'

His face was working again; the pain of his breathing tore through him like a knife. He stood forcing himself to quiet, taking in steadier breaths, letting them go again until he could speak once more.

'Into his body with the red-hot iron; into his very guts. Do I offend your delicacy, Madam?' Again his smile was dreadful. 'The horn would tell no tale. No mark upon the body . . . No mark save the agony on his face so that no man could know the face as his; not even I, his son! Oh it was clever, Madam! Whose wits planned it, yours or his—the man for whom you slew my father? Yours, I'll wager; he was not clever!' And still he could not bring that hated name upon his tongue.

'Have you ever thought upon it, Madam—the agony, the live flesh scorching, burning, stinking? And the bleeding; the hidden bleeding? There must be left no mark! And the cries for mercy. And no mercy. No mercy! So to murder a man; any man! But . . . your King and mine; your husband and my father? I could not do it to a beast let alone a man; not to *him,* even. I might have commanded it and no man blame me; but I could not do it. *That man* died a merciful death; for that be grateful. But my father, my father! The way he died; doesn't that deed turn all sweet things to rottenness, all beauty to foulness, all your prayers to blasphemy? Do you sleep at nights. Madam? Me, I cannot sleep!'

In the midst of her own anguish, her own fear, she wanted to comfort him—he was after all her son, her young son. She half put out a hand; saw the disgust upon his face and the way he shrank, as though she were a leper, from her touch.

'But you; you sleep! Why not? You are not a woman; you are an animal, a savage beast. And so the people name you. *She-wolf!*

But they wrong such beasts; for they are, as God made them, innocent. You are a were-wolf, rather; a damned creature that goes about her familiar friends to drink their blood.'

She stood there, unhearing; mercifully, his words flowed over her head. Hardened as she was, cruel as she could be, her mind could not, as yet, encompass that death so horrible, so appalling; so, for all the clear detail, not to be imagined. She was filled with loathing; loathing of herself that, asking no question, had let it happen; loathing of Mortimer, of him even, that had commanded it to happen; loathing of him that had been made to suffer it.

Vomit filled her mouth. She threw out her hands. She went down into the darkness.

Chapter Forty-Six

She lay back in the great chair. Save for the high painting of cheek and mouth she was grey head-to-foot; grey as the gown she wore, gown of the Grey Friars though she was no religious, and if she lived a thousand years, never would be. It was a dress she affected, fancying so to spread some odour of sanctity, to inveigle God's forgiveness; never would she forgo her small cunnings. And the gown did double duty, covering shrunken arms and bosom that once had been the loveliest in Christendom; no more than her small cunnings could she forget the beauty that had been hers.

She was sixty-three and Mortimer dead these twenty-eight years. She was old, she was weary to the bone, and she repented of her wickedness, God knew. Yet, were it all to do again, still she must do it for love of Mortimer, gentle Mortimer. And she forgot, being told and at times half-crazed, that from the first he had never been gentle, that he had used her to serve his ambition and his lust. She forgot that, cruel and brutal, he had with lies dragged her into a fearful murder. And she forgot, also, the loathing she had felt for him when first she heard the truth of her husband's death.

Yet she did truly repent. Remorse fed upon her heart like an obscene bird gorging itself full. There were times when, if she were not to go mad with the pain of it, she must sit rigid, the tears pouring down her face, not daring to move until the monstrous thing had departed. Thereafter she would sit whispering, whispering to God. And seeing her weeping for no reason, and talking as they thought to herself, they called it madness.

Madness? My bitter repentance, my conversations with God? And this, too, I must accept, part of my punishment. I am glad to accept it; for surely, the more I am punished now, the less my punishment thereafter. Twenty-eight years of punishment endured. It is a long time; but longer, eternity.

Twenty-eight years since Mortimer died. My son bade me hasten to Windsor lest I meet face-to-face my love's rotting head. I did not wait for that. When they went to take down the body they found the gallows empty. Myself a prisoner, still I had means to command a service. He lies now in the church of the Grey Friars and there, at his side, I hope, one day, to lie. He was my true husband.

Twenty-eight years. And he is dead and I live still. I had not thought that possible. But we live from day to day; and the days pass into weeks, into months, into years; and the years pass, somehow they pass.

My son, they said, was merciful to me. I think it was less mercy than shame; shame for his behaviour in the Tower. When he came to his senses, he believed I knew nothing of the way his father died. But even then he did not entirely acquit me; nor does he now. That time in the Tower I can neither forget nor forgive—the way he forced the truth upon me, the brutal truth in all its horror. Had he meant to punish me with life-long torment he could have done no better. For it was my soul he punished; not my body. My body he kept close for three months; and then, free to go where I would. But the punishment my soul must bear for ever.

Those months at Windsor he never came near me; no, nor sent to enquire of me. Night after night lying sleepless, the scarifying image of that murder burning into my brain, burning as with that same hot iron they used there in the dark cell. Lying there and crying to God to let me die before my wits cracked . . . and all the time knowing I did not dare to die, that I was afraid to die. Lying there in the endless dark wondering what punishment my son had devised; like all his house he has a cruel streak.

Those nights I died a hundred deaths; and all needless. Pope John, good Christian man, asked my son to let all rest in silence; that a man shame his mother is unchristian. And who dares disobey the lord Pope? My son lifted the blame from me to set it fair and square upon Mortimer. There was a document . . . *Mortimer alone brought all the evils upon the land. Malicious and lying, he persuaded Madam Queen Isabella that the late King sought her death. For this reason alone she absented herself from her husband's bed. . . .*

But it did not say into whose bed I went!

A smile brushed the painted lips.

It did not say that before ever I set eyes upon my love I hated my husband; and with reason. Nor that it needed no man to tell me the Despensers watched to make an end of me. Nor did it say that were there no Mortimer to love, no Despensers to fear, not God Himself had brought me to my husband's bed.

A reasonable document, false and lying and sealed with my virtuous son's own seal! And, having proclaimed my innocence he must abide by it.

After those three months at Windsor he let me free. But first he robbed me of my lands and dowers—even those that were my unalienable right. And who got them? Who but my son's wife Philippa whose money runs through her fingers like water—and nothing to show for it but figures that don't balance in her accounts and items set down to charities. She dresses sober as a merchant's wife and her jewels are laughable in a Queen. For her—everything that was mine; for me—a dole insufficient for my state.

Well, but I was free; free to go where I would—save that I must keep from London. Did he fear the heart of London would turn to me again? Or that I would contaminate his virtuous Philippa? Or that I would dip my fingers in the political pie? My fingers were burned enough already.

Poor, besmirched for all the whitewash, I yet made a good showing. . . .

She sat there, smiling, remembering how she had ridden the countryside with a great train—knights and esquires, ladies and waiting-women, household officials and servants—her own court. She'd stayed now at one house her son had lent her, now at another; when her beggarly allowance had run out she'd announced herself a guest at some great house. And always the people had come to pay their respects; but not their love.

Not their love.

She stopped her smiling.

MORTIMER AND THE QUEEN 389

My son need not have feared. The people loved me no longer. It hurt; surprisingly, it hurt. Vanity; vanity, only. I never pretended to love the garlic-stinking mob; not even when they bawled themselves hoarse for me—*the Good Queen!*

And she remembered that soon she had given up processions and progresses, telling herself that they were too costly for an impoverished Queen.

. . . But it was partly pride because I did not choose to face a people that had no love for me; partly because since Mortimer died I took no joy in such affairs. I was content to stay at home; content, above all, to stay from London where they hated me with an undying hatred.

And wherever I made my home my son would visit me, as still he does, coming in state, showing all due respect; respect but no love. An unloving heart, my virtuous son. He allows no word to tarnish my good name; but even now he keeps his wife from me. Madam Philippa sends her respects, sends her gifts; but herself comes never. Too busy about her good works!

And good works no doubt they are; but somewhat odd in a Queen. She should have been a merchant's wife, that one! She'd not been here a couple of years before she was sending home for weavers in wool—masters with their journeymen, to come and settle with their families. She paid them well to teach their mistery. Soon less and less raw wool was going out of the country, more and more money coming in. And money breeds money—no-one can quarrel with that. But I like a more royal way. Still, money is money!

She has her eye on the main chance, the so-good Philippa; she cares little for the glories of war; instead of knights she keeps merchants to give her advice—and no doubt more substantial benefits; she keeps scholars and poets to sing her praises. She has Messire Froissart running at her heels like a little dog, proclaiming her virtues to all Christendom.

Good works and yearly pregnancies—her history. Fertile as a gypsy! So many children; impossible to remember them all—I've never been allowed near them!

Twenty-eight years since the power was snatched from my hands.

And my son John lies sleeping in his fine tomb—a kinder son than Edward; and Joan, my little one, lies sick to death.

And she forgot that her little one was thirty-five and a grand-mother.

Children die; and children are born. My son's eldest boy—the only one of my grandchildren I've ever seen and then by accident—I could have doted upon; the handsome child! A tall young man he must be now; a bonny fighter they say, and a wicked look to his eye like a blood stallion. Black armour he has, from Florence; his father gave it him. *The Black Prince* they call him—a name to stir the blood.

She found herself wishing that, him at least, she might see; she dearly loved a handsome man. As for the others, she cared not a fig! But all the same the insult rankled.

There was a small sound in the room; a little page came quietly in. Careful, he carried a cloak and laid it upon the stool at her feet. A small cloak it was; a child's, rich velvet lined with cloth-of-gold.

'Madam, the things you asked for! Here's the cloak; the books are in the anteroom.'

She smiled at the pretty boy. 'I have to be certain all is at hand. You see I am making my will; for who can hope to escape death? But all the same I do not like to think upon it!'

You are very old; it is time. The young face spoke clear; but well-trained to courtesy he said, 'Madam Queen Isabella need not fear to think upon death. Madam is very good—forever at her prayers!'

'There are many,' she said, her smile wry, 'that would not agree with you!'

'Then they are fools!' he said at once, being too young to know the tales about her. 'Or else they do not know you!'

'Maybe they know me too well. But there's none so bad he couldn't be worse; and none so good he couldn't be better! But it isn't only bad they call me; mad, they say that too! Do you think me crazy?'

'No . . .' He was a little doubtful. 'Madam talks to herself at times, but I think it is not foolish talking. I think she talks to God!'

'They say I am crazy because I weep without cause.'

'We all have cause to weep.'

'So young and so wise! Well, it seems I have one friend at least! You are a good page; one day you will make a good knight!'

'I would like to be your knight, Madam; to serve you with my life!' *But you are old . . . too old.*

She knew the thought; how should she not? She sighed. 'Life goes by . . . so *quick*. You'd not believe *how* quick!' She picked up the little cloak. 'I was married in this!' She stroked it with a gentle hand.

His eyes widened. 'Such a little girl!'

She nodded. 'Happy and innocent; but neither for long!' And now she spoke to herself, forgetful, as was her way at times. 'But because of that short happiness, that short innocence, I must be buried in it. They must lay it about my shoulders. It will reach, perhaps, to my waist.' She was silent a while; then, remembering the boy she said, her voice clear and direct, 'Have you bid my priest to me?'

'Madam, he lies sick abed. But there's a friar below in the kitchens; comes from Gloucester way he says. Would Madam Queen see him, perhaps?'

'Perhaps. See that they look to his needs. Yes, bring him later . . . later. Go now!'

Upright in the great chair Isabella regarded the little cloak. In the dim room it shone—a small sun. She turned a restless head from side to side as though to shake away pain.

The little cloak. It brought everything back. The young child kneeling by her groom—so handome a prince, golden Edward—in far away Boulogne.

Tears stung the old eyes.

A good child. . . .

She considered the word *good* with care.

. . . not always good; but a *will* to goodness; and that's the thing that counts. A loving child wanting to be good.

The tears fell faster, remembering what that child had become.

A child that had asked nothing but to love her husband; to be a little loved and to serve him with all her heart . . . and, in the end *how* had she served him?

The restless head moved yet more restless, the grey face twitched with pain.

The child grew up; the little cloak fitted her no longer. She grew beautiful. *Isabella the fair*. But, for all that, unloved of her husband and slighted still; a woman crying in her heart for love and finding none; a woman the world praised—a woman alone.

Alone. Familiar misery bridged the long years; she came back to the empty room.

But even then I did my best; and it was not so poor a best. I made peace between the King and his barons; I made peace between England and France. I would have prospered the King and prospered the country but that vile favourites brought it all to nothing. . . .

She sat there sending her thoughts back, further back, beyond the Despensers.

Not Piers. He was never vile; wild, only, wild. There was good in him. Piers I won; but it was too late.

Now she was muttering in the way they called crazy. She could hear it for herself, the whispering in the empty room; hear the black angel's wings beating within her head. If she didn't stop now, while she could, the whisper would rise to a scream and she wouldn't be able to stop it. Scream after scream until they came and tied her with a cord and put her into the dark. Above all things she hated the dark; she feared it. It was as though they shut her living into the grave.

She bit upon her lips, bit until the blood ran salt in her mouth; the whispering stopped.

But not the thinking. That went on and on.

Lonely. Unloved. Humiliated. And then—Mortimer.

She was old, she was grey, she was drained of life. Yet remembering Mortimer her body grew soft again, open and desiring.

Even now, death at her elbow, she could not forget her love for him, nor the passion there had been between them; neither forget nor regret, not though she prayed for forgiveness until the knees shook beneath her.

Yet God should forgive; they call Him merciful. And for that thing we did together we paid in full—he with a shameful death, I with the terrible loneliness; and the black angel that beats in my head and the black raven that sits upon my heart. Torment beyond endurance, so that, at times, I must run from wall to wall, beating my head against the stone, driving away the black angel; beating my clenched fists upon my breast, beating out the black raven; wailing like the lost soul I am till they come and put me away unto the dark.

I hear the dark wings louder, louder; the great bird presses ever more heavy upon my heart. I feel the madness rising. It is always so when I think of *him,* of gentle Mortimer. Keep my thoughts from him. Wipe the mind clean; blank as an egg. Sit unmoving, still as the dead. . . .

She sat bolt upright, eyes closed; save for the paint bright upon cheekbones and mouth, a mask of death.

The long moments passed.

The black angel departed, the black raven eased her of its weight. Without stirring, her eyes opened; she looked about her. She saw once more the little cloak; her thoughts came lucid now and calm.

Edward. I set my wits to prosper his affairs; but useless, useless! Goodwill thrown back into my face, work all come to nothing. The crown, the crown even, in danger! What wonder that I turned to *him,* to him that already had my heart. What Mortimer wanted, I wanted. Except one thing. To put an end to the man that was my husband. Let him die and I'd not grieve—so long as I had no hand in it. That I did not want; God Himself knows it! But I could not save him. He was doomed; he had doomed himself.

The bright dazzle of the cloak confused her; she shut her eyes against it. At the thought of that death, old as she was, indifferent, for the most part, to pain and pleasure, she sickened.

But *did* he die in agony there, in the dark dungeon?

For the hundredth, hundredth time that question.

There's some to say he escaped. Well, that's all one now! He must be dead, it's all so long ago; and we shall never know. But sweet Christ, if I might believe he lives! And yet, why not? His own brother believed it, swore he'd seen Edward's self—and for that belief, he died; but Kent's wits were none too bright. Yet Melton of York believed it and Gravesend of London believed it, they'd known him since a boy; shrewd priests both, judges of men, hard to deceive. And the Pope; the Pope at Avignon believed it. If he believed, great lawyer that he was, who should doubt?

Edward escaped to France—so the story goes; in Avignon the Pope sheltered him, honoured him. And such a man did appear at Avignon and the Pope did shelter him, honour him—so much we know! Why? Was it Christian charity to a crazed soul? Or did he know the man? Rumour said much; the Pope himself—nothing. To all enquiries a smile, a smile, only.

And yet it could be true. . . .

She was desperate to convince herself.

There were tales enough, God knows! A second attempt on Berkeley; armed men attacking and rescuing the King. At Berkeley they swore there'd been no such thing, ever; that the prisoner died peacefully in his cell. But all men lie to save their skin; and it might well be true. For why did the Pope command my son to declare me innocent in the matter? And why was no-one ever punished? Ogle and Gurney were tried and convicted—and allowed to escape; why was Maltravers, prime mover in the affair, also allowed to escape? Why was he left safe in Flanders? Why was his wife left to enjoy his incomes? Why was he allowed home, at last, his lands restored, himself honoured?

No-one was punished because there was no murder. And that is why my son was glad to obey the Pope and why he allowed me a Queen's dignity—some cold justice he has!

But, if it is not Edward that came to a hideous death—who is it that sleeps in a martyr's grave?

Her thoughts went round and round in her head like rats biting each other's tail.

. . . Surely it must be Edward. Or, if not, he must have died soon after the rescue. Of this be sure—had he lived he had never had held his tongue. The first cup of wine—and out the tale would come!

Well, whatever happened, Mortimer died for it; and still I bear my punishment. I grant it not unjust. But what of punishment to come? If there's no murder on my soul, will God, in the end, forgive me?

Sitting upright in her chair, she began to pray desperately that, if the final evil had come to pass—the evil she had lifted no hand to stop—she might not burn to all eternity.

A knock fell upon the door. 'Madam,' the little page said, 'I have brought the priest.'

It was a tall man that entered; so tall he must bend his cowled head in the doorway. He stood in his Grey Friar robes, hands folded within his sleeves. The cowl shadowed his face; she did not find this strange. There were some orders where a brother must cover his face before a woman. She rose to greet him. They stood face-to-face and both in the Grey Friar robes.

Brother and sister of the same order . . . so it would seem; save that I am no holy woman.

'Madam,' he said. And then, 'Daughter, you wish to make confession?'

She did not answer. The confession she had in mind was not easily spoken; nor one to make to a stranger.

She said, in order to gain time, 'Father, will you not be seated?'

'Soon we are to kneel,' he reminded her.

'Yet be seated,' she said.

'Madam,' and still he stood, 'we move towards our death; and for some of us time is all but done. The thing you would confess, I think, lies heavy on your heart.'

She said nothing; she was greatly troubled. For nigh on thirty years the thing had lain unspoken; how could she now bring it upon her tongue? But, *We move towards our death; and for some of us time is all but done.* The truth must be told. And soon. Soon. And what better time to tell this unknown priest she would never see again?

And when still she did not speak he said, his voice gentle, 'Madam, shall I help you? Does the matter concern the late King?'

She made no answer. It was not his words that troubled her—she scarce heard them. It was his voice. She had never heard it before and yet it troubled her.

She said, at last, very low, 'There is much upon my soul.'

'Which one of us must not say the same? Madam, shall we not kneel?'

She knelt upon the stool that still held the little cloak. He stood above her, quiet and grey . . . *like a ghost; we are both ghosts.*

Between them like a flame the little cloak lay unheeded.

He had not put back his cowl. She was glad of that; it was easier so. She began to speak, her voice so low he must bend to hear.

When she had made an end, he gave her no absolution; instead he made her a sign to rise. He said, 'Daughter, were you willing for the deed?'

'Unwilling, father; I was not willing here!' She touched her forehead. 'Yet I was willing, too . . . lust, lust drove me. *He* . . .' and even now she could not say his name, 'refused me his bed until the thing was done. But, before Christ, I was not willing for the manner of his dying. I did not know it. I swear by Christ, I did not know it!' And when he made no answer to that, she said, very slow, 'My son told me . . . a tale. Most horrible. I cannot and I will not believe it—no devil out of Hell could be so cruel! And why should I believe it? There's no man knows the truth!'

'There's one man knows the truth.'

Her head came from her hands. She stared at him. What did he mean by that? What *could* he mean save what anyone might mean —a putting together of old tales, a guessing at the truth? No more.

But for all that she began to shake and could not still her body. The voice; the voice that, from the first, had troubled her. The voice and the height of him!

'God is all-merciful. He that searches the inmost heart will forgive you, so you truly repent. And be sure that he who was your husband forgives you also.'

. . . your husband forgives you. . . .

She went on staring, her eyes enormous and darkened with fear.

His hands came out from the wide sleeves; hands long and fine, craftsmen's hands. They had aged but still she knew them.

The room began to rock; and, in the vortex of whirling wall and floor and ceiling, she saw those hands outstretched to help.

The room stopped its mad whirling, came back to ordered stillness; and in the stillness she said his name. She saw him faintly start at that. The years had disciplined him—but not to the sound of the name he had once borne.

'Sir,' she said and went down upon her knees.

'Never kneel to me,' he said. 'Kneel to none but two Kings;

first the King of Heaven and then the King of England. As for me, I am nothing but a poor friar of Gloucester.'

'Sir,' she said again, 'sir . . .' and knelt still.

He went to her then; he held out both hands and raised her to her feet. The shivering took her again at the touch of his hand, She said, wholly fearful, 'Will you not put back your hood?'

The cowl dropped. For the moment she was not quite sure; lacking the beard the face had a strange, a naked look. Then she saw the noble head and her eyes came back to the face, the handsome face she had prayed never to see again. A petulant face it had been; now it was a face of mercy. The hair was white, the hair that had flowed in bright locks; the eyes were faded that had once been blue as the flower that country-folk call forget-me-not . . . she had not forgotten. There were lines upon that once-smooth forehead; lines of pain stitched deeper than mere years can bring. The once-rosy, well-fleshed cheeks were pale as ivory, were hollow so that the bones showed through beautiful and clean. Old and humbly clad there was a nobility about him he had never had. He was, every inch, a King.

She said, 'Sir, will you, for old time's sake and to show your forgiveness, drink a cup of wine?' And while he hesitated, she said, sorrowful, 'Will you not take so simple a thing at my hands? For if I mark no forgiveness in you that I see with my own eyes, how shall I believe in the forgiveness of God my eyes cannot see?'

He nodded at that. She went to the table glad to perform this so-small service for him and poured a cup of fine Bordeaux. And all the time she stared at him as if, even now, not believing the thing she saw, so that the wine brimmed and spilt upon the table. She brought him the cup and, a little doubtful, he set it to his lips. He drank thirstily, draining it like a man that loves wine and sees all too little of it. With a little sigh he put down the empty cup.

'Sir,' she said—and she could no longer call him *Father*, 'they speak of miracles at Gloucester. Well—and why not? That you should be here together with me in one room, isn't that a miracle in itself? But those other miracles—what truth?'

'Miracles!' And she caught a glimpse of the old impatience. 'What need of miracles? The world God made—isn't that miracle enough? Yet—and especially it is so with the poor—a miracle is a blessing and a wonder upon a hard life.' And there was a sweetness in him and a strength, also, she had never seen before. 'As for the miracles at Gloucester—true or not, the minster grows in beauty on the fame of them; the very stones blossom like a tree reaching up to God Himself.'

'I think,' she said, 'all of us need a miracle, whether we be rich or poor, simple or wise, humble or proud. And I—I need it more than any. And to me it has been given. To see you alive—it is the greatest miracle of all.'

'One that you welcome?'

'Can you doubt it? For though the sight of you cannot cleanse my soul, some guilt it takes from me. Now I cannot question the mercy of God. I know if repentance be deep enough and prayer long enough, He will forgive even me.'

For a while they sat in silence. Then she said, 'Sir, will you not explain your own miracle?'

'Who can explain a miracle save in the first term and the last —the mercy of God?'

'Yet still there's something to tell.' Unthinking, she put out a hand and lightly touched his knee. She saw him start from her touch as though she burnt him with fire.

'You have not forgiven me after all,' she said. 'Well, I could not expect it!' She fetched a sigh from the depth of her being.

'My soul forgives you . . . but the flesh is not so quick as the soul.'

She poured him a second cup of wine and, kneeling, offered it. He drained it even more thirstily than the first. She poured another, waiting for the wine to do its work. For all their will to repentance she had not forgotten her slyness nor he his delight in wine.

The wine easing his strict discipline he said, 'The thing I speak of must never pass your lips. It could bring great trouble upon the land; and most of all upon the King . . . my son.' And upon those last words his lips trembled. 'It could be death to him; or to me. For myself I care little; any time is not too soon. But for him I care very much. And for the country still more. That it should be torn by war again—God forbid! Yet it would be so. There are always those to take one side or another; two Kings at one time cannot be.'

'No word shall pass my lips. As I hope for the mercy of God, I swear it!'

'It was all so simple,' he said. 'So simple you'd not believe it! I walked out of the cell and out of the gates. Simple as that! You see I had my friends; and by God's kindness the turnkey was one —he was a new fellow. The old one was sick; a cruel fellow, he'd nigh done me to death. Had he stayed longer there'd have been no need of escape nor yet of murder! This new fellow told me that friends worked for my escape; but I must wait, he said, until I was fit. And, indeed, I could scarce stand upon my feet—despair and foul conditions had so wasted me. He brought me food from his own table; but more than that he brought me hope! Food and hope! Givers of strength, both!

'One day he came with news. That very night—late, Gurney would come with one other to murder me. But they should find their bird flown. Before ever they came I should be free. He brought me some clothes—his own. And how they stank! Well, God knows I was used to foul smells. I'd not quarrel with any stink that brought me life and freedom. He took the chains from me; he would return at dusk, he said.

'Dusk or noonday; in that place it was all one. How long I waited I could not tell. I thought it must be midnight; when I heard footsteps at last, I thought it was Gurney come to murder me. But God be praised; it was my friend the turnkey—his name I must not say, being under oath. He went first from the cell and I followed. All went well until the outer gate; and there the porter challenged me. I had to kill him; God assoil him and me also. There was no other way. It was him or me and the friend whose clothes I wore . . . and one other waiting outside and both risking their lives for me!

'So we walked out and there was my friend waiting. His name, also, I must not say; but his brother died for me. He wore a friar's gown and he had one for me, also; and we walked away together. And that was all. Two friars walking the roads—who should think to question them?' He gave one of his well-remembered shrugs.

She thought, Nor time nor adversity can change us. This is
that same Edward that could never close his mouth upon a secret.
He names no name; yet he all but shouts the name aloud! Ah well,
it's long ago and no harm done! She smiled, and in that smile was
something of tenderness, as for a child's fault long forgiven.

'At first I wore the gown for safety, only; it is easy for a friar
to catch the news as it flies and run from danger. Nor will he ever
lack food or a bed; he is welcome everywhere. But soon God
worked His miracle. He touched my heart to turn it to Himself—
and there's a miracle indeed. So I wandered here and there praying,
but preaching never; binding up wounds—I was quick to learn,
being skilled with my hands; doing all those things that friars do
until I grew weary. A man grows older and years of prison do not
add to his strength. And Gloucester drew me. I always loved the
minster . . . and there was the tomb.'

'Who lies within it?'

'The porter; who else? They had to hush the matter up—my
escape and his corpse. What better way? He was a tall fellow, like
me, and like me grey; the face all marred with shock of his violent
end. They didn't recognise the King—those that came to pay their
last respects. Well no wonder!' And he chuckled.

'But the death . . . the fearful death? Mortimer confessed it.'

'He did right to confess it. He planned it. He thought the thing
had happened. But God had mercy upon me; and upon him,
upon him also, to prevent so monstrous a stain upon his soul.'

'Sweet Christ be praised!' She took in her breath on a great
sigh.

'So now the porter, poor fellow, is a saint, and works his miracles.
And I hope the glory pays for his death! It is not given every man
to lie in a King's place beneath marble and gold in a great church;
nor to be worshipped by pilgrims from far and near. He was no
saint while he lived; now he has a fine chance of salvation!' He
smiled the smile she knew so well—the lazy charming smile so that
her eyes stung with sudden tears. To this she had brought his
crowned head!

And now he was grave once more. 'The tomb. I cannot keep
myself from it. It draws me like a lodestone. I stand, often, within

the shadow of the pillars; I watch and say a blessing for all that kneel to pray!'

He stopped. He said. 'My son comes; at least once a year, and sometimes twice. And always his wife with him; you chose well for him, better than I—I would have married him to Spain. And for that I thank you. And they bring their children—though they are children no longer. They come in state, those two with all their fine sons, but best of them all, the eldest. A great fighter he is; the best knight in Christendom. He's like his father and my father. God be praised he's not like me! Though—' and he was wistful, 'I wish he might feature me a little—the old Adam dies hard.'

She found that infinitely touching. 'I wish too, he featured you . . . a little. You were the handsomest man in Christendom. There was never another so handsome!'

'Handsome is as handsome does—it's an old saying. By that reckoning I am not worth much!'

'You live a holy life,' she said, 'and you have not lost your looks. By any reckoning you will do!'

He smiled at that, shaking his head.

'So many years carrying your secret. In any man a marvel . . . and you were always a free talker.'

'Another miracle?' And he was teasing her a little. 'Yes, I've learnt to hold my tongue—prison's a wonderful discipline. But for all that it's been hard, hard. There was one time I almost declared myself. It was when our daughter came—all the long way from Scotland with that fine young man her husband. She was pregnant; and not much more than a child herself! There she knelt heavy with child and weeping above my tomb. I couldn't take my eyes from her; so sweet a face; not handsome but *good*, a face to love. I wanted to make myself known, to comfort her, to touch her; I'd never wanted anything so desperately in all my life . . . except, perhaps, my freedom. But I stood still in the shadows; and I prayed and blessed her—her and her young husband and the child she carried . . . and all the time the heart was breaking, within me. May God put it to my credit that I made no sign!'

They were silent for a while; then he said, 'All England blamed you that you made peace with Scotland and sealed it with our daughter's marriage. But you were wise! We cannot hold Scotland nor could we, ever. In war some great deeds are done but more foolish . . . foolish and cruel. War brings death and sorrow and hunger. So the best deed of all was the peace you made. For our son's marriage and for our daughter's marriage, I thank you; and all England should thank you!' He bent with his courtier's grace and kissed her hand.

'But our own marriage,' she said. 'You never thanked me for that! If you had . . . if only you had!'

'I did you a great wrong,' he said.

'And the wrong I did you—what of that?'

'It cancels out. I forget it. And God will forget it!'

Again there was silence between them. Then, 'You never came to my tomb,' he said. 'I waited; but you never came.'

'I did not dare. I feared God Himself would make a sign—the marble crack, the corpse bleed.'

'At first I waited that I might curse you. Then I waited that I might forgive you. And, at last, when sickness and grief fell upon you I remembered that it was you . . . in your way, that brought me to God; and I waited that I might bless you.'

'Will you give me that blessing now?' And her head went down upon the hand he had kissed.

'It was for that I came.'

When he had blessed her and signed her with the cross, he said, 'Will you come to Gloucester . . . some time?'

She shook her head. 'I am too old, too sick. I am not able.'

'Then it is Goodbye.'

He bent again to salute her hand, She felt a tear drop and sting like acid and did not know was it her own or his, so blinded she was she could not see. Between them like a flame, the little cloak . . . and still he did not see it; or, seeing, did not recognise it. He raised his hand in benediction; and now he was neither King nor courtier. He was a priest.

At the door he turned for a last look at her that had been his wife; and so they stood looking one upon the other that had been each other's bane. And now he saw the little cloak, knew the little cloak. He took a step forward, looking upon it with a sort of wonder. He bent and touched it with a gentle hand, as though it, too, received his blessing.

She watched him pass through the door, watched the door close behind him. She would see him never again. She felt the tears run down her cheeks and upon her hands; tears lay in dark spots upon the little cloak. Grief she knew still and must always know; but it was no longer a carrion bird, a biting, burning, devouring thing. And the black angel had spread his wings and departed. For what she had said was true—knowing his forgiveness she could lean upon the forgiveness of God. Always she must repent; but no longer in agony, in despair, in madness. Like a blessing tears had washed the dark anguish away; only pure repentence was left.

She turned to her prie-dieu. For the first time her prayer was not an asking nor a bargaining; it was a thanksgiving and a praise.

Notes

The King's Poem

'The Song of King Edward, son of King Edward that he himself made'
It has long been a point of argument whether the poem bearing this title is,
indeed, the King's own work. But the chronicler Fabyan says this:

> Then Edward thus remaining in prison at first in the castle of Kenilworth
> and after in the castle of Berkeley took great repentance of his former life
> and made a lamentable complaint for that he had so grievously offended
> God. . . . These, with many others after the same making I have seen.[1]

The Anglo-Norman original of the poem is in the Longleat collection,
where I have seen it. It was studied by a modern scholar, Paul Studer, who
in 1921 published the text with a commentary. He believes that the poem
is certainly the King's own work.

The supposed death of Edward II in Berkeley Castle.

When news of the death of King Edward II broke upon a shocked country it
was commonly supposed that he had been murdered.

But did he die at Berkeley?

There is good evidence that the King was alive long after his supposed
death. We may perhaps discount the testimony of his brother Kent who
swore to having seen him, with details of time and place—Kent's wits were
not of the best. But we have contemporary testimony of two most eminent
Englishmen who swore that they had seen and recognised the King in later
years—Archbishop Melton of York who had known the King from
boyhood; and Bishop Gravesend of London who knew the King well.
And what of Pope John the shrewdest lawyer in Christendom? He received
a stranger at Avignon, questioned him and accepted him as the King. It was
on the special intercession of this Pope that Isabella was declared innocent.

[1] I quote exactly but have modernised the spelling.

There are other pointers of interest.

Edward had escaped once from Berkeley, why not again? In that case would his gaolers have admitted to Mortimer and the Queen their appalling ineptitude?

It was commonly said that the face of the dead man exposed in an open coffin was unrecognisable.

No-one was ever punished. Even Mortimer was hanged on charges of treason, the death of the King being barely mentioned. All the others managed to escape abroad; Maltravers lived very comfortably in Flanders whence some years later he was brought home in honour, served his King on diplomatic missions and sat in Parliament. Is it likely that Edward III would have dealt thus with the murderer of his father?

And finally, T. F. Tout, greatest historian on this period, has said in his essay on Edward II's captivity:

There are exceptional reasons for believing that Edward II escaped the doom allotted to him at Berkeley.

The Queen's wedding-cloak.

She asked in her will that it be buried with her.

Some books consulted

Annales Londinienses; in *Chronicles of Edward I and Edward II*, Rolls Series I 1882

Camden Miscellany; Number 15, 1929

DENHOLM-YOUNG, N., (ed.) *Vita Edwardi Secundi*, 1957

DIMITRESCO, M., *Pierre de Gaveston, Comte de Cornuailles*, 1898

DODGE, W. P., *Piers Gaveston*, 1899

Flores Historiarum, Rolls Series III, 1890

FROISSART, J., *Chronicles*

GREEN, M. A. E., *Lives of the Princesses of England*, 1849–51

HARDYNG, J., *The Chronicle*, 1812

JOHNSTONE, H., 'The Queen's Household' in Tout, T. F., *Chapters on Medieval Administrative History*, 1930; 'The Queen's Exchequer under Three Edwards' in *Historical Essays in honour of J. Tait*, 1933; *Edward of Carnarvon*, 1946; 'Eccentricities of Edward II' in *English Historical Review*, 1933

MCKISACK, M., *The Fourteenth Century*, 1959

MOORE, T. DE LA, 'Vita et Mors Edwardi II' in *Chronicles of the Reign of Edward I and II*, Rolls Series I, 1882

PLANCHÉ, J. R., *Regal Records, Coronations of Queens*, 1838

POWICKE, M., *The Thirteenth Century*, 1962

ROBINSON, C., 'Was King Edward II a Degenerate?' in *American Journal of Insanity*, 1910

RYMER, T., *Foedera*, Vols II and III

SCHRAMM, P. E., *History of the Coronation*, 1937

STRICKLAND, A., *Lives of the Queens of England*, 1851

STUDER, P., 'An Anglo-Norman Poem by Edward II' in *Modern Language Review*, 1921

TOUT, T. F., *Palace of Edward II in English History*, 1922; 'Captivity and Death of Carnarvon' in *Bulletin of John Rylands Library*, 1920; *Chapters on Medieval Administrative History*, 1930

WALSINGHAM, T., Historia Anglicana, Rolls Series, 1863

WILKINSON, B., 'The Coronation Oath of Edward II' in *Historical Essays in honour of J. Tait*, 1933